SHIFTING GEARS

Sarah Kohnle

www.CleanReads.com

SHIFTING GEARS
Copyright © 2014 SARAH KOHNLE
ISBN 978-1-62135-554-0
Cover Art Designed by FOR THE MUSE DESIGNS

This is a work of fiction. Names, places, characters, and events are fictitious in every regard. Any similarities to actual events and persons, living or dead, are purely coincidental. Any trademarks, service marks, product names, or named features are assumed to be the property of their respective owners, and are used only for reference. There is no implied endorsement if any of these terms are used. Except for review purposes, the reproduction of this book in whole or part, electronically or mechanically, constitutes a copyright violation.

For my family and the One who makes everything possible.
Hebrews 12:1-2

Many thanks to Amber M. Dlugosh for graciously lending the lyrics to "Oh, My Soul."

One

Step One: light a candle.

Meg Albertson smoothed out the folds in the hospice center's typed instructions and reread the sheet, faded and fuzzy from a trip through the washing machine.

Light a candle. Say a prayer.

A box of matches sat on the mantle next to a ceramic jar, the size of her palm. Meg reached for the jar and matches then carried them over to the coffee table next to the candle. She sank down on the couch, her fingers curled around the matchbox. With her other hand, she caressed the smooth sides of the jar.

Light a candle. Say a prayer.

She struck a wooden matchstick. Wind rattling down the chimney snaked out the open flue and snuffed the flame. Another draft shivered across her neck. Meg didn't budge. She sat and stared at the burnt match while the memory candle mocked her from the mantle. Perhaps she should get up and close the flue and light the candle.

Behind her house, pine trees dotted the edge of the frozen lake, a lake as silent as a dead man. The sky was like the gray film of dust that clung to the family room baseboards. Inside, yellowed newspapers, tightly bound with rubber bands, covered the coffee table. Fast-food wrappers stained with grease and splotches of catsup littered the floor.

Maybe a real fire in the fireplace would take the edge off the mess, make it seem festive. If she waited long enough, maybe someone would build one for her.

Loud pounding on the front door saved her from having to endure the obligatory candle ceremony and the rest of the steps.

"Meg Albertson, you home?"

Meg darted behind the draperies. The doorbell rang in three quick bursts. Nothing good ever came from an early morning visitor.

Pound, pound, pound. The visitor reverted to the original technique.

Meg peeked down the hall to the front door window. With relief she saw a friendly face, someone to light a fire for her. She swept a comforter from the back of the couch and draped it around herself. She pulled the door open and a gust of wind swirled in.

"Did I wake you?" Her husband's old friend, Chip, stood on the front porch, stomping snow off his massive boots. The two men had been buddies since second grade in Lake Devine, tucked in the northern woods of Minnesota.

"Heavens no, up for hours. Since the sun rose." Meg, bundled in the comforter, leaned against the doorframe.

"It sure is a cold one." Chip rubbed his gloves together. Then he stomped his boots again. "Um, can I come in?"

Meg flushed. "Excuse my brain lapse. Of course." She waved him into the hallway.

"Before I forget Meg, Merry Christmas. Well, tomorrow I guess." Chip hesitated and then reached out to hug her. The warmth of his embrace seemed to seep through his down parka straight through the comforter and into Meg's thin robe. She needed his touch, anyone's touch. Two bright patches of scarlet flashed across the frosty pink and white on Chip's cheeks and he pulled away. He inched closer to the front door before he tugged off his wool cap and reached to scratch his head.

"Gee, sorry we haven't stopped in to see you lately. It's been busy down at the hardware store. Jean's been busy too, all the holiday stuff." Chip looked down at his feet. "But here." Chip thrust a small package into her hands. "Robert made me promise I'd deliver this for Christmas."

"Robert?" Meg tossed the package back, like a game of hot potato.

Chip leaned over and forced the package back in her grasp. Meg stared at the object and began to sway ever so slightly to the cadence of the clock on the wall. The ticking grew louder. Meg squeezed her eyes shut to stop the noise.

Chip cleared his throat. "Meg? Meg?"

She opened one eye. Chip still stood there and she still held the package.

"But, Chip?" Her palm moved up to cradle her jaw as she stumbled over a response. "What's this all about?"

"Beats me. I'm just the delivery boy, but call Jean if you need anything. Okay then, I'm off." Chip scooted out the door. Meg watched him leap over a snowbank and jog to his truck. Dual plumes of exhaust puffed behind it as he tore out of the driveway. When the truck was no longer visible, Meg turned away.

Robert, what this time? Meg pulled the paper off as she walked back to the family room, leaving a trail of gold foil. With an index finger, she stroked the white label on the gift, a DVD. "For Meg, Merry Christmas." It was Robert's scrawl. She cradled the DVD in her hands and drew it to her chest. Maybe he transferred a copy of their wedding video. After a few minutes, she popped it into the player, unable to wait. Whatever was recorded, she had to see it.

Meg grabbed the remote and teetered inches away from the screen.

Robert looked at her, his face drawn and gray.

"Hi honey, I guess if you're watching this, I must be dead."

Two

Meg bolted from the TV. Tremors rippled through her nervous system to the tips of her fingers and she fought to keep the remote still. Finally, she pushed Stop. With her sleeve, she mopped her drippy nose and dabbed at the sudden cascade of tears down her cheeks.

Tea, strong tea, that's what she needed. Maybe a Bloody Mary. She discovered a crusty bottle of mixer behind the pickles in the refrigerator and made herself a drink. Meg inhaled deeply, hoping to find a sense of calm. She perched on the edge of the couch and hit Play.

"I hope things aren't too bad for you and Josh. Everything should be fine financially. Oh, I almost forgot, Merry Christmas! That's the whole reason for this DVD. I figured out an incredible gift. Okay, if Josh isn't there with you, stop this and grab the boy."

Always one to follow Robert's orders, Meg obediently stopped the DVD and went upstairs to Josh's room. She tapped on his door with her finger and waited a moment before entering. Meg drifted over to the side of his bed. Only the top of his head was visible. When she nudged him, he escaped farther under his blankets.

"Josh, you won't believe this."

Josh groaned and burrowed deeper. Meg sat down on the edge of his bed and began to stroke his shoulder through his covers. She reached to knead the muscles in his neck like she once did after his hockey games.

Josh wiggled away. "Mom, stop it. You're being weird."

"Josh, look at me. Chip brought over a present from Dad."

The teen rolled over to meet her gaze. "What'd he give me?"

"Not you," Meg said. "Us. I think."

Josh propped up on an elbow and blinked a few times before he struggled out of bed. He grabbed the top blanket and wrapped it around his body. He trailed Meg down the stairs. She motioned into the family room.

"What's the deal? Where's the surprise?" Josh scratched his stomach and yawned loud enough to launch the cat from its perch on the couch.

Meg sat down and patted the spot next to her. "Sit," she said. He took a step and faltered by the coffee table.

"Why'd you move it?" With a swift scoop, he picked up the ceramic jar and returned it to the mantle. Satisfied, he landed on the opposite end of the couch, as far from Meg as possible without landing on the floor. Meg pushed Play again.

"Josh, you better be here. Are you?" Robert asked from the TV screen.

Josh's face crumpled and he pulled the blanket up over his head. The blanket muffled his voice. "I didn't realize how sick he looked, Mom. I hardly recognize him."

Meg paused the DVD and waited for Josh to resurface. When she saw his red-rimmed eyes again, she hit Play.

"Listen son, I'm glad you're there with Mom. She needs you. You need her. I've got a great plan. First, go in my office and get the Lance Armstrong book from the shelf. Hit Stop now."

The two obeyed and searched his bookshelves, mottled with dust. As they pawed through all the self-help titles of financial freedom and persuasive control, an uneasy feeling dominated Meg's stomach. It reminded her of the many times they waited for the oncology reports. It was the type of ache that starts in the heart, is magnified by the brain, and cramps the stomach.

With book in hand, Meg started the DVD.

"I hope you found it because I just realized I don't have a Plan B," Robert said. "Okay, look in the middle."

Meg passed the book to her son and he withdrew an envelope. He tapped it on the coffee table, ripped open one end and withdrew a stack of bills and a smaller envelope. He flipped through the wad and his eyes widened with each one-hundred-dollar bill. Then he picked up a check and whistled at the amount before he passed it to Meg. Meg gasped and began to fan herself with the check.

"Bet you're wondering what that's all about." Robert chuckled. "Listen, this summer, I want you two to take a bicycle trip. It will be a chance for you to get to know each other again before Josh takes off for college. The money is for fancy new bikes and whatever gear you need. The check is for the bike shop on the square."

Josh jerked the remote from Meg's hand and paused the recording. "How could Dad do this? You on a bike? Tell me he's joking."

Meg tried to ease the moment with a slight laugh. "What's your problem with a bike ride? How hard could a little ride be?" She cringed as Josh scanned her from head to toe.

"Okay, so maybe I've gained a few pounds." She sucked in her stomach and covered her thighs with the quilt.

"Yeah right, just a few."

"It's those silly church ladies and their hot dish."

"Whatever." He resumed his spot on the couch and pushed Play.

Robert continued: "Listen, both of you. I guess this sounds kinda crazy. But consider it my last request. Josh, go online and plot a course. Start out west and end up in St.

Louis. And, this is the best part. Take my ashes with you. You did have me cremated, right?"

Meg glanced toward the mantle before she met Josh's stare. She'd love to forget that terrible day. The gray-suited funeral director, hiding behind his mask of stoic professionalism, moderated the mother-son showdown. Robert had insisted on cremation, but Josh had come unglued at the funeral home.

The DVD continued: "Anyway, take my ashes to Busch Stadium. That was the last one on our list. I guess you could say our final inning. That's where my ashes are going."

Robert's voice changed to a more solemn tone. "I know this whole DVD thing is pretty strange. Geez, it feels pretty bizarre to be talking about my own ashes. But listen, bottom line, I love you guys."

His image disappeared and Meg turned off the player. She reached toward the screen and traced where Robert's face had been. She choked back a sob and glanced at her son. The blanket had slipped off his head and a solitary tear escaped through his clamped eyelids.

Three

Meg tucked her hair into her wool cap and swung herself out of the black SUV's warmth. To see Robert's image after so many months unnerved her, made it crucial to escape, to flee the encroaching walls of the home they once shared.

Snow crunched under her boots as she stumbled along the street rutted from snowplows. Dingy giant candy canes, their red and white stripes now a nondescript swirl like chewed bubble-gum, whipped back and forth in the wind from the wires strung across Main Street. Bundled people jumped out of their cars and scurried into the shops along the town square.

Meg ducked into the corner drugstore. The sight of 'their booth,' with its cracked red vinyl seats, jolted her. It'd been a year since she'd slid across those seats. She longed to sit and share a cup of strong black coffee with Robert, laugh about nothing, maybe run across to the floral shop and grab another poinsettia, and then down to Bjorn's Bakery for a fresh coffee ring for Christmas morning. She wanted to dash into the dime store for silly stocking stuffers and then onto Super Value for cranberry sauce that no one ever ate but tradition was tradition, and pick up mustard for leftover turkey sandwiches because they never remembered to buy the mustard on the first shopping trip, but heavens to Betsy, when you're spending a million bucks on groceries you should remember to pick up everything at the same time.

Meg sank down into the faded booth and yanked her cap down to her chin. *Shut up mind, stop your babbling.*

At 4:01 p.m. the phone rang, shattering the stillness of the afternoon. Meg had retreated to bed after the numbing trip to the drugstore. She grabbed the cordless phone, ready to face her daily dose of phone therapy.

"Oh, hi, Aunt Naomi. Of course I knew it was you."

"Honey, you're just sharp as a tack. Caller ID?" Naomi asked.

Meg's aunt had never adjusted to the phone company's deregulation. Long-distance calls were reserved for after 5 p.m., Florida time. With the phone cradled on her shoulder, Meg headed into the kitchen to brew a cup of tea. At least the call could pull her through that depressing hour between day and evening. That depressing time when the blackness of the winter woods closed in if she didn't shut the blinds quick enough.

Meg sat down at the worn pine table in the kitchen and kicked out another chair for her feet. Her thumbnail traced the letters left years ago in the wood when Josh had practiced his second-grade spelling words.

"So, how'd the cards go yesterday? You play?" Meg asked. Naomi played poker with the girls in the clubhouse every Friday. Since retiring in Delray, Naomi had become somewhat of a hustler.

"Sure we played. Those girls, they're all a bunch of patsies. I bluffed my way through today." Naomi chuckled.

After tossing a few "oh-reallys?" into Naomi's latest medical update of her neighbor's hip replacement and another resident's quadruple bypass, Meg stood up and moved to the computer table. She muted the sound so she could play solitaire while she talked.

"Yes, I'm taking care of myself," Meg said. "No, I don't plan to date for a while. Really, are you serious?"

Meg clicked on New Game after seeing it was an instant loss.

"Listen, Harry and I want you and Josh to spend the rest of the holidays with us. I know it's an icky time for you. Florida will give you a change of pace." Naomi inhaled her cigarette with loud gusto.

"What a generous offer. But no."

"Now, honey, listen to me. I promised your daddy decades ago I'd look after you if anything ever happened." Naomi, true to her word, had booked a flight the minute she heard her brother, Meg's father, had lost a wager with a thunderstorm on the seventeenth hole at the golf course.

Naomi hacked and hacked across the wires, sending tobacco-laden drops so viscous Meg held the phone away from her ear and grimaced. Naomi regained her breath and continued, "And now, what with you alone in the big cabin on Lake Devine. Well, you know. So, consider this my official family role. I insist, jump on a plane today. There might be some last-minute cancellations."

An engine whined past the back of the house. Meg pulled apart the horizontal slats of the blinds and watched a snowmobile cross the frozen lake, its taillights disappearing in the darkness.

"Really, no, we can't take off now, besides it wouldn't be Christmas break without snow."

"Snow, shmoe, who needs it?"

Something about her aunt's argument made sense, Meg thought as she eyed the snow that reached the railing on the back deck.

"For heaven's sake, Margaret, you're as stubborn as my brother was. You don't need snow at Christmastime. Besides, you should see the condo. I put up lots of darling decorations. I'm getting good with plastic canvas. I sold 23 tissue covers just last week at the mall. They look like little log cabins, and the tissue comes out of the chimney, you know, like smoke. These people down here are ga-ga for that north woods look. I'm surrounded by snowbirds. Wait, let me pull off this earring, it's killing me."

During the lull, Meg tried to get a word in, but Naomi was quick.

"I'm looking online right now. You could catch a flight down here tomorrow. Meg, did you hear me?"

"Naomi, that's Christmas. Those seats will be too expensive and I can't get both of us ready to leave tomorrow."

"Can't or won't? Harry and I think it's time for you to get on with your life. You're young, you can find a new man. And that new Mayo clinic has a lot of handsome young doctors.

"Why, I never thought I'd be happy after Eddie left. And just look at me and Harry, a coupla lovebirds."

"Divorce has nothing over death."

"Oh sweetie, you know I didn't mean it like that."

"I know, I know. You're just trying to cheer me up. After all, 'tis the season."

"See, there you go, Meg. That's the attitude."

Once the good-byes were out of the way, Meg hung up. Not satisfied with just a cup of tea, she searched the cabinets and found a box of cereal. She reached in for a handful and dumped the cereal on the counter. Wisps of dried insect wings hovered in the air before they drifted back into the pile of chocolate puffs. With a leftover set of chopsticks from carryout, Meg plucked one puff and popped it into her mouth. And then another and another, careful not to disturb the fragile wings.

Four

Christmas Eve, Meg watched Josh wad up newspapers and stick them in the fireplace under the kindling. The flames took hold and crackled to the logs. With a poker, Josh adjusted the wood until he finally stood up and pulled the screen tight in front of the fireplace.

"Eggnog?" Meg asked. A carton and two glasses waited on a tray on the coffee table.

"Ick, that's nasty stuff." Josh returned to his pile of presents.

Before they sat down, Meg had turned on Christmas music, in the hopes of inviting some holiday spirit. Now the music just made her feel tired and lonely.

"Let's see what Aunt Naomi made this year," Meg said. "Grab that bag. On the count of one, two, three..."

Meg and Josh pulled their presents out of tattered and faded gift bags, slightly recognizable from previous Christmases.

"Isn't this nice," Meg said as she separated the tissue from her gift. It was a wall calendar made of bright yellow yarn on blue plastic canvas with a space for a photograph on the top. Josh eyed his gift, a wallet made from forest green yarn on plastic canvas.

"Well, it's the thought, remember," Meg said.

"Maybe it would've been better if she hadn't thought."

"Josh, come on, she loves you and wanted to make you something nice. That probably took her quite some time to stitch, or whatever the technique is."

He tossed the wallet on the coffee table and groped for other packages. Then he snatched a box labeled with his name. He shredded the paper off and whipped out a black-and-red jersey.

"Wow. Awesome. Chicago Black Hawks, how'd you know?" He modeled it over his T-shirt and danced around the room.

Seeing happiness return to her son's face tugged at her heart and Meg choked to speak without sounding too emotional.

"I'm relieved you like it. I had no clue. I called your hockey coach and he suggested that."

"Oh, I should've known." The smile disappeared from his face and Meg regretted revealing her source. Just once she'd like to be the favorite parent, even if she was the only parent now. He reached under the couch and shoved a familiar rectangular box in her hands. "Chocolate. Your favorites."

When Meg woke up on the couch, carols rang out from the television. Meg tried to clear her head. Like some character in a Dickens novel, was today Christmas or did she miss it?

She pawed along the floor until she reached the remote. In one quick movement, the silence returned. Then she realized she missed the Christmas Eve service. Perhaps she should've slipped into a back pew last night, hidden in the shadows of the candlelight. Just this time.

Meg struggled to sit up, hampered by Chester the cat, nestled on her ankles. She pushed him aside and folded the faded comforter, setting it on the back of the couch. Last night, Meg had decided to break with tradition and open gifts on Christmas Eve.

Hours ago, the fire had died and the cold now pierced her bones. Wax from the memory candle splattered the mantel.

Now, alone in the family room, Meg stared at the box of chocolates on the coffee table, next to the plastic creations. They really were her favorites, maybe because they had been a standard present for every occasion for the last eleven years, ever since the Alexanders opened their candy shop on the downtown square.

The remains from last night's ice cream congealed in the carton and the idea of more sugar seemed repulsive — even if Christmas meant dancing sugarplums tickling the taste buds. She tossed the box in the trashcan, but then retrieved it. Since it was still swaddled in plastic, she stuck a bow from Aunt Naomi on top.

"Bonus for the garbage collectors this week," she told the cat.

She scooped up the shreds of paper and jammed them into a plastic bag. One holiday down. A jillion to go.

Five

Five, four, three, two, one! Meg counted down the seconds with the revelers in Times Square before she snapped off the television. "Time for bed and a new year," she declared.

The week had crept along, as slow as a novice cross-country skier learning to traverse flat land. Not like the fast, fluid movements of the downhill skiers Meg admired.

New Year's Eve. Another unnerving time for tradition so close on the heels of Christmas it just wasn't fair. The Albertsons usually celebrated with Chip and Jean. Jean would always create something exotic she discovered online. Even if they didn't attend a gala black-tie party, they could at least eat like they did. They would deal endless games of whist, waiting for midnight to strike. This year, Meg had begged off from the celebration.

Outside a horn honked and Josh bounded down the stairs.

"Honey, where are you headed?"

"Out." He pulled on his jacket.

"I realize that. Out where?"

"Some people are hanging out at Joey's for a while."

"And then what?"

"Dunno. It's New Year's."

"Be careful. Don't come home too late."

"Look, I'm outta here. Erik is waiting."

"Maybe you could call me later and let me know where you'll be?"

"Yup." He shut the door.

To block the sudden rush of cold air, Meg pulled the comforter around her shoulders. She cradled the remote and turned the TV back on, punching in the number for Court TV.

How could Robert just die on her? Leaving her alone with a teenage boy? Didn't Robert always say they were going to be like the old married couples pictured in the weekly newspaper? *We didn't even make it to our twentieth. What am I supposed to do now?*

Meg wound up her arm and threw the remote at the wall. The cover popped off and the batteries scattered across the carpet.

Six

Robert's old parka hung on a wooden peg by the back door. Meg grabbed it and pulled it on over her sweat suit, stepped into a pair of clunky boots and headed out to the frozen lake. Her ability to concentrate had departed. *Departed?* It was dead. Perhaps a walk in the crisp air would awaken some brain cells. That's how Robert always operated. Whenever that ribbon along his jaw pulsed, Meg knew he was in the midst of a serious internal battle. He'd bolt from home and ramble along the shore, through the woods to untangle a real estate mess. He never shared specific details with Meg, but he'd return smiling, saying 'situation resolved.'

Situation resolved. What exactly did that mean? For her not to worry? Some business partner she was. A smooth indentation in a pile of snow caught her eye, and she glanced around for animal tracks. When Josh was eight, and much more pleasant, he told Meg how muskrats enjoyed sliding in the snow. She remembered listening for a half hour as he explained. He was already preparing to be an animal biologist. Her boot caught a long tree limb tangled in the brush and brought her back to the present. She freed the branch and was pleased to find it made a perfect walking stick.

High atop a naked willow, a crow squawked its annoyance at Meg's arrival. Its *caw-caw-caw* rang out across the frozen air. The cold slapped Meg's cheeks and she fastened the parka's hood tighter around her face and buried her chin and nose into the collar.

Armed with the walking stick, she picked her way along the rocky shoreline. Several times she had to plant the stick to offset the imbalance caused by Robert's size 14 boots. Robert was the last person to wear those boots, and her toes curled knowing she should've checked for spiders first.

The spiders are probably all dead and gone. Like Robert, dead and gone.

And what about that man's asinine proposal? Forced to refocus on her objective, Meg continued her walk along the shore. A trail of smoke from her neighbor's chimney hung in the air.

Meg whacked at the frozen ground with her stick, frustrated by her inability to bounce Robert's proposal off someone. Anyone. When she had started dating Robert, he guarded every minute with her, and never even wanted to double date. One by one her friendships had dried up.

Dead leaves crackled at her feet, a dervish dancing to a tuneless song. A torrent of wind swept off the icy lake and forced Meg to turn back toward home. As she passed the boathouse, she peeked in the window and was reassured all was right.

Hoping for gloves, she reached into Robert's pocket. Her fingers touched a crumpled piece of paper and she fished it out for closer examination. She pried the foil off of a lump of gum as gray as the winter skies, and stuck it in her mouth, hoping to remember the taste of Robert's last kiss.

Seven

Monday morning Meg arose with a tiny spark of conviction. Josh came into the kitchen just as she slipped a plate of scrambled eggs on the table.

"You know, maybe it's time to clean, get a new start for the new year," Meg said.

Josh glanced around the kitchen. "Huh?"

"Maybe it's time for a change," Meg said.

"Fine with me, if it means you're going to start fixing me breakfast again."

Josh grabbed a bottle of catsup before he sat down. He distributed the catsup in three equal circles on his plate. With his fork, he lined the eggs into a rectangle. "Just let me know next time so I don't have to brush my teeth twice."

Ten minutes later, Josh jumped in his car to race to school. Resolute, Meg stacked up his dishes and stuck them in the sink before attempting to unfold the wooden stairs to the attic. A wall of brisk air tumbled down the stairs and slammed into her early-morning conviction.

She hesitated mid-step, but decided to push on to the chore. At the top, a dead sparrow pointed belly-up, a black spot exposed on its gray breast. Meg found a paper towel wadded in her robe pocket, unfolded it and covered the bird. As she stood, she gingerly picked her way across the plywood planks Robert had placed across the rafters.

A cardboard box filled with his clothes sat in a corner. The men's group from church had packed his things, but Meg was reluctant to dispose of everything. The men suggested donating it all to the homeless shelter in the city. But what if she bumped into some bum wearing one of Robert's favorite shirts? Besides, Josh might like to have his dad's things. Eventually.

She bypassed that box and headed toward one she knew contained a jumble of things, from Josh's crude elementary school artwork to his English papers and correspondence from relatives. Everything was tossed into boxes over the years, never sorted. Meg fished out one large manila envelope marked "Mom and Dad." A familiar yellowed piece of paper slipped out. Meg held the brittle clipping, torn from Parade magazine. The Sunday after Meg's father died on the golf course, her mother had tacked the quote from Rose Kennedy inside the bathroom medicine cabinet.

> *Of knowing that tragedies befell everyone, and that, although one may seem singled out for special sorrow, worse things have happened many times to others in the world, and it is not tears, but determination that makes pain bearable.*

Meg's mother recited that quote out loud at least once a week. Now Meg hung to it like a lifeline. *It's not the tears, but the determination.*

"Meg," her mother had said. "Just know God will never give you more than you can handle. Bad things happen to everyone, think of poor Rose Kennedy and all her tragedy."

Her mother's optimism in the face of tragedy was of no real consolation. What did God have to do with her load anyway?

The cold air in the attic snapped Meg out of her reminiscent mood. As she stepped over the dead sparrow to retreat to the warmth downstairs, she misjudged her footing and knocked over a stack of snow skis and poles. And suddenly the floor under her feet disappeared.

Eight

The wipers groaned and skipped across the frozen chips of ice on the SUV's windshield. Meg squirted washer fluid to try to remove the debris from the winter road crew. Each attempt decreased her visibility, until she finally was forced to pull to the side of the road.

Muttering, she grabbed an ice scraper and jumped out of the vehicle. "Why Minnesota? Tell me Robert, why? And why didn't you ever look into the defrost gizmo on this thing?" She scraped a small patch in the windshield and hopped back into the still-warm vehicle.

A long procession of snow-topped cars inched behind a van with out-of-state plates. Once traffic cleared, Meg pulled out and continued toward the town square. Before she had left home, Mr. Halvorsen had assured her he could patch the ceiling. She just hoped the evidence of her stupidity would be gone by the time Josh returned from school. She had dangled for just a few minutes, catching her breath before she pulled herself back up into the attic.

Today, as part of her grief recovery, she had decided to follow more advice from the hospice volunteer. The mission was to set goals. One at a time. Today's goal was a stop at the bookstore in town. Meg had argued it was just as easy to order something online. But the volunteer had warned her about becoming trapped in her own house. Especially out on the lake like that, with so few neighbors.

She cautioned her about sitting inside watching the blustery snow and entertaining thoughts of insanity. Becoming desperate like the women who trekked west in the 1800s and survived by eating animal hides off the walls during those long, miserable winters. Meg assured her it would never be that bad.

So today she was buying a book, or at least looking around, since the attic adventure was a major disaster. She pulled into a diagonal spot right in front of Ned's Book Nook. Because her plan was just to step in for a minute, she considered leaving the engine running. But in a flash of conservatism, she turned the key off and put it under the floor mat.

A few other people tramped along the boardwalk, tourists passing through town for the winter carnival, bundled up too much to be natives. She ducked into the shop and wrinkled her nose at the odor of burnt microwave popcorn.

A voice called out, "Hey there, make yourself at home. I'll be up front in a sec."

Meg obliged and started walking past the displays. A prominent table showcased books by local authors. The rack of current bestsellers had a few bare spots, for No. 1 and No. 3. A cover piqued her interest and she picked up the book.

"Oh, now that's a good one there." A thin man hovered over her and pointed to the book in her hand. Then he gestured to the blackened paper bag in his other hand. "Guess it was ten seconds too long," he said. His reading glasses balanced on the end of his long, rather rectangular nose, caused Meg to think of a myopic aardvark.

He whirled around and picked up a book from another shelf. "If you like that kind of style, I bet you'd like this one. What are you looking for anyway?"

"Just looking around," Meg said.

"People don't just look around. Believe me. I've owned this shop for just six months, but already I've learned people come in here for a reason. Maybe they don't know it instantly, but there's a reason they're here. That black SUV yours?" He gestured out the front window. "Haven't seen it around here, but I know it's local by the dealer's decals. You like it? I had one a few years ago, loved that thing to death. Drove it into the ground too."

Meg opened the book he handed her and started to read the first paragraph.

"Do you always do that with a new book? I don't. I like to wait until I buy it. Of course I will read the synopsis on the flap. And the bio in the back. But of course I usually will have read a review even before then."

Meg closed the book.

"Didn't catch you, eh?" the aardvark said. He moved over to another rack.

"How about this? It's a new one, *121 Ways to Turn Up the Heat in Your Relationship When it's Way below Zero*." He stared at Meg over his glasses, waiting for a response.

"No, I don't think that's quite what I need," Meg said. *Oh brother, I bet he's into speed dating too, complete with a timer.*

"Oh, I see. Not in a relationship, or not in one that needs a little revitalization? I've been dating the same woman for nine years. We've talked matrimony, but she doesn't seem ready to commit. She's from the city. I think it's the idea of living in the lake area that scares her. What lake are you on? Or do you live right in town?"

"Lake Devine," Meg said.

"Fine lake, that Lake Devine. Lot of pretty homes around there. I've got a pretty home on Misty Lake. I bought it at auction and I've been working on it for several months now. I'm just about done with the hardwood floors. I study remodeling here, during the day. At night I go home and apply all that knowledge. You should see the view I have from the living room. I can hardly wait until I finish that place. I'll be able to sit in front of the fireplace while I read and watch the lake."

Meg tried to inch her way toward another aisle of books. A section of self-improvement and exercise books caught her eye. She approached the rack and pulled a title on bicycling. Maybe it could give a hint into Robert's wild plan.

"Oh, cycling, the lure of the open road, the adventure, the exercise." The aardvark hadn't left. "Is that book a gift for someone? I used to bicycle. A lot in fact, when I was in college. I lived way off campus. Due to some mild youthful indiscretions, I wasn't able to use my car, so I logged a lot of miles on my old ten-speed. That was a great bicycle. I developed quite a lot of muscle too. Probably the best shape in my life."

"You know," Meg said. "I am ready. This book is exactly what I'm looking for."

The aardvark took the book and carried it to the cash register. "See, what did I tell you? Everyone is really looking for something when they come in my shop. They just don't know it when they walk in."

Nine

Every day since Christmas, Josh played the DVD over and over and over hoping for more clues. Josh knew his mom didn't notice the little envelope addressed to him. That was for his eyes only. He unfolded the letter and reread his dad's handwriting:

> *Dear son, I'm sure this whole plan probably feels like a sinister plot to you, but you are head of the family now and I think you are the only one who can reach your mom. My cancer took a lot out of her, and I saw her age as I got sicker. This bike trip might be the ticket to help her reclaim her spirit, to shift gears from a caregiver to a vibrant woman. I hope you do deliver my ashes to St. Louis. We both know you could jump on a plane to do this. But I loved to bike and this trip might be what your mom needs to snap her back. Just think of everything you'll see and share.*

Out for his morning run, Josh passed the old Larson barn and laughed at Dad's comment. Think of everything he'll see? Yeah, right. Mom sweating and whining on a bike? Share, like her stash of junk food?

A row of spruce trees protected the lake road from the wind. Josh jogged along the top of the crowned road, trying to sidestep the snowplow ruts. Josh still couldn't believe Dad made him do this. Did he hate him or something? The last thing Josh wanted to do was travel across the country with Mom, much less on bicycles.

Josh rattled off the negatives. First, she wasn't in shape. Far from it. She was so uncoordinated she fell through the ceiling, although she never confessed. Thanks to Mr. Halvorsen and his inability to shut up, Josh learned the truth behind the fresh paint.

Second, sorry, but Mom wasn't that much fun. She wasn't any fun, when he really thought about it. He swore out loud. Ever since Dad had died, she'd been nothing but a big pain. All she did was sit around and eat and whine and complain.

He passed the Johnson's house and waved to Stephanie, paper shopping bags dangling from her arms. She always sat next to him in French, their last class every other day. The teacher, Mr. Gustafson, was a joke. His French was corrupted by a Scandinavian accent. Josh and Stephanie passed notes and killed time doing stupid stuff. His mom hadn't even noticed the time Stephanie painted his fingernails black.

Third, he had better things to do. Much better.

It was his last summer of freedom. And time to escape to college. The University of Miami let him know before Christmas that he was accepted. He and Dad visited campus when they flew down to watch the Cardinals play the Marlins last summer. Josh knew that was where he wanted to study and he'd gone with the early decision plan.

He sprinted for a few yards. "Forget it. I don't have time for this trip."

The man in the little boat in the middle of the lake appeared so serene. Water rippled around the small craft.

Josh eyed the illuminated beer sign on the wall and wished himself to the land of sky blue water. It had to be way better than facing his friends now at Chuck's Pub-n-Grub. He released the dart from his grip and launched it on its way to an easy twenty bucks. The tip struck the center and stayed.

"Yes," Josh said and danced back to the booth where his friends sat. That is, he thought he was dancing, but his tennis shoe stuck to the vinyl bar floor and caused him to trip. His hip caught the edge of the shuffleboard table and he bounced toward the booth.

"Hey Chuck, you better cut off Albertson. He can't walk anymore," Erik jeered. He lifted up his mug and saluted Josh.

"Funny," Josh said and feigned a punch to Erik's chin. "Chuck, you should mop these floors sometime."

"Yeah kid. That'd be the day. Probably the same day I serve you real beer." Chuck snorted.

"You mean this is fake?" Erik lofted his mug again.

"You kids are so funny. You know it's my famous rootbeer. Now shut up so I can listen to my man Bobby."

"That guy singing about some dude and his knife? I wondered what you had on the jukebox," Josh said. "Make that a junkbox."

Chuck wiped his hands on the bar towel in his waistband before he withdrew it. "Don't knock a classic." He snapped the towel at Josh. "That's Mack the Knife you're hearing."

Chuck's Pub-n-Grub was their standard gathering spot. In the middle of lake country, the bar was actually part of Chuck's home. Chuck lost his liquor license years ago, but prided himself on his homebrewed rootbeer. No one really came for the grub, not since the grill fell apart, reducing the choices to bologna on white bread and pickled eggs out of large glass jar. Not even twenty-four years of grease could hold it together. Josh turned back to the bar.

"Hey Chuck, any chips back there?"

Chuck tossed the bar towel to Josh. "Here, wipe the counter while I check."

Josh flipped the towel back on the counter without wiping. While Chuck was in the back, Josh slipped a flask out of his pocket and added some vodka to the pitcher. Then he wandered over to the corner near the pay telephone, its black receiver dangling by its cord, rendered useless and superfluous with cell phones. Josh could never recall anyone using it. But he did remember its magic. When he was a kid, every now and then he found a quarter in the change return.

Out of habit, Josh stuck his finger in and dug around the coin return slot. *Nada.* Next to the phone, the walls were plastered with dusty dime-store frames holding old photographs from endless seasons at the lake. Walleyes and northern pikes—forever immortalized by taxidermists—stared with glass eyeballs from their mounts on the wall. Josh backed up to look again at one of the photos of a prize-winning catch. He must've been in first grade when it was taken. His dad's hair curled over the collar of his shirt. A sun-burnt Josh held up a northern with both hands.

Erik walked up. "Albertson, isn't that you? Someone said you were on the wall at Chuck's. Guess I never looked before."

"Nah, just a kid who looks like me."

Erik leaned over to peer at the smudged glass. "Yeah, that kid looks too normal to be you." Erik dragged Josh back to their booth and pushed him to sit. Chuck had left several bags of chips on their table and the guys ripped off the tops. Content with a mouth full of chips, Josh reached for the pitcher.

"Nothing doing. First you gotta tell us the wild story," Erik slid the pitcher away from his grasp.

Josh strained again to touch it, but Erik said, "Seriously, dude. What's this about a bike trip? With your mom?"

Josh leaned back, his spine pushed against the booth. His hands splayed on the tabletop. With a finger, he began drawing circles in a few dribbles of rootbeer near his empty mug. The other guys grew silent. The man on the jukebox was finished and the only other sound was Chuck whistling in the back.

"So?" one finally said.

"First, don't 'dude' me. Second, it's really stupid," Josh said.

"Yeah, that's what we heard too," Erik said. He pushed the brim of his Twins cap up on his forehead.

"I'm just going to tell it to you once. And that's it. And nobody better bring it up again." Josh with his still-empty mug and a salt shaker, illustrated the story for his friends.

"This," he rattled the mug, "is Mom. And this shaker is me. Note the difference in size. Erik, fill up the mug, add some weight."

Erik looked over for Chuck and then swiftly pulled a bottle out of his jacket. He dumped some into the pitcher and replenished the rootbeer; Josh continued. "Now this pepper shaker over here is my dad. See how the salt and pepper shakers are alike? Well, the insides of this pepper shaker turned bad." Josh unscrewed the metal lid and poured the pepper into a glass ashtray. Then he screwed the lid back on and slammed the shaker down. "All that's left is a container, nothing. That's my dad. Well, except they burnt up his container. So, forget that illustration." Josh tossed the pepper shaker over his shoulder and it hit the floor.

"You kids stop it out there." Chuck hollered from the back.

The guys laughed and waited for Josh to continue.

"Before Dad left he made a DVD. And get this, he ordered me and Mom to take a bike trip and deliver his ashes to St. Louis. At least he left some money for it."

The guys all stared at Josh, except for Erik who kept his head down. Then he looked up and met Josh's eyes. "Albertson, too bad your dad did this to you." Erik took a long drink and wiped the foam off his lips with the back of his hand. With his other hand, he pushed the pitcher across to Josh.

"Yeah, talk about a nightmare, a nightmare on wheels," another guy said.

But, they all agreed on one thing: You had to honor your dad, even if he was dead.

Ten

"Hello, this is Mrs. Albertson. I'd like a double sausage pizza, extra cheese." Only one pizza shop delivered to the lake area and Meg had them on speed dial. "The door is open so come upstairs."

"What do you mean you can't do that anymore? I'm stuck in bed." Meg's frustration started to mount. "And no, there is no one else around. Remember? My husband is dead." She decided to go for shock value. Then she switched tactics.

"There will be a substantial tip. What? For heaven's sake. Just leave the pizza on the floor and your check will be by the door."

While she waited for the doorbell, she plucked up the wads of tissue littering her bed. Three days of a classic film fest on TV cleaned out her tear ducts. The doorbell and the phone rang at almost the same instant. She let the phone continue to ring while she perched on the top step watching the front door.

A hand reached in to pick up the check and exchanged it for Meg's pizza. When she could no longer hear the delivery vehicle, she bounded downstairs for dinner. She carried the box back up to the fort in her bed. When the phone rang again, she toyed with the idea of not answering. On the fifth ring, she relented and greeted Aunt Naomi.

"There you are," Naomi began, "have you done anything about Robert's Christmas present?"

A few days after the holidays, Meg had let it slip to Naomi about his final request.

"If you're going to do it, you better get your fanny in gear. Do you have any idea how long it will take you to get in shape?"

"Not exactly. I—"

"There's a nice young man who leads my water aerobics class. I told him all about you and the ride. He said it will be tough."

Meg muttered a few syllables into the midst of Naomi's volley of words, but that didn't stop the older woman.

"Now, what you need to do is get out a calendar and work backward. Did Josh find a route yet? If you figure out when you need to get to St. Louis, then you can figure out when to start. What about equipment? Have you thought of that yet?"

Like taking her turn on a schoolyard merry-go-round, Meg jumped in the conversation. "No, for heaven's sake, Aunt Naomi, this whole thing is ridiculous."

"Meg, honey, listen. I think I figured out what Robert had in his head. You and Josh need this trip. Do you honestly want that boy heading off to college while he still hates you?"

Silence lingered on both ends of the phone connection. Finally, Naomi plunged on.

"It's a great adventure, Meg. The idea about the ashes is rather strange. I don't know what our pastor would've thought about that. But your husband had a good motive."

"I don't think Josh hates me. It's just one of those stages, you know, the terrible twos, the torturous teens." Meg put down the box of pizza and licked tomato sauce off her fingers.

"But don't you think this might work?" Naomi said. "Josh is an athlete, he could do it. You once were. Didn't you run track in high school?"

"That was a lifetime ago."

"What size do you wear now? I hate to say this, but at the funeral it looked like you've let yourself go, just a bit."

Heavy footsteps on the stairs startled Meg. She shifted in bed to check the time: 3:35 a.m. "Josh? That you?"

"What do you think?" Josh leaned in her bedroom doorway.

"Josh, where in the world have you been? I've been worried sick. You never answered your cell phone."

"Whatever. I'm 18, remember?"

"You've never been gone this long before. And this sure seems like an odd time to come home."

"The party just broke up, okay?"

Meg sighed. "I wish your father were still around."

"Maybe you should've let Dad go down to Mexico for treatment. Maybe then he'd still be here," Josh said.

Meg was instantly wide-awake. "Josh, for heaven's sake, not this again. You know it wouldn't have saved him." She pulled on her robe and met Josh in the hall. She leaned forward and sniffed. "Have you been drinking?"

"Nope," Josh said.

His glare sliced through Meg. His shadow, enlarged by the hall nightlight, loomed over her.

"Listen, hon, how about a truce? Be nice. We're all we've got now. Please?" Meg moved closer to touch his arm. "I know, you're probably hungry. Let me fix something for you. Hot cocoa and cookies?"

"Mom, forget it. I'm not your little baby." He jerked away and stormed to his room. Moments later, boisterous bluegrass music rumbled from his room. The framed photograph of Robert and his bicycle taken when he finished RAGBRAI trembled on the wall.

Eleven

Just like they always had, Meg and Robert sat side-by-side in their rockers, watching the morning sun tiptoe through the bare branches across Lake Devine. Closer to the deck, the fresh trace of pine drifted on the crisp air. Meg gathered a faded quilt around her shoulders, tucked in her stocking feet and pulled her knees up to her chest.

A blue jay darted by and grabbed a peanut from a feeder hanging on a nearby birch. After Robert had died, her neighbor George Halvorsen declared his personal mission to surround Meg with bird feeders. One for the small birds; one for the large birds.

"Nature is soothing. Healing for the soul," he said. He visited daily to fill the various feeders he had placed throughout the yard.

Spring teased the air and Meg wanted to extend its courtship into something permanent. Much of the snow had melted, except for the gray mounds next to their drive.

The old wooden chair squawked as Meg rocked back and forth. Robert's chair was silent, his remains concealed in the jar on the seat cushion. A spider crept down from the overhang on a wisp of a web. It rocked in its slow descent with each slight puff of a breeze. It finally reached the wooden timbers under Robert's chair and slipped between the cracks.

So many thoughts clashed in her mind. A major battle, with her sanity at stake. Today would've been their twentieth anniversary. *Wood, china? Does it really matter?*

"Twenty years," she said. Before coming outside, she had grabbed their wedding album off the walnut bookshelf built in the den. The hospice volunteer's parting words rang in Meg's head: 'Memories are important, dear, hold onto them. Don't suppress them by letting the holidays and anniversaries slip by. Take that time to remember.'

Meg balanced the album in her lap and drew hearts in the dusty cover before she turned to the first page. Her parents looked about her age now, young and smiling at the camera. So proud. She and Robert seemed mere children. He had been her first boyfriend, her first real boyfriend. He made her feel like a princess. At restaurants, she loved how he always ordered for her. And he was an expert picking out her clothes. He always knew which sweater was the most flattering. Robert called Meg's long hair, the color of coffee with a splash of cream, her best asset, and made her promise never to change it. That and her petite figure, the way his hands could encircle her waist just so. Sighing, Meg reached to pinch the extra skin that now folded over her waistband. For years she feared she'd gain weight and lose favor with Robert. *Like that matters now.*

They had married when they were still at the University of Minnesota. February 22 at 2:22 p.m. That had been another one of Robert's ideas. Of course, the wedding guests all felt the need to discuss the odd time. Plus, Robert's curly brown hair reached his shoulders, which set her grandmother on edge. 'I can't have my granddaughter marrying a hippie or a druggie. What will my friends think?'

So Grandmother Ethel skipped the wedding in protest, eliminating her participation in the family photograph. Aunt Naomi had been in the Orient with her first husband otherwise, she assured her, she would've been there with bells on. The photographer had posed them in the church parlor after the ceremony, while the guests headed to the reception at the country club. Of the six smiling faces, Meg was the only one still alive.

Twelve

The late-night news crew was all a twitter with the winter weather warning. Turquoise, pink, and white bands spread across the weather map. Dangerous wind chills and blowing snow threatened to make travel impossible. Meg dozed in and out awaiting Josh's return. She hit Redial for his cell phone every hour, but he never picked up. With the phone on the pillow next to her she awaited the state troopers' call. The TV was left on, just in case they broke in with details of a fatal crash on the icy highway.

Around 2:00 a.m., the door to the garage beneath her bedroom rumbled up its tracks. Meg tensed until she heard the familiar step of her son coming upstairs. His door slammed shut and Meg popped out of bed. Inches away from his door, she hesitated and then crept back to her room. Breathing a prayer of relief for Josh's safe return, she pulled back the curtains and stared at the heavy snow blanketing the area. If she were a photographer, she would've taken a picture of the swirling flakes in the shadow of the moon. But she wasn't. Robert was. She flicked off the television and returned to bed, tugging the comforter up around her shoulders.

Several hours later she awoke, curious about the weather, and turned on the television and saw live shots of the storm. A rookie reporter shivered on an overpass, getting whipped by the wind and falling snow, while she warned viewers to stay home. Traffic crept beneath her and the ditches along the highway were crowded with vehicles. The list of school closings crawled along the bottom of the TV screen.

"Don't go out unless you have to," the reporter said and flipped up the fur-lined hood to her parka.

"You think?" Meg stared at the screen for a while watching the unnecessary advice. Her feet slid past the cat burrowed near the foot of the bed. Meg reached for the remote and did a quick spin around the channels before returning to the area closings. Life around the lake just shut down. No need to wake Josh to tell him. In elementary school, he loved hearing the announcement. Snow days were fun, too. At first.

Their routine had always included making hot chocolate on the burner with milk and chocolate syrup and lots of miniature marshmallows. Wrapped in blankets, they'd huddle on the couch watching the storm report and checking out the window every five minutes. Josh had feared school would be back in session when the snow stopped because he knew the teachers didn't want to be home. They wanted to be at school with the kids.

Snow days had meant wrestling Josh into his snowsuit and then out of it. And then back into it. Aunt Naomi kept the boy supplied in knit wool mittens, connected on a string. The odd smell of wet mittens and sweaty boy came back to Meg and she longed for those winter days with that little flush-faced boy.

By noon, the storm had dumped 12 inches of snow. Visibility was limited with winds at 20 mph. No one was going anywhere. The Minnesota Department of Transportation finally had to yank its snowplows off the road.

When the flurries slowed, Mr. Halvorsen struggled over from next door to fill up her bird feeders. Meg saw him through one of the windows in the living room and he waved. She held up her mug and pointed to it. He nodded and plodded through the deep snow.

From the backdoor, Meg beckoned him. "Come in, come in Mr. Halvorsen. Here, step right here. Don't worry about the snow."

Heavy clumps of snow slid off his boots onto the rug. "Oh mercy, it's a cold one out there," he exclaimed. "We haven't seen snow like this in years. I was worried about the little birds. They need seed to keep their bodies warm. Thanks."

He accepted the mug from Meg. "Oh," he said after a sip. "Hot chocolate. I guess I thought it'd be coffee."

"I'm sorry. I should've warned you."

"Oh no, this is wonderful. I enjoy a cup of cocoa every now and then. And on a day like today, it's perfect." He beamed his approval and struggled out of his outer layers.

Meg directed a path of scatter rugs to the table so he wouldn't have to remove his snow-caked boots. It wouldn't have made much difference, since the snow clung to his trousers as well.

"Did you hear about the guy at Spruce Lake? He was clearing snow for his little old neighbor lady and his hand got stuck in the snowblower. The ambulance drove behind the snowplow to get to him. I hear they're still working on him at the hospital."

Mr. Halvorsen settled into his story. "And then that poor guy down the road. You know, what's the name of that little town? Doesn't matter. Anyway, the gal on the television said he was shoveling, you know, with a shovel, not a blower, and he has *the big one* right there. Wasn't anything they could do. No one could reach him in time. Horrible shame. It seems we always lose a couple of people that way each winter.

"I hear thirty-one rigs spent the night at Emma's. I bet that place is hopping now. Wonder if she ran out of pie?" He drained his hot chocolate and smacked his lips. "Any more of this?"

Meg stirred the thin film on the top of the hot chocolate and refilled his cup.

"Cookies?"

Mr. Halvorsen smiled. "You betcha, that'd be great. If it's not too much bother. I wouldn't want you to go to any trouble now."

She rummaged in the freezer until she unearthed a plastic bag. The wealth from the church ladies continued. She plopped a handful of cookies onto a plate and warmed them in the microwave.

"Oatmeal raisin," Mr. Halvorsen said, biting into a steaming cookie. "Absolutely my favorite." He grinned across the table at her.

"So Meg, tell me. How's it going? Really."

Meg sipped her cocoa and wiped her mouth with a paper napkin. "Oh, you know, we're getting along fine."

"But how are you? This house seems pretty empty. Is your boy even around anymore? I don't see him too much. Hear him just fine, though. Those speakers in his car are something. I always know when he's coming. Don't kids worry that will make them deaf?"

"I know, the sheriff was after him again about the noise restrictions. Josh figures as long as no one is out there with a tape measure, he's fine. Who's to know if the car is 75 feet away?" Meg shook her head. "I swear he'll lose his hearing before he turns twenty. Even if his music is just the twangy kind. Here, have another." Meg passed the plate of cookies. Mr. Halvorsen's arm shot out to grab another cookie.

"You know Mr. Halvorsen, I worry a lot about Josh."

Her neighbor stuffed the cookie in his mouth before he replied. "Please, drop the Mister part. I'm not that old, for crying out loud." He beamed at her again, bits of raisins stuck between his front teeth. "What's to worry about? He'll be gone before you know it. How old is he now? Time for college?"

Meg nodded.

"Okay then, you're set. Now, let's get back to you. What are you going to do when he is gone? You can't just sit around here and mope. You need a game plan. You need to get out, see people. Start living again."

Meg nibbled on another cookie. "What about you? How long ago did your wife die?"

"Years ago. Took me a while, but I bounced back. I wasted a lot of living. Now I play bridge every Tuesday and Thursday. I even joined a dinner club. Say, that gives me an idea." His eyes widened. "How would you like to be my guest? We're meeting at my house Friday. I'm preparing an Italian special, *Costatelle di Maiale*, or however it's pronounced. Pork chops, really. I saw a recipe for brains, but I didn't think that would go over well."

He raised his eyebrows and leaned toward her, his hands reaching across the table. "Maybe we could get something cooking, hmm?"

Thirteen

Heavy snow caused power to sputter throughout the house and die once more. Meg tugged the pillows behind her back to prop herself up in bed. With a flashlight balanced on her shoulder, she flipped to the word challenge in the magazine. A candle illuminated yesterday's mug of blackberry tea on the nightstand.

She was about to circle the word 'mercy' when, Josh burst into her room. The cat vaulted off her bed and the flashlight fell from her shoulder. She grabbed it and shone it in Josh's face.

"What on earth?"

"Get that thing out of my eyes first."

Meg lowered the flashlight, its beam bounced across the glass on the family photo before it rested in the dresser mirror and illuminated the room.

"It's like this. I've decided. We have to do this for Dad," Josh said.

"Come here honey." Meg patted the rumpled covers next to her. "What made you decide?"

Josh walked over to her, but refused to sit. Instead he kept swiveling his head around the room.

"Man, what stinks?" Josh finally said.

"Fresh floral mix." Meg pointed with the flashlight to a stick of incense smoldering in a saucer on her dresser. Piles of magazines and catalogs competed for space next to boxes of unsent Christmas cards, dirty cups and an array of burning candles.

Josh pinched the tip of the glowing stick and returned to tower over Meg. She pulled the bedcovers around her neck and shrank into the sheets.

"Here's the deal. First..." He held up his index finger. "Dad and I were trying to hit all the National League ballparks. We had one stadium to go."

She flicked the flashlight to Josh's face, eager to read her son's expression. His eyes shone back with fury and he darted to wrench the flashlight from her hand.

"I just wanted to see your face." Meg hoped she had stifled her whine.

"I'll control the light," he said. "Be happy I don't show you what it's like to be blinded."

With a hum, the electricity resumed throughout the house. The room lit up and the Beach Boys blasted from the radio.

"Stupid surfing music." Josh flipped off the radio on Meg's nightstand. Its digital clock flashed 12:00.

"It's been nice in a way, hasn't it honey, not to have power? Like the simpler times," Meg said.

Josh ignored her comment and held up two fingers. "Second. This would be the only time I could travel. I'll have a real job next summer, probably on campus."

Suddenly aware that the full light exposed her eating orgy, Meg slipped a pillow over the evidence on the bed.

"Just like I thought." Josh grabbed the box of cookies and shook it. Bits and pieces sprinkled her bedcovers and he pointed to Meg's chest. She glanced down. Crumbs clung to the front of her gray sweatshirt.

"And third." He pointed three fingers at Meg. "You really need to get out."

Fourteen

An empty plastic bottle bounced out of his locker as Josh dumped off stuff and glanced in the mirror stuck inside the door. He slammed the metal door shut and walked to the classroom where Biology Club met.

Two cheerleaders clapped and chanted in one corner. Josh wished they would just shut up. He walked past three guys and joined their complaining about the ref's call last night at the basketball game. He glanced at the couple they called Meldrew, Melissa and Andrew, climbing all over each other in the back of the room.

"Hey everybody, let's be cool now." The sponsor, Ms. Dorland, never forget the Ms. part, not Miss, clapped her hands and then let go a whistle that threatened to destroy Josh's eardrums. When Josh looked at her, she motioned him to the table at the front of the room. The other officers were already there.

While the club secretary read the minutes, Josh drew along the border of the agenda. With the side of his pencil, he shaded in the bottlenose dolphin he just sketched next to the words Shedd Aquarium.

"Mister president, mister president?" Some freshman waved her hand under Josh's nose. He stopped shading and pushed her hand away. Josh had been elected president around the time Dad died. Now he was just waiting for the new president to take over.

Spit flew out of the freshman's mouth and she couldn't get her words out fast enough. "What if we have a fish bowl toss during Spring Fling? You know, toss little balls into fish bowls?" Josh realized the agenda must be on fundraisers now.

Before Josh could talk, his neighbor and vice president, Stephanie, jumped up. "Shouldn't we, as representatives of all that's good for biology and the animal kingdom, ban such a game? What kind of quality of life is that for the poor Beta fish to live in such a tiny world?"

Josh was training Stephanie to take over the presidency. He often let her handle the discussions. Of course, Dorland agreed with Stephanie about the plight of the silly fish. The debate continued until the delivery guy arrived with a thermal bag of pizzas. Dorland was smart. Since Biology Club met right after school, she always treated them to pizza. Membership grew and now the club was pretty popular. On his college applications, Josh made sure to include president of Biology Club, the high school's most successful club.

During Josh's junior year, his dad had met the sponsor at open house and declared her 'as cute as a button.' *Button* was not exactly the word Josh would use. Her hippie skirts bagged out all the way to her hairy ankles, exposed in the leather sandals she wore even if there was a foot of snow. Josh didn't even want to think about her hairy armpits. And she smelled weird.

"Josh, you set for college?" Dorland placed her hand on his shoulder and guided him away from the kids crowded around the pizza. "I know things have been difficult for you."

"Difficult? Because of Dad? Nah. It's cool. It was his time. Time to check out." He held up a slice of sausage pizza, "Hey, thanks for the pizza again."

On his way home, Josh decided to investigate the bike shop. Part of his brain considered doing the trip alone in order to honor Dad's dying wish. But right now with nothing but gray in the sky and snowdrifts along the street, the idea of cycling rated a zero.

Why not a scuba trip in Hawaii? Isn't his major marine biology? Think of diving while working on a tan. What was Dad thinking of?

Warm air blew through the vents by the time he found a parking spot in front of the bike shop. A wrinkled-up lady, as old as Aunt Naomi, shuffled on the sidewalk. Josh sat in his car and waited to see if she would fall on the ice. The last thing he wanted to do was have to play hero and hang out in the cold until an ambulance came. When she inched past, Josh popped in a piece of gum and jumped out of the car. In the store's front window, an old high-wheeled bicycle almost touched the ceiling. Josh recognized Lance Armstrong on a faded poster on the glass. Someone had drawn a black mustache on him.

Inside, the place was dead, as dead as a frog after bio lab. Maybe Dad was trying to give the guy a break and send him business. Hey, wait a minute. He and Mom didn't have to buy top-of-the-line stuff, did they? Who would know? Maybe he could spend less on Mom and get some money back.

Josh wandered past displays of sleek bicycles and racks of clothing. He stopped and turned around. A sweet green bicycle on the end beckoned. He followed the bike's curves with his hand, from its curled handlebars to its pointed leather seat. Josh flipped over the price tag dangling from the handlebar.

"No way, man." It cost the same as a good used car.

"Oh, she's a beauty, isn't she?"

Josh looked up at a smiling guy with bright white teeth. It was the first thing he noticed. Second thing was the dreadlocks. Not too many people around Lake Devine wore dreadlocks. The white kids who tried looked pretty lame. And black kids, well, there weren't many around.

"Is that seriously the price?" Josh asked.

"Oh yes. She's brimming. Top-of-the-line components, stem to stern." He continued to smile. "Were you looking for anything in particular today?"

Josh shook his head. "Nah, just dropped in. You're not from around here, are you?"

The guy's hair bobbed as he laughed. "You noticed? The accent gives me away all the time. When people discover I'm from Jamaica, the first thing they want to know is if I'm on a bobsled team or if I play soccer."

"And do you?"

"Bobsled, no. I did play soccer. Now I just play around when there are no customers." With that, he slipped a small cloth ball out of his pocket and dropped it to his foot. His right knee caught it and he juggled the ball back and forth between his feet and knees.

"You?" The guy passed it to Josh and Josh caught it with his instep before sending it back.

"This your place?" Josh flicked the sack back.

"No, no. I just assist the owner. He allows me to stay here in exchange for some work. I live upstairs. I go to the university. A bit of a commute, but I love the lakes out here. And I have the entire second floor to myself. Can't find anything like that by the school for this price. I'm Duda, by the way." He stopped the game and grasped Josh's right hand.

"I'm Josh Albertson. Do you know anything about a deal with a guy named Albertson? Maybe there's a note somewhere?"

"Albertson, Albertson. You know, I think that sounds familiar." Duda ducked behind the counter. "Found it." He surfaced with an envelope in his hand.

"We wondered when someone would come in. When I started working here last fall, Jerry, he's the owner, enlightened… Is that the word? He told me about this story. I get it now. Sorry, I guess this means your father passed."

"Yeah, he did." Josh studied the floor.

"Sorry, man," Duda said.

When Josh looked back up, Duda grinned. "So, when do you begin the adventure?"

Fifteen

Two days later, Josh dragged Meg to the bike shop.

"Mom, this guy's pretty cool. He has tons of ideas. You gotta hear his accent too," Josh said while he parked the family vehicle.

Inside, the two split up after Meg officially met Josh's new idol. Meg headed to the back of the shop and waited on a battered stool. With her toe, she followed an indentation in the worn uneven timbers stretched across the floor. The place had been a grocery store when she first moved to town. Faded red brick peeked through the walls. Bits and pieces of the conversation floated over.

"Well, first I need to know. You camp or you motel—stretch the plastic a little?"

She leaned over to look at him, amazed that the bike shop employee didn't seem stunned. Instead he just grinned at them. Everyone else thought they were silly. Meg spotted a pair of pink shorts hanging on the end of a rack.

"No way," Meg said, moving to touch it. Then she backed up. *Why not? The whole idea of the trip is a joke anyway.* She grabbed the pair of shiny shorts, ablaze with hot pink hibiscus flowers.

"Mrs. Albertson, you looking to try something on?" Duda asked. He gestured toward the back of the shop. "Bathroom's through there."

Meg closed the door and almost crashed into the sink. A cracked mirror hung above it and two worn toothbrushes nestled in a plastic cup next to the faucet. The scent of coconuts drifted from a canister near the toilet. She pulled the shorts on up over her thighs and hips. *I pity the person who looks at me from behind.* With that, she decided she should see what a stranger would see. Meg flipped the lid down on the toilet and climbed up. As she swung around to check the back view in the small mirror, the lid slipped and she tumbled.

"Mrs. Albertson, Mrs. Albertson, that you? What in mercy sake's happened? You okay?" Duda tried to get into the bathroom.

Meg lay sprawled in front of the door. Each time Duda pushed, the door banged her in the back.

"Blame it on the spandex" she hollered. "And quit pushing that door."

Sixteen

"Miz Albertson, those pork roasts you like are on sale today." Bob, the meat man, leaned around the display case.

Meg looked at him. "What did you say?"

"I thought you might like to fix a pork roast for that boy of yours. Add some potatoes and carrots, real easy."

"Do you think I should?"

It had been so long since Meg had cooked. Lately she dashed into the grocery mostly for milk, bread, and sandwich meat. She had almost forgotten about pork roast. Josh did seem to enjoy that. She eyed the boxes of cereal in her cart and looked back at Bob.

"Okay, I'll grab a coffee while you wrap one up for me." She coaxed the last of the coffee from the urn into a paper cup and stirred in two packets of sugar.

Hearty laughter and a shock of cold air blew in through the door with construction workers on lunch break. Rosy noses punctuated their lined faces. They headed straight to the deli counter for the fresh roast beef sandwiches Bob's wife made every morning.

The tune playing was one of Meg's favorite songs from college. She bobbed her head and joined in the chorus. The song had topped the charts the summer she and Robert decided to marry.

"What's that you say?" The cat lady, hobbled by arthritis, stopped her shopping cart mid-aisle and squinted up at Meg.

"Oh nothing Miss Betty." Evidently the singing was not just in Meg's head.

The back wheel on Meg's cart skipped a beat and her stomach slammed against the stopped handle. She hoisted the cart and dropped it until the wheel bounced back into alignment. As she wheeled around the corner, she mentally reviewed her list. Since she knew exactly where everything was, Meg bet she could shop blindfolded. Canned soup, vegetables, and fruit down aisle two, baking goods aisle three, frozen pizzas in the back. Nothing ever changed. Even the cat lady looked the same as she did when Meg was a newlywed. The woman lived alone in a rundown mansion. Well, not entirely alone if you factor in the 14 cats. *Is that my future? Old, nearly blind, surrounded by felines?* The hair on Meg's arms itched at the thought.

Meg closed her eyes and held on to the cart as she walked down the aisle. *See, I could live on my own when I get too old and Josh never visits.* Periodically she touched the shelves with the very tips of her fingers so she knew when the aisle ended. When she turned the corner to the cereal aisle, her cart hit a wall. A wall of cans. The tower toppled and cans clattered to the floor.

"For Pete's sake, when did they start putting stuff here?" Meg asked the cat lady. The older woman trembled and wobbled away from Meg.

On her hands and knees, Meg scooped up wayward cans. She looked up to see Bob approach in his blood-speckled apron. He cradled a roast in his arms and gently placed it in Meg's cart. Then he shooed her away from the tumbled Lenten disaster of cans of tuna, cream of mushroom soup, and packages of egg noodles.

Meg slunk to the empty checkout lane where Alison towered on her blue heron legs. Meg would give anything to have legs even half the length. Alison was another one of those things that never changed. Always efficient, never too nosy, just friendly enough.

Alison scanned the first frozen pizza and stopped with it mid-air. "What's up with all this frozen stuff? Shouldn't you be eating all healthy now?"

"Pizza's not that bad," Meg said.

Alison clicked her tongue. "Just don't read the labels. Your son was in yesterday and he was telling his buddy about that bike trip." Alison grabbed the roast wrapped in white paper and passed it across the scanner. "Oh, at least you thought to purchase some real food then."

Meg leaned across the counter until she was inches away from Alison. "Does everyone know about this?"

The clerk shrugged and scanned Meg's boxes of cereal.

"Alison, this is all so confusing. And embarrassing. What would you do?"

At that, Alison smiled. "Go for it. How often do you get the chance to get out of this town?"

Probably more than you, Meg wanted to say.

Alison rang up the order. "Did you want to sign for it today?" Alison signaled a high school boy to finish bagging. Meg recognized him from church. Years ago, when Meg taught third-grade Sunday school, he always rearranged the flannel characters on her storyboard before class to his classmate's delight.

The boy carried out the grocery bags, lifted up the tailgate and gently positioned each bag, as if they each contained a dozen eggs. He closed the gate to her vehicle. "Drive safe, now, Mrs. Albertson," he said.

Adverb, Meg wanted to shout out, *use an adverb*. Instead, she just smiled and hopped in the driver's seat, leaving the boy and his outstretched palm behind.

The plastic handles chewed into her palms as Meg juggled the bags in an effort to make just one trip from the garage to the kitchen. She unloaded the groceries and flipped on the television, clicking through the channels until a shopping show caught her interest.

On one stool sat a woman about Meg's age hunched over, and hands folded in her lap. Her hair, the color of a cloudy January sky, swept past her waist. Her mouth was a solid line, as if someone colored it on with a marker.

On another stool perched a woman with a military-straight back and the excited expression of a kindergarten teacher on the first day of school. Her shiny hair reflected the studio lights and her swollen lips glistened with coral gloss. Meg stepped closer to the TV. Nobody was born with lips like that.

The shiny woman balanced a jar on her right palm and gestured to her guest with her other hand. Second by second, traces of the plain Jane disappeared as the host, Felicia, Meg learned, scurried about applying various products.

If it works for that frump... Meg left the rest of her thought unfinished and tore a scrap of newspaper to write down the toll-free number while Felicia took a call.

"Well hello, sweetie. Ladies, this is one of our faves." Felicia's camera-smile almost looked real. "So Naomi, what would you like today?"

> *"Felicia, this I can say*
> *my wish for today*
> *is cream to keep the wrinkles at bay*
> *until the end of merry May"*

Felicia pressed her palms together and clapped her fingertips. "Isn't she something? We've got your order coming dear."

Lovely poetry, just lovely. Meg's snort disturbed the cat and he jumped down from his perch atop the couch. With the remote, she changed stations to her favorite, Court TV, and returned to the kitchen to assemble dinner before immersing herself in a show.

En route to the refrigerator, she crumpled the slip of newspaper for the beauty products and tossed it in the garbage can. She had just tucked the roast in the oven when the volume on the TV went up a notch. A breathy voice said: "And coming up next, an intriguing tale of deception."

Meg dashed back to the family room to catch her favorite legal reporter, a woman about her age, noted for her crisp suits that always hung just so, and hair with every strand in place.

"That could've been me, Chester. But I'd be known for my professional expertise, not just my wardrobe."

The cat had returned to his post on the back of the couch, and Meg rubbed the thin tips of his ears back and forth between her fingers. "If only I pursued my law degree."

Robert's sick chair reminded her of her newly single status, and dreams of continuing her education twittered through her head. She shook the thoughts away, instead remembering the long hours Robert spent in that chair, his emaciated body wrapped in his raggedy robe. He had declined her offer to buy him a thick, fleece robe. He said he preferred the comfort of the thin fabric close to his skin.

Another look at that blasted sick chair forced Meg into action. Enough was enough. Tugging on the armrest and pushing with her hip, she inched the heavy lounge chair to a corner and pulled over the couch and a leather club chair. She tested the club chair in its new location, her gaze glued to the action on Court TV. After a few good nudges, it was finally in a perfect television-watching spot.

"Something smells good around here." Josh headed in from the garage door toward the oven to investigate. "I thought the food from the church ladies ran out a long time ago. What's up?"

"Don't you think it's time we had a real sit-down dinner?" Meg paused from setting the table, her hand clutching the silver utensils.

"Yeah, sure. No big deal though. I leave in thirty minutes." Josh grabbed a carton of milk from the fridge and gulped loudly until he emptied the carton of milk. He wiped his mouth with his sleeve and tossed the cardboard carton in the sink.

"But you just got home."

"It's okay. I eat fast. Let me know when it's ready. I gotta shower." Josh ran upstairs. Ten minutes later, he bounded down the steps as canned laughter erupted from the family room TV. Meg fussed around the kitchen, checking the meat thermometer every two minutes. Five more minutes should do it. Soon the canned laughter was interspersed with little grunts. When the grunting stopped, Meg stuck her head around the corner of the door. There was her son, plunked on the couch in front of the TV and Robert's sick chair, back in its original spot.

Seventeen

Meg tried to escape Aunt Naomi's regular phone checks. If she refused to answer, Naomi ringed again in five minutes. One day Meg timed the intervals between calls. Each time Naomi let the phone ring four times and never waited for the click of the answering machine. Meg answered the phone while she idly shuffled through channels with the TV's remote control.

Words spilled out of a breathless Naomi. "Listen, I just thought of a great idea. Escape the bleary winter and fly down here, like the baseball teams do. Spring training! You could exercise everyday outside. We've got a weight room you could use. Does Josh have a break coming up? You probably don't want to leave him alone. Easter is early this year. Check his calendar and plan to come here for spring break. Remember the trainer I told you about?"

"The swim aerobics teacher?"

"He's really a trainer and he might be able to work with you. Let me know, dear. I'll call you tomorrow to check."

As Meg hung up, she admitted it might be appealing to break out of the Minnesota gloom.

To Josh, the idea was anything but appealing. "Why would I want to spend my spring break with a bunch of old people?"

"Old people? Aunt Naomi is family."

"As if that matters. Boring is boring." Josh opened a cabinet for a glass, but withdrew an empty hand.

"Is every glass we own in there?" He pointed to the sink, crowded with dishes, crusty from the roast dinner several nights ago. "Maybe someone around here should think about doing some dishes."

His question hung in the air while he rummaged through more kitchen cabinets. Meg considered several responses but disliked the idea of haggling with her son again. After much grumbling about the absence of food, Josh surfaced with a tin of sardines. He pulled back the lid and popped one in his mouth.

"I don't know how you can stand those things. They smell like cat food." Meg shuddered. "And their little heads are still on."

Josh picked up another one and eyed its face, before he chomped off its head. He licked his fingers and grinned.

"Joshua Robert Albertson, how repulsive." Her face scrunched at the display.

Josh laughed. "Have you ever studied a can? See how precisely the little guys are lined up? Perfect order?"

"Your father got you started on that."

"Sardines?"

"No. Trying to make perfect order in the world. He showed you how to line up the cereal on your high chair tray. It must've stuck."

The cat circled Josh and stood on its hind legs, pawing Josh's calf. Josh reached down to let Chester nibble on his fingers, and continued with his list of excuses for spring break.

"Besides, I have to stay here for hockey. Our team has playoffs that week," Josh said. "But you probably forgot that. You don't even come to my games anymore."

For too many years, Meg had endured too many hours sitting on cold, stiff bleachers. How three twenty-minute periods could feel like nine hours still stumped her.

And she hated to see Josh being forced to sit on that penalty bench. What an embarrassment. She had wanted to shout at the referee, but she'd be the first to admit she couldn't even recall what icing was. Robert had to miss most games, but Meg was always there, cheering on Josh. When the boy started glaring at her when he skated past the glass, Erik's mother encouraged Meg to just leave. "That might teach him something," a teammate's mom had suggested. "Make him treat you with more respect."

Meg now pleaded. "But honey, I thought you didn't want me there."

Josh dangled a sardine in front of the cat. The cat flicked a paw and Josh jerked away the sardine. Then the boy lifted his chin, tilted his head backward and looked down his nose at Meg.

"Yeah, but what was I supposed to do when I needed money for food after the game?"

Eighteen

Meg jumped on the plane bound for Florida, eager to put as many miles as possible between herself and her son. She was proud of booking her own ticket online until the flight attendant pointed to her seat. Now she remembered. Robert always asked for an upgrade at the ticket counter. She started past the spacious leather seats and had to turn sideways to side step with her bag as the aisle narrowed for the cloth-covered seats. She grabbed the next flight attendant.

"Miss, is it too late to take one of these seats? I have the money with me. Cash."

"I'm sorry, dear, you'll have to keep moving." The attendant glanced at the boarding pass Meg clenched in her hand. "Seat 27B is back toward the rear of the plane."

Wedged between 27A and 27C, Meg tried to focus on the cycling book from Ned's Book Nook. The chapter titled "When Things Go Wrong" alarmed her so much she stuffed the book deep in the seat pocket and grabbed the in-flight catalog. Soon executive gadgets replaced the images of broken limbs and blistered derrières.

Once the seatbelt light flashed off, Meg looked at her seatmates and contemplated escaping to the lavatory. Passenger C was sprawled and snoring. Passenger A was awake and alert.

"I'm on my way to Florida," Meg said.

The woman nodded. "Honey, that's good 'cause that's where this plane is going."

Meg fanned herself with the catalog, hoping her blush wasn't too evident. "Of course. I meant to say I left my son."

"You what?" The woman twisted in her seat, her knees touching Meg's.

Meg pulled away, ever so slightly so as not to offend the woman.

"No, no. Not like that. He's a big boy. He's at home by himself," Meg stuttered.

"But a boy? Honey, there are laws against that."

Meg drew her legs in closer and placed her palms on her knees. The catalog fluttered from her lap to the floor under the outstretched legs of Passenger C. The man remained motionless, his eyes closed.

Meg tried again. "Actually, he's a senior in high school. He has hockey practice over break. I don't." Meg chuckled.

The woman didn't return Meg's laugh, but folded her arms across her chest. And waited.

"I'm heading to my aunt's for spring training," Meg said.

At this the woman smiled. "Oh, so you are going to Florida to catch some pre-season baseball. That sounds nice, honey." The woman patted Meg's hand and pointed her knees toward the window. Then she pulled out a pair of headphones from the seat pocket and inserted them into her ears.

Strange, Meg thought. *They don't appear to be connected to anything.*

Naomi and Harry met her at the Fort Lauderdale airport by the luggage carousel. Harry grabbed her bags and led the way out. Shuttles and taxis jockeyed for positions. Diesel exhaust, honking horns, and whistling blasts from security officers filled the air. Despite the chaos, an oasis of calm settled around Meg. She looked up at the palm trees and breathed in the humid air.

Naomi hugged her. "Honey, this week I want you to concentrate on yourself, forget you're a mom. We'll get some color in your face, a sparkle in your eyes, a flex to your muscles. Why, you'll be another Arnold." Naomi giggled.

Harry maintained a steady travelogue, while Naomi's driving was anything but steady. Punctuated with starts and stops at unexpected locations, Naomi barreled along in her luxury sedan to their seaside condo. Meg closed her eyes after one-too-many near hits with motorists at the intersections. Naomi wasn't the only southern Florida driver who misjudged her ability.

After taking the grand tour of the retirement village, exclaiming over the six shuffleboard courts, three swimming pools, one craft room, and one platform tennis court, Meg closed the guestroom door and heard it latch. She hefted her suitcase on to one of the twin beds and unzipped it. With relief, she slipped out Robert's old shirt and held it to her face. If she tried hard enough, she could still smell her husband. With a look toward the door, she folded the shirt and tucked it under the mountain of pillows on her bed.

The balmy Florida temperature and the change in scenery activated an attitude long dormant. She pulled on her new tennis shoes and each tug on the lace infused her with energy. It would be possible to return to Minnesota, to come back a new woman, to show Josh she could do that blasted bike trip. Naomi met her at the front door of the condominium with a plastic bottle of water.

"At the end of our block you'll find the quarter-mile track, over to the left. It has that nice squishy surface," Naomi explained. "Don't try the fitness course in the middle. Gloria, from next door? She broke her wrist last month trying to jump over the logs. The doctors put her back together with pins."

Meg started out strolling on the track. One by one, the older residents passed her. By pumping her arms, she increased her pace. One time around didn't seem too bad.

A few yards ahead, a woman ran with her arms flailing back and forth across her body. Meg locked in on the woman's orange shirt and soon fell in step with her. The older runner glanced at Meg and flailed her arms even more, propelling herself at least two strides ahead of Meg.

Two can play this game. Meg matched the woman's speed and upped the ante by loping a few yards. Sweat stung her eyes and a cramp seized her calf. Meg collapsed on the nearest bench. The older woman raced away, raising an arm in a victory salute.

A shadow fell over her. Meg looked up to see a muscle-packed figure standing there.

"Hey, you Meg?"

What, no verb? Meg held her tongue and used the nice Meg response, "Yes."

"Naomi told me I might find you here. She comes to the big pool every Tuesday for class. I teach that just for kicks. I'm really a personal trainer." He looked at her through his sun-bleached bangs and stood with his hands at his hips. "So, what do you need?"

"Need?" Meg stared out at the other fitness buffs on the course and contemplated a variety of responses. *I need my husband back, I'd like my son back, most of all I'd like my life back.* She folded her arms. "I don't need anything. I'm here just for some sun and relaxation."

"That's not how Naomi explained it. She said you have a big bike trip coming up and I need to help whip you into shape."

The trainer is a little too obvious, Meg thought, as she watched him scan her body, top to bottom. When he finished his surveying, he said, "Are you sure you're up for something that demanding? She said you had to cover hundreds of miles."

"Of course I'm up for it, if I decide to do it. I'm still undecided. But why am I telling you this? It's none of your concern," Meg said.

"Whoa, take it easy, woman. I'm here to help, that's all. Do you think I'm hitting on you, or something?"

Although the thought was miles away from her mind, Meg suddenly felt as old as Naomi and her friends. "Later," she said to the supposed trainer and headed back to Naomi's condo. When she walked in, Naomi's smile stretched from one dangling earring to the other. "Well," she said. "Did you run into anyone interesting?"

"Interesting? If you can call a muscle-bound egotistical poser interesting." Meg noticed Naomi's eyes and mouth take a sudden downturn, but the older woman quickly recovered.

Meg sat down on the tropical print sofa and pulled off her running shoes. A TV hummed in the corner, and Meg instantly remembered Naomi's addiction.

"Still ordering all those crazy gadgets?"

Meg's aunt was one of the first people she knew who actually bought a set of knives that could slice through a tin can and a tomato, simultaneously. When Meg had left for college, she became the only student with a complete set of the knives, plus a collapsible fishing rod small enough to stuff into a pocket.

Aunt Naomi snuffed out a cigarette burning in an ashtray and cleared her throat so many times it sounded like a motorboat engine off to a hard start.

"Oh, honey, not gadgets. Marvelous beauty products. All natural ingredients. Come here, I'll show you." Naomi pulled Meg's hand and yanked her off the couch, down the hall, and into the bathroom.

"What in the world..." Meg's jaw dropped as she looked around in bewilderment.

"Oh those?" Naomi waved her fingertips toward an array of alligator parts. "That's Harry's little collection."

An alligator stood on its hind feet with a roll of toilet tissue hanging from its snout. Another alligator head decorated the counter and toothbrushes popped up from an alligator foot. Several lengths of back scratchers with alligator feet and claws hung near the shower. When she reached number eleven, Meg stopped counting the alligator heads.

"He keeps busy with those and never badgers me about my little collection. It all started when Harry accidentally hit a small gator one night. We stopped the car and scooped it up in a beach towel from the trunk. He was dead instantly. Course, now Harry wants to be a gator wrangler... Now, why are we here?"

Naomi tapped a rose-polished fingernail against her matching lips several times. "Oh yes." She opened a door and reached inside for a light switch. At first, only a narrow closet, almost like a store's display case, was visible. Shelves laden with boxes of feminine hygiene products stymied Meg. *Surely Aunt Naomi is past all that.*

"Watch this." Naomi pushed on the right side of the doorframe. "Just like in the movies." The back of the closet swung around and revealed another closet, this one long and narrow.

"Those boxes are empty. Girlie stuff makes Harry nervous so he doesn't even dare get closer." Naomi pulled Meg into the closet. "After my first husband died, I hired a man to remodel this closet into a safe room, you know, somewhere I can hide if someone is after me. When Harry came along, it made sense to use it for storage. No need for him to know all of my secrets."

Naomi rolled out several plastic bins crammed with boxes and jars ranging in size from grapes to oranges. She pawed to the bottom of one bin and fished out a container.

"Now this, this is the crème de la crème. Take a whiff." With a deft flick of her wrist, she untwisted the lid and stuck the container under Meg's nose.

"Bahama breeze. Guaranteed to soothe your skin and soul."

Meg misjudged Naomi's reach and goo shot up each nostril. With the back of her hand, she wiped away the blobs.

"Just blend it in. It even works for colds and allergies." Naomi held the container up to her own nose and inhaled loudly. "I can feel it tingling now."

Naomi opened a compact and swiped a fingertip across a chunk of powder. "Look at this." She tested it on Meg's inner wrist. "That would make your eyes stunning."

"No thanks, I don't use makeup."

"Oh." Naomi lowered her glasses to her nose and peered at Meg. "I guess you don't, do you?" Naomi continued, "Whenever I order something, I always chat on air with Felicia. Someday I think I'd like to meet her."

"For heaven's sake, Aunt Naomi, she's just an on-air salesperson."

"Well, she is still quite nice. She gets so excited for me when I try a new product. Sometimes I order express delivery because I can't wait either."

Naomi whisked a canvas bag off a shelf and pulled out a tube. "Say, this would be perfect for your trip. It's a small blush, like a lipstick tube. *Très* easy to pack. Step out to the mirror. Now suck in, so I can see where the hollows of your checks should be."

Meg faced the mirror, edged in individual alligator teeth, and Naomi swiped the makeup against Meg's cheeks.

"See how cute you can be." Naomi gushed at her handiwork. Then she reached up and placed a hand on each of Meg's shoulders. "We need to talk," Naomi said.

Those four words always prefaced something horrible. Whenever Robert said they needed to talk, something weighty burdened his thoughts. Meg knew if she kept her mouth closed, her husband would handle both sides of the discussion. Early in their marriage, she had mastered the technique and successfully avoided conflict for years. Maybe the same approach would work with her aunt.

"Margaret, my girl, it's time to do something about that hair of yours."

Meg opened her mouth, but her words got stuck behind a lump of surprise.

"Now, before you say anything," Naomi paused. When Meg didn't comment, she continued. "I made an appointment with Jack. I had to pull some strings to get you scheduled, but it will be worth it. I want him to chop off that shaggy gray hair of yours, give you your old color back. Honestly, you look like you should be living around here, and honey, I know you're not that old."

"But, but, Robert loved my hair." Meg reached to grab a strand.

"Meg, look at yourself." Naomi pushed her toward the mirror. Two older women stared back. Meg *yelped* and jumped away.

"I'm sorry to force you to face up to it like this, honey. But I bet you didn't know how bad you look. Well, I don't mean bad. I mean you don't look your best. You've slipped. Such a pretty girl."

Any self-esteem Meg once possessed shriveled to a raisin of assuredness.

"Now, will you go see Jack tomorrow morning? I bet he can find the old Meg."

"I suppose… for you," Meg said.

After bagels and coffee, Meg let Naomi drive her over in the baby blue convertible. "Don't you just love this car? It's my in-town car. I brought a scarf so you can protect your hair on the way home. Now, I'll drop you off at the front. I already arranged this with Jack, so just go in and ask for him. I need to run to the deli while you're there."

She steered the car in a wide arc and it hopped the curb by the entrance. "Oops. I'll be back in awhile. Enjoy."

Meg swung open the door to the salon. The sharp aroma of permanent solution and nail polish escaped out onto the street. The receptionist scanned Meg from head to toe while she checked her in and then nodded to the waiting area.

In the corner, Meg grabbed an empty chair and sat and studied the scarf from Aunt Naomi. A map of France was printed on it. Meg's father once talked about something like this—maps for downed pilots. Escape maps for enemy territory. Well, if this wasn't enemy territory now, what was it? Meg stood up. An exit sign was lit up near the back.

"Mrs. Albertson? Jack is ready for you." The receptionist pointed out Jack's booth, the largest one in the salon. Thatched grass partitions, decorated with tiki lanterns, separated his domain from the rest. Fresh exotic plants, unlike anything growing in Minnesota, fringed the entry. A man at least six inches shorter than Meg, his shirt buttons barely holding back his furry tummy, flagged her into the cubicle. The refrain from an old toy commercial popped in Meg's head and she clamped her lips for fear of letting the words wobble out.

"You must be Naomi's niece. Wonderful, please sit down." Jack swirled the cape over Meg and adjusted it in the back. He gently lifted up locks of her hair.

"Okay, girlfriend, what are we doing today? The works?"

Meg nodded. "I guess so. Whatever you think."

Jack rolled her hair with pieces of foil and painted on *Skinny Latte*. "No fattening products on my girls," he explained. Meg sat under the dryer, reading the latest fashion magazine. Just as she was about to doze off, Jack lifted the dryer hood to examine her hair. "Oh, it's going to be perfect. Let's rinse." He directed her to a basin and signaled to the shampoo boy, lurking nearby.

"How about if we tackle those eyebrows of yours? On the house." Jack applied hot wax and yanked out the excess hair.

After her shampoo, he grabbed Meg's hand and led her back to the leopard-printed chair. He hummed and snipped away. "Oh, your ears have such lovely pores. I'm always afraid when I cut hair off that my client will have an ear full of revolting blackheads."

Meg squirmed in the chair. "Yuck, that's somewhat disgusting."

"It is. Then I have to use a bobby pin to clean them out. You're lucky," Jack said.

Meg's hair floated to the ground. Armed with a blow-dryer and curling iron, Jack shaped the remaining hair. With a flourish, he twirled her chair toward the mirror.

"So, what do you think? A regular beauty queen?"

Just then Naomi breezed through the door and scanned the salon before heading back toward Jack's chair.

"Meg, it's beautiful." She reached out to touch Meg's short hair. "Oh, Jack honey, you do wonders!" She hugged Jack in excitement and thrust a roll of bills at him.

Now Meg recognized the person in the mirror. It was someone she once knew.

"Hey, lucky me. Babe One and Babe Two. I'll be the envy of the neighborhood," Harry said when Meg and Naomi returned. Meg felt a blush creep up her neck.

"Did Josh call while we were gone?" For the last three nights Meg had tried to reach her son back in Minnesota, but she kept hearing his recorded message.

"No, sweetie," Harry said. "Sorry. If anything bad happened, someone would call us immediately. Speaking of calling, I hope he calls or visits when he's in Coral Gables in the fall."

"You'll almost be neighbors. I'm sure he'll call when his funds dip, before he resorts to selling plasma," Meg said. A look of confusion flashed across her aunt's face. Meg reached out to hug the older woman.

"Thanks for the new me. I need to pack."

On the way to the guest room, Meg collected her belongings and knocked the sand out of her tennis shoes. She took another look in the mirror before heading toward the laundry room. Naomi, bent over her writing desk, hummed along with the TV.

Meg glanced at the screen, a fitness show this time. A woman with ribs poking through her old-school leotard swung back and forth on an apparatus, like something out of the circus. She pushed with her arms while her legs worked in the opposite direction. Almost like trying to run through a slushy parking lot in the spring, but the woman kept a smile on her face while zipping back and forth.

Fitness, fitness, fitness. Meg could scream. Yet another image to taunt her lack of it.

Meg turned away from the TV. Naomi clenched a pencil between her lips and had a stack of 3 x 5 cards spread in front of her.

"You're deep in thought." Meg moved closer to her aunt.

"Hmm, right. As soon as this fitness segment ends, the Beauty Be Mine show comes on. I'm ready to call in my comments. I have it all detailed on these cards. This one is for the lipstick." Naomi held up a card with LIPSTICK on the top in capital letters. A second card had swatches of color down the left-hand side.

"I put the rose, burgundy, and pink lipsticks on this card, to trigger my memory. I also included what occasions I wore these colors. You know, to make it more personal... Now, this card is for moisturizer." She flipped up another card.

"No matter what products they air, I'm ready in a second."

"You mean you're the one with the rhymes? I heard you a month ago." *So this is what retirement looks like.* Meg could feel Naomi studying her.

"Speaking of products, honey, go help yourself. Fill up a bag with whatever you want. After the show, I'll give you a little advice. Beauty tricks."

The idea of having to pass all those grinning alligator heads again was enough to stop Meg from filling up a bag with Beauty Be Mine. She'd rather envision them with all their little friends, cavorting in the swamp.

Nineteen

Back in Minnesota, Meg dutifully reviewed the list of spring classes at the big Y in the city. Aunt Naomi made her promise she'd do a little something for herself, before outdoor training officially began. Goodness knows Josh wasn't about to do anything for her. He had barely uttered a few words since Meg returned. Enough to inform her of his hockey team's success over break. Beyond that, Meg didn't care to know what occurred while she was gone. Sometimes it is better to be left in the dark.

Her finger traced each listing: step aerobics, kick boxing, water exercise. Meg reviewed the descriptions and stopped at Pilates. It was being revived in Hollywood lately—at least that's what she'd read at Jack's salon. Pilates sounded the least stressful of all. She knew she'd lose her balance in step aerobics. Kick boxing sounded too *twenty-something*. And water exercise—those pasty, cold bodies in the dead of winter—forget it.

Forty-eight hours later, Meg sat on a foam mat surrounded by strangers. The instructor reassured everyone they'd learn the moves, the moves would come to them. Then everyone removed their shoes.

Meg gulped. A sea of pristine socks and bare feet with polished toenails surrounded her. Her white socks had been tossed in the washer with Josh's jeans months ago. Now they looked like something the cat dug up from the yard. Taking them off wasn't an option either. No way was she revealing her gnarled winter toes.

The instructor flipped on the music and they began. Rather than risk falling on her face, Meg stayed on the mat on her back most of the time. It gave her time to study the ceiling tiles and odd bits of dust plastered on the vents.

"Concentrate. Focus on your abs." The instructor's voice broke into her tile examination.

As Meg struggled to lift her legs off the ground, she glanced at the woman next to her. Her legs thrashed through the air and her gray sweats drooped to expose dingy socks.

"Breathe, one, two, three, four, five." The instructor was long and graceful, everything the written description said Pilates could accomplish. Meg attempted to bring her legs up over her head and toes to the ground, almost a backward roll. Only her legs were going nowhere. With one good grunt, Meg tumbled over. She caught a glance from the woman next to her, also crumpled over. They started giggling.

"Uff da. I thought this was supposed to be easy." Meg gasped for air between laughter.

"Where did you ever hear that?"

"Ladies, be quiet and concentrate on how our bodies feel." The instructor towered over Meg, her long brown ponytail dipping toward her. "Let's roll over to your stomachs, arms stretched overhead."

Meg obeyed. Her partner in crime had rolled over too, and now they faced each other.

"Feel free to move your mats if you get too close to each other." The instructor's words floated away while Meg and her new friend traded conspiratorial grins.

"I'm Meg. And obviously this is the first time I tried anything like this."

"Hey, I'm Christy. Believe it or not, I used to be thin and athletic. A few kids, a husband, not enough time in life, and look at me." She smiled and wiped her sweaty face with the back of her hand. Mascara smudged under her eyes.

"Ladies, really." The instructor clapped her hands, flustered at the lack of attention.

"Hey," Meg said to Christy. "I think she means it this time. I'll shut up and do the swimmer or whatever this move is." Meg stretched her body. Her arms pointed to Christy and her toes to the wall.

Christy whispered, "Now flail like a dying walleye on the shore."

After class Meg and Christy both threw their parkas over their sweats.

"You don't use the locker room either?" Meg asked.

"No. I usually head home. There's no need to strip down in front of strangers. Didn't you have enough of that in high school P.E.?"

"Yeah, you bet. I hated those days. Today was a flashback. I was even embarrassed about my socks."

"Oh, I know. Mine could have been pulled from the same heap of laundry." Christy giggled. She stopped at the door and looked at Meg.

"Do you want to get a pedicure? Or let's run to that strip mall across the street, buy socks, and grab a latte."

The two women dashed into the discount store and each took an aisle to scan for socks. A bundle of socks sailed over the shelves and landed at Meg's feet.

"Christy, what are you doing?"

"Wrong size?" Two more bundles flew over.

Meg hustled to the adjacent aisle and grabbed Christy's arm. "Enough, we'll get kicked out of here."

"Next up, coffee," Christy said and steered her next door. Meg hesitated in the entryway while her eyes became accustomed to the dark interior.

"Make up your mind," someone hollered. Meg jumped and followed Christy to a booth.

"Christy," she whispered. "What kind of place is this?"

The woman pulled Meg into the booth and smiled. "Just wait. And you'll probably get too hot in that parka of yours."

"I thought we were going for coffee," Meg said. Just then their server walked over and Meg broke out in a sweat. Besides a winter scarf wrapped around his neck, he wore a pair of flannel boxers. Nothing else. Not sure where to look, Meg focused on his eyes, but she couldn't help stopping for a glance at the muscles in his chest.

"Nice, huh?" Christy rubbed her hands and laughed at Meg's reaction.

"What will you ladies have? I guess you'll like your regular, right?" He nodded to Christy.

Meg blurted, "Just black coffee. Hot. Strong."

Christy giggled as the server walked to the kitchen. "A little too obvious there, Meg. I will agree though, Santiago is one fine piece of chiseled perfection."

"I guess you come here a lot," Meg said. She shrugged out of her parka and let it slide off her shoulders into the booth. "I can safely say I have never been in a place like this before."

"Safety has nothing to do with it," Christy said. "You need to live a little. It's just harmless fun."

Santiago returned with orange juice for Christy and a small stainless pitcher and a mug for Meg. He winked at Meg as he poured her coffee.

"Just juice, no coffee?" Meg asked Christy.

"Believe me, it's not just juice, honey. Santiago knows what I like. Want a sip?"

Meg checked her watch. "I really need to go soon."

"Relax. The world can wait. Now, tell me, what's your story?"

"Story? What do you mean?"

"Okay then, I'll go first. I have two daughters. One is in nursing school and the other married after high school.

Why, I don't know. But we couldn't stop her. We, I said, but there's no more we."

Meg started to utter her condolences, but Christy held up her hand.

"I left my husband after I discovered he had a cyber honey. I started getting suspicious when he spent so much time on-line. Odd bits of time. I'd wake up in the middle of night for some O.J., and there he'd be, glued to the screen in the dark house. At first I thought he caught auction fever and was spending our retirement money on-line." Christy stopped to signal Santiago. "Hey, how about some of those chocolate chip muffins?"

Santiago plopped a woven basket in the center of their table. Meg chomped into a hot muffin, and felt the chocolate melt.

"Doesn't this negate the sweat equity?" she asked.

"Don't go out looking like that." Christy pointed at Meg's mouth. Meg took a gulp of coffee and swished it around in her mouth.

Then Christy waved at the muffin. "Forget the guilt. The heat of the coffee forces the calories to pass through fast, so fast they don't have time to stick." Christy took another bite and a chocolate chip fell out and rolled across the table. Christy reached over and popped it into her mouth.

"Back to my story. That night, Bill didn't know I came downstairs. He usually rocks out with headphones. I was a few yards away, in the dark hallway, when he left the computer and went into the kitchen.

"I tiptoed over and saw his messages on the screen. Do you know he was sending instant notes to that woman? All sorts of sappy things: 'You're the only one who understands me. You know what I'd be doing if you were here next to me.' Things like that." A shudder rippled across Christy's body.

"What did you do? I can't imagine the situation."

"I crept back up to bed. I couldn't think straight and I didn't want to confront Bill until I knew what action to take." Christy finished her muffin and licked the tips of her fingers. She pressed a finger on each crumb remaining on her plate until the plate looked like it had just come out of the dishwasher. "Boy, aren't their muffins deluxe?"

"Muffins, shmuffins. Don't leave me hanging. What happened next?" Meg said.

Christy emptied her drink. "I need a refill, where'd that guy go?" She held up her glass for Santiago and continued talking.

"I thought about that saying, *are you better with him or without him?* I realized I was better without. The girls were grown and our married life wasn't too cozy, if you know what I mean." Christy smirked.

Meg felt her face flush and she looked down at her mug, studying the chip in its lip.

"So, I left him and that's that." Christy finished her story with a flip of her hand.

"And now. What about you? I'm trying to recreate myself. What brings you to the big Y?" Christy prodded.

Silence hovered about them while Meg fiddled with the rest of her muffin until it crumpled apart. Then she lined the pieces along the edges of the paper plate.

"Gee, honey, I didn't mean for it to be such a tough question. Look you don't have to tell me your life's secrets. I just wondered why you signed up for the class. Nothing more."

Meg shrugged. "No, I'm just so tired of telling people about my husband's idea. You see, he died awhile ago."

"I'm sorry. Accident? Illness?"

"It was the big C. Cancer." Meg took the last sip and grimaced at its cool temperature.

"That must have been tough. Any kids?"

"Just one. Josh. He graduates high school in May. He and his dad were pretty close. And we're anything but."

"So, you decided to get out of the house. Escape life and this dreary winter. Exercise. Get the blood flowing," Christy said. "Am I close?"

"In a sense. Actually the exercise is part of exercise in a larger sense. In an immensely larger sense." With a deep breath, Meg continued. "This is the part where most people start laughing, so please show some restraint."

Twenty

The wind wailed and rammed a tree limb against the bedroom window. The constant creaking and scraping had woken Meg and she sat up to listen, pulling the covers snug around her neck. Robert never did trim that branch like he had promised. Now fully awake, Meg fought the necessity to dash to the frigid bathroom. Several winters ago, Robert had set the thermostat to automatically drop to 62 overnight. By 6:30 a.m., the house would gradually warm up. Just how much money did that really save? At least her sweat suit helped lessen the initial impact from the icy sheets each night. Maybe she could figure out how to reset the device tomorrow.

The longer Meg waited, the more her need intensified. She braced herself for the abrupt change in temperature. At least she might be able to find a pain reliever to tackle the abuse Pilates had wreaked on her body. Finally, Meg nudged the bulky cat dozing next to her so she could bolt to the bathroom in one swift movement.

Her bare feet skittered across the bathroom floor, the tiles as smooth and frigid as ice. The cold rippled from her toes to the tip of her runny nose, and Meg raced back into bed. Gone was the singular comfort of returning to a cozy bed and clamping onto Robert's warm back and feeling his sleepy legs automatically tangle with hers. That all-consuming wave of security had always lulled her back into a peaceful sleep. She reached for Robert's old flannel shirt under the pillow and drew it to her chest. Determinedly, she bunched up her pillows and held on, willing the return of the depth of sleep she once enjoyed. As she waited for sleep to take over, her conversation with Christy replayed itself. For once, Meg hadn't felt like a fool. Christy had actually clapped her hands and said she was impressed with Meg's determination. Very impressed.

Twenty-One

The *clink, clink, clink* on the glass of the aquarium drew Josh away from calculus homework to his hermit crabs. Flecks of moonlight glinted off the banjo in a corner near the window. Josh picked it up and flicked the strings to see if it was in tune. He adjusted it with the pegs until he was satisfied. He stretched his fingers with the exercises Mr. Kowalski taught in keyboarding and warmed up with a forward roll on the instrument.

The crabs tapped again and Josh stopped playing. Curly and Moe skittered in the sand, past their water dish. The third Stooge crab, Larry, had died a couple of months ago when Josh accidentally flung him to his death. After a night at Chuck's Pub & Grub, Josh had checked on the crabs before he fell asleep. He stuck his hand in the aquarium and grabbed Larry, who in turn latched onto his thumb. The pain was unreal and Josh whipped his hand, sending Larry crashing against the wall.

Now Curly, Josh's favorite crab, scooted next to one of the empty shells and poked it with a claw. In a flash, the creature abandoned his old home and crawled into a new one. It'd be something to get a fresh start just like that. At least in college he could reinvent himself. For once he was in control. The realization he was in charge of his destiny startled him. What if he wasn't ready? Josh stroked the inside of his right palm under his thumb, sore from banjo playing.

Josh reached in and pulled Moe up by his shell. The crab retreated until Josh blew warm breath on it. When Moe uncurled his limbs, Josh gently placed him on the floor. Moe waved his claw and then ducked back into his shell. Mom was like that, hiding from confrontation, avoiding disturbances. *She's supposed to be the parent around here, but ever since Dad died, that shell just keeps getting thicker.*

Twenty-Two

A week later, upon Aunt Naomi's suggestion, Meg removed all the drapes and curtains and proclaimed it time for spring cleaning. She jammed what she could in the washing machine and armed with a duster, returned to clean off the wooden windowsills. In the midst of a sneezing attack, Meg grabbed her abdomen and waited for the muscle cramp. Another sneeze, another pause. Nothing. Maybe she was developing abs of steel, thanks to that Pilates class.

Next on the list was the front hall closet. She stood on her tiptoes to pull a duffel off the top shelf, but she misjudged its weight and the bag slipped through her fingers to the floor.

"How many times have I told that boy to keep his gear in his room?" Meg bent down and unzipped the bag.

"Oh," she said. Instead of hockey equipment, she discovered Robert's cycling gear. Intrigued, she sat down next to the closet with the bag between her legs. One by one she pulled out the contents, as images of Robert and his biking treasures came racing to her mind. Her finger traced the cleat on the bottom of a biking shoe and she remembered the excitement in Robert's voice when he explained how it improved his style.

She picked up one of his old helmets, like a white bubble, and plopped it on her head. He looked so silly in that helmet, almost like he had a turtle shell on his head. It was a big relief when he finally updated his look. As she buckled the old helmet under her chin, she closed her eyes. A vision of a healthy Robert pedaled up to her, and she thought, perhaps he finally is well, just like he said.

She jerked off the helmet and opened the front door, eager to take a break from the memories.

Rusty screeching of blue jays punctuated the air and an earthy scent of spring drifted through the woods. Green tips of the daffodils burst through the winter-weary soil near the maple tree. Meg took it as a sign to begin her outdoor training. Tomorrow.

Six o'clock Monday morning, she stretched on the front steps, ready to sneak out before the rest of the world awoke. A quick glance to the right told Meg she was too late. With his flannel robe flapping around bony knees, her neighbor scurried out to refresh the suet for the woodpeckers.

"Meg, what on earth are you doing at this time of morning, dressed like that? You been watching that Richard Simmons fella on cable again? It's still dark out, too."

Meg waved and continued walking. The plan was to walk to the end of the lane, where the yellow school bus picked up the kids. The last time she jogged was at Naomi's condo complex. At least here she didn't have to worry about anyone passing her.

She felt inspired to jog in front of her neighbor. She loped across the yard and sprinted until she hit the bend in the road. Away from Mr. Halvorsen's watchful eye, she collapsed and gulped in the cool air.

Twenty-Three

Meg met Christy thirty minutes before the spinning class at the downtown Y. This was another one of Christy's ideas. She told Meg that if she planned to ride cross-country she better get her hiney on a bicycle ASAP. Empty stationary bicycles in a semi-circle pointed toward one bicycle in the dark and quiet room. Floor-to-ceiling mirrors lined three walls. Christy selected a bike near the far side.

"Here," she said. "This is a good spot. Notice the bulletin board behind this bike? That means no one can watch my lardo rear in the mirror while I jiggle away on the bike seat."

Meg raced to the bicycle next to Christy, hopped on the seat and twisted to look at the wall behind her. Her lucky day—the bulletin board extended behind her bike too.

"I'm claiming this baby."

When they had checked in, the front desk clerk gave them water bottles and towels. The bleached white towels were still warm from the dryer. Meg buried her face in hers and Christy looped her towel around the handlebars. "I have to run back upstairs. Save my spot," she said.

Meg nodded and started to pedal. She played with the levers and knobs on the bike, experimenting with different amounts of tension. Christy returned to the classroom as more people began to enter. A twenty-something man with close-cropped hair and well-developed calves walked around, greeting everyone. He moved toward Christy and Meg.

"I'm Bradley. Welcome to spinning class, where sweating is an adventure."

Christy reached out to shake his hand. "Hi. I'm Christy, and this is my friend Meg. What level of class is this anyway?"

"All levels. Just do what's comfortable. Holler if you have questions."

Everyone else seemed to be wearing tight black shorts. And no one wore regular tennis shoes.

"Hey, Christy," she whispered. "Notice how everyone is dressed? How'd we mess up again?"

Christy looked around and motioned Bradley over. "Should we be wearing special clothing and shoes?"

"No," he reassured her. "You don't have to wear biking shorts. The shoes and sandals you see are the type that clip into the pedals. But you don't need those. Just slip your feet into the toe clips on the pedals. That will hold your feet in when we speed things up."

He adjusted his headset and walked over to the stereo cabinet. "This will get us moving." He flipped up the volume and the sudden beat throbbing out of the speakers jolted Meg.

Bradley jumped on his bike. "All right everyone, start pedaling. Remember to take a drink of water whenever you need one."

Meg stopped and got off her bike to retrieve the water bottle she had left by the wall. Everyone else was still pedaling. Meg noticed they slipped the bottles back into carriers on the handlebars.

She hopped back on and tried to get comfortable. First she moved the seat forward and then backward. And then the pedals seemed too far away. Meg stopped to dismount. Everyone else kept going faster and faster and faster.

Christy's latest post-exercise excursion lasted three hours, exactly two hours beyond Meg's threshold. Mercifully, Christy didn't drag her to ogle Santiago and his flannel boxers. At least not this time.

While Christy shopped for new linens, Meg had spotted an electric blanket on a nearby shelf. Robert had always nixed the idea of electric blankets, saying they were too dangerous and too expensive. Well, she showed him today. The price was no more than a reasonable lunch out for two in Minneapolis.

Now at home, Meg ripped off the plastic bag. It floated until it landed atop the escape ladder curled in the bedroom corner, leftover from the days when Robert conducted monthly fire drills.

Meg dragged the comforter off their bed and shook out the new electric blanket over the sheets. Satisfied it was smooth across the top of the bed, she redid the covers and plugged in the blanket.

She pulled up the chair on Robert's side of the bed, to wait and watch for the sparks Robert said were sure to come. Her toes bumped into the fire extinguisher tucked under the bed. Meg reached for it, and her fingers brushed against a pair of reading glasses, one of Robert's many. She plunked them on to inspect the expiration label on the extinguisher. Six more months of readiness. She pushed the extinguisher back under the bed and retrieved the wrapper to the blanket.

The cat leaped to the bed and meowed at Meg. She reached over to scratch his head.

"Time for food, huh Chester?"

Meg checked the clock. Already 4:30 and she didn't have a clue what to throw together for Josh's dinner. She fretted as she walked to his room. Out of habit, she peaked in. Scanning the room she spotted only two crabs in the aquarium, a baseball bat, a banjo, and an advanced biology textbook next to his bed. Biology. That's it. She skipped out of his room and bounced down the stairs to the kitchen.

"It's Bio Club day," she said to Chester, "and thankfully you're the only one who needs feeding tonight." Meg scooped a handful of cat food into his bowl on the countertop. She trailed her fingers through the fur on his back while he gulped down his dinner.

Next to the coffee maker was the cycling book she had bought at Ned's. Meg tucked the book under her arm, grabbed a box of crackers, and retreated upstairs.

She pressed her palm to the comforter and felt a slight glow of warmth. Inspired, she peeled off her workout clothes and launched them onto the floor. Naked, she dashed into the bathroom to turn on the shower. While the water warmed up, she pawed through the clean laundry basket for a fresh nightgown and hung it on the back of the door.

Twenty minutes later, a refreshed Meg slid between the covers, and out of habit, braced for the cold sheets. Instead, a warm pocket enveloped her. She pulled the blanket around her neck and tucked a hand under each thigh. Chester nudged his way under the covers and nestled across her chest.

"Chester," she sighed. "Why haven't we discovered this before?"

She stretched her legs and pointed her toes to the wall. Then she rolled over and drew Robert's shirt from under his pillow and wrapped her hands in it.

"Hey, you sick or something?" Josh stuck his head through the doorway.

Meg opened one eye. "Just resting."

"I'm home," he grunted. "Big exam tomorrow."

At least he was home, even if he didn't care to communicate. Meg flicked off the bedside lamp, ready to fall asleep for real; content her home was once again full.

Flames jumped higher and higher, licking the ceiling. Meg struggled to shout, to flee. Her legs were trapped and she couldn't move. Once more she tried to yell, but her lips refused to cooperate. From deep within her chest, a guttural sound emanated.

Meg bolted upright in bed, soaking wet. Perspiration dripped down between her breasts and in the small of her back. She gulped in the chilled air and forced herself to look to the ceiling. Its darkness held no trace of fire. The only glow came from her bedside clock. She made herself inhale deeply.

"There is no fire. There. Is. No. Fire," she said out loud. No flames. Chester stood on the bed, the fur along his back spiked and angry. Meg reached out to let him sniff her hand. "Didn't mean to scare you buddy."

No flames. She reached over and shut off the control to the electric blanket. Too weary to change clothes, she left the wet gown on and scooted to a dry part of the mattress.

Spring in Minnesota was like a game of chance at the state fair. Meg never knew what weather would meet her at the door. She kicked at a clump of gray slush behind a parked car and wind swept into her unfastened parka and pierced her cotton T-shirt. With one hand, Meg clutched the edges of her jacket and shuffled faster toward the Y entrance.

"Hey Grandma," a woman called from across the lot. Meg's head swiveled toward the source.

"Oops," the woman said. "I thought you were a friend of mine. Her daughter just had triplets, so I knew she'd be thrilled if I called her grandma."

"Three would be thrilling," Meg agreed as she held the door open for the older woman. Meg followed her and nodded to the desk attendant and grabbed a fresh towel.

"Ladies, no cycling class today, if that's where you're heading. Bradley got sick and there's no one to sub," the attendant said.

Meg's first thought was to turn around and go home. Instead, she hung her parka in the locker room and headed toward the open exercise area for a stationary bike. As she warmed up, she sneaked a peak in the mirrored wall in front of the exercise machines. "Grandma, really!" she said as she discreetly examined herself. She reached up and followed the furrows in her brow with a fingertip. The more she pedaled, the more indignant she became. "That woman had to be at least 10 years, 20 years older. And she didn't even apologize to me. Of all the nerve!"

Meg flipped through a fashion magazine left behind in the reading stand. As she thumbed through the pages about age-defying overnight creams and plastic surgery and injections, she smarted. "Is it the hair? But I cut it all off. Maybe I should wear makeup." Meg pinched her cheeks and massaged the grooves in her face. The results in the mirror did nothing to boost her spirits.

Maybe it's the clothes, Meg thought. She glanced around at the others in the workout room. A few women wore halter-type bras that showed off tan and well-defined muscles. Then she noticed even the people with flabby arms and extra insulation wore the same type of outfit. Not many wore gray sweat suits like hers. Maybe if she dressed younger? But what would that be? The woman who insulted her was running on the treadmill in a sports bra and tight workout shorts. Many of the men dressed in post-frat boy uniforms of faded T-shirts and baggy shorts. *Men can get away with anything,* Meg thought as she looked around.

She glanced at the time and caloric expenditure on the bike's small monitor and decided it was time to quit. She had come to a decision. One decision that would make her feel better. Instantly. On the way home, she would swing by the drive-through and order a bag of french fries and a double cheeseburger.

Twenty-Four

Chester the cat landed on the kitchen floor with a soft thud. Meg opened a can and scooped out some tuna delight to add to his crunchy morsels. He circled and rubbed her ankles in gratitude. She reached down and scratched him behind his ears.

Every morning after Josh left for school, Meg flipped on the morning news show to fill the empty spaces in her house. Today the newscaster chatted in high pitches about the Minnesota spring thaw.

She stopped listening and looked out at the lake. Mr. Halvorsen was down near the shore, gesturing to two men in black wetsuits, chest deep in the water putting in her dock. Herb Larson stood nearby and caught Meg watching. He waved and trotted toward the back door. Mr. Halvorsen left his post and began to race. Meg groaned. Just what she needed now – dueling do-gooders. She stood at the door as the two men rushed to greet her.

"I didn't realize the dock was going in today," she said.

"Hey, Meg. I thought it was time so I called Halvorsen here." Herb stood ramrod stiff as he spoke. His military-cut blond hair had not changed in years, except for the flecks of silver. "Got to take care of our widows and orphans, you know."

"Sure, that's what you said before. Thanks for trimming those trees over the deck last week. Listen, what do I owe you guys this time?"

Mr. Halvorsen stepped in front of Herb and reached out to touch Meg's sleeve. "Nothing, honey. You know I like to take care of you. "

Herb butted in and removed Halvorsen's hand. "Don't mind him, Meg. Old age is getting to his brain. He's really harmless."

"Sorry, guys. No time to visit today. I have a full agenda," Meg said. "Thanks, though. I promise to have cookies later." She slid the door shut and watched the men lumber off toward the dock, swatting each other with their caps.

As soon as the men were engaged with the dock workers, Meg grabbed a jacket from the closet and dashed to the shed. The minute she yanked open the door, months of abandon careened out. Remnants of dead rodents made her eyes tear and forced her to cover her nose. Undaunted, Meg pushed past the riding lawn mower and stepped over rakes and shovels. She paused in front of a baby bassinet. Robert often got impatient when she wondered aloud what the other child would've been like. His standard reply was that it just didn't matter. *A miscarriage is a miscarriage, no reason to wonder 'what if.'*

In the back of the shed, Meg spotted her goal—a bike propped against the wall. A network of thick webs darkened its once beautiful frame. They had bought it for Josh's twelfth birthday, when his growth spurt kicked in early and he had outgrown his discount-store bike.

Half-wheeling and half-carrying, she managed to wrestle it into the house. Thirty minutes of scrubbing was enough to encourage the paint to sparkle again. The next hurdle was what to do about the flat tires. Then Meg remembered passing a pump in the shed and hurried back out to retrieve it. The whine of Mr. Halvorsen's weed whacker filled the air and she could see him tackling the growth on the far side of her house again.

After fiddling with the valves, she pumped life into the tires. She opened the door and waited in the hope of avoiding another one of her neighbor's chance encounters. She paused to listen for his weed whacker. Its *whirl* was just a distant *hum*. Satisfied he was far enough away, she put her jacket on, ready to take the bike outside for a spin. The old frame creaked as much as Meg's did after her first day at the gym.

The lake road offered two options, south past Mr. Halvorsen, or north toward the girls' camp. She headed north and began to pedal with ease. *What was Josh so concerned about? There's nothing to this biking.*

Halfway up Johnson Hill, her years of inactivity struck her right over the handlebars. Not wanting the hill to claim a total victory, she dismounted and walked the bike to the top. From there, she could see pontoons and fishing boats on neighboring lakes. Meg turned the bike around, and coasted toward home. *Now this is biking.* She flung her feet off the pedals, and in that one swift gesture, she remembered a time in fifth grade when she had tasted that same downhill liberation.

Twenty-Five

"Wait," Meg hollered. She sprinted after the ice cream truck, its merry melody spilling from its speakers. When the driver stopped, Meg pointed to a photo and asked for two of them.

"Boy, you took off after that thing like a missile," Christy said when Meg rejoined her on the park swings.

Meg handed her a sundae in a cup. "It's not often you can catch one before the summer. And look, I'm not even breathing heavy."

"Did you measure before this started? I bet you're firmer than ever, even if you think the scale hasn't changed. Don't you feel any different?"

"I don't sleep during the day. I suppose that's a good sign," Meg said. "What was with that spinning routine today? Class was brutal. I still have no idea how all this is going to help me bike across America."

Meg was not the only one who had doubts. The local newspaper had gotten wind of the challenge and hoped to do a story on Meg, start to finish. The reporter was a new one, fresh out of Bemidji State, ready to save the world, but faced with the reality of reporting for a small-town weekly.

"Did you know that pesky little reporter asked me how much I weigh? And how often I exercise?"

"What did you say?"

"I about hung up on her. And get this, her name is Candy Cane."

'The adventures of an overweight sedentary housewife would be entertaining,' the girl had said. She didn't actually phrase it as such. That was Josh's interpretation. The girl formulated the concept of a before-and-after approach and wanted to come out to the lake for some photographs. She had promised Meg she would photograph her in a positive manner.

Christy tossed her ice cream container on the ground. "It's that whole accountability thing," she said. Meg jumped off her swing to retrieve Christy's trash and tucked it in her pocket.

"Accountability?" Meg asked.

"The more people who know about this—the deeper you're in. How can you back out if the whole town knows about this plan?"

That was precisely the problem. Meg didn't want everyone to know. She could just imagine their collective eyes rolling as she pedaled around town. People nudging each other with their elbows, whispering, 'Isn't that the overweight sedentary housewife?' It was bad enough to share Robert's plan with family members. Pretty soon the news would spread around the church ladies. Maybe she should sell the house and move.

Meg sat on the swing and pumped her legs, reaching for the sky. Next to her, Christy stretched further and then shouted, "Watch this!" With that Christy launched herself off the swing.

When Meg returned home from the emergency room, she checked phone messages. Another one from Candy.

It was Meg's idea to get Christy checked out at the hospital, but the only thing she had injured in her flight from the swing was her pride.

Meg jotted down the phone number and noticed it was already written at the top of the note pad. She gnawed on the pencil, and dialed the number. The minute Candy picked up the phone, Meg hung up. What possessed her to return the calls? Seconds later, Meg's phone rang.

"Hi, this is Candy. Something must've happened to our connection. Thank goodness for caller ID. Look can we meet somewhere to talk? I'd like to outline our plan for the series."

"Series? That's why I was calling," Meg said. "I don't think there's a story in this. No one would be interested. I'm really a boring person. Pretty plain-Jane."

After talking in circles a few more times, Meg agreed to meet at the coffee shop of the Grande Hotel, just so she could tell Candy 'no' in person.

Before the interview, Christy came over to coach Meg. "Don't look matronly," she cautioned, and pulled out a few things from Meg's closet. "Or wait, maybe you should look that way for the first interview and photo. Then the after ones will be incredible. We'll do a makeover on you and everyone will be amazed. That will give people something to talk about!"

Meg loved the idea. It was brilliant. If she didn't change, she could fake it. She pulled on fresh pair of sweats and jumped into the SUV. In the hotel parking lot, she tried to run a comb through her hair but gave up and stuck on a baseball cap. She pinched her cheeks for a little color and went up the steps to the old hotel.

Inside she scanned the lobby before heading to the coffee shop. Through the glass-paneled French doors she spotted a table of retired farmers next to a group of women in red hats. At one table, a girl about the age of Josh, and dressed in a bright sweater and short skirt, sat alone. Meg bit the inside of her lip and tried to work up a smile.

"Hi, Candy?" Meg asked.

The girl bounced up and pumped Meg's hand. "Oh my goodness, I can't believe you actually made it here. This is so exciting!"

Meg snorted, and then worried if Candy heard it. "What in the world is exciting about this?"

"This story could be big. This could be my ticket out of here. Someday I plan to work in New York, for a fashion magazine. My uncle lives there. When I graduated he gave me a subscription to the Sunday New York Times. I just gobble it up, like the club scene and the clothes. I can't wait!"

Meg struggled to make the connection between her sorry tale and Candy's break in the big city. "I'm not sure I understand."

Candy flushed and tucked a wayward bang behind her ear. "I know, I go on and on. That's something they warned me about in my public relations class. But sometimes I get so excited by the possibilities!"

A waitress appeared near Candy's elbow. "Miss, what can I get you today?" Candy scanned the menu and decided on a diet cola. Turning to Meg, the woman said, "And what about you, Ma'am?"

Any shred of confidence disappeared. At what age did she become a 'ma'am'?

"Just coffee," Meg said with a wave. The waitress lingered.

"We have some fresh apple pie, hot from the oven. People say it's the best. Even the newspaper voted it 'Number One in the county.' Its cinnamon crunch topping is to die for."

Meg weighed the caloric value while she studied Candy's trim shape. Who was she kidding? No amount of training could ever bring back her youthful body. With a sigh, Meg nodded at the waitress's suggestion. "Ala mode too, please."

Candy cleared the silverware and flipped open her spiral reporter's notebook. She placed a small tape recorder in front of Meg. "Do you mind?"

Meg shrugged. "Whatever." She glanced around the room, remembering all the Saturdays when her daddy had brought her there for the breakfast smorgasbord, just the two of them. It seemed so elegant then, with crisp white table linens, silver bud vases with a fresh rose at each table. Her mom had always polished Meg's patent leather shoes and pressed her best dress before shooing them out the door. Meg had loved walking into that hotel, holding her elegant father's hand. She often dreamed the other guests in the restaurant would wonder who that sharp little girl was. Maybe an actress, or visiting royalty.

"Mrs. Albertson?" Candy looked puzzled. "I was afraid I just lost you there. Are you ready to answer some questions yet?" She clicked on the recorder. "Test, 1, 2, 3, test." She rewound it. "Don't you just hate how your own voice sounds on tape?" She slid the player closer to Meg.

"Here's the deal. My editor told me about your story. I thought it'd be interesting to see how someone your age could consider such a wild plan. A cross-country bike trip? And this summer too? That's going to be short of a miracle, isn't it?"

"Well, it is a challenge I'll admit." Meg's index finger played with the cuticle on her thumb. She stabbed a forkful of the steaming apple pie and pondered a response. But Candy was just getting started.

"I think we should do a photo shoot of you before and if you do make it, we can do an after shot and story. I think I can convince my editor to schedule a photographer. If not, I can do it myself.

"Okay then, let's go. First, tell me the basics. Who, what, when, where, why and how? I have the who—you and your son, and the what. The where we can plug in later. The big W is the why. Have you given any thoughts to this?" Candy paused with her pen.

Meg swallowed another bite of pie and cleared her throat. "Why? I guess because my husband asked me to. It was his last request. When I see him again in heaven, I don't want there to be any regrets."

"Isn't that a little weird?" Candy asked. "Excuse me, if that's how you believe, fine, but come on now, really? He died last year. You don't believe you have to do what he said? My grandmom was like that, always doing this and that for grandpa. She even ironed his boxers. Can you imagine? She died a nervous wreck trying to please that man. But everyone always said, and I quote 'Such a dear lady, never a bad thought about another person'."

Meg started to retreat again, wondering if all reporters were like this. *So this is why Candy works on the local weekly and not in New York.* Robert's DVD replayed in Meg's head.

Candy snapped her fingers under Meg's face. "Whew, you're back. Any other reasons why? What about your son? I hear he's a hottie. Why is he doing this?"

"A hottie? What's that?"

"You know, he's hot, cute, sexy." The tips of Candy's ears flushed. "I should probably interview him for a sidebar, you know, those little stories that run next to the big story."

Oh, so that's where this interview is going. She just wants access to Josh.

Meg scrutinized the reporter. "He was blessed with good looks, I will say that. I think he's looking forward to this. You'll just have to ask him yourself."

"You think so?" Candy's eyes brightened considerably and she touched her hair.

Twenty-Six

Saturday morning, promptly at eleven, the doorbell rang. Josh's mom had warned him about the interview. Why did he have to get up so early to talk to the reporter? Mom assured him it would be painless, maybe even fun. *What's the point?* The whole town would be laughing at the stupid plan, especially once they saw a photo of Mom, the overweight sedentary housewife.

He crawled out of bed and saw an unfamiliar car in the driveway. With a quick sniff of his armpits, Josh raced across the hall to his bathroom. He peeked though a small crack in the door. A girl decked out in smiles, purple, and a fluffy scarf, greeted his mom. Josh quickly shut the bathroom door and started the shower.

"Oh hi," Josh said minutes later walking into the kitchen. "I didn't realize anyone was here."

Candy flipped her hair before she strode over and stuck out her hand. "Hi, I'm Candy Cane. And yes, that's really my name," she said when Josh laughed. "My parents thought it was a pretty cute name for a Christmas baby."

"Well, I supposed it could've been worse. Something like Jingle or Tinsel."

Candy giggled at his lame joke. Her nose flared in a cute sort of way too.

Definite possibilities here. His mom motioned to the table and placed two mugs of steaming coffee. "Josh? It's hazelnut today," she asked.

"Nah, I'll snag a pop." He grabbed one from the refrigerator.

Candy perched on her chair, ready to start. Josh noticed she licked her lips when she looked at him. He looked back at her with more interest.

"I just had the yummiest doughnut," Candy said, "but I think there's still cinnamon sugar all over my lips. Here, I did bring extra." She handed Josh a crumpled paper bag, spotted with grease. "I treat myself on Sunday mornings to doughnuts. You don't think it could hurt me, could it?"

Josh shook his head.

"Let's start. Your mom told me the background, but I want to hear from you about this adventure. First, what do you think is your biggest challenge? Conditioning?"

Josh stuffed a doughnut in his mouth and washed it down with pop. He laughed at her question. "Conditioning's no problem. I'm in decent shape. I lift all the time and play a ton of hockey. My legs can handle a little bike trip. The biggest challenge won't be for me." He jerked his thumb at his mom. "It'll be for her."

Candy jotted this down in her narrow notebook. "So you're not doing anything special to get ready for this?"

"Nope, not yet, but once it warms up I'll probably go bike a little."

The phone rang and Mom excused herself to answer it. She carried the cordless phone into the other room. Candy scooted her chair a little closer to Josh. "Can you tell me why you're doing this?"

Josh played with the tab on the empty can, working it back and forth before it broke loose. "Here's the deal. Dad told me to do it. The guy is dead. But before he died he made a DVD about delivering his ashes. The two of us always went to baseball games every summer. One big away-trip a year. St. Louis was the last stadium on our list. And then he got sick. It's kinda spooky I have to do this for a dead guy, but that's what my friends say."

Candy reached out and patted his arm. "I think that's sweet. You must really miss your dad."

Josh tossed the metal tab from hand to hand. "Yeah, I guess. We were pretty tight. I can't believe he's already been dead for so long. You know it's weird. In one way it feels just like yesterday we were sitting at his funeral. You should've seen how many people were there. Man, Dad would've been proud."

Josh saw Candy's eyes start to mist so he looked out the sliding glass doors to the lake. Several small fishing boats were returning home after a morning of puttering around the glassy lake.

When he glanced back at Candy he continued. "On the other hand, it seems like he's been gone forever. I'm ready to be gone, too. I'm sick of living at home. This fall, I'm out of here."

His mom returned too soon. "All finished?"

"Just about Mrs. Albertson. I need to know some more about the logistics of the trip."

Candy scribbled a few more notes. Josh walked over to the computer desk and picked up a green folder. He studied his printouts. The trip didn't excite him, but his research did. Dad would've been pleased. For the last three years, he had let Josh plan their baseball trips and bargain for cheap room rates.

Late last summer they had to eat their room charge when Dad suddenly got sick. Josh knew his back had bothered him for a while. They had been loading the old van for one more trip before they traded it in. Suddenly, his dad had gasped and doubled over. Rivers of perspiration raced down his pale forehead. Josh had grabbed an arm and eased him to the ground.

His dad had tried to reassure him, said it was only indigestion, but just the same, he wanted to sit for a bit next to the van. Josh had sprinted inside to find Mom. Together they helped Dad back in the house and into the leather chair in his den. Mom had insisted they call the doctor, but the pain soon disappeared. That was the last Josh heard him complain about it. Until it was too late.

Twenty-Seven

Before Candy took off, she posed Josh with a set of hand weights for a photograph. Josh had stripped off his sweatshirt and wore just a thin T-shirt and baggy shorts. "Nice definition," Candy said.

The reporter asked Meg to pick up a weight for one photo, but she felt rather silly posing. "Just one," Candy coaxed.

The weekly paper didn't come off the press until Friday. By Wednesday, Meg had destroyed her cuticles and shredded the inside of her mouth. By Thursday, she was a sleepless wreck after rolling all night in bed, like a rowboat caught in whitecaps. Her churning tangled the sheets, leaving the cat disgruntled and displaced. Thursday night, snippets of her insipid interview with Candy taunted her brain. Desperately, Meg willed her internal Stop button to work. Unable to completely erase the image, Meg bolted upright and yelled out loud.

"Robert, how could you?"

She snapped on the bedside lamp and stared at his smiling photo on the dresser. It had been Robert's idea for the three of them to pose in bulky matching sweaters for their Christmas photo. He had even ordered the sweaters, knit by some peasant women in a remote country.

The only problem with the Albertson Christmas photo was the timing. Under the heavy wool sweaters, the three Albertsons had dripped with perspiration, despite the fans swirling in the photo studio. The air conditioner struggled to keep up with the July heatwave. The photographer had distributed handkerchiefs so they could dab their shiny faces between shots. The uninspired poses failed to capture any joy. Robert's smile concealed his discomfort, while Meg had tried not to think of it as their final family photo. Josh's lips bunched in a contorted effort. The photographer's corny knock-knock jokes only served to enhance their grimaces.

Not the type to burden others with personal circumstances, they had fled the studio, leaving behind a photographer clueless as to why the session had been so awkward.

By the time the neighbors were stringing Christmas lights, Robert was long dead and already situated in his jar on the mantle. Meg had lacked the strength and desire to go through the annual greeting card ritual.

Meg continued speaking to the photograph, "I appreciate what you were trying to do about the bike trip and the whole mother/son adventure, but now everyone will know. And frankly, they'll think we're all a bit strange—I mean, the ashes. Did you have to include that?"

Meg reached under the pillow for Robert's shirt and brought it up to her face. The thought of her husband being reduced to ashes undid her. Why did she have to let the part about the ashes slip to that young reporter?

By Friday morning, the combination of no sleep and lots of caffeine had left her a jittery wreck. She paced with a cup of coffee and looked out the front window every thirty seconds for the paper carrier. At last a red van turned up the drive. An arm popped out the window and launched the paper toward Meg's front porch. Even before the vehicle pulled away, Meg scrambled outside and snatched the paper from the cold ground.

The pictures were good of Josh, but Candy let her down. She looked every part the overweight sedentary housewife. Meg pitched the paper in the trash and marched upstairs to change into her gym clothes.

The drive allowed her time to decompress. At the Y, she ran her membership card through the scanner. The clerk, without looking up, tossed a towel at her. The anonymity of the city was a relief. The workout room hummed with activity and young, lean bodies sweated away to the pounding music from the television. Meg found an unoccupied stationary bike and nodded to the overweight housewife next to her.

As Meg adjusted the seat, she felt the stares of the other woman. Meg entered all the pertinent data on the bike's computer and started pedaling. She caught the woman looking again. Meg strained harder and tried to get in the rhythm of the music video on the large screen. Sweat soon rewarded her efforts. When she toweled off her face, she couldn't avoid the woman's intense gaze.

"Is there something wrong? Am I breaking out in hives again?" Meg asked.

The woman looked down and continued to pedal. "I have to confess, this is my first time here. I hate to exercise. But this morning I was reading the paper and there was a story about a woman in our area. She kind of looks like you. But you're not as large as she was."

Meg slowed down. "So, if you hate to exercise, why are you here?"

"Because of the story. If she could train for something like that, I could at least try to lose a few pounds by exercising. I didn't mean to stare. I just thought you might be that the woman. So brave."

Twenty-Eight

Sunday was her day of rest. Monday, Wednesday and Friday were Y days. That left Tuesday and Thursday for bicycling outside, but the pain from outdoor training threatened to disable her. Meg unloaded her bike and wheeled it into Duda's shop.

"I can't feel my hands anymore," she said, and shook them to illustrate her point. "The blood's not flowing."

Duda rose from behind the counter and enveloped her hands between his two large ones. "Ah, such delicate hands. Are you sure you want to do this biking thing anyway?"

Meg instinctively pulled her hands away. "I'm beginning to wonder myself. If this is how I feel already, what will it be like later? And now, my rear is sore and my hands tingle every time I ride."

"Ah, I was just teasing you. We'll get you ready for this enormous task." Duda beamed at her.

Most Saturdays, the bike shop was a haven for granola-eaters who gathered to swap stories over Duda's free organic coffee. Today the shop was quiet.

"Where is everyone?'

"The heart foundation is sponsoring a century today."

"A century of what?"

"No, no. A century bike ride. Riders go 100 miles, or they can do a half-century and even a quarter-century. You should probably try one," Duda said.

"One step at a time, buddy, one step at a time. I'm not even up to twenty-five miles without some part of my body yelling for me to 'stop, stop you crazy woman'."

Duda laughed and spun around to grab a pot of coffee from the counter. His movement accidentally sent a stack of energy bars tumbling to the floor.

"How about a cup of coffee? Let's sit and talk." He motioned to two webbed lawn chairs in the work area. With his other hand, he scooped up the bars and cleared a spot back on the counter, crowded with assorted tools, catalogs, and advertising promotions.

"Now, let's talk about this ride and that child of yours. I heard him—you know, in Jamaica if we ever spoke to our mama like that, ooh, boy. I would not be here to talk to you today, I can tell you that."

"He's a handful, and it's only gotten worse since his dad died last year. Now he thinks he's lord of the house."

"Oh, there can be only one Lord of any house."

"Please, not you too." Meg poked her finger through a dime-sized hole in the frayed webbing and played with a loose piece of nylon string. "No religion for me. I've been there, done that. And what did I get?"

"All right, no Jesus talk. We just talk biking." Duda's hands quickly skimmed along the flat tire he was fixing.

"Did the boy pick out a route yet? I know there are many excellent websites he could use."

"He said he has some good ideas."

"Wonderful. On to you, your hands." Duda beckoned to Meg. "Show me how you ride. But first we put your bike in the stand."

After Duda lifted her bike and secured it into a stand, Meg stood next to it and swung a leg over.

"Now hop on, you'll be safe in that stand. Pretend you are riding."

Meg put her feet on the pedals and hands on the handlebars.

"Aha, that is it!" Duda danced, delighted with his discovery. "Look, look at your hands! The nerve is getting compressed, making your hand quite sleepy indeed. You need to change the position, move your hands many times while you ride."

Her knuckles turned white when she gripped the bar. Then she loosened her grasp and experimented putting her hands close together and than far apart at several intervals along the handlebars.

"Don't collapse your hands so." He lifted up her wrists. "Now, what about gloves?"

"Gloves? They're packed away with the down parkas and fleece hats."

"No, biking gloves. Here try these." He flipped a package to her. "Let's see how they fit."

Meg tugged on a pair of black, padded gloves, the fingertips missing. She resumed her riding position and bounced her hands along to check the padding.

"Very nice." She wiggled her hands along the handlebars.

"Now time for more talk," Duda said. He helped her off the bicycle stand and led her back to the lawn chairs. Meg inched the gloves off her hands and held them up for Duda.

He raised his hand, palm toward her. "Nope. They're yours."

"But can't I even—?"

Duda cut off her response and took both of Meg's hands in his and gently massaged them, working one finger at a time.

"You could do this yourself. Maybe the boy could?"

"Are you kidding? Josh cringes if he accidentally bumps into me. There's no way he'd rub my hands," Meg said.

Duda continued massaging. His touch was soothing, yet embarrassing, since after all, he really wasn't a massage therapist.

"My, it's getting warmer in here," Meg said. *Please not a hot flash. I can't be that old.* Perspiration collected in her armpits and she couldn't look at Duda. She flushed and glanced out the shop window. Herb Larson, head of the church trustees, stared directly at Meg, his mouth a gaping chute of amazement.

Twenty-Nine

"Who was that fella who just lost his eyeballs?" Duda hopped up from his chair. The front door to the floral shop next door swung open and a delivery boy sprinted by with a bouquet of daisies. The door smacked Herb and he collapsed in a disheveled pile in front of the florist.

Duda vaulted over the counter and out the door, Meg on his heels.

The boy hollered over his shoulder "They're for the Festival Queen. It's an emergency. She just had her tonsils out. Sorry." Then he jumped in the delivery van, idling at the curb. Duda tried to scoop up Herb, but the man whacked Duda on the arm.

"Meg," Herb said. "What in the world is this guy up to? Halverson said something about you going a little off the deep end. I hope this isn't part of it."

Meg assured him everything was fine. Herb brushed off his slacks and stood up.

"I was on my way to pick up the altar flowers. You know, I do it every week. That's part of my Christian duty. And when we're through with them I deliver them to the shut-ins. Many of them are just like you, widows."

"Herb, Duda. Duda, Herb," Meg said. "Duda is helping me with Robert's project."

Duda stuck out his right hand toward Herb and Meg saw Herb hesitate a moment too long before he shook it.

Once Meg and Duda settled back down in the lawn chairs, Duda reached over and patted her arm. "Here's what we are going to do. We are going to make you a strong biker lady. No more shaky hands, sore rumps."

Duda leaned back and grabbed a newspaper off the counter, searching for a blank place to write.

"Here, take this," Meg said. She handed him a grocery-shopping tablet.

"Oh good one. We are shopping for a new biker lady." Duda flashed his big smile. "Now let's plan. When does the big adventure begin?"

"June 1."

"Okay, and today is..." Duda glanced at the big calendar hanging on the wall. "Ooh."

Meg flinched in her chair. "Umm, not much time for training. Not much at all."

"No, no, no. Plenty of time. You be ready. Just wait and see." Duda twisted one of his dread locks while he plotted. With a red marker, he stood up and moved to the calendar.

"Here we are." He put a small X on the date. "Now," he skimmed across the poster, "here is D-Day, or B-Day, Bike Day." He drew a big X on June 1. "Now, the big question. What are we going to do between now and then?"

His eyes held no glints of sarcasm or scorn, so unlike the eyes of her soon-to-be biking companion. Meg stood up and started to pace.

"Goodness if I know," Meg said. "This is all making me a little crazy. When I first saw the recording, and heard Robert's wild plan, I thought there'd be no way Josh and I could do this. I didn't think we'd even consider it. And now, here I am, in a bike shop actually entertaining the wild notion. All my friends think I'm insane. I think I'm insane."

"You're not insane."

"If Josh wasn't taking it seriously, I know I'd never do it. I just couldn't."

"Miss Meg, you gotta be strong. We get a plan, you follow it, you do the ride. You happy to finish. See, end of story."

"Easy for you to say."

"Ahh, but I didn't say it would be easy to do. It will take discipline and sacrifice."

By now, Meg's pacing had grown to the perimeter of the store and she lengthened her stride. Duda kept in step until they walked past a rack of bicycles.

"This is what you need." He pulled out a brand new bicycle. "Your boy bought a new one for himself. It's only fair that you get one too. You can't keep riding that old bike."

She eyed the bike and its narrow seat then pointed to a seat almost double the width of the others hanging from the wall. "What about that model? Even a walrus would enjoy all that cushioning. I'd never get sore on that."

"That's a little old lady bike saddle, perfect for zooming around the block, but not across the country." He patted the seat on the bike. "You'll see. This will be great. Hop up, let me see how it fits."

Duda held the bike while she climbed up. The saddle curved in all the right places.

"Anatomically designed," Duda said. "This is perfect. I take your old bike and recycle it for Pedals for Progress. You help someone across the world instead of filling up a dump somewhere. Everybody happy."

Josh pulled open the door to the bookstore at the same time someone was pushing it.

"Come in, come." The man waved him in. "I saw you walking down the street and I just knew you were going to turn in here. Welcome to my shop. What can I do for you today?"

With the back of his hand, the owner pushed his glasses back up his nose. His fingers glistened in the bookshop's bright light. "Cookie dough," he said in response to Josh's stare. "Marketing, you know. I thought if I baked and gave away cookies, more customers might stop."

"You might be on to something there," Josh said.

"I even turn on a fan to circulate the good smells. The only problem is," the man paused to lift up his fingers, "when the dough gets under my nails. Maybe if I kept them short."

Bing. A timer sounded somewhere from the back of the shop.

"Just wait. You've never had anything like my cookies. I'll be right back."

The shop owner scuttled toward the back of the shop and Josh ran to the opposite corner. A sign announcing MUSIC dangled from the ceiling. Cardboard boxes of old LPs were stacked below and on top of a table. Josh pulled out an album, its cover rippled with water damage, aged with brown mildew. He slipped out the record and examined it for scratches. Then he held it up to the window and rotated it. Too many scratches would make the needle on his dad's old turntable skip around too much.

Josh slid the record back into its cover and reached under the table. Hand-lettered brown file folders separated the albums alphabetically. He crouched over a box and thumbed through letters R-T.

"Awesome," he exclaimed under his breath and withdrew an album.

"You can never go wrong with Scruggs. One of the finest ever was. Did you know he was only 6 when he started banjo? Me, I started when I was 5, but I never became a star. Course, if I would've practiced a little. Everyone knows it's a difficult instrument." To Josh's regret, the shop owner had completed his baking experiment.

"My grandmother taught me." Josh stayed on the floor, hunkered over the box of records. "It wasn't too bad."

"Well, of course, that's what I meant." The man withdrew a platter of steaming cookies from behind his back. "I meant, some people find it tough. Not I. Cookie?"

Josh eyed the plate, but the image of dough under the guy's ragged thumbnails chased the taste of chocolate chips right out of his mouth.

"No, thanks. Gave it up for Lent." At school some kids said that about chocolate. He didn't have a clue what it meant. Right now it just meant salvation.

"Didn't figure you for one of them religious types. Can't argue with the church though. That's The Church, capital T, capital C. I've known people who've tried, and next thing you know, they're excommunicated." The shopkeeper nibbled on a cookie and warm chocolate melted across his lips. "Some valuable records tucked in there."

Josh balanced two albums on his knees. He flipped over a third album to see who played backup.

"I once dated a girl who performed with that group, probably on that album." The chocolate smear across the shopkeeper's mouth continued to grow. Josh thought of Jimmie Klimstak back in elementary school. The kid couldn't make it though snack time without wearing half his snacks. The teacher gave up with napkins and began handing him complete rolls of paper towels.

Josh looked at the date in the lower left-hand corner. *Uh huh, sure you did buddy. That'd make you what, at least 90?* But he didn't want to get into it with the guy. Josh scanned the list of artists and pulled another name out of his elementary class. "I bet it was Jiffy Johnson, right?"

The guy blinked. "Righto, how'd you guess?"

"Lucky." Josh straightened up and the owner peered at him, nose-to-nose, first through his glasses and then over the glasses.

"You're that boy." The shopkeeper clapped his hands, in three short bursts with each word. "You're going on a journey with your mother. The lure of the open road."

The man scurried over to the counter and reached toward the cash register. Josh groaned when the man picked up a newspaper. *Not again.*

"Look." The man tapped his chocolate nail at the black-and-white photo. "That's you. Although I have to say this boy looks more muscular. Especially lifting weights. I'll be. Another celebrity in my store."

The pause hung empty in the air while Josh refused to fill it with a question.

The man tried again. "I get a lot of them you know. Celebrities."

Josh grunted a slight *uh-huh*.

The shop owner changed tactics and said, "The last winner from American Idol came in many times."

Finally, the shop owner gave up. He traced the newspaper with his finger, leaving a trail of chocolate across Josh's photo.

"Oh, oh. Look what I did. I just mutilated it. How can you sign it now?" The man whipped a handkerchief out of his pocket and tried to wipe away the smear. The newspaper ripped.

"Oopsy whoopsy. It's my last copy. This thing has been selling faster than lefse at the Christmas bazaar." The man shifted back and forth on his toes and his glance darted about the shop. Josh resumed looking through the records. *Let the guy figure out his own problem.*

"I've got it." The man clapped his hands again. Just one burst. "Would you mind if I run into the drugstore? It's just down the square. I bet he has a copy you can sign. I'll frame it and put it up on the wall."

The man disappeared without an answer from Josh. Within minutes, the shop phone began to ring. Josh considered the options and decided to let the phone ring. After five rings, it quit. Maybe the answering machine picked up. Josh crouched over the carton of albums again. He had just reached the double album from Woodstock when the phone began to ring and a gust of wind accompanied a shopper through the front door.

Josh considered a quick exit through the back door, but the phone became silent. The customer began to walk around the displays.

"You. Where are your souvenirs? I need to find a shot glass from Minnesota. Got anything with a walleye on it? Maybe one of those black-and-white birds? Wait, how about a giant mosquito? Your state bird." The stranger covered his belly with his hands while he laughed.

The phone on the wall began to ring, one of those old-school drilling rings.

"Aren't you going to get that kid?"

"No, sir, customers come first." *Where'd that line come from?* "We don't have any souvenirs like that. Some books about Minnesota, right there." Josh pointed to the large display at the front of the store.

"Nah, my kids wouldn't be too happy with a book. Before I hit the road for Illinois, I loaded up my suitcase with all the shampoos and soaps at the hotel. That'll make my daughter happy. The boy, he collects shot glasses."

"Try the drugstore. Out the door, turn left, giant orange sign on its front." The phone rang again and Josh turned to answer it.

"Hello?" He couldn't remember the new name of the store. Each owner called it something different.

"You're supposed to say, "Ned's Book Nook'," the caller said.

"Okay then, the guy isn't here. Call back later."

"Wait, this is Ned."

"You said you were coming right back." Josh walked as far as the phone cord would allow him. This guy needed to start living in the real world and get a cordless.

The voice at the other end spoke again. "Boy? You still there? I can't find a paper anywhere. I'm going to jog over to the hotel." He hung up before Josh could tell him he had to take off.

All of a sudden, Josh grasped the situation. This had to be one of those reality shows, *Living in the Real World*, or something like that. He replaced the receiver and looked around the store for a camera. He knew it would get more insane by the minute and the audience would be waiting for him to explode.

Two can play this game.

Josh located the camera on a ledge above the doorsill, but kept his glance moving, so the audience wouldn't realize he was in on it.

The phone started ringing again, just as a tour bus pulled up in front of the shop and parked next to the curb, blocking several diagonal parking spaces. The bus driver jumped out and held out his arm to assist a bunch of little old ladies, all looking like Aunt Naomi. *Sweet, this is perfect.*

Josh ran to the door, flipped the cardboard sign to CLOSED and locked the door. A woman with a nametag bouncing around her chest and a clipboard wedged under her arm hustled to the door. Her fur hat, looking a bit like the Johnson's Maltese, slipped over one eye. He pulled down the shade in the door.

A polite rap of knuckles sounded on the door.

"Young man, I know you're in there. We just saw you. This is one of our official stops for the Marvelous Minnesota Movie."

Josh scoffed at the likely cover. Who would pay to take a bus tour of movie sites near Lake Devine? It all looked the same.

The knocking continued, although a little more intense. Josh plastered on a smile and opened the door.

"Come in. I've got movie soundtracks right here." Josh shuffled through the box of LPs while the women streamed into the store. He stopped in the Os, snagged an album and jumped up to the turntable, just like the one Dad nursed along to play his jazz albums.

"This guy was crazy. Ate heads of off birds on stage. I'll play it for you."

Josh placed it on the spindle and set the arm down on the edge of the vinyl. Music spewed from the tiny speakers and the women covered their ears to the clash of chords. A kitchen timer went off, its *bing* competing with the incessant ringing of the phone. Then a smoke alarm began to wail. Josh dropped the albums and raced toward the back door. He ran past the toaster oven on the countertop in the workroom, and stopped to grab a towel to pull out a tray of black lumps, their smoke filling the shop. Then he pushed open the door.

"What's going on?" Ned, the shop owner, stood there with a stack of newspapers, his mouth agape.

"Funny. You tell me. I saw the camera."

"Camera? I don't know what you're dreaming about, but I must help these customers." Ned rushed past Josh, fanning the air with his newspapers and sweeping the turntable's arm across the album, screeching it into silence.

"Ladies, please don't leave." Ned grabbed the coat sleeve of the woman with the Maltese on her head and clipboard. "Just a minor misunderstanding."

"What an odd way to welcome tourists. I thought the company phoned last week to arrange our visit. And this young man." She pointed at Josh. "I never."

Ned jabbed a thumb in his own chest. "I'm Ned, the owner. This boy just came in off the streets. He's a troubled youth I'm counseling. He has much to learn about customer service. I've set aside several autographed copies of the book they made about that movie. For all the confusion, I'll give you a 10 percent discount. Plus, I'd be happy to entertain you with stories about the wonderful time we had when the actors came to town. We shared many good times over glasses of the finest wine."

"Ladies, what's the consensus?" The tour leader scanned her group.

Ned reached behind the counter and pulled out a bottle in each hand. "And you all may enjoy that same fine wine. My treat."

Josh lingered long enough to hear the women agree to stay. Now he remembered the one movie. His biology teacher had a role because of her hippy-dippy looks. She later told the class the actors kept their distance and complained about chummy townspeople. *I bet they were complaining about this guy.* Josh slipped out, leaving Ned to charm his customers.

Thirty

Meg juggled two trays of cookies and pulled open the backdoor to the church kitchen. A handful of women milled about the center island in the kitchen.

"Oh. Oh, hi. I didn't realize anyone was around." Meg held up the pans. "Peanut butter. I saw in the church newsletter that you needed hundreds of cookies for the kids' spring program."

"Well, well. If it isn't Meg." Two women hurried over to embrace her while she put down the pans.

"Honey, it's been a long time since we've seen you. Where have you been keeping yourself?" As the woman spoke, Meg caught another one nearby signaling her. "Oh, I didn't mean it in a bad way. I know it takes time to recover when you lose your spouse." The woman spun around to dry off glass platters in the sink.

Jean, Chip's wife, came over and touched Meg's sleeve. "I'm sorry I haven't been over much since the funeral. You know how life is. Here and there. Between two kids in jazz dance and piano and one girl in basketball and literary club. Well, you know. Life as a chauffeur. You're probably coasting now, since Josh can drive."

From across the kitchen, Grace called out, "Is it true what I heard? Herb said he saw you with that black fella at the bike shop. It's probably time you were interested in another man. You can't mourn forever. And heavens to Betsy, is he a looker."

Mortified, Meg raised a hand to her cheek. "No, no, you don't understand," she stammered. "He's half my age. He's been helping me on a professional level."

"What? He a part-time counselor or something?"

Meg's gaze darted around. The room was getting stuffier and quieter by the minute.

"Well, I heard something completely different," responded a woman getting fruit punch out of the double-door refrigerator. "But frankly it's so bizarre, I don't believe it. I think that newspaper reporter just made it up."

The room was completely silent now. Meg held her breath, braced for the inquisition.

"Meg, sit down. You look a little pale." Jean gestured to a tall stool by the counter. "Now, tell us. What in the world is going on?"

Meg yanked at a short lock of her hair, twirled it around and around while she tried to figure out, for the umpteenth time, where to begin her sorry story.

"Before Robert died, he arranged a cross-country bicycle trip. For the two of us. Not him. I mean for Josh and me. He explained it all on a DVD he recorded."

Jean nodded. "Chip said he delivered something at Christmas to you. That must've been it."

"Bingo," Meg said.

"There's more to the story, isn't there?" Grace, her old friend from the mothers' study group, sought to encourage her with a hand on her shoulder.

"Robert wants us to go where the St. Louis Cardinals play, their baseball stadium. We're to deliver his ashes."

A collection of gasps filled the kitchen. Meg pushed on, eager to finish her story and escape their so-called concern.

"There's one catch. We have to travel by bicycle, from Oregon to Missouri."

"You're not going to do it, are you?" asked the one with the fruit punch "I mean, we're not kids anymore. And wouldn't that take forever? All that time with a teenager? I'd go crazy."

The woman drying dishes piped in. "Isn't that rather dangerous? Just the two of you? What do you mean by cross-country? How long will you be gone?"

"The whole summer. We'll be back in time for Josh to get ready for college."

A small *humph* rolled out of Jean's mouth. "Well, I know I could never do something like that. How could I just drop everything and go?"

Several women bobbed their heads in agreement.

"I guess when your spouse dies, priorities change." Meg headed for the door.

Jean added one more punch. "That's just like Robert, anyway, isn't it?"

Meg stopped. "What do you mean by that?"

"I know he always went on those long bike trips in Iowa. Now he's making you do it."

"Nobody's making anyone do anything," Meg said. She turned to leave again. "Well, good luck with the program."

Jean followed Meg to the door and gripped her arm. She lowered her voice. "You know, Meg, maybe you should talk to my cousin Marjorie. She's a counselor, has a little office above the bakery downtown. You're just setting yourself up for a big disappointment with this asinine plan."

Meg ducked out the door, but Jean continued to follow with advice. "You need a more appropriate way to channel that grief. Maybe Grace was right about you getting hooked up with another man."

Thirty-One

Days after the encounter in the church kitchen, Meg let the answering machine pick up her phone calls. Finally, the women quit calling.

She dumped a load of laundry in Josh's room and noticed Chester sitting upright facing a corner. The cat's tail twitched like a metronome.

"What's up little buddy?" Meg moved up behind him. There in the corner behind a baseball bat was one of her son's crabs. The creature was tucked in its shell, hiding from the curious swipes of Chester's paw.

"Good job, Chester." She patted the cat's head. She glanced around Josh's room and found a paperback book on his chair. *Marine Biology Adventures*. She deftly swept the creature onto the book, lifted the lid and returned the crab to the aquarium. Once she closed it, she examined it for escape hatches.

Once she finished her morning chores, she stuck her bike in the SUV and drove to town, careful to park far away from the church. With a lookout for potential gossipers, she unpacked her bike and climbed aboard.

The crossing guard held up the stop sign and Meg waited as the school children walked across the street. Next up was Bjorn's Bakery on the square. Meg pressed her face against the window watching the baker's assistant zig-zag frosting atop the cranberry walnut bagels, steaming from the oven. If she leaned hard enough, she could almost smell them. The assistant stopped and waved to Meg. Caught in her weekly routine, Meg parked her bike outside and went in for just a taste. That, combined with a cup of their house blend, made the morning exercise palatable. It also gave her time to rest her tingling hands.

At the bike shop, she explained her cycling routine to Duda. He grinned and patted her on the shoulder.

"Oh, Miss Meg. That will take you nowhere. Except to a bigger size of short." He pretended to peek around at her rear, before he peppered her with questions.

Meg walked over to a sunglass display and removed a pair with amber lenses. She looked in the little mirror on the stand. *Probably need to pick up a pair before D-Day. Departure Day.*

"That man from your church. He okay?"

"Herb? The one who tripped out front?" Meg hoped he was still sore. "He's well enough to gossip. I got an earful at church when I dropped off food for a program."

"Gossip? I thought you said at your church he was a column."

"Pillar," Meg said. "What's gossip got to do with church?"

Duda lifted a sheet of bubble wrap out of the carton and folded it in thirds before sticking it under the counter. He looked directly at Meg. "Christians need to control their tongues. Gossip is a sin."

"Oh please," Meg said. "Sin is pretty strong. Save that for the murderers and rapists. Not the gossips."

Duda grabbed a box cutter and slit open another carton sitting on the floor. He rocked back on his heels to peer up at Meg. "Miss Meg, you're a momma. When your boy does wrong, does it not hurt you here?" He thumped his chest. "Jesus, our Lord and Father grieves too, every time we sin. Big. Little. It's all the same."

In order to avoid the bakery's allure, Meg decided to venture out on the bike trail near town. Plus, she figured no one would recognize her in a helmet and sunglasses. What she hadn't realized was how difficult the first step would be. It looked like everyone from Lake Devine was on the trail today. She sat in her vehicle in the parking lot and watched. If she counted 10 people in 10 minutes, she'd leave. Too many people made her nervous. A pair of women pushed strollers. Meg hesitated in her tally, would that be two people or four? A bike gang whizzed by, seven members strong and sleek in matching green tops and black shorts. Meg unpeeled a banana as she watched the bikers dissolve into a blur down the bike path. A glance at her watch told her two more minutes and one more person and then she could go home.

It's now or never. Do or die. I can do all things through Him who strengthens me. Just do it. By the time she unloaded her new lightweight bike, Meg ran out of sayings. She strapped on her bright yellow helmet, pulled on the new gloves, and slipped her right foot into the cage attached to her pedals. Someday, Duda had told her, she would get the special clip-in pedals and shoes, like Robert had. First she had to learn how to pull with these.

Armed with Duda's training schedule, Meg was ready to advance beyond novice rank. Duda recommended the bike trail so she wouldn't have to worry about traffic. Or in her case, he joked, fresh bagels.

The plan was to pedal to the bridge and back to the parking lot. Her only stop would be the turn. Meg checked the trail's flow both ways before she straddled her bike. At least the weather cooperated. Clear skies, sunny, and surprise, no wind. Another rare Minnesota spring day.

She concentrated on staying to the right side of the path. Soon, she caught up with the two moms, their hands moving in animation and their babies asleep in strollers. Bits of their conversation floated to Meg.

"And then, he spit up all over me, just as I was on my way to the meeting," one exclaimed.

The gap was now less than three feet and Meg slipped her feet out of the pedal cages, prepared to stop.

"Excuse me," Meg called out. "I'm sorry, but I am right behind you. I need to pass, please don't move."

The young women jerked their heads back and shuffled farther to the right.

Meg glided past them and gave a little wave of thanks. *Not bad.* Gradually she loosened her grip on the handlebar and willed her shoulders to relax. A pair of chickadees darted along in the underbrush. Other bird songs floated out of the budding woods, and the chorus of spring surrounded Meg.

When a slight tingle vibrated up her fingers, Duda's instructions flashed in her head, "Remember to change your hand position frequently." Meg looked down at her hands. Her palms lay flat against the handlebars. She shifted her hand placement. Relief instantly replaced the numbness.

Near the next mile marker, a woman marched on the right, her head bobbing in a steady beat. As Meg drew closer she heard show tunes. "Willkomen, bienvenue, welcome..."

A miniature schnauzer minced along the left side of the trail, catching smells from previous animals. Inches away, Meg realized the schnauzer and singer were attached.

"Watch out, behind you, behind you," Meg hollered. The singer headed for the grand finale now, complete with arm gestures.

"BEHIND YOU," Meg bellowed. The singer ripped off her headphones, her eyes as wide as pancakes when she saw Meg bearing down on her. First she danced to the left, and back to the right, while the little white dog zipped back and forth.

Meg squeezed on the brake levers, but it was seconds too late. She flipped over the handlebars and landed in the brush alongside the trail.

"Oh my heavens," screamed the singer. "Look what you've done to my precious Petey."

The dog's leash was tangled in Meg's front wheel, still on the trail with the rest of her bike. Petey jumped around on the shortened leash. The woman rushed to extricate him from the bike.

"Oh my little baby. I can't believe what that mean biker lady did to you." She cradled him in her arms and nuzzled his face.

Meg, sprawled on the ground, could do little more than stare at the show-tunes devotee. Her head throbbed and her left knee was covered in blood.

She looked up at the sound of voices. "And then that crazy biker plowed into them," an older man explained to the onlookers. "She came out of nowhere. And next thing you know, *BAM*. She smacks into them and then she flies off her bike."

With that, the crowd collectively turned to Meg, motionless in the brush.

"There she is. Over there."

Two people rushed to her aid, and one said, "Now, I've had a little CPR training. Do you need any of that?"

"No, no, I'll be fine," Meg assured her rescuers. "I just need a little help getting up. I'm stuck in this old tree limb."

A woman gasped. "Oh honey, look at the poison ivy, wrapped around that thing. You are in for it now."

Meg looked around. Just about every part of her body touched the noxious vine.

Thirty-Two

Muted strains of Schubert drifted across the room. Layered with coats of cortisone cream, Meg teetered on a leather couch, fearful of smearing the ointment. The poison ivy branched up her legs, but stopped at her hips. Over the angry blotches, Meg wore a coordinated workout outfit she had ordered online. After several weeks observing the fit regulars at the Y, Christy declared it was time to update their exercise fashion and break out of their sweat suits.

Coming here was all Duda's idea. He suggested she pump up her routine a notch or two. The trip was in jeopardy otherwise, he cautioned. At the very least she'd be facing too much of a mental and physical challenge.

So today she waited to meet her new personal trainer. The first phone call was difficult. The notion of a trainer seemed somewhat silly and pretentious. Like the idea of a personal assistant or something like that. This had to remain confidential. She studied her gnawed fingernails, pulling at the cuticles.

"Mrs. Albertson?" A woman, approximately Meg's age, popped in the room. Meg stood up to shake her hand.

"Please sit." The spiky-haired trainer, armed with a clipboard, motioned to the couch, but remained standing. She removed the pen from behind her ear.

"I'm Greta. How much weight do you want to lose?"

"I thought Duda called you," Meg said.

"He did mention he was sending a cyclist over. That's not you, is it?"

""I'm pretty sure it is. Or it was." Meg stood, ready to leave. Greta pushed her back down on the couch.

"Sit. Silly misunderstanding. Between supplements and super sessions, I can whip you into prime shape."

Meg looked at the glossy photos on the wall behind Greta. Several men and women in unnatural poses smiled at the camera.

"Prime shape like that?" Meg jerked her thumb toward the photos.

"Not exactly," Greta said with a smirk.

"Thank goodness."

"Mrs. Albertson, Meg, maybe we need to start over. Tell me what you hope to get out of our sessions. Then we can set some goals."

As Meg explained, Greta took notes with small precise movements and nodded numerous times. When Meg got to the point about the timing, Greta held up her hand.

"Hold up a sec. When do you depart?"

"Wouldn't you be more comfortable sitting?" Meg said.

"Standing is a more efficient manner to expend calories."

Meg leaned forward to push off from the couch. Greta stopped her with a hand on the top of her head. Then she pulled out a calendar.

"You start when?"

"June 1, right after my son's commencement."

The trainer tapped her chin with the pen and flipped through her notes. "Hmm, I see."

"Not good?"

"It's right around the corner."

"I'm ready to work hard. I can be here every day. I'll do whatever it takes," Meg said.

"I'll tell you what it will take. It will take a miracle." Greta collapsed on the couch next to Meg.

"I hate to say this Greta, but it's like a nightmare that haunted me in high school. I'd wake up in a cold sweat, dreaming about being in the state finals in track but with no training. On the morning of the run, I would stumble after the *pop* of the starter's pistol. The only way to finish was to crawl."

A spot no larger than a jellybean began to pulsate under Greta's cheek. Meg studied the muscle and began to count how frequently it moved.

"When was the last time you ran?"

"Competitively? High school. I didn't run in college. I did play tennis, intramurals. I played tennis for many years, right up until my husband got sick. And skied."

"And now you're doing?" Greta paused, pencil poised above the clipboard.

"Now, well." Meg matched Greta's pause. "I've participated in some classes at the Y, but my workout buddy, Christy, had to leave town for some family emergency. Plus that bicycle class killed me. All that up and down, up and down. And then I became quite sore, if you know what I mean. I don't know if I will ever heal, which worries me because what if that happens when I'm on our big ride? What then?"

"I'm sure Duda will get you properly outfitted so you'll ride in relative comfort. My job is to help strengthen your legs, abdomen and back. We can work on strengthening while you take a break from the bicycle. Let's check out the machines."

Meg followed Greta into the weight machine area and listened to her explain each piece's function. Then she instructed Meg to sit on each apparatus while she adjusted the settings. Each setting was duly recorded on the clipboard.

Two days later when Meg returned, Greta barked out instructions for the workout. With a pencil, she beat a staccato rhythm on the leg press machine as she counted Meg's repetitions out loud.

"Meg, we work three times a week. If you give up, you're on your own. Now move it."

Thirty-Three

A coyote's cry drifted across the inky lake, answered by the bark of a dog. Josh dangled his feet over the dock, his banjo cradled in his lap. Slight ripples on the lake's surface caught the glow from a slice of moon. Wind rustled the branches in the trees behind him.

He picked out a little tune and the spirit of Earl Scruggs danced atop the water. Josh loved the crisp sound—so precise you could hear every note. Midtune, Josh stopped to flex his right hand and massage a tender spot on his thumb. His little finger returned to its resting place on the banjo, the spot worn smooth by his grandmother. Thanks to her, his fingers knew their way around a banjo. Nana could pick with the best of them, until arthritis hobbled her fingers and stopped the music. Then she placed the instrument in his arms.

Bright lights flickered across Lake Devine. Probably a raccoon tripping the security lights at the Happy Trails girls' camp. Summer nights after midnight Josh used to sneak out in his family's canoe and paddle to the camp. The junior counselors, always up for excitement, responded to his *hooty-hoo* signal from the water. They showed him where to beach the canoe to avoid activating the lights. Life always seemed more fun and easy in the summer.

During the school year, girls just complicated things. Take prom, for example, a simple dinner and a dance. But the girls fell for the hype, the big magical night where everything had to be perfect. He always interrupted the girls in Biology Club when they started buzzing about their dresses, nails, hair, and everything else for prom. Their buzzing was almost as bad as the mosquito that circled his ear. He slapped at the bloodthirsty little sucker. Least skeets were better than those stupid black flies that feasted on your ankles and made a boat ride miserable.

When he was a little kid, Josh loved to go out in the boat with Dad. The water was always so clear they could watch turtles paddling below the surface. Josh had learned early on to cast far away from the boat if he wanted to attract a walleye.

Back and forth, Josh's index and third finger joined his thumb in the basic roll, the first pattern Nana had shared with him. He warmed up and let his fingers fly across the strings. Once a month he joined a bunch of bluegrass lovers over on Sunset Lake. They'd pick all night. It was kinda nice, being the youngest one. But nights like this, alone with his banjo on the dock, were true gold.

Josh still couldn't comprehend why Dad didn't trust him to handle this trip on his own. He'd have no problem delivering the ashes to Busch Stadium. Now he faced three months stuck with another person. And that one person had to be Mom. *What's the point?*

He switched automatically to one of his favorite Scruggs tunes, the theme from an old TV show about some hillbillies who moved to Beverly Hills. He used to watch the reruns at his grandparent's house, just to listen to the music. The day Nana had pulled out her banjo blew him away. Right behind him, the strings rang out, and there she was, walking and playing the banjo, in sync with the guys on TV.

She died. But she was really old. Dad died, and he wasn't. *Okay, God, one question, how does that fit into your will?* He sat on the dock and waited for the proverbial lighting strike to come and claim him too.

Thirty-Four

With Duda's encouragement ringing in her ears, Meg decided to get back on her bicycle, but not on the trail. Picking a route shouldn't be too difficult. The garage walls were covered with maps of the area lakes. Robert had tacked them up so he could check on the properties. Meg scanned the map, noting the blue stars, red stars, and gold stars. Some associate she was. She didn't have a clue what his star coding meant. Just like his bland response, 'situation resolved.' Meg blew out a quick breath, blotting out further thoughts of her husband until she came to 'You are Here', penciled in red on one of the maps.

Yes, I am here. You are not. She blew out another breath and tried to remember the cleansing breaths from the yoga class she and Christy dropped in on at the Y. *In and out. In and out.* Her chest rose with each in, deflated on the outs. *In and out.*

Five cleansing breaths later she was able to focus on her cycling agenda. With an ink pen, she plotted a route on her forearm. The road meandered around a nearby lake and would take her farther out into the countryside. She patted her bike hanging on the hook and returned to the kitchen until Josh was awake.

The boy lumbered down the stairs, his body heavy with sleep. Meg poured cereal into a bowl and set a spoon next to it.

"I made you breakfast," she said.

"This?" Josh pulled a stool up to the counter. Meg forced herself to smile.

"I couldn't find any eggs. I guess we need groceries. Milk?" She opened the refrigerator. "White or chocolate?"

Josh mumbled so she gave him both cartons and retreated upstairs.

When he shouted 'good bye', she rushed down the stairs to hug him. She swung open the front door, but all that remained was the sound of his car rumbling off to school.

In and out, in and out. Two more cleansing breaths.

The lake sparkled under the morning sun and a long-legged heron skimmed the water with a fish in its claws. Meg sat on the deck with a stationery box in her lap and reflected on the last few months. The mere mention of Robert's name no longer caused her tears to spill. At the grocery store she could zip past Robert's favorite ice cream without feeling the need to pick up another half-gallon.

As she nibbled on a pen she contemplated the first sentence for the next thank-you note. Only seven more notes before she could check off this final task. After Robert's funeral, someone from the church had addressed and stamped the envelopes for Meg. At least Meg guessed that was the source.

With a flourish, she licked the last envelope and stood up, energized by her accomplishment. Inside, she stacked the notes on a table next to the front door and went upstairs to change into biking clothes.

Reluctant to hit the trail again, Meg pedaled away from the lake. She hung close to the shoulder, startled by an occasional truck or car. With each rise in the road ahead, a bicycle came into view. And then the image would vanish.

Ten miles later, she passed a bike propped in a clump of forsythia in full lemony bloom. Ready to offer assistance and take a break herself, Meg stopped pedaling and coasted. As she neared, the rider jumped out from behind the bush. His hands gripped the sides of his coat and stretched it as wide as the span of his arms. And underneath, he had no secrets.

Meg slammed on her brakes so hard they squealed.

"Mr. Svenson. You stop that."

The old man grinned and held out his arms. "Care to tango?"

"It's me, Meg Albertson."

"Thought I was scaring me a new one." He chuckled and pulled his worn coat around his skinny frame. "My eyes are getting kinda dim nowadays."

"That's why you better get on your bike and head home."

"I ain't got no home."

"The new place. Where they cook for you." She held out her watch and pointed to it. "I bet it's time for lunch now. Chocolate cake on Tuesdays?"

Mr. Svenson smacked his lips and widened his eyes so much Meg could see the cataracts that clouded them. He waved over his shoulder and took off for the home, his bike wobbling side-to-side.

It was after 4:00 p.m. when Meg pedaled up her drive. She hung her bike up in the garage and called the Golden Years retirement home and the sheriff's office to make sure Mr. Svenson came back this time.

Before Robert had needed her constant attention, Meg volunteered once a month at Golden Years. She had started volunteering when her pastor needed someone to deliver tapes of his sermon to the home after Sunday service. Since Golden Years was on her way home from town, she had made the perfect candidate.

When the Y fell off of the sign in front of the ivy-covered mansion, Meg had considered organizing a craft project with a Golden Ear idea. Sort of a Van Gogh theme. That was right before Robert's diagnosis.

Thirty-Five

Duda spun the bike wheel with his left hand and adjusted the gauge with his right. He explained to Josh how to true a wheel while it was in the stand. He cocked an ear to the stand, and listened for the wheel to bump the indicator.

"Duda, I don't get all this God's will stuff." Josh scratched his neck. "At the funeral, wrinkled up old ladies came up to me, patted my cheek and told me it was God's will that Dad died."

"That's a silly thing to say at a funeral. They should've just hugged you. That's what a body needs."

"I thought God was supposed to be a loving being."

"Whoa, man. Where'd that come from?" Duda stopped working at the stand and stared at Josh.

"Do you think it was God's will that he died?"

Duda dragged two chairs over to the work area. "Sit. Now, this is how I see it. How my mama taught me. And she learned in Christian schools, just like I did."

"That's kinda weird. Thinking about Christian schools somewhere like Jamaica."

"What's so funny 'bout that? We're not primitives, running around with bones through our noses."

"No, I didn't mean anything..." Josh held up his hands. "Please."

"Sure I know I talk funny, look funny, but we're all God's children. I don't get it all, but I will trust God. He's bigger than me, wiser than me, so I can submit to Him, follow Him. Just like Jesus said, 'Not my will, but thy will.' "

Duda returned to the truing stand, and worked in silence, adjusting the gauge. He abruptly stopped. "Hey, you know what? You need to know this. Come here."

Josh bounced up and joined Duda at the stand.

"Call me Doctor Duda, I dispense advice. You need to know there are things, like a bad woman, that can cripple you. But out in the middle of nowhere, it's not the ladies—you get a flat, break a chain, snap a spoke. You in trouble if you can't fix them. Watch what I do and then imitate me."

Josh manipulated the spoke and Duda made him work on another.

"Now I'll show you how to fix a chain," Duda said.

"Yeah, and the next thing you know, all the shop's work is done and your fingers are clean." Josh laughed.

"Good one, very funny. Now back to your questions. If you want to bring God's will into this, God's marked out a course for you to run. Right now your course is loving and supporting your mama, while drawing closer to Christ. Turn to Him. Believe in His promises."

"But I..."

Duda stopped Josh. "I know it's hard, but it's the next leg of your race. Let's close shop. Fifteen minute break."

He turned the clock hands on the 'Will Return' sign to 3:30, pulled the door shut and locked it. Taking Josh by the shoulder, he pointed to the drugstore.

"Man, I love that place. I'll buy."

Duda beamed feel-good waves to everyone he met. People on the square just couldn't help returning his smile. Even the crabby ones they ran into cracked a smile. Maybe the guy should turn his charm into cash, make some money in toothpaste commercials.

They perched on stools at the soda counter while the girl scooped ice cream for their order. With one hand she shot whipped cream from a canister and then with her other hand, stuck a slice of kiwi on top.

"My signature." She placed the glass dishes before them and bowed. Duda clapped. Josh bent over and stuck his tongue in his sundae, ready to let a blob melt down his throat.

Old-time music played over the speakers, the kind Mom liked about surfing, girls, and bikinis. Silence would be better than that stuff. Tapping on the linoleum countered the beat of the music overhead. Soon the *clickety-clack* was louder and louder, until it stopped right behind him.

Josh spun around to check it out. Mrs. Wheeler, his former piano teacher, tottered in her tiny high-heeled shoes. Maybe her tiny shoes were to blame and she'd be more pleasant in something suited for Big Foot. Regardless, her expression never changed. It was always the look of 'stay away, I'm constipated and nothing works.'

Mom had forced him to take lessons from that woman for too many years. After his last session, he had slipped a package of laxatives out of his pocket and left it on the piano bench.

"Hello, Mrs. Wheeler," Josh said. She blinked and snapped her head in a curt nod. Then she peered up at Duda. "Joshua, this isn't one of your classmates, is it?"

"No, ma'am, this is Duda, he works in the bicycle shop."

Duda extended his right hand, his smile connecting his ears.

Mrs. Wheeler said, "I didn't think so. I wasn't aware of any new residents of Lake Devine." She glanced down at Duda's outstretched hand, thrust her own hand into her coat pocket, and *clickety-clacked* away.

"How do you put up with stuff like that?" Josh asked Duda. "That woman is just plain ignorant. That's one reason I'm eager to get out of this area. Stupid people like that. But you, you chose to live here."

Duda shrugged. "I don't let it get to me."

"Wow, that's seems impossible. Don't you want to just punch them in the face?"

"Let me tell you something I learned when I first came here from Jamaica. It was a cold, cold day. I thank God for spring days like today. At least it is green out now. Could be warmer, lot warmer." Duda rubbed his hands together.

"Anyway, I retreat to Jamaica in my mind. I can battle the gloom and the cold, and people like that. Their ugly attitude can't take my spirit, my soul, my heart."

Josh let Duda's words sink in while he watched Mrs. Wheeler disappear down the street. He coaxed a melted lump of ice cream onto his spoon and slurped it.

Duda continued his story. "When I first felt trapped here, I remembered the stories passed down through my people. Their bodies might have been trapped, but their spirits were free. Even if they were slaves, they were still God's children and for that, they could sing and dance, even if sometimes it was only inside their bodies. They knew salvation and freedom awaited them. Someday, they'd be dancing with Jesus."

With his spoon, Josh drew ice cream curlicues around the kiwi slice in the bottom of the glass. Then he snatched it and popped it in his mouth. "You know, you sure have made an impression on my mom. It's Duda this, Duda that."

Duda licked the back of his spoon. "She said you don't go to church."

"Nah, we don't. I was never too big on it, too many hypocrites. Too many restrictions. She quit going, never said why."

"She's searching, that's for sure. What about friends?"

"Not my mom. She's pretty much a loner. Glued to Court TV. Course now that she's exercising, she's a little better. Sometimes she talks about someone at the Y. Nothing churchy though." Josh stood up.

"Before we go back, I need to pick up some food for the crabs."

"Next to Ned's bookstore? I always enjoy checking on my little buddies down the street," Duda said.

At the pet shop, Josh stuck his hand against the wired cage to let a German shepherd puppy lick his fingers. A dog was at the top of his list. Someone to sleep on his bed, keep him company. Hermit crabs were pretty boring, but Dad approved them, so Josh hadn't complained at the time. But the minute Josh signed the lease to a place of his own he was heading to the pound to rescue the first dog that smiled at him.

Duda signaled Josh over to the birdcages. "Remember what I said about feeling trapped? Listen. These finches still sing a happy melody. You know, I just thought of something else that's different about this place."

"This shop?"

"No, no, no. This part of the world. Not only have you cold temperatures, but everyone act so funny, so cold to each other. When your mama told me she hired a trainer, I tried to hug her, it made me so happy. I don't think she like me anymore."

"She has a trainer?" Josh knew she was taking the trip seriously, but she never said anything about a trainer. Not that he'd been around home much. When he was, he'd throw a pizza in the oven or make a box of macaroni and cheese and eat it next to his keyboard and computer. His mom tried to get him to sit down with her, but her diet was pretty strange. The last time he opened the refrigerator, heads of lettuce and too many other green things bounced out. Mac-and-cheese was a perfect meal.

Thirty-Six

From the walkout lower level, Meg watched the whitecaps on the waves surrender to the beach. Spring winds whipped the lake into a frenzy, but a row of pines Robert had planted years ago protected the yard. Next door she could see Mr. Halvorsen clad in a little swimming brief, perched on his lawn tractor. A multi-colored umbrella hat protected his neck and face. His bare back and stomach were already a blotchy pink. With one hand on the steering wheel, he maneuvered around the trees, and pulled up his tall tube socks with his other hand.

Meg noticed dried fish scales still clung to the cleaning station next to the downstairs kitchenette. When the oncologist gave them the news, Robert had made a list of things to do, 'just in case' he said. He wanted to take a thermos of coffee out on the pontoon boat and wait for the sun to rise. He wanted to drop in a line and maybe hook a walleye.

With her fingernail, Meg scraped the leftover scales and watched them disintegrate. Robert's muddy boots still sat next to the sink. One of these days, Meg figured, she should probably sort the rest of Robert's clothing. Except it was going to be a long time before she returned to the attic.

With her pinkie finger, she played with a buttonhole on the flannel shirt. The shirt came out only when Josh wasn't home. She never washed it, hoping to retain Robert's smell. At night, she hid it under Robert's pillow. Sometimes she would fall asleep with her face nestled in the fabric. Other times she'd just wrap her hands in its soft folds. Robert always wore it over a white cotton T-shirt and faded jeans. His weekend outfit, when he looked most handsome.

An urgent tapping rattled the sliding door. Mr. Halvorsen, still atop his mower, knocked on the glass with the end of a rake. A plastic garbage can was tied to the back of his mower, loaded with all the tools necessary to maintain his show-quality yard. Last summer he had won the Lake Devine title for outstanding yard. The trophy stood in his front bay window, visible to the road.

"Meg, open up," he hollered.

Meg slid open the door and poked her head out. "Careful with that rake, now."

He planted the rake back in the garbage can.

"Meg, isn't it a glorious day?" He swiveled around and inhaled deeply. "Just smell that, Minnesota gold. Anyway, I thought maybe you'd want to go with me into town. Chip at the hardware store called this morning to say my order is in. I saw the neatest gadget on TV to pull weeds and he was able to get me one. Maybe you and I could grab a cup of coffee or something downtown?"

Meg stepped out and watched a hawk circle in the sky. Mr. Halvorsen followed her gaze. "Isn't that a beautiful sight?" He looked to Meg for agreement. "Now, it will just take me a minute to throw on some clothes and then we could be off. Or..." He paused. "Do you sort of like me in my French swimming suit?"

She didn't know where to look. If she met his eyes, she knew she'd blush, and she didn't want to look down in case she accidentally glimpsed his swimsuit and then he'd think she was interested in his physique. She focused on the hawk.

"I do take care of myself. I know I'm just a little older than you, but you know..."

Older by at least two decades, Meg snorted, *and shorter by at least a foot.* His flabby stomach and bony arms and legs looked much better in the winter, concealed by layers of clothing.

"And kiddo, ever since you started this training routine, you're looking pretty good yourself. And that hair of yours, so flattering." He reached toward her.

Meg jerked her head back. "Thanks, but I have to go back inside. I think I hear the timer on the dryer and I need to grab some things before they wrinkle." She darted in and closed and locked the door.

The nerve of that old coot, teasing her like that. The scale hadn't changed in weeks. But she knew the hair was good.

Thirty-Seven

By now, Meg rode every day. The idea of cycling to a different town each day kept it pleasurable. Her pace improved too, thanks to Duda's insistence that she use a cycle computer. He mounted the device on her handlebars. Watching those digital numbers flash right under her nose encouraged her to maintain a steady speed.

While Greta, the trainer, helped Meg tone her muscles, Duda kept her focused. Three to four times a week, he challenged her to ride long distances. On the other days, it was her choice—speed work, hills, or a leisure pedal along the trails.

Today's assignment was to log forty miles. Since music was her sole companion, she stuck the Porgy and Bess tape into the cassette player in her fanny pack and looped the headphones around her neck. It would be nice to have a riding partner, but Christy said 'no way' and Josh trained on his own. *At least he better.* It was going to be hard enough to get herself in gear. Thank goodness she still had her old cassette player.

Heeding the advice in the cycling book from Ned's Book Nook, she scanned the kitchen for a nutritious snack. Something to help when she'd hit that caloric deficit. She smeared peanut butter inside a bagel and packed a chocolate oatmeal cookie and an orange for lunch. At the last minute, she stuck in a small bag of potato chips.

Careful to avoid the congested route near town, Meg took the trail in the opposite direction. The bike trail, on an abandoned rail bed, threaded through the woods around the lake towns. It sheltered Meg from the hazards of motorists and provided her the freedom to think. Or not. She could mindlessly pedal and purge her mind of clutter.

Every now and then other cyclists greeted her, traveling the opposite way. Soon the trees parted and the trail opened to a field of prairie grass. Meg shifted on her saddle and tugged on her cotton shorts to separate her sweaty underwear from the seams. Now she knew why Duda said biking shorts were imperative. This must be how elderly residents at Golden Years feel when they're forced to wear adult diapers. She knew Mr. Svenson didn't wear a diaper, that's for sure. *Someday the sheriff needs to arrest that man for exposure.*

Meg leaned her head back and coaxed the last few drops out of her water bottle. In her early training days, it took several attempts before she mastered grabbing the bottle while the bike was in motion. It helped to practice during spinning class when her body was in motion, not the bike. Just think how cranky Josh would have been if she needed to stop every time she was thirsty.

With twenty more miles to go, Meg realized the shade had bailed on her, and a blazing sun had jumped onboard. With an index finger, she poked her forearm. A dot of white appeared, swimming in a sea of scarlet. Her bangs were plastered to her forehead, and perspiration trickled into her eyes. Her eyes crossed as she watched the droplets skim down her nose to the trail below. With a little practice, she was able to aim the blobs of sweat to land in the dent in the middle of her handlebars. After six droplets hit the target, she declared herself a winner.

A trailside marker indicated a stop sign and intersection ahead. She blew through the empty intersection and swung left to escape the sun in a thicket of pine trees. Tucked under the trees sat a small church, its paint curled in faded strips and its windows shuttered with plywood. The bell tower sagged on collapsed timbers. A narrow path off the bike trail led to the church's gravel parking lot. A pickup truck, its original color no longer distinguishable from the rust, sat next to a white-painted school bus, dented and listing to the right.

Meg armed herself with the pump off her bicycle and crept past the junked vehicles, ready to wallop any watchdog. She twisted the spigot outside the building and let the water gush out into the gravel.

The backdoor to the church swung open and a boy stuck his head out. "I thought I heard the water running. Go ahead, help yourself."

"Thanks," Meg said. "I can't believe how hot it is today. Plus, I ran out of water miles ago. You probably saved my life."

He laughed. "It couldn't have been that bad! Although it is unusually hot for this time of year. You're welcome to rest in the shade here. Want some cold pop?"

"I guess I'm not on a real schedule. Just as long as I'm back to Lake Devine by three. It does feel nice to get away from that sun for a while. I didn't think to put on sunscreen." She lifted up her scarlet arm. "Can you tell? It just seems too early in the year for that."

"I know what you mean. I thought summer doesn't hit Minnesota until the fourth of July. At least that's what I had always heard. I'm Malachi by the way. I'll get you a pop and be right back."

Malachi returned with a plank of wood and a can. Meg took the cold can and pressed it against her forehead. She studied Malachi and realized he wasn't a boy. *Maybe twenty-six, twenty-seven?*

Malachi held up the plank. "I'm making a sign for the church. The Church of the 4Ls," he said. "Church for the lost, the least, the last, and the lonely." He outlined it with his fingertip. "Four Ls. I fell in love with this abandoned church when I saw it on-line. I hope to rebuild it. Don't you just love how it's nestled under these evergreens? And I can see a lake from the pulpit. There's something about preaching while being able to look beyond to the lake.

"I hope to reach out to those who feel the church has let them down. People who are dissatisfied with organized religion. You know, all the rituals that can get in the way of true worship and love for one another. It's almost like we're back in the Old Testament days with all these different rules. Why can't we just worship and praise God?"

He paused. "I'm preaching, I know. Sometimes I get carried away. My wife, she works in the city, says that will drive away people."

Meg nodded, plotting her escape while she gulped the rest of the pop. "Well, gee, thanks for the drink and the water. I'm set now." She stood up and adjusted her helmet. "I need to roll."

"So soon?"

"Daylight's burning. Many more miles to go. Thanks." Meg jumped on her bike and sped away.

Satisfied enough miles separated her from the preacher, Meg dropped her bike along the trail, ripped open the bag of potato chips and let the salty goodness fill her mouth.

Thirty-Eight

Duda grasped the OPEN sign, ready to flip it and signal an end to Saturday. Josh wiped his hands on his jeans, eager to be finished fiddling with bike tubes and tires. He stepped away from the door to return a wrench to the workbench.

"Something's wrong with my wheels, Duda."

Josh spun around to see a man steer in a bike, plastic dairy crates strapped to the frame and bulging grocery bags lashed all over.

"Thought I could fix it, straighten it out." The man shrugged and lifted up his palms, then he bent over and tugged on a rubber band circling his right pants leg.

Josh figured the guy to be at least 80. Maybe 90. Thin lines etched his tanned face and when he removed his battered white helmet, a thin gray braid fell to his shoulders. The fluorescent lights glared off the rest of his head, bald except for a few wisps by the braid. Another one of the hippies, just like his biology teacher.

"Let's take a look." Duda wheeled the bicycle over to the work area and lifted it onto a mechanic's stand. He spun the front wheel. "I get it. Two spokes are ready to snap."

"I'd been bending them a lot, trying to get extra miles out of them."

"Take a seat," Duda said. "Help yourself to some coffee."

Josh moved closer to the door. "Duda was just about to close."

"Josh, no problem." Duda shushed him with a hand. "Samuel, meet Josh, my assistant for today."

"Assistant?" Josh sputtered.

"Why not grab a bottom bracket wrench from the backroom, Josh. Over on the wall."

Samuel landed in a lawn chair and waved a hello to Josh. Josh lingered behind the bedspread hanging from the doorframe until Duda began to speak.

"The kid is struggling. His papa died. He's alone with his mama. And the papa is making them bicycle together, a long journey."

Josh returned from the backroom. "Couldn't find it."

"I guess I was mistaken." Duda wiggled the spokes into place and spun the wheel. "Sam my man, I think you're ready."

Samuel clasped Duda's hand and arm. "Thanks, man. I owe you one."

"Wait," Duda said. "I almost forgot." He sprinted over to a battered refrigerator in the corner and swung open the door. He held up a plastic bread bag.

"Bologna sandwiches. And two apples at the bottom. See?" His fingers curled around the apples in the bag.

"Duda, too much."

Duda waved a hand. "No, I was expecting a big crowd today and no one came. Except for Josh here. I have lots of sandwiches."

Samuel placed the bag in the basket attached to his handlebars. "Next time," he said and wheeled up the ramp and out the door.

Duda followed him to the door and flipped the sign.

"Finally," Josh said. "What's the deal? I thought we were going to a movie? Now it's too late."

"Actually, I think it's a perfect time. Sit."

Josh sat in the lawn chair Samuel had vacated. "Okay, lay it on me."

Duda patted Josh's shoulder and grinned.

Josh pointed at Duda's mouth. "There you go, flashing that smile. I'm in trouble, right?"

Duda brushed aside some catalogs on the counter and hopped up. He leaned toward Josh before he picked up a pamphlet next to the register. Josh squirmed in his chair waiting for Duda to speak.

"There are some things about Christians you need to know. Idea of grace, faith, and works. God loved us so much he sent his own boy. And he wants us to have a relationship with him. And with others. We do that through love. Like what I did for Samuel. Our eternity is guaranteed through God's grace, nothing we do."

Josh snorted. "Yeah, try telling that to Mister Larson, the old guy from church. He's earning his way to heaven. He says so all the time."

"Doesn't work that way," Duda said. "We all screw up. Christians don't have a free pass."

"What about him? He's like all the rest at church. Denial of reality. Bet he never struggles a day, wears his morality on his sleeve, that is, his prep school polo shirt sleeve."

"That's the problem. It should be his immorality," Duda said. "We're all broken. That's what the gospel teaches us. You ever read the Bible?"

"Duda, please, no more."

"Let me say one more thing. There's a guy named Paul. He wrote a bunch of the Bible, he shows his transparency. He said that he desired to be good, but couldn't do it on his own. If this guy, who hung out with Jesus, had a hard time, what about us? Think of the people you know who say they are Christians."

"I'm thinking of some. They talk about being Christians, but they get drunk and high all the time." Josh pushed up from the chair. "We finished here?"

Thirty-Nine

The flow of company died after Robert did. Except for an occasional church lady bringing comfort in a hot dish, no one ventured to Meg's front door. And after a month, the calls from the hospice volunteer ended.

Today was different though. Today Christy was coming out to the lake. When Meg had called to invite her, Christy squealed and made Meg promise they'd go fishing. Meg hadn't fished since late last summer, when Josh took the whole family out on the lake. With any luck, Meg's license was still good.

Meg unplugged the battery charger for the trolling motor. The 10-footer boat was flipped on its side next to the boathouse. Robert had bought the little 'pond jumper' for her, in case she wanted to go fishing on her own when he was tied up with a client. Since it was just the two of them today, Meg opted for the fishing boat instead of the ski boat. She pulled it down to the water's edge and guided it next to the dock. She had just secured the line when a blast on a car horn announced Christy's arrival. She kept honking until Meg was next to the car.

"I didn't know if there'd be guard dogs out here in the wilderness. Didn't want to take any chances," Christy said. She jumped out of her car and modeled her khaki vest with pockets plastered across her chest.

"Look, here's some licorice, and this is where I'll keep my cell phone. Isn't this the coolest deal? I bought this at that big outdoorsy store. Who would've thought they had a shirt like this?"

"I don't know. Maybe the people who fly fish," Meg said. Her dry response did nothing to dent Christy's enthusiasm.

"And, ta-da." Christy pulled out a package of green, yellow, and orange artificial lures.

"What in the world?"

"The night you called, I couldn't sleep. Caffeine overdose. I caught a great show on TV. Wait until you see their natural swimming motion." She tossed the package to Meg.

"These would be great if we were going in the ocean." Meg laughed. "There's nothing here that could bite that."

Christy's shoulders slumped. "I always get suckered into those infomercials."

Meg collected the rest of Christy's gear and carried it up to the house. Christy suddenly stopped and *yelped*.

"What's the deal? You were holding out on me. You said you lived in a cabin. This... this..." Christy gestured toward the lake home while she searched for a word.

"This IS a cabin. See the logs?" Meg pointed to the front of the two-story house. The women walked inside and Christy twirled about. "What a glorious combination of light and wood. Windows everywhere."

They walked past the family room. "And this room. Look at that fireplace and the ceilings. I love those rustic open beams." Christy craned her head back.

"Just don't let me know about the dust and cobwebs. I haven't gotten into cleaning yet."

Christy ran her hand across the top of a leather club chair and held up a finger. "I see what you mean." Christy brushed the dust off on her shorts. "Oh well. Life's too short to be too clean." She walked closer to the windows.

"Look at that view. Oh my goodness, look at that. Meg, does your neighbor always mow naked? Except for some ridiculous socks."

Through the trees, they could see George Halvorsen perched on his lawn tractor mowing diagonal stripes in his yard.

"Just ignore him. And he probably has on his bikini bottoms. Whatever you do, don't let him see you watching." Meg pulled Christy away from the window.

The boat, tied to the dock, rocked in the gentle wake of a passing boat.

"After seeing the house," Christy paused.

"You what?" Meg said.

"I just thought your boat would be a little, shall we say, more glorious? You even named it, Bob or John or whatever."

"Jon. That's what it is. A Jon boat." Meg tossed in a seat cushion. "Hop in."

Christy jumped off the dock and the boat tilted side to side.

"Sit down. Now," Meg said.

Christy immediately sat. "Bossy, aren't we?"

Meg ignored her and said, "We'll putter around the lake and see what we can shake up. This time of day is good. It's cooling off and the fish should be surfacing."

Meg loaded the fishing poles and a tackle box and stepped in. She engaged the motor. The sun clung to the bottom of the sky and enriched the blues and greens of the lake.

"Have you ever been fishing?"

"Nope," Christy said. "This is my maiden voyage."

"How could you grow up in Minnesota and not fish?"

Christy shrugged. "I don't know. Didn't know that made me dysfunctional or anything. Didn't know you were Queen Angler either."

Meg didn't know how to respond. So she didn't. She stepped on the pedal to the motor and guided the boat close to the shoreline and released the pedal. The boat stopped.

"That's a pretty nifty motor," Christy said. "And now it's so quiet out here."

The boat's wake tossed ripples toward the shore. Meg opened a margarine tub and withdrew an earthworm, wiggling toward escape. She threaded the hook the length of the worm and handed the pole to Christy.

"Such the Queen Angler." Christy eyed the worm dangling on the line. "Worm slime doesn't even make you flinch."

"Years ago, Robert taught me everything he thought there was to know about fishing. Probably so I'd quit bugging him. He liked his quiet time on the lake." Meg wiped her palms off on her shorts. When she looked up, Christy's worm dangled three inches away from her face.

"Toss your line into the water," Meg said. "Port side." Christy plopped her line on the right side and smiled.

"Left, port, right starboard," Meg said.

Christy bowed on her seat, pole in hand. "I'd curtsy to Her Highness, but I'd probably sink the boat."

"Stop it with the queenie stuff," Meg said.

"Whoa." Christy held up her hand. "You don't have to snap at me. "What's eating you anyway?"

Meg didn't answer, but swiveled and cast her line close to shore. She waited for the worm to settle on the bottom. After a few minutes, she slowly turned the crank and reeled in the line.

"Meg, you okay? I'm sorry if I upset you."

"It's fine. You just reminded me of Robert. Something I somehow forgot. He mocked me like that. He'd start out joking and then turn nasty."

"Meg, I'm so sorry to trigger that," Christy leaned to pat Meg's knee. "I was just being stupid. And a bit envious. You're impressive with all this fishing jazz. And your humongous —" Christy paused to draw imaginary quotes, "— cabin is impressive."

Christy picked up her fishing pole and jiggled it, dipping the end of the pole in and out of the lake. And just like the pole, the worm on the end of the hook jumped in and out of the water.

"Forgive me?"

"Yeah."

"Then watch this, just like the infomercial, natural swimming action." Christy's pole swept the water's surface and she brought the worm to rest just below Meg.

Meg stared down at the water, beyond her reflection, at the lifeless bait. "One problem. Worms don't swim."

Christy swung the pole back, dipped it a few more times in the water and reeled in the line. She rested the pole across her knees.

"There's something I don't get, Meg. At first I understood why you were going on the bike ride. You had to escape, run away. But this..." she spread her hand across the lake, taking in the wooded shore. "This is already an escape. People pay to vacation in places like this."

Meg cast again, a few feet away from her first toss. The line jiggled in her hand and she yanked to set the hook. "Got 'em. The trick is waiting for the fish to take the bait," Meg explained.

Christy *whooped* and clapped at the catch. Meg brought the fish in toward the boat and scooped it up in a net. "It's a sunnie, you want to eat it?"

"Are you kidding? Look at his eyes? How could I eat something that's watching me?"

"Fine." Meg wrapped her hand around the fish to unhook it and placed it back in the lake. She swirled her hand underwater to rinse it. "We'll just catch and release. Better toss your line back in."

"That's what I did with my husband. I caught him and released him." Christy rocked in mirth, making the boat bob in the water.

"Funny." Meg wished for the fishing trip to end, but at that moment Christy's pole sprang to life.

"Pull it back and crank," Meg commanded.

Christy soon had another sunnie near the boat. She pulled it close to Meg. "Please, set him free? And I promise no more queenie jokes."

Meg reached over the side to liberate the fish. It floated briefly before snapping its tail and swimming away. Then she pulled a night crawler out of the plastic tub and baited Christy's hook again. The minute the worm was submerged, the line grew taut.

"Hot dog, another." Christy jerked the rod. The hooked fish flew out of the water and landed in the boat by her feet. It flopped and gasped. And then it was still. "I killed it." Christy nudged it with her toe. The fish didn't move.

"Maybe it's just stunned," Meg said. "Swing the pole over here."

Christy obliged and Meg unhooked the fish's bloody lip and slid it back in the water. It floated away. Sideways, then belly up.

"I can't believe I murdered it." Christy hung her head.

Meg reeled in her line. "Maybe we should go."

"No, I came here to fish," Christy proclaimed. "I'll just fish without bait. Practice." Christy tried to imitate Meg's movement.

"Hold the pole behind you, like this," Meg said. "Snap your wrist."

She watched Christy launch it a few times then returned to concentrate on her own fishing. A deer on shore bent to lap water. She whispered, "look" to Christy just as something stung her ear. Meg swiped at it and her hand brushed against fishing line. Not a mosquito.

"Meg, don't move. I don't know what to do, but I do know this, don't move." Christy's face blanched as she stared at her friend and at the fishing line connected to her pole.

The slightest tug on the line sent twinges up to Meg's ear. She was stunned. First by the pain and then by her friend's ineptness. Not even Josh, when he was a little kid, hooked anyone. Meg continued to gently explore the hook's location with her fingertips. It was firmly attached to the cartilage.

Christy started giggling. "Now that's a fashion statement. Kinda a Goth-Minnesota pierced ear. Can't you just pull it out?"

"No. I can't. The barb is lodged in my flesh." Meg spoke through gritted teeth. She expelled a deep breath and pointed to the tackle box. "Grab the lineman's pliers out of there."

Christy started to rummage through the box. "Lineman's what?"

"That's what Robert called them. Josh and I just call them snoops. Funny looking pliers. The ones with a red handle."

When Meg was no longer connected to Christy's pole, she piloted the boat back to the dock. She grabbed the pliers and headed inside to the guest bath near the front door. Christy trailed and *cooed* sympathy every other step. Meg adjusted a mirror and clamped down on the barb with the pliers. Once her ear was free of the hook, she doused it with hydrogen peroxide over the sink.

Forty

On Monday, Meg was folding Josh's laundry when the doorbell rang. She pulled aside a curtain. A delivery truck idled in the driveway.

"Josh, it's here, it's here." She bounded down the stairs. Breathless, she flung open the front door and met the courier.

"It's a big one Mrs. Albertson. Do you think you can handle it?" He pulled a pen from behind his ear and waited for her signature on the clipboard.

"Just set it right there on the porch. And thanks."

The driver touched the brim of his cap and trotted back to the truck.

The tape refused to give up its grip on the box, so Meg went to the kitchen in search of a knife. Properly armed, she slit open one end of the large box, careful not to slide the knife too far. Tugging on the plastic inside, Meg pulled out one sleeping bag and then another. At the bottom of the box was the tent, the deluxe version that cost more than she ever spent on one item in her life.

Duda had guided them through the comparison process of various brands and prices. Weight was a prime concern, since they would be carrying their gear on their bicycles. But they also wanted a tent with plenty of room. As Josh put it, the idea of waking up nose-to-nose with his mom was frightening. Hours later, Meg had thought of a smart retort, but the boy was already gone.

In mid-thought, Meg stopped unpacking the camping gear and climbed the stairs to Josh's room. Halfway to his room, she changed her mind and went down the hall to her room to snatch a sweatshirt.

Cross-legged on the porch, she studied the instructions for the tent. Mr. Halvorsen was at work by the road, replacing the battered mailbox that appeared to have lost to yet another baseball bat. The last few weeks the newspaper reported there'd been a rash of mailbox smashing on their road. Every house had been hit except hers. The vandals most likely felt sympathy because she was a widow.

The pounding from Mr. Halvorsen continued for five more minutes, and Meg grabbed the tent and directions and headed to the far side of the house, away from his view. In a bright sunny spot, she unfurled the tent and carefully laid out the poles. No way was she going to wait until the trip to discover if they bought a dysfunctional tent.

The pieces all matched up with the sketches in the pamphlet. The directions appeared pretty straightforward so Meg started to unfold the poles. In no time, the long poles took on a life of their own. They quivered in six directions and collapsed whenever she picked one up. How hard could it be to erect a tent? She would fare better without the directions.

She stuck one pole through a sleeve on top of the tent. Then she tried maneuvering a second pole into another sleeve. With her left foot, she trapped the lower edge of the first pole at the bottom of the tent. Just as the tent started to take shape, the other edge of the pole flew straight out and flattened the tent. Exhausted, Meg flopped back in the grass and waited for Josh. After a few minutes, she rolled over and reached for the pamphlet. No way would she concede defeat this soon.

She studied the sketches closely and read the instructions aloud. Nodding, she clicked her tongue and followed the step-by-step directions. Finally she placed the additional covering over the top of the now erect blue tent. The fly, she read, could help them weather almost any storm.

Satisfied, she positioned the tent so one door faced the lake and one faced the road. Then she crawled in, closed the door to the road and zipped the screen at the opposite end. Hidden from view, it was just like being tucked in a little fort, almost like when she and her best friend Mary Jo were 10. The girls had pounded nails and 2 x 4s into the old tree in Mary Jo's backyard. Leftover plywood sheets completed their rickety hideout. Girls Only, because they had serious business. They were secret agents, ready to save the world.

Earlier that morning, she had awoken to the sounds of Josh clomping up the stairs, and was unable to fall back asleep. Now inside the sun-warmed tent, an afternoon nap sounded delightful. She unzipped the top halves of the side windows to ventilate the tent, but not enough that someone driving by would see her. The domed tent was made for at least four campers, and Meg decided to check out its spaciousness. Starting on the roadside of the tent, she rolled side-to-side. The tent was even roomier than she thought and she picked up speed as she rolled across the tent.

Her last rotation landed her on the wall of the tent and it started to topple. It was then she remembered she was on the steep sledding hill next to the house, and the unstaked tent bounced down the grassy slope. A strong gust of wind hurled the tent to the edge of the yard, where it dropped over a small cliff and landed on the flat sandy beach.

Forty-One

As Josh opened his eyes, he realized he was looking at the bottom of a toilet. He brought himself up to kneel on the cold tile floor and the urge to retch overcame him. He winced at the emptiness in his gut and hung his head over the edge. Convinced there was nothing left, he pushed off the floor and stumbled to the sink. The cold water did nothing to erase the pounding in his head and he flung open the cabinet looking for some relief. He cupped water from the faucet and swished down two pain relievers.

Last night's activities were a blur and the cautionary words from Duda kept ringing in his head. Not only did alcohol make him do stupid things, he was stupid for drinking. Not only that, he was underage. Duda was right. It was time to be the man of the house like his dad asked. That meant rising to the challenge of the bike trip and getting in supreme physical shape. Josh looked at his eyes in the bathroom mirror, still puffy and red. With the back of his hand, he wiped off his mouth and promised the end of his stupidity.

In his room, he pushed the window wider for freshness to clean out his sour lungs and body. When he looked out toward the lake, a tent sailed by and disappeared over the sandy ledge. In disbelief, he rubbed his eyes and looked again. Then he grabbed a pair of jeans and a T-shirt and dressed as he hobbled down the stairs.

Near the beach, he spotted the tent upside down in the sand by the dock. Seagulls dipped in the water and *squawked* at the rocking tent. Suddenly, a door unzipped and an arm popped out.

"Just great. This better not be our new tent," he said.

His mother struggled to escape, her sweatshirt twisted around her body. If only Mom could see her hair now, you'd think a magpie built a nest there. A dazed look crossed her face.

"I don't know what happened. All of a sudden the tent started rolling down the hill. Thank goodness it didn't make it into the water. That'd be something." She attempted to stand up.

"Are you serious? Don't you realize how much damage you caused by being stupid? Get away from the tent and let me look at it."

Mom crawled across the shore and pulled herself onto the dock. Slowly she brushed away the sand embedded in her knees. A lone seagull floated on top of the water, a glassy eye watching her.

With one hand, Josh righted the tent. He glared at his mother before he tossed the tent back up on the grassy yard. Hand-over-hand, he carefully examined every inch of fabric, shaking off sand and swearing.

"This trip is gonna be so lame," he muttered.

Mom called over from the dock. "What?"

"Nothing," Josh said.

"You know, honey, the tent looks fine from here. I hardly think that could've wrecked it," she said.

"We'll see." He continued his close scrutiny. He decided to give her the silent treatment, although he wanted to yell at her until her eyes popped out. She was truly insane. This proved it. The tent appeared fine, but he didn't want her to know that right away. Let her suffer for a change. After all, he was the one who had to suffer along with this stupid plan. He planned to wait Mom out. He knew she sat on the dock, watching him. Her eyes widened when she met his glance. Wordless, Josh bent back over the tent.

"Oh, hey there." Mr. Halvorsen waved from across the yard and pulled up on his lawn tractor. He cut the engine. "Oh my goodness. What a handsome looking tent, but is that big enough for the two of you? When I was a scout, we had immense canvas tents. Talk about spacious."

He slipped one leg across the top of the tractor and jumped off. "Nice dismount, huh?"

Josh just shook his head and kept focused on the tent.

"Oh hi, Meg," Mr. Halvorsen said. With a playful whack on Josh's shoulder, he added in a low voice, "I didn't realize your mom was over there." He licked two fingers and smoothed down the hair around his bald spot before he headed down to the dock.

"Whatever," Josh said. The guy was just creepy. Did he really think he was a player? *Too weird. And that other joker from church?* Their voices buzzed as they sat next to each other on the dock. Occasionally he caught them looking his way. Mom was using her hands to pantomime the tent's trip down the hill. Mr. Halvorsen nodded a few times and then stood. He offered a hand to Mom and pulled her to her feet. Josh ducked his head as the two of them came up the hill.

"Pretty staggering story, Josh. Those winds can be something this time of year. I still can't believe your mom after such a tumble." He ran a hand across the dome. "Tent looks fine. But it must've been just awful for her." Mr. Halvorsen shot an admiring glance at Josh's mom. "She's some woman. A divine creation."

Forty-Two

It was the stillness that reeled her back to reality. No birds twittered back and forth among the trees that lined the trail. Nothing, except the sound of her tires snapping an occasional twig on the path. Meg scanned the sky and continued to pedal through the dead air.

Then, almost imperceptibly, the clamminess lifted from her arms and cool air settled around her. The fresh earthy smell of incoming rain surrounded her. First the birch leaves began to tremble in the intensifying wind, and then Meg's body began to tremble. It was just plain careless to be out on the trail now. Just plain clueless. Robert would've berated her for not checking the weather before she left home hours ago.

Meg was almost to the Church of the 4Ls when lightning flashed across the sky.

"One thousand one, one thousand two," Meg began to count. She tried to remember the odds of getting struck by lightning and wondered if her father felt it before he was struck. Thunder rumbled in the distance. She quickly pedaled the last few yards to the turnoff to Malachi's church, just as the light rain formed into pellets. With a firm yank, she whipped open the door to the church.

"Hello? Is anyone around?"

She wheeled her bike into the entryway. Malachi rounded the corner from his office. "Oh, hey, it's you," he said. "I didn't think I'd see you again."

"I was lucky your door was open. I didn't want to be stuck on the trail in a storm. I know what they can do. Years ago a storm roared through Itasca Park, shearing hundreds of trees. I hate storms. I always have." She took off her helmet and shook out her hair, just slightly damp.

Malachi motioned to a cluster of mismatched canvas director's chairs.

"Sit, I'll get you a towel. Then we'll talk about storms."

She sighed, fearing more proselytizing, but she started to shiver in her damp clothes. It was a toss up, what was worse?

"I've got some hot water going for tea. Would you like a cup?" Malachi called out.

"Hot tea sounds wonderful."

Malachi returned with a tray of mugs, a teapot, and a plate of cookies. His wife, Rachel, trailed him with a stack of folded towels. A faded green sweatshirt sat on top of the pile in her arms. She smiled at Meg. "So, I finally get to meet the mystery biker. Perhaps you'd like a warm layer?" She offered the sweatshirt to Meg. "We keep extra clothes around here for the people Malachi drags in. Sometimes it's the only change of clothes they get. There's a bathroom around the left if you need to take off your wet top."

Meg went through the dark hallway to the bathroom and felt along the wall for a switch. She frowned at her soaked self in the mirror and eagerly changed shirts. The dry sweatshirt felt heavenly next to her damp skin. Over the sink she wrung out her soggy T-shirt until the dripping slackened. She wrapped her shirt in paper towels and blotted water from her legs.

Malachi and Rachel were sitting knee-to-knee and holding hands. Meg hesitated and then plunged ahead, eager for the hot tea. Malachi dropped his wife's hand to toss a towel to Meg. "I'm glad you returned. I was afraid that I might've scared you with my preaching. We got off to a rough start," Malachi said.

Rachel gave a knowing smirk to Meg. "He does have that effect on people."

Rain drummed against the windows and the lightning increased. Meg counted out loud, "a thousand one, a thousand two." At 'a thousand three', a clap of thunder rumbled through the church. Meg jumped.

"Whoa, you're certainly skittish," Malachi said. "There's nothing to be afraid of here. You know, a friend of mine wrote this song, 'Oh, My Soul'. Hang on a sec. I have a guitar in my office."

Of course he does. This is going to be another one of those insipid church camp, Kum Ba Ya sessions. Meg grabbed the terry cloth towel and rushed to squeeze the water from her T-shirt wrapped in paper towels. Another roll of thunder made her realize she was stuck until the storm dissipated. She dropped the shirt and concentrated on the mug of hot tea, hoping the lemon aroma could pacify her.

Malachi returned with an acoustic guitar and plopped down in the chair between Meg and Rachel. "I think you'll get a real sense of comfort from these words."

He strummed a few chords before he sang:

> *Why do you fear being alone?*
> *Trust that your heart is always at home.*
> *And why do you dread this downpour of rain?*
> *To know the depth of Joy you must shake hands with Pain.*

Malachi stopped singing. "Boy, listen to that rain coming down."

The *rat-a-tat-tat* of the rain's drum solo switched to an entire drum line from a marching band, minus a conductor. The windows in the sanctuary rattled and the lights flickered and died an abrupt death. A tumultuous explosion rocked the aged church.

Darkness enveloped the three. "What in the world was that?" Meg asked. She tried to control the pitch of her voice. "Where are you two?"

"We're right here," Malachi said. "Let me get some candles out of the sanctuary. You stay put. Rachel and I will see if there's any damage."

"Don't leave me alone," Meg pleaded. Illuminated by occasional flashes of lightning, she inched her way through the dark building and followed the acrid air. Smoke poured out of the basement. Malachi met her at the top of the stairs with blazing candles.

"Meg, quick—call the fire department. I'll grab an extinguisher."

Meg punched in the numbers on her cell phone. From the basement, Malachi called up to her. "Meg, we need your help, Hurry, there's still time."

She hesitated at the door. "The smoke's too thick down there. You two need to get up here fast."

"It's not that bad. And I have to get all of these out." She could hear shuffling along with his grunts and groans. "Please help me. Please."

He ran to the top of the stairs. "Here, take this." He handed her a plaster object. "It's the babe. Put him somewhere safe while I get the rest of them out of here."

In her arms was the Baby Jesus.

Forty-Three

With a loud click, Meg snapped her helmet under her chin, straddled her bike and waited her turn. A group of cyclists whizzed by, their matching jerseys blurring into a splash of color on the trail. Positive no more were coming, she switched on the bike computer, and began to pedal north. Peals of laughter resonated behind her. Soon a line of three bicyclists was even with Meg. She eased off her pedals and coasted to the edge of the limestone path.

"No, no, stay on your bike and keep going," the lead one called out.

Obediently, Meg kept her pace with the women. The lead rider wanted to chat, but Meg was afraid to look and lose control.

"Don't you ride here a lot? I know I've seen you several times," the woman said. "I recognize your yellow helmet. Can you believe that storm we had last night? We were up most the night making calls for the fire squad. Lot of lightning damage. I'm Mimi, by the way. That's Beth and Suzie."

"You're with those fast riders who flew by a bit ago?"

"Oh, those, those are the animals." Mimi laughed. "We stop and smell the roses."

"And eat," Beth added.

"Right. We're trying out a new café just eleven miles away. Everyone says the pastries are to die for. Join us?"

Meg hesitated. Clueless about the technique of riding in a pack, she was nervous on the trail crowded with numerous children weaving in and out on bikes. Meg slowed down just as the group approached a family.

"Fall in behind us," Mimi, the leader, called to Meg. "We'll pass them single file on their left. Be sure to watch the wheel in front of you."

Mimi hollered to the family, "On your left, four of us."

Instead of pulling to the right and creating a passing lane, the family split in the middle. Two adults went left; two children went right.

Mimi yelled, "No one move. We're going down the middle."

The family stopped, suspended as if in the middle of a game of freeze tag. Mimi and her gang sailed past them single-file. They continued to negotiate the clusters of walkers, bikers, and talkers on the trail. Meg concentrated on the back wheel of the woman in front of her. Debris from last night's storm littered the trail and murky water trickled in the adjacent drainage ditch.

Meg swerved to miss a splintered branch hanging over the trail. A flashback of the storm and the memory of baby Jesus in her arms crowded out all logical thoughts. People often talk about signs from God. Was that one? She remembered the weight of the plaster son of God. She'd been afraid to handle it like a sack of potatoes from SuperValu. Her natural instinct was to cradle the bundle. Just what did that mean?

Mimi waited on the edge of the trail for Meg. "We ride here every Saturday. Join us anytime," Mimi said. "What was your name? And look, here's our turn. Girls, it's time for pie."

Forty-Four

Balance was the lesson for the day. According to Duda, riding with full panniers might be tricky at first, so he advised Meg to calculate how much weight she had to carry. In Robert's study, she stacked real estate books on a bathroom scale and then filled the panniers attached to the back of her bicycle.

Ready for a test ride, Meg took to the trail and pedaled to the church turnoff. Next to the building, Malachi stretched to trim shrubs brushing against a window. She slowed down just as he put down the clippers.

"Hey Meg! Stop for a cold one?" He grinned. A soaked red bandana covered his head and sweat trickled down his face. "Come on, I know I could use a break."

He dashed up the steps to the church. When he returned, he carried two cans of pop high overhead like a tennis champion displaying the silver platter.

"Rachel was glad she met you, although that turned out to be one strange night. Let's go sit under those trees by the lake. We'll get a breeze off the water."

Meg parked her bike against a tree and reached for a can, its coolness calming the tingling in her hands.

"Hey thanks again for helping get the nativity set out during that storm. I got so excited when I found them in the church basement. I'm working to restore them. Rachel is a great artist and is going to help."

Mid-step, Meg paused. "You mean there wasn't anything significant when you handed the infant to me? Like God's will?"

"I think God's will is that we're fully happy in the moment, living as children, forgiving others."

"That was such a scary night. I thought maybe the storm was God's will and I was going to die like my husband."

"That wouldn't be God's will."

"I was never so relieved to get home. I'm so thankful my son came to give me a ride. Did the church have much damage?"

"Nah. Thanks to the extinguisher, the fire stayed out. The fire fighters came out just in case."

"That's good. I'm glad it wasn't worse." She sipped her pop and hesitated. "I guess I'm ready for you to explain again about your church. What's up with the least, the last, the lonely, and the whatever."

"The lost. In Psalm 51 it talks about teaching transgressors, or rebels, God's way so they can find their way home. I once bargained with God using that. I'd slumped to the lowest rung, so I asked God if he helped me, I would help others find Him.

"Now I do a lot of my work after normal hours. Hang out in the taverns, get to know the regulars."

That explained his thin face flecked with stubble and his shaggy hair. He didn't resemble any minister Meg knew. Most of them carried that scrubbed and fresh look, as if God could drop out of clouds any minute and bless them.

Malachi smiled. "I'm just a regular guy, like them. We talk about anything and everything. Gradually I might discuss religion with them. Sometimes I invite them out here, not to go to church but to go fishing." He stood up and pointed to a small rowboat on the shore. "See that? I like to take it out on the lake. It's not the conventional approach. Do you have a church?"

"I did. I just haven't been there for a bit. I agree about the conventional part. I can't imagine our church welcoming people off the streets. Course there doesn't seem to be much of that problem around here."

"You'd be surprised," Malachi said. "It caught Rachel off-guard at first too. Now she leads a Bible study for economically challenged women. If young mothers attend, we give them a package of diapers. Maybe you'd like to help her with childcare?"

"Childcare? That'd be the last thing I'd enjoy. I'm still caring for my own child and the results are less than impressive."

Forty-Five

Raindrops chased each other down the windowpane over the kitchen sink. Meg rinsed out her coffee cup and returned it to the cabinet. Because the forecast called for a day of solid drizzle Meg planned to skip training and shop with Christy.

At ten, the doorbell rang. But instead of Christy on her front porch, there stood Duda, smiling in the rain.

"Did we have plans? Did I forget about something?" Meg asked.

"The rain led me to a great idea," Duda said. "But I must warn you. You might hear from friends at church."

Meg shrugged. "I've gotten so used to being called crazy. They all think I'm nuts. The thought I was dating you was easier for them to digest than the idea I was taking this bike trip. To be honest with you, people don't know how to act around me. When Robert started getting sick, really sick, people scurried away. They were there in the beginning, always coming around with food and things. And at the end, after he died. But no one was *there*, you know what I mean?" Meg clapped once. "Enough about that. Why are you here?"

"Meg, everything okay over here? I was working on the gutters," Mr. Halverson appeared right behind Duda on the porch.

"Everything's fine, fine," Meg said. "This is Duda. Duda, Mr., uhm, George."

Duda pumped Mr. Halverson's hand. He held up two yellow packages. "Presents for Meg and Josh," he said.

"Okay then," Mr. Halverson muttered and stepped off the porch. Meg motioned for Duda to enter.

"The man can be a little territorial," she said.

"No bother. Look, rain suits for you and Josh. The shop is checking out this brand, and we need hamsters. They're supposed to be breathable, so you stay dry inside and outside."

"Guinea pigs and you want us to go cycling now?" Meg sputtered. "But I'm not training today. Christy and I are going shopping."

"How are you going to reach your goal if you don't make some sacrifices?" Duda opened the packages and laid out the suits on the back of the couch.

A loud sigh slipped out of Meg. "In the rain, really?"

"Really," Duda said.

Meg phoned Christy to cancel the plans, but promised she'd make it up to her. The minute she hung up, Duda was at her elbow. "Training takes discipline. Besides, have you ever ridden in the rain?"

"Not intentionally."

"Then you must. On the trip, can you just stop when it rains? No, because your trip could stop for long time. Where's Josh?"

Meg thumbed toward his room upstairs. "First door on the left. Go get him if you want. I'm not."

Duda bounded up the stairs and soon returned with Josh.

"And Duda is here because?" Josh glared at Meg and rubbed his eyes with his fist.

"Don't look at me. I had my own plans."

Duda butted in. "Today you and your mom are going to get a lesson about riding in the rain."

"You got me out of bed for this? Duda, c'mon, who doesn't know how to ride in the rain?"

"This will be good, just wait. You'll thank me later. Here." Duda tossed a rain suit to Josh. "This is yours."

Meg pulled the suit over her clothes and spun around to model it.

"Oh perfect, matching ones," Josh said. "Let me at least grab some cereal and chocolate milk."

The rain was still coming down when they left the house fifteen minutes later. Mr. Halvorsen waved from his picture window and gave them a big thumbs up, a double thumbs up.

"We'll turn left at that road there," Duda said. "Slow down as you reach the corner."

He pointed to an oily rainbow on a puddle. "When the rain first starts, oil floats up and makes the road slick. We should be fine since it's been raining all day. The gunk is probably washed away. But lots of stuff stays slick. Railroad tracks can be a big problem. You might want to dismount and walk across."

Josh sped ahead of Meg and started to weave around the puddles on the road. "Duda, this is pretty elementary stuff. I'm going home, back to bed."

"Just don't aim for the puddles," Duda said.

"I'm not afraid of getting wet." Josh hammered toward a big puddle. There was a loud clunk. The front wheel twisted under Josh and he flew off the bike.

Duda shook his head. "But sometimes you should be afraid of the deep holes under the puddles."

Forty-Six

High-pitched *yips* and *yodels* of coyotes in the woods interrupted the cool stillness of the dawn. Meg wrapped her jacket tighter around her and loaded the SUV. The plan was to gather at the gas station at 5:45 a.m., to caravan to the ride's start. Participants would ride a sixty-five mile loop both days and could camp or stay at the lodge.

Last night, water-logged after Duda's challenge, Meg called her new riding partners to cancel. It was the longest back-to-back ride she'd ever considered. 'That is precisely why you must do it,' Mimi had said.

Meg's stomach wobbled now as she drove to the gas station. The uncertainty of her ability, coupled with the uncertainty of everyone else's speed, tumbled around inside her.

When Josh heard about the ride, he bet Meg she wouldn't even register. In fact, he was so sure, he wagered a week's worth of his laundry. A reprieve from the boy's never-diminishing mountain of dirty clothes was tempting. When Meg realized she had nothing to lose, she made the call and now, here she was.

A sliver of moon clung to the sky. Under the gas station's glowing sign two vans were parked next to each other. Meg slowly drove up and rolled down her window a crack, until she recognized Mimi at the wheel.

"Hey, Meg," said Mimi. "You made it. Super. Jump in with us? The storeowner said we could leave vehicles here overnight. They'll be fine."

Meg parked and collected the gear she'd thrown into a carry-on bag. Mimi helped Meg stick her bike in the van. "Meg, say hi to Kate, this is her first big ride too. I'm going to run in and get a cappuccino. Any takers?"

Meg waved to Kate in the front seat and slid into the middle row. Both women ordered hot chocolate.

"Are you escaping from your family for the weekend? I've got two teen-age girls and couldn't wait to leave. This will be good for my husband," Kate said.

"I just have one at home. Only he has a hockey tournament this weekend in St. Paul. He and some buddies drove over."

"You mean you didn't have to go? It seems I have to be at every volleyball practice, every game and every tournament for the girls. My husband feels one of us has to always be there."

"Whatever for?"

"In case something happens to one of them. When the oldest was eight, she jammed a finger during practice. Of course, we weren't there. It was just a practice, for crying out loud. You would've thought the world was coming to an end. She wanted to quit but my husband made her tough out the season. Now, the girls are so superstitious they think nothing horrid will happen if we're there. It's bad enough they have their lucky socks, lucky underwear, lucky hair ribbons. I am so relieved to get away this weekend."

An extra burst of speed thrust Meg against the car seat. Mimi said, "You know, at this rate, we'll be there in no time." She drained the last of her convenience store coffee.

"Anyone need to stop? We're getting pretty close. Did you two know you have the option of taking an easier route this weekend?" Mimi looked over her shoulder at Meg.

"Although I think you both could handle the entire route. Kate, you wouldn't believe how many times I've seen Meg out on the bike trail. She practically lives out there."

Kate turned around to face Meg. "Doesn't that get boring? I can't imagine staying on the trail all the time."

"No, I have different routes, destinations. And it's a lot easier to just keep pedaling one direction, instead of figuring out where to turn out in the country. Plus, you don't have to watch for cars or anything like that," Meg said.

"I suppose. And I guess you don't have to worry about dogs, either. Man I hate dogs when I'm biking. They just sneak right up next to you. Next thing, you know they're chomping your foot," Kate said. She flipped open the illuminated mirror on the visor and applied a layer of mascara to each eye. "It was too early to put on makeup first thing this morning."

Meg reached around in her pocket for a tube of medicated lip gloss. "I know what you mean." Meg circled her lips with the gloss. "About the makeup, that is. But you know, I did have a dog encounter on the trail."

Kate put on a fresh layer of lipstick, "What happened? Was it loose?"

"No. The owner was in her own world and the dog was traipsing all over the trail. Unfortunately, the dumb thing was still on its leash. I'm riding along and next thing you know, I get between the woman and her dog."

"No kidding, that was you?" Mimi looked at her in the rearview mirror. "We heard about you at one of the bike club meetings. We've been on the lookout for that woman since early this spring. Didn't she have a white terrier or something like that? I can't believe how idiotic people are. Did she send you an apology?"

"Apology? No way. She threatened me. Said if Petey, the dog, was hurt, she was going to collect. Course I'd slap her with a counter suit for the pain and suffering from the poison ivy. Did you know there's almost no place on your body immune from the rash? And girls, I mean no place."

"Hey look, here we are." Mimi pulled in alongside numerous parked vehicles with bike racks. People in bright-colored outfits milled around.

"Some of these people look pretty fit." Meg chewed the inside of her bottom lip. Kate turned around and locked gazes with Meg. Then she plucked at her thumb and dabbed at the sudden drops of blood.

Mimi chuckled. "Oh, don't fool yourself. Most are just regular people, like us. You'll see." She hopped out and headed toward a table with a small line of people.

Kate looked at Meg. "I guess we should follow her, huh?"

The two meandered up to the line to receive their materials. Meg unzipped her registration packet and found a wristband for the lunch stop, bandages, aspirin and a real estate agent's business card. She carefully folded the route map and stuck it in her pocket. She sent the business card sailing into a garbage can.

"I'm going to pump air into my tires," Kate said, and left to work on her bicycle. Meg glanced at her watch. It was almost time for the mass start. She dashed to the lodge's bathroom. By the time she jogged back, Kate was already straddling her bike.

"Oh, Kate, I'm so sorry. It's almost time. Everyone is lined up. I think I'm going to throw up." Meg heaved in deep gulps of air.

"Meg, catch your breath. We still have ten minutes until the official start. And even if we miss it, it's no big deal. We can start when we want."

"Are you sure?"

"No problem. It might be smart not to get in the middle of all of those riders. Can you imagine the tangle if someone goes over? Mimi is up toward the start with some friends from her office. Now, get your helmet and gloves on. Did you want any air in your tires? They look a little low."

"No, no, I'm sure they're fine. I don't want them to explode," Meg said. She plunked her helmet on. "Let's do it!"

Kate adjusted the mirror on the end of her handlebars. The two women approached the mob at the start just as a huge green flag swept through the air.

"Well, I guess we missed it. Do you still want to ride?" Meg asked.

"What? Are you serious? Of course we're going to ride. We woke up at the crack of dawn and we're going to do this. We can't quit before we even start." Kate stared at Meg.

"Okey dokey. Just kidding."

When they finally left the lodge property, the crowd had thinned. Several clusters of bikers rode ahead and Meg and Kate pedaled past a family. The dad pulled a trailer with two toddlers in it.

"Morning." Everyone nodded and exchanged pleasantries. "Beautiful day for a ride, isn't it?" the mom said.

"Exquisite," Kate said. She and Meg wove past the family and soon overtook another pack.

"This is kind of fun," Meg said. "I didn't think we'd pass anybody." She shifted gears and pushed a little harder as they swung around a group of older women dressed in purple tops and bottoms.

"Passing on your left," Kate called out.

"That's all right honey, feel free to pass. We're just happy to be out here rejoicing in the glorious day the Lord hath made. We might look old, but deep down, we're just kids having fun on our bikes," said a woman in the front of the group. Purple feathers and glitter adorned her helmet. "You two girls enjoy today, and don't work too hard." Her purple fingernails glimmered when she waved goodbye.

Meg wondered if one of those ladies would like to join her in Oregon. They'd be fun to ride with. Maybe one of them would even take her place.

Birch trees flecked with morning sun towered over the bikers as they followed a two-lane road. The trees cleared and exposed a body of water as flat as the road, and surrounded by homes. The road was clear of traffic, except for the support vans with flashing lights, sweeping the route for stragglers or casualties.

The digestive juices no longer burned and churned in Meg's stomach and her breathing had stabilized. Her computer displayed a distance of thirty-five miles. No wonder she finally felt confident.

"Hey, Meg, guess what?" Kate said. "Our first food stop is coming up. Can you believe it? The route sheet said it was at the fifteen-mile mark. Keep your eyes peeled and watch where everyone turns."

"Fifteen? We've already done thirty-five."

"Better check the reset."

Another arrow *zinged* Meg's armor of biking confidence. After she rounded the next curve orange rubber cones marked the entrance to a long driveway. Three cyclists leaving the food stop yelled, "Just follow the road."

Meg and Kate picked up their pace as they pedaled down the narrow road. Numerous bikes were strewn on the ground around a smattering of picnic tables and a gray concrete building.

"So this is where everyone is," Meg said. "I wondered what happened to the crowd."

The two women set their bikes down in the grass, removed their helmets and shook out their hair. People with handfuls of cookies and orange slices thronged the large coolers marked Water and Sports Drink. Plastic bags with sandwich bread sat next to opened jars of peanut butter and jelly.

"I need to hit the john before I eat." Kate trotted toward the gray building. Meg followed and noticed Kate's black shorts were speckled with white blobs.

"Umm, Kate," Meg leaned close to her riding partner. The door swung open and a woman with a long gray ponytail and a face spotted from years of sun got in line behind them.

"Sister," the woman said looking at Kate's shorts, "you might want to rub in that cream next time."

Kate gasped. "Meg, why didn't you say anything?"

"I didn't want to embarrass you."

"Like I couldn't be any more embarrassed." Kate ducked into an empty stall and kept talking. "Mimi said to use diaper ointment so I wouldn't get a rash. The more, the better, I thought."

By the time Meg remounted, she was forced to share the road with more and more pickups and cars. Eager to get off the bustling road, Meg ticked off the miles to the next stop.

"All this traffic makes me nervous," she said to Kate. "What if I hit a rock and fly into a car?"

"I know," Kate looked over with wide eyes. "What if one of those trucks plows into us?" With that, Kate's front wheel caught the edge of the shoulder. She overcorrected her steering and her bike wobbled.

"Hey, just stay over on the shoulder," yelled a biker blazing past. "If you can't ride, you don't belong out here." He and five other bikers, decked out in identical clothes, sped off in close synchronization.

Forty-Seven

The mileage from the weekend bumped Meg's total right in range, according to Duda. She had called him from the road to let him know she survived. Only one more month of training before she'd be on the road for real.

Meg lowered her arms, rubbed her shoulders and rolled her neck in circles. The drive back to Lake Devine worsened the kinks and now every tender spot screamed. Next time she'd bring a change of clothes. Chills, caused by her damp and sweaty clothes, raced across her body. A hot bath was a priority and she clambered up the stairs to start the water.

As the tub filled, she flipped on the classical radio station and lit two candles on a ledge. Soon, they flickered to the smooth evening jazz. Meg stretched out in the bathtub and closed her eyes. Warm water lapped against her shoulders and the lavender bubbles perfumed the bathroom. To stretch her calf muscles, she pointed her feet to the ceiling and then to the wall. Her body, sore and stiff, slowly snapped back to normal.

After the soak, Meg bounced down the stairs to the kitchen. Her son stood at the kitchen counter and stared at her.

"I can't believe you made it," he said. His look soon turned to scorn. "Or maybe you cheated."

"I'll have you know we did not flag down the support wagon, or the sag wagon as they call it. We rode the entire route. Some guy's bike broke down and he had to catch a ride. But not us." Meg raised her arms and danced a little two-step. "Want me to fix you a salad while you do your own laundry?"

"That's not fair," Josh said. "I still think you cheated."

"No one likes sore losers. We made an honest wager over that load of laundry. Wait, I forgot to ask – how was hockey? Let's talk while I chop some carrots and celery for a nice salad."

Josh snitched a carrot from the cutting board. "Nah. I have some things to take care of. Be back later."

When she rinsed off the cutting board, she remembered she left her water bottle on her bicycle. She swung open the door to the garage. The bottle, with an inch of liquid, was still in its cage on her bike. As her hand closed around the bottle, she took another look across the garage. The hook where Josh's bike usually hung was empty.

Josh stuck his tongue out to catch the salty sweat dripping down his face. He kept his daily bike rides a secret from his mom. Sometimes he even ran with Candy. She was the one who convinced him training might make the ordeal a little less painful, from a physical standpoint. The mental aspect didn't faze him. That's what headphones were for. He could shut out Mom and ride along in his own peaceful world.

Dad was a genius for suggesting they splurge on the bicycles. His old bicycle was probably still in the shed. Fenders and all. Compared to that heavy old thing, this bike was like riding on air. Josh increased his speed to overtake the cyclist ahead. Maybe there were some races nearby. Maybe he'd outrace everyone. Josh maneuvered around a fallen tree limb on the trail and admired his own bicycle handling skills. That's it—he'd out maneuver his competitors. He couldn't wait to ask Duda.

Forty-Eight

A smile crossed Meg's lips as she looked across the table at her son. For the past several weeks, she noticed Josh had been taking his bike out, although he never mentioned it. She knew she was the reason for his sudden interest in training, but she stifled her desire to tease him. Josh unfolded the map on the kitchen table and smoothed the creases with his palm.

"That's our starting point." He pointed to the northwest tip of Oregon.

Meg sipped her tea and gazed at the map. Her brain wanted to lock out the reality of the impending trip and an army of fire ants marched through her nervous system. "So, we just fly our bikes there? That's it?"

"Yup. Piece of cake. Remember I found some great maps for us. Plus, we'll probably run into people on the road." Josh had definitely warmed up to the adventure.

"But what if we don't know where to pick up the trail? That looks like a pretty large area."

"We won't be looking for a trail, you goof. We'll be watching for road signs, you know, the little state highways. Nothing is off-road."

Meg had renewed her old habit of lip biting the week before. When she pulled in her lower lip, the extra piece of skin was already chewed off.

"Josh, I don't know about this." Meg stood up and pushed her chair away from the table. She searched in the refrigerator for a piece of reassurance. A leftover slice of apple pie was tucked behind odd bottles of salsa and spaghetti sauce.

"Oh, you found it." Josh eyed the last piece in her hand. "When I picked that up from Bjorn's I didn't think you'd want it. You know, with your new training routine and all. Now I can't believe that's all that is left."

Meg reluctantly did the proper Mom-thing and set the piece in front of her son.

"You're right. But I would love to know when I'll see the results of training. This has been a royal pain. About the only reason I'm looking forward to the trip next week is that it means training is officially over." She returned to her mug of tea on the table.

"Any more ice cream?" Josh looked up, expectantly.

"Let me check." Meg jumped back up from the table. After she pulled out the vanilla ice cream, she removed the plate from under Josh's nose.

"Hey, no fair." He grabbed it.

"I was just going to warm it up in the microwave." Meg directed her best whammy eye.

"Oh, right. Good idea."

She set the steaming pie in front of him and plopped a mound of ice cream onto the flaky crust. The drool pooled in Meg's mouth. *Just one more week.* She tried to focus on the map and topography.

"Wait a minute," she said. "Just wait one doggone minute. What is this doing here?" Her finger jabbed at Mount Hood on the map.

"Well, sure, we'll have some climbs. Didn't you look at any of the research I printed out for you? You didn't think the whole route would be flat, did you?" He licked the last of the ice cream from the plate.

"Oh, that looks nice," she reprimanded. He glared back.

"Josh, I don't think I'm up for this trip. It's one thing to bike on abandoned railroad beds. But to go up mountains? I haven't practiced on anything steeper than Johnson hill."

"It's all in the gears. Just remember that."

His comment did little to reassure her. Her stomach felt like a dryer with tennis shoes bouncing around in it.

"I'm off to bed. Be sure to turn off the lights and check the doors." With any luck, he'd at least put his dishes in the sink so she wouldn't have to face a mess in the morning.

He'll be gone in the fall. And then I'll really be all alone.

Forty-Nine

Meg circled the block a third time before she spotted the spa's sign tucked between a video store and dry cleaning business. She pulled into the lot and waited for Christy. This was another one of Christy's ideas, but at least she offered to treat Meg. At the front counter, the two women were whisked away and ushered into a room lit with too-few bulbs. In minutes they were seated side-by-side. Meg dipped a toe into warm water and pulled her sweatpants up to her knee. Sudsy water swirled around their feet while the technicians massaged their calves and shaped their toenails.

"Well, maybe this idea wasn't so bad." Meg adjusted the vibrations on her chair.

"Stick with me honey." Christy gestured toward herself. "I can always find fun. But you, I can't believe how disciplined you've become. I thought the Y was tough enough. And then you tell me about your training sessions too. You must be super woman by now. C'mon, flex. Show me the results."

"Oh stop," Meg said. "You would've done the same thing if you were in this situation. And believe me, you can thank your lucky stars that you're not."

Meg and Christy sipped iced tea and soaked up the pampering. The repetitive music from the speakers soothed Meg and she listened to the recorded sounds of birds and trickling creeks. The other clients spoke in subdued tones.

Except for one person engaged in a loud conversation on his cell phone.

"Why do people do that?" Christy shot an evil look. "I mean, what's so important that the rest of us have to hear?" She signaled the man to walk outside to finish the call.

"Hush," Meg said. "Just ignore him."

The man caught Christy's gestures and stuck out his tongue. He continued his call.

"That does it." Christy stood up in the soapy water. "We're trying to relax in here," she yelled.

Meg reached over and yanked Christy's shirt. "Sit down, before someone gets in trouble. It's no big deal. He's not that loud. Please, you're making more of a scene than he is."

Christy sank back down. "If you think so..." She reached for her iced tea, but after one sip, she slammed the glass and the tea sloshed on the tray. She continued to glare at the cell phone talker.

"C'mon Christy. Forget him. Let's enjoy our visit. Who knows when I'll be back? Or if I'll be back."

Christy shrugged. "Yeah, I guess you're right. There's just something about that guy that bugs me. He reminds me of my ex. Always trying to be the center of attention."

"And see what you did? You let him know he commanded your attention. If you would've ignored him, he wouldn't have won the little game."

"True. You'd think I would've learned by now."

"Ladies, time for polish," the technician said. Christy pointed to a bright bottle. "That one there, for her. Isn't that Naughty Blush? I'll have the same."

Meg's toenails turned pink with the long even strokes of color. Christy swiveled in her chair to face Meg. "Back to your big adventure. Are you all packed?"

"Not quite."

"Do you think you have room for this?" Christy reached next to the chair for her purse and pulled out a small package.

"Oh Christy, you shouldn't have. That's awfully sweet of you."

Christy grinned and handed over the wrapped gift. "Wait until you see what it is before you thank me. I did have to fight the crowds at the megamall for it though."

Meg unfolded the paper and a bundle of silk plopped into her lap. Her hand darted out to conceal it before anyone else noticed. She raised the edge of her hand.

"What exactly am I looking at?"

"Lingerie," Christy said.

"I realize that, silly."

"Thong underwear. You know, in case you meet up with someone out there, during those long lonely miles, empty nights. Maybe some night you could be a woman instead of a mom and get your own motel room."

Meg snorted. "I assure you, the last thing on my mind will be sex."

Fifty

Graduation morning, Meg stepped out the front door and inhaled. *Okay Robert, now I get the whole Minnesota appeal.* Even a movie director couldn't have envisioned a prettier day. She reached down to pluck a violet. A long blade of grass clung to it and Meg brought it to her lips and whistled.

Mr. Halvorsen hollered from his garden, "Big day today. The boy left hours ago. Shouldn't you be at the ceremony too?"

"Just a quick run down the road, get my blood flowing before I have to sit for hours." Meg jogged away from her neighbor.

When she returned, she swiped a washcloth across her face and under her armpits and slipped a dress over her head. On the drive to school, Meg reviewed her checklist for the bicycle trip. Every time another item jumped to mind, she jumped on the accelerator. The sheriff, sitting in his car, wagged his finger at her as she squealed into the school parking lot.

The lower bleachers were already crowded, with people bunched up, shoulder-to-shoulder. Meg scaled the bleachers and scanned the audience from her perch. To her left sat the Fitzpatricks. Meg flashed a quick smile. *Thank goodness Josh's relationship with their daughter didn't last be-*

yond junior year. That girl, with her odd sense of humor and shrill laugh, was rather intense.

A jumble of scents hovered around Meg in the warm gym. An overdose of cologne swirled with nervous perspiration and too many years of dust and mold. The whirl of the big overhead fans added to the tension.

Meg fanned herself with the program to keep awake. *Too many speeches given by too many administrators.* Finally the valedictorian jumped up, but his speech lacked enthusiasm and originality. If only Josh's grades were just a tiny bit higher, he'd be up there impressing the crowd.

While Mrs. Christianson, the principal, gathered her lists with names of the graduates, Meg plotted her route to the roped off photo area. She made it down as the principal read the As.

At "Emily Elizabeth Albertson. Joshua Robert Albertson," she raised the camera and snapped away. Josh placed the tassel on the other side of his mortarboard and she gave him a thumbs-up sign. His eyes flickered toward her before he strode away, his gown swinging over the tops of his tennis shoes.

"Can you believe it?" a mom next to her said. "After all these years, our kids are finally finished."

Mrs. Christianson made a final plea for graduates to act like the adults they now were, but they pulled out the cans of ropy string and filled the air with goopy cobwebs.

After the ceremony, Meg reached Josh as he and his friends posed for photographs. "One more." Meg gaily pulled out her camera.

Josh glared at her. "C'mon, Mom. Can't you see we're finished?"

Fifty-One

At 1:30 a.m., Meg awoke to the sound of tires spinning on the gravel road. She dashed to the window in time to see the flash of taillights from a pickup truck trailing a fishing boat. No Josh.

Departing the day after graduation was a horrid idea. *Maybe the whole trip was a bad idea.* What if the hospital calls to tell her they have Josh in a hundred little pieces? Then what?

With that thought, Meg snapped on the bedside lamp and picked up her phone. Maybe there'd be a message from Josh, she hoped. Seeing nothing new on the screen, Meg tossed the phone on her bed, disgusted at her son's lack of courtesy.

A tiny germ of an idea suddenly planted itself. What if Josh was unable to ride? All these weeks of planning and training wasted. Once again the folks of Lake Devine would have something to gossip about, giggling over the silly 'overweight, sedentary housewife,' who thought she could pull off such an adventure. Meg would show them. She could do it by herself.

She skipped down the stairs, excited at the possibility. But when she flipped on the switch to the light in the family room, the old Meg returned. The sight of all the cycling gear mocked her as much as the memory candle had so many months ago. She took a detour around the equipment and headed into the kitchen.

In the freezer, she found a carton of frozen yogurt. When she reached to open a drawer, she tugged and tugged. Finally, it pulled loose and a box of plastic forks and spoons popped open and rained on the floor. That was the last trick she had tried for Robert before he died, when he complained that everything tasted metallic.

Fifty-Two

Before they left, Josh dropped the cat at Chip and Jean's house. They had keys to check on the house and Meg hired their daughter to collect the mail and feed the hermit crabs. They stopped the newspaper delivery and turned off the water. With a start, Meg realized they should've contacted the stadium manager to see about releasing Robert's ashes. *We probably won't get that far anyway.*

A week ago, Duda had removed the pedals and handlebars and carefully packed their bicycles to ship them to Oregon. Now at the airport, all they had to do was check in their bike packs. Meg stowed her medications and bare essentials along with a new mp3 player in her handlebar bag to carry on.

At the security checkpoint, a clerk flagged Meg aside and searched her bag.

"Ma'am, can you come over here?" Bushy eyebrows framed the security clerk's beady eyes. Her standard-issue khaki skirt clung to her hips and revealed an outline of her underwear.

Meg followed her command and stood by the wall. Other passengers stared at her as they breezed through the checkpoint. Soon three uniformed guards surrounded Meg.

"Caesar, Gate Nine," one guard spoke into his radio.

A German shepherd pranced in place on his handler's leash. He sniffed Meg's legs and hands and moved on. The beady-eyed clerk passed Meg's handlebar pack to the dog's handler. The gloved-handler rummaged in Meg's pack and withdrew a plastic bag.

Fifty-Three

"How was I to know it looked like drugs?" Meg asked Josh. She trembled from her run-in with the authorities. "Did they think I was a donkey?"

"The term is mule. And duh, the ashes look suspicious. The whole thing is pretty weird anyway. I can't believe you're carrying Dad around like that. And why a ziplock bag?" Each syllable was laced with disdain.

They raced up the ramp to the plane. When they entered the cabin, the other passengers glared and pointedly looked at their watches. An attendant directed them to their seats. Meg blushed and tried to stammer an apology.

"It was all a mistake, really," she explained as she walked down the aisle. "I was carrying my husband's ashes," she said to the woman already belted into the window seat. The woman's eyes bulged and she quickly snatched the in-flight magazine from the seat pocket.

Meg plunked down in the middle seat. Once Josh was situated on the aisle seat, she whispered, "I figured a bag would be easier to carry on the bicycle. Plus it wouldn't break." They strapped themselves in, while the flight attendant rattled through the list of instructions.

"Yeah, whatever." Josh leaned back and closed his eyes. Meg smiled at the perky attendant and tried to listen to the safety instructions about loss of altitude. She knew she'd definitely put on her facemask before assisting Josh. That boy was on his own.

Fifty-Four

Aunt Naomi insisted on reserving two rooms at a bed and breakfast to launch them in style. The B&B's shuttle picked them up at the airport right on schedule. Gingerbread lattice covered the inn, and flowers dotted the trellis along the wraparound porch. After they checked in, Meg carried up her gear before they walked to the bike shop to retrieve their bikes.

"Do you think the bikes arrived already? I hope they're fine." Meg's pace quickened near the bike shop. "It'd be a shame if we made it this far and couldn't continue because the bikes were damaged or something."

"They're fine. Drop it."

The clerk led them to two cardboard shipping boxes leaned against a wall behind the store's counter. Josh tore open his box and pulled out the bike frame. In minutes, his bike was reassembled and ready to roll. Meg managed to get her frame out of the box, but struggled to adjust the handlebars. She fished the pedals out of a plastic bag and tried to screw them back on the bike.

"You'll need a wrench for those. Remember to check the direction you tighten them," Josh said. "I'm going to try my bike outside."

Relieved to pay the shop mechanic to assemble and tune up her bike, Meg returned to the B&B an hour later.

Her goal was to stay clear of Josh until morning. His disdain slapped every one of her questions and concerns. Meg's stomach had enough turmoil of its own.

Armed with a turkey sandwich and the local newspaper, Meg locked herself in her room at the top of the third floor. The mattress on the four-poster bed was taller than her hips. But height had nothing on comfort. At 5:00 a.m., she conceded and tip-toed downstairs, guided by a small reading light in the library. A silver tea service reflected the soft light. She rifled though tea bags and poured hot water in a china cup. While the tea steeped, she searched through the titles on the oak shelves.

A volume labeled *Meditations for Travelers* jutted out an inch away from the other books. Meg thumbed through it until she reached a section on anxiety. Someone had underlined a Bible verse, from the sixth chapter of Matthew:

> 34 *Take therefore no thought for the morrow: for the morrow shall take thought for the things of itself. Sufficient unto the day is the evil thereof.*

Easy for you to say. Meg replaced the book, but it stopped short of the back of the bookcase. She withdrew the book and a crumpled piece of paper, once wedged in the spot, tumbled out.

> *Select a rock and remember God, your refuge, your strength, your safety.*

Meg repeated the written words and then folded the paper and returned it behind the book. She sat down in a wing chair and pulled a knit lap robe over her knees, closed her eyes and held the cup of tea under her nose.

When she awoke, the blanket was tucked around her shoulders and the light was off. Breakfast smells of just-brewed coffee and bacon on the grill drifted up from the kitchen. Rays of sun bounced off a cut-glass bowl near the window and cast a rainbow on the wall. In the bowl was a collection of colored pebbles. Meg fingered through the bowl and unearthed a pebble the size of her thumbnail, polished to a smooth finish.

Meg pocketed the pebble and returned to her room at the top of the stairs. After she wiggled into her black shorts, she slipped the pebble in the middle pocket of her jersey. Duda's cautionary tale about saddle sores convinced her to always wear the shorts biking. But she still couldn't believe that she, the 'overweight sedentary housewife' conceded to wearing spandex. At least that perky reporter from the weekly paper wouldn't be around to take photos.

Meg touched her toes a few times, did some windmill stretches and drew in three deep breaths to disable her fear. Downstairs she found Josh at the breakfast table engrossed in conversation with another person dressed in spandex.

"About time you woke up," Josh said. Meg sat down and opened her mouth to explain, but reconsidered.

"I hear you two are doing the big trip," the other biker said. "This is my second time. I first crossed five years ago. You'll love it." He chomped into a hearty muffin and sunflower seeds fell onto his plate. "Here, try these." He passed the basket to Meg.

The smallest muffin was larger than the size of the man's fist. Meg pinched off an edge and stuck it in her mouth. The nibble lodged itself in her throat and she grabbed a goblet of water to force the bite on its way.

Another cyclist lifted the lid to a chafing dish filled with scrambled eggs swimming in water. "Eat up, Mom," Josh said. Hash browns tumbled out of his mouth. "We leave in forty-five minutes."

Meg's stomach buckled and she raced to the bathroom.

After splashing water on her face, Meg returned to the table. The hostess flitted back and forth, refilling silver platters with warm pastries. Her caftan floated in her wake.

The woman drifted toward the kitchen and waved at Meg to follow. In the hallway, she gave Meg a small paper bag.

"Here toots. I've seen that look of terror before at this table. You're scared to death, and now it's even worse, because you can't eat, but yet you want to make sure your body doesn't poop out on you today. Once you start riding, your stomach will settle. Bananas and a bagel with peanut butter. It will get you through the day."

Meg hugged the soft pillow of a woman. "How did you know? I can't thank you enough. Someday I'll return and spend time here."

"Now shoo. And God be with you."

Meg scooped up her gear and met Josh in the front of the house. Their bottles were filled with water and the panniers on the back of the bikes already bulged with their belongings. Meg jammed in the rest and attached her smaller bag to the handlebars. Before she zipped up the handlebar bag, she leaned over and stroked the plastic sandwich bag nestled inside. "This is it Robert. This is for you."

Linda, one of the bikers from the breakfast table, stood nearby. "I thought I'd ride with you two for a little while, if that's fine."

"Sure," Meg shrugged. "The more the merrier." She began to mount her bike and then stopped. "Wait." Meg pawed through her pack for her camera, gave it to Linda. "Please, could you?"

"Sure, get over next to your son. Big smiles, get a little closer together now."

Meg threw an arm over Josh's rigid shoulders. His body locked in position. Once the shutter clicked, he ducked under her arm and spun away.

Fifty-Five

Too fast, too slow, never just right. Meg stopped at a roadside picnic table and tore off chunks of the bagel and devoured it before she even sat down. Her first day on the road, and already she rode by herself most of the time. Even Linda took off. At least Oregon had nice paved shoulders, almost like biking on a bowling alley next to the road.

Josh kept riding ahead, unable to adjust to her pace, which even Meg had to admit was slower than a turtle. Her bike reacted like a different animal with all the extra weight of their gear. Sacrifice, Duda kept reminding her, will get her to the goal. Did that mean tossing out any self-esteem she had around Josh?

She finished the lunch from the B&B, crumpled up the paper bag and aimed for the garbage can. She missed it by five inches. Two cyclists pulled up to her picnic table, but Meg wanted to enjoy her pity party.

"You best be on your way mortals," she shrieked at the newcomers. "I fear danger lurks here. Wait, I hear them coming." Meg jumped up and shook her head until she was dizzy. When she stopped, the bikers were gone. "Thank you cat lady of Lake Devine," she said.

Alone again, Meg unzipped her handlebar pack and removed the bag containing Robert.

"So far, Robert, this is one of the worst ideas you have ever had. Josh isn't even with me and my body is screaming in pain. And we're supposed to make it all the way to St. Louis?"

Traveling for long solitary hours provided plenty of time for thought. Duda's words came back, but tangled with those from Malachi. Both seemed like they wanted her to succeed. Both seemed like they worried about her spiritually. And Malachi did say he was a pastor. Duda was just a bike-shop employee.

Meg tucked Robert back in the bag, and reached for her mp3 player. She scanned the menu until she landed on Gershwin's biggest hits. She tucked the player in a back pocket of her jersey. Then she threaded an earphone under the helmet strap and left the other one to dangle.

Meg mounted her bike and turned east. Ten miles later, a smattering of civilization appeared and a campground's sign announced RV hookups, hot showers. Josh's bike leaned against the post. This must be the place he talked about days ago, or maybe just hours ago.

A vehicle pulling into the campground kicked up clouds of dust and Meg swerved to avoid a mouthful of grit. She glanced to her right and saw the bathhouse. Across from her, campers and trailers were parked and plugged in. A television flickered from one campsite and a family sat outside, glued to the large screen on their picnic table. Tents dotted the other side of the campground. Josh was fastening the fly to their tent when Meg reached him.

"Finally," he said.

Meg leaned her bike next to a nearby picnic table and joined Josh by the tent. "Josh, I was thinking. Maybe we should stay in a motel our first night."

"And take down the tent? I just got it up. You've got to be kidding." He tossed the tent bag to her. "Stow this inside."

When Meg popped back out of the tent, Josh pointed to the shower house. "The punch code on the door is thirty-five-nine, but you have to hit it exactly, or you're locked out unless someone is inside. The showers aren't bad."

Meg recited "thirty-five-nine" six times before Josh yelled for her to stop.

"Sorry," Meg said. "I just don't want anything to prevent me from getting a hot shower. Thanks for leaving your bike for me at the entrance."

"Yeah, I figured you'd probably forgot the name of the place and would ride by. Course at your cruising speed, you probably had time to read every letter on the sign."

Meg grabbed a towel off the top of her panniers and swatted him. He grabbed his leg and affected a limp. Then he jogged away. He returned with his bicycle and parked it against a tree. Meg was still rummaging through her panniers when he took his off the bike and dropped them near the front of the tent.

"I'm heading into town. Want anything?"

"Food would be nice sometime," Meg said. First she wanted a shower. Armed with towel and toiletries she marched to 'thirty-five-nine, thirty-five-nine, thirty-five-nine.'

Water pelted her tender body and she tried to adjust the flow. Not even her sunscreen had held out today. She felt abused inside and out. Water gathered at her feet and she stood on tip-toes until her feet gave out and forced her to finish in the fungus-laden water backed up from the drain.

In Minnesota, everyone told her she'd get stronger each day. Right now, that seemed far from being possible. Meg rinsed out her biking shorts and walked back to the campsite. She hung the shorts from the handlebars and ducked into the tent. With nothing left to do, Meg twisted the valve to inflate her mattress, unrolled her sleeping bag, and took a nap.

The smell of fried onions and hamburgers revived her. Josh fanned the fast-food bag under her nose and she followed him outside to a table.

"There's a group of musicians—banjos, guitars across the road," Josh said. "That's where I'll be." He stuffed the last burger in his mouth and left before Meg could respond.

From the bottom of her left pannier, she pulled out a paperback novel and read until it became too dark. Inside the tent, Meg placed her handlebar bag near her head and laid out her clothes for the next day. She transferred the polished pebble from the B&B into the back pocket of a fresh jersey. She rolled up extra clothes and stuck them inside a T-shirt, soft with age, for a pillow.

She switched off her flashlight and stretched out on the sleeping bag and listened to the evening insects. Much too soon, the natural symphony was interrupted by the people in the tent next to her.

Their voices got louder and louder, almost as though Meg was right in the tent with them hearing bear stories. One man claimed that just the other week, a bear came right by his tent and sniffed around. Someone else talked of a place where the tents were inside a chain-link fence to keep bears out.

Just great, now bears? Meg checked the zipper on the tent door. A motel would have been a fine idea. She rolled over. Every rock and root seemed to poke through her sleeping bag and kept her from sleep. A trip to the bathhouse meant having to walk past her neighbors and their raucous party. Meg tried to convince herself she didn't have to go, but that was like trying to suppress a cough in a room filled with silent people.

"Thirty-five-nine, thirty-five-nine, thirty-five-nine." Meg bounded out of the tent toward the bathhouse. As long as the neighbors were noisy, no bears would consider coming around.

When Josh returned, she pounced on him. "Why couldn't we spend tonight in a motel? I saw one right around the corner when we turned into this place."

"We haven't earned the right."

"What right? It'd be a privilege to sleep in an air-conditioned room, on a bed, with no neighbors. We'd start off with a good night's sleep."

"Like I said, we haven't earned the right."

"You are as stubborn as your father was. As stubborn as he was about Mexico." Meg turned away and zipped up her sleeping bag. Sometime in the middle of the night, she woke up. Her sleeping bag had slid off the mattress pad, and she was flat against Josh's back. She tried to wiggle back in her bag.

Josh stirred. "What in the world are you doing?"

"Nothing, nothing," Meg said. "Go back to sleep."

Day one, but who is counting?

Fifty-Six

Meg hollered up to Josh, "Can we stop? This heat is about to kill me." She tried to pedal faster to keep up with him.

"You know, that's one of the things I don't like about you. You're always whining about stuff you can't change." Josh glared back at her.

"Whining? Me?" Meg was surprised.

"Is this how it's going to be? We've been on the road just a few days," Josh said. "But already you've jammed your chain and blown a tire. And I can't believe how slow you are. No wonder that lady rode ahead."

Despite the hours of conditioning with Greta the trainer, Meg's quadriceps were ready to rupture right through her skin. She longed for a stream to soak her feet, burning with each revolution. Every bone ached and her eyes were on fire. The mosquitoes swarmed so thick the previous night that Meg rubbed repellent all over her face. Now the repellent, loosened by sweat, dripped down her face. Her entire face felt masked with hives.

Josh fell in pace alongside Meg. "What, you're wimping out again? Or are you thinking about Dad?"

"I am not crying. However, I think I could. And no, your father is the last thing in my mind. No wait, I take that back. He's the one responsible for this blasted trip. He's the one responsible for my agony."

Josh changed gears to slow his pedaling speed to match hers. "But we're just starting out. What's the deal with your face? It's getting kinda red and puffy."

"That stupid repellent I used last night."

"You mean you didn't wash this morning? There was a fresh water pump at the campsite."

"I know. I regret skipping it now. I just wanted to get out of that spot. Who were those people?"

Three cyclists were already at the site when Meg and Josh had pulled up the night before. After Josh helped set up their tent, he walked over and made friends. He waved Meg over and she shook hands all around. They offered her a cold drink and passed around a bag of tortilla chips. One of the cyclists was a female about Josh's age. The two others were men in their twenties. All they wanted to talk about was components and gear ratio and other things. *One would think after sitting on a bike all day they could think of something besides bikes, but no, let's just keep the misery going.*

Josh brought her back to present day. "They were from Canada. You should've stayed up to visit with them."

"I tried, hon. But frankly, bike talk bores me."

"We talked about more than that. Their stories were incredible. They've traveled together for years, each year a different adventure. One year they went to Turkey."

Meg stood up on the pedals to relieve the soreness in her back. While her bike coasted, she drifted behind Josh. Soon she was forced to pedal hard to reach him again.

"They were stopped by armed bandits. They convinced them they were poor bikers, not rich tourists. 'Just look at our clothes,' they said, they wiped out earlier in the mud. They knew the area was dangerous, almost like the Wild West, so they hid their money in a spare bike pump."

Meg rued her jump to assumptions. And now she had missed a chance for interesting dialogue.

"Where are they now? Maybe we'll meet on the road today," Meg said.

"They planned to leave early. In fact, they packed last night. You should see some of the stuff they have. If we were just starting out, I'd be a lot smarter about gear."

"I don't think we're doing too badly," Meg said.

A pair of turkey buzzards circled overhead.

"Don't they look like bomber planes from a distance? As they glide along?" Meg asked.

"I wouldn't go that far."

"What else did the Canadians have to say?"

"Not much."

"How do they like America?"

"Don't know."

"Did you talk for a long time?"

"Nope." Josh shifted gears and eased ahead of Meg.

"Did you get enough sleep last night? I woke up at two and didn't see you."

"Listen, I need to keep moving. This pace is about to kill me," Josh said. "You can catch up to me later. Look for my bike in about an hour or two. I'll put it in a spot where even you could see it."

Over a slight rise in the road, he disappeared.

Fifty-Seven

"I just want to go home." Wind whipped Meg's face and tossed her words over her shoulder. Farther up she could see Josh, head down, plunging ahead, his body curled to cut through the headwind.

Somewhere around the western edge of Idaho, the feeling in her hands committed mutiny, and now her rear threatened to join the rebellion. The one positive note was the lack of traffic on the road, just as the guidebook promised. *Thank you, God, for the little things.*

She willed her feet to keep moving, but she knew she was losing speed. A slight elevation to the road didn't help either. She turned on her mp3 player, anything to remove the focus from the drudgery of pedaling. Something landed on her back, and she reached behind to flick it off her jersey.

Her hand touched flesh. And it wasn't hers. Someone else's hand was planted on her back. She screamed and swerved and the bike toppled to the shoulder.

"Get away from me," Meg yelled at the man who stopped his bicycle next to her. She jumped up and righted her bike, careful to keep it between her and the stranger.

"I thought you could use a little push."

"A push?" Meg fumbled for the mace in her handlebar bag. "You better get back on your bike and leave. I'm armed."

"I guess I shouldn't have surprised you like that. I only thought to help you move. Honest. No harm intended." Most of his features were hidden behind his expensive wraparound sunglasses, just like the glasses she wanted. Hers came from the gas station, thanks to Josh. An array of silver earrings dangled from almost all the exposed parts of his ear. A salt-and-pepper goatee covered his chin. His bright turquoise jersey matched his bicycle.

"You think you could've said something first?" Meg brushed road debris off her leg. "Where'd you come from anyway? I didn't see anyone around."

"I've been behind you for a while. I had to stop to change a flat, but I knew I'd catch up eventually. Weren't you with someone?"

"My son." Why did that boy have to pick this particular time to disappear? She was about to get murdered on the road at the hands of a strange man. Then Josh would be sorry.

"I'm sure he turned around and is coming back for me."

"Or I could keep you company until you reach him?"

Her alternatives were limited. "He'll probably realize I'm not around and start searching for me. That kid has lots of energy. I'm about ready to die, myself."

"Don't worry. The feeling passes. I felt like that for my first week. Oh, I'm Vincent, by the way."

"I'm Meg. From Minnesota. My son is Josh. He'll be going to college this fall." Meg kept talking while she eyed the road for other cyclists. She pointed to the back of Vincent's bike. "What's the trailer for?"

"It's easier to carry my gear behind me. And when I stop, if I find something small and intriguing at an antique shop, I don't have to ship it back home."

"You stop at shops along the way?" Meg was incredulous. With Josh, it was 'pedal, pedal, pedal.' No stopping except for a little food and an occasional pit stop. And the trip was still in its infancy.

"Doesn't everyone?" Vincent said. "Boy, you are missing a lot. What about all these interesting towns you've been through? Haven't you stopped for one latte and a look around? Some even have Native American pawn sales." He pulled up his sleeve to reveal his wrist, adorned with three ornate silver cuffs.

Meg reconsidered her perspective. Maybe this guy was harmless after all. She propped her bike up with one hand while she scanned the gravel where she tumbled. Satisfied that nothing had tumbled out of her packs, Meg got back on her bike. Vincent was already on his bike.

"Get behind me in the air pocket. It will be easier for you." He eased his bike onto the road in front of her.

"Hey," she called up to him, her fear of murder dissipating. "What was the deal about the hand on my back?"

"I was pushing you, to give you a rest. You looked like you were struggling. Want to try it again?"

"No, it's fine this way." Meg drafted behind Vincent. As long as she kept her wheel in the perfect spot, she didn't have to work quite as hard.

She rode in silence and concentrated on staying in the air pocket until Vincent signaled her to move up next to him. "Listen. There's supposed to be a great place ahead. Are you interested?"

All Meg could see was her reflection in his sunglasses.

"Well..." Meg's voice dropped. The thought of getting off her bike delighted her, but she wasn't sure if she should trust Vincent. Plus, she would have to face the biting wrath of Josh if she lagged too far. It was a toss-up, her son or a potential murderer.

"Why don't you call your son? You can use my phone." Vincent patted a back pocket on his jersey.

"How'd you know I was thinking about him?"

"You're a mom, right?" He grinned, a testament to either good genes or years of orthodontia.

When they reached the edge of town, Meg pointed to the shoulder. "How about stopping there and I'll try to call him. I've got a phone."

Josh's voice mail clicked on, asking Meg to leave a message.

"Hon, this is Mom. I'm stopping in..." Meg didn't know where they were.

"Sweet River," Vincent said.

"Sweet River," Meg said. "Call when you get this message." When she disconnected, she realized that was silly. No one listens to messages anymore.

Fifty-Eight

Josh felt his tire go flat. Another one of those stupid goat head thorns. A cyclist from Idaho warned him several times when they chatted on-line. In her last message, she insisted he carry a lot of extra tubes for his bike.

He pulled over at a shady spot to repair the damage. One thing about this trip, at least he was getting pretty fast at changing a tire. His record was seven minutes. He scanned the two-lane road for his mother. Always behind. For a brief second he considered changing his method, maybe he should ride with Mom. Every morning, they started out together. By afternoon, many miles separated them. It worked because they both knew where they would end up at night. Would Dad think that was enough?

Grit built up in his mouth. With each swallow, it felt like the thorns had penetrated his throat. He grabbed a water bottle out of its holder and found an envelope of sports drink in his left pannier. He tapped a few grains of the powder into the water, just enough to give him a little boost and soothe his throat.

He flipped open the map and studied it. Only thirty-five more miles to go for the day. Not bad at all. He could handle that without going crazy. This solitude was getting to him. Too much time to think about a lot of nothing.

A truck with a semi trailer filled with cattle honked a friendly toot. Josh waved back. By now Josh had learned the difference between the horns, the friendly and the not. Sometimes the not-friendly toots included a cup of ice flung in his face.

Still no sign of Mom, so he decided to get back on his bike and log some more miles. His stomach started to rumble. A green sign announced the next town in seventeen miles. A burger would be good right now. Josh adjusted his gears to hammer into town. He figured he could fly over the flat surface in well under an hour, at least he could if his bike wasn't so loaded. He bent down over the handlebars. *Hey, think of this as a training device. Pack your bike with tons of stuff and you work harder. Maybe the U.S. cycle team will call you.*

With each stroke of the pedal he envisioned cruising over the flat stretches of the Tour de France. Lance had such a good run at the title for so many years, and then he blew it by being stupid about steroids. Josh shook his head. *All that natural talent and now he's stripped from the history books.* Maybe it was time for an American to go for it again. A drug-free one. Josh nodded to the cows along the road, imagining their cheers of encouragement.

Maybe he could live in France and join the French team. *"Bon jour, bon jour,"* he called out. With that he recalled the first conversation Monsieur Gustafson made them memorize. It all came back now. 'Hello, my name is Pierre. And you, what is your name? How are you? I am fine. Do you know what time it is?'

As the miles disappeared, Josh plotted how to race and attend college part time. Take classes in the morning and train all afternoon, lift weights at night. Of course, he wouldn't have time to work. How much money did Dad really leave? Maybe he didn't need to earn a degree. Maybe he could just be a professional bike racer and not worry about anything else.

Just as he reached to accept the winning yellow jersey, a sharp horn blasted. He wasn't on the winner's podium; he had drifted across the middle of his lane, almost hugging the centerline. The horn blared again as Josh pulled over to the side. Although both lanes were empty with no vehicles for miles, the driver laid on the horn again. The truck slowed to Josh's speed. The red-faced driver glared out the passenger side.

"Stupid biker. You don't belong out here. Get off the road." His sneer exposed stained and gnarled teeth. He drove with his left hand on the steering wheel while the rest of his body leaned toward Josh. "I could knock you over if I wanted to. Don't wanna deal with the mess on my truck."

The more Josh was forced to ride on the edge of the pavement, the more he feared additional thorns in his tires.

"Ma appelle es Pierre. Comment allez-vous?" Josh said to the jerk.

"Should've figured you're one of them pesky foreigners." With that, the trucker unleashed the wad of tobacco he stored in his gums. The black tarry blob hit Josh on his left arm and the driver squealed away.

Fifty-Nine

A tornado siren began to blare, disrupting the tranquility of the small town Meg and Vincent just entered. Meg scanned the sky, bluer than Lake Devine.

"Must be noon," Vincent said. "Might as well stop anyway. Coffee or lunch or play?"

Stopping purely for fun wasn't in Josh's playbook yet. Meg planned to enlighten him once they reconnected.

"I heard there's a great coffee shop right off the main drag," Vincent said. "That should be our first stop. Last one there pays."

Meg's bike vibrated with each brick in the street as they bounced around the town square searching for the shop. Finally, Meg spotted an outline of a coffee cup painted on the window of a building wedged between an Eagles Club and a boarded-up hardware store. She eagerly rode over and left her bike against the wall. After she removed her helmet, she shook her head to let the air circulate under the layers of her hair.

"Oh. My. Goodness," Meg said. She closed her eyes and breathed deeply. "Fresh baked bread!" She unfastened the small bag from her handlebar and raced for the door.

Vincent placed his bike and its trailer against the building. He flashed a broad smile at Meg and took off his helmet and clipped it to his handlebars.

Inside, a faux finish on the walls created an Italian village and bright yellow ceramic tiles topped the tables. A tray of scones rested on a cooling rack.

Meg pointed to an overstuffed couch and mismatched chairs. "Could we sit there? It looks just heavenly."

"Wonderful idea. What sounds good? Mocha, latte? They have it all." He recited the list on the chalkboard. The coffee shop, an oasis in a sea of rural cafes where coffee was limited to regular or decaffeinated, delighted Meg.

"It all sounds good. Pick anything." Meg handed him a five-dollar bill.

He pushed the money back. "My treat."

Meg headed to the couch while the barista steamed the milk for an espresso. She sank down, relaxing in the comfort of the cushions. All of a sudden, she jumped up.

"Restroom?" She mouthed the words to the girl behind the counter.

The girl pointed to her left. The bathroom mirror confirmed Meg's thoughts. Her raccoon eyes were rimmed in white, protected by her sunglasses. She washed her hands and face, and splashed some water in her armpits. With her elbow, she punched the control for the electric hand dryer and dried her sweaty head. After she smoothed her hair back into place, she fished in her bike bag and found a tube of lip gloss and smeared it across her lips. A smile crossed her lips as Meg thought of Aunt Naomi. She'd be so proud of Meg's beauty routine, albeit a baby step.

Vincent sat in a chair in front of two steaming mugs on a coffee table. Mounds of whipped cream, dusted with chocolate sprinkles, covered the cups. Meg grabbed a cup and sat down to take a sip. She closed her eyes to savor the taste, but popped them open when she felt something on her lips. Vincent leaned over her and his index finger swiped her lips. "Whipped cream," he explained.

Meg recoiled and grabbed a napkin to scrub her lips to remove any traces of the cream or Vincent's touch. His move dumbfounded her. No one in her hometown would have been that forward. Not even Herb or Mr. Halvorsen.

"Sorry," Vincent said. "I didn't mean to startle you. Just helping out."

Meg swung her legs away from Vincent before she responded. "You just caught me off guard, that's all." Meg eyed the newspaper on the table. She recalled a self-protection demo when a woman defended herself with a rolled up magazine.

Sixty

Josh raised his arm at the truck driver fleeing in a cloud of dust. Mumbling a chain of words, Josh snatched his water bottle and squirted off the blob of chew that clung to his arm.

With each stroke of the pedal, Josh plotted revenge. He considered calling 9-1-1 on his cell phone to report a suspicious driver. Get that guy in some real trouble. Then he'd be sorry he ever messed with a biker. Or, maybe he could catch up to him at a diner or somewhere, drop a laxative in his coffee when he was in the bathroom. But first he'd have to buy the stuff. Forget that.

Semi-trucks passed him, creating sacks of air that pulled him along. But he stayed focused on his mission. His speed increased with each idea. He took a stick of gum from the back pocket of his jersey and let the wrapper float away. The more he chewed, the more he schemed.

After fifteen miles of wheat fields, a grain silo popped into view. Parked right in front of the town's diner sat the snaggle-toothed truck driver's heap.

Josh swung around to the rear of the diner and left his bike against the building. Armed with his tire pump, he crept across the gravel lot. With a loud creak, the diner's screen door swung open. Josh ducked behind a pickup.

A pair of farmers in overalls and seed caps came out. "Boy howdy, it's good to be back in the fields," the taller one said.

His buddy agreed and slapped the back of his truck. "Yup, time's a wasting. Catch you later." The men left and Josh continued toward his target.

Crouching behind the truck, Josh twisted off the cap to the valve and released the air from the two back tires.

Meg followed Vincent along the aisles in the antique store. Books with brown covers and yellowed pages crowded the shelves. Racks bent with the weight of too many forgotten old clothes. Tacked below the ceiling, tin signs advertised field corn and farm implements. Meg spotted a tea set like the one she had unwrapped on her sixth birthday. She picked up one of the delicate cups and turned to Vincent. "This is just like—" she said to dead air.

Vincent had disappeared. Too slow even for him, Meg thought. But did he need to play schoolyard games and drop her like that? At least all she had to do was keep the afternoon sun at her back, stay on the same route, and she'd eventually make it to their overnight stay.

She returned the teacup to the display and picked up a dishtowel with cartoon figures from the 1950s. A woman was greeting a man at the door, removing his shoes, handing him the newspaper and a pipe. The towel read, "Remember, he's the king." She could just imagine Christy sputtering with laughter. Then she recalled something Duda said when she accidentally complained about Josh. She called him the lord of the house. *Why had Duda held up his hands at that one? More of his religious babble? Why balk at that?*

Figuring the towel would be perfect for Christy, she knew she could fit it somewhere, just roll it up and tuck it in. She heard voices and turned to follow the source. Vincent bent over a glass counter, exchanging words with an older man.

"Ah, Meg, there you are," Vincent said. "Bob White Cloud here makes this jewelry. What do you think of this piece?" Vincent held up a silver bracelet and flipped it over in his palm. "Bob also does a lot of nice work with gemstones."

Vincent displayed a turquoise piece. "Bob, I'll take this thin bracelet, and then those other two I looked at. Wait, don't ring me up yet. I just noticed something over there." Vincent dashed down the aisle toward the entrance.

Meg waited at the counter with Bob. "Your work is very nice." She eyed a bracelet and contemplated buying a souvenir for herself. Then she looked at the price tag.

"Oops, Robert would shoot..."

"I thought he said his name was Vincent?"

"It was. It is. I'm sorry." Meg stepped back from the counter.

The last time Meg had gone souvenir shopping was when the family drove west one summer vacation. At the edge of the Teton mountains, Robert had given her spending money. In town, a young Josh had begged for a leather vest with a silver sheriff's star, and leather chaps. The cowboy hat he picked out slipped over his ears. And just like that, the spending spree was over. Not that she wanted anything for herself. But Robert couldn't believe she spent all the money in one quick stop. Now mice were probably burrowing in that outfit up in the attic by the school boxes.

Vincent returned carrying a mirror with beveled edges. Its wooden frame was inlaid with pieces of silver and a green stone.

"You don't see much of this stone," Vincent said as he set his treasure on the counter. "I'll take this, but you better ship it to me. Don't want to risk carrying this beauty."

Bob totaled the purchases, and the old-time cash register bell rang and the drawer popped out. Outside, they rearranged their packs to accommodate their purchases. Vincent handed a package to Meg. "I want you to have this."

"No, I can't."

"Can't or won't? Just open it," he said.

Meg unwrapped the tissue. The silver bracelet he had shown her glinted in the sun. "Now I know I can't, or won't," Meg said.

"If it's the money thing, *achk*," Vincent made a guttural sound. "Money is meant to be spent. I invested well over the years."

Meg looked at the bracelet, delicate in her hand, bands of silver twisted in a spiral.

"When I saw that, I thought of you and your son."

Meg turned the bracelet over and over. "My son?"

"Sure, the two of you are family. You should bind together and strengthen your efforts. Like the silver."

The analogy made sense to her, but it was too expensive. "I saw the price," she said.

"Well, pretend you didn't. Pretend it was 75 percent off. Pretend you found it on the road and there was no one to be seen for miles."

She slipped the cuff bracelet over her wrist and pressed on the edges to make sure wouldn't fall off. "Thank you. That was a generous gesture."

"My pleasure. Now let's ride."

They rode several miles with little traffic. Occasionally they passed a farmer in a field with swirls of dust behind him. They traveled two abreast until they approached a hill.

"Better ride behind me, just in case some nut job is barreling toward us taking up both lanes." Vincent eased his bicycle in front of Meg's. A car gunned from behind, honking as it passed. Teen-age boys hooted, arms sticking out the windows, clutching brown bottles. Then in a flash, several bottles flew from the car and exploded on the pavement. Vincent and Meg swerved to avoid the glass and pulled to the side.

"What a bunch of idiots," Vincent shouted. "And now we have to stop before we get to the top of a hill. I hate that. There's no way we'll get the momentum to continue. Not with these loaded bikes."

Vincent looked at Meg. "Are you ready to continue?"

"Are you serious?" Meg's body still shook. "I still can't breathe."

"I hate jerks like that," he said. "Drink some water, you'll be okay. We can just walk slowly. Be sure to squeeze your rear brake. Last thing you want to do is roll backward."

They crested the hill and Vincent swung a leg over his top tube. The car was a blur down the road. Near the bottom, Meg felt her bike slow, once the road leveled off. Vincent had already edged over to the shoulder and stopped.

"Well, those kids got us. Our tires are flat. We better pull out the glass and patch them or change them." Vincent's face took on a grim line.

Meg leaned her bike over in the brush and undid the quick release to remove her front tire. "Vincent... there's a problem. Josh always did this for me."

"Just watch. And learn."

Meg was right about the wrath of Josh. When she told him about stopping for coffee, his face grew red and he shook a finger in her face. "Don't you ever go off with a stranger again." She didn't dare tell him that Vincent was in the same motel.

One at a time, he wheeled their bikes into the motel room, locked the door and drew the curtains closed.

"What's the problem now?" Meg said.

"You don't know about the people around here. Just a bunch of hicks. And the ones who aren't hicks are lunatics." Josh walked to the window and peeked out between the curtains. "Bunch of farmers."

"Boy, when did you become mister glass-half-empty?"

"Not even close, Mom. Nice try."

Josh picked up the plastic folder listing local services and paged through the contents.

"Pizza?" He paused over the room phone and picked up the receiver.

"Let's go out, walk around town." For the first time, the day's miles didn't cripple Meg. She pulled a hairbrush out of her pack and began to smooth out her hair.

"We can't," Josh said.

Meg grabbed a clean shirt. "I'll just take a minute in the bathroom. I promise."

Josh was still standing over the telephone when she returned.

"Combo okay?"

"Josh, don't be silly. I wasn't gone that long. We still have plenty of daylight to walk to a restaurant. Let's go."

"I don't think we should. That's all." Josh hung up the receiver and flipped open a small opening in the curtains. Meg went over, stood behind her son and looked out. The parking lot was empty except for three pickup trucks, a van, and a motorcycle. She reached around to feel Josh's forehead.

"Stop it Mom." He swatted her arm away. "Let's just order pizza, watch TV."

Meg shook her head, but kept quiet. When a knock came on the door, Josh jumped up and peered through the eyehole. Then he opened the door, paid the delivery guy, and closed and locked the door. He carried the pizza to the corner table. Meg grabbed bath towels, thin as tissue paper, and sat down at the table. Josh stood over her and placed both hands on her shoulders.

"If you hear anyone at the door again, do not answer." Josh lectured. "I'm serious Mom. Under no circumstances."

Later, after Josh fell asleep, Meg stayed up rinsing out clothes in the sink. Before she shut off the lights, she grasped the desk chair and propped it under the doorknob.

Sixty-One

Although Meg blamed male hormones for Josh's strange behavior, she decided to bite her tongue and let the subject disappear along with the mile markers and Vincent.

The two experimented with riding styles. Some mornings she hit the road before he did. When he caught up, she'd enjoy a few miles with him before he got bored at her pace. Then it was time to pull out the Gershwin. Thanks to Duda, her new mp3 player was packed with tunes.

"My Man's Gone Now" carried Meg right up to the gates of a state park, their spot for the night. When she checked in, the ranger handed her a note from Josh. He was already off fishing with some people from Germany. At least the boy erected the tent before he disappeared.

Meg toted clean clothes to the campground services for a shower. According to a sign, three minutes of water flowed from the coin-operated shower for a dollar. Meg fished out two dollars worth of quarters from her ditty bag, careful to pluck off bits of crumpled tissues and assorted fuzz. She stepped into a stall and lathered on body gel before she started the water. Arching her back, she stretched her shoulders as warm water cascaded down her torso. She dumped a handful of shampoo on her hair when suddenly the water turned frigid and shut off. Blinded by soap, Meg felt along the ledge next to the bottles for her four last quarters and inserted them one by one. The final quarter slipped and bounced off the floor. With her foot, she patted the tile and inched around the shower stall. Except for the dripping from the shower, the bathhouse was silent. Meg snaked her foot over the drain and under the next stall. Her toes found the quarter.

"What in the?" The person in the next shower stomped on Meg's foot.

Meg jerked back her foot. "I need my quarter."

"What some people won't do for a little loving. Perv."

"No, seriously." Meg shivered in her stall, soap congealing on her skin. "Just kick it back to me."

The quarter slid under the stall and hit Meg's foot. Quickly she bent over to retrieve it and engaged the water once more. When she finished, she listened again. Convinced she was alone, she dressed and rushed to her campsite.

"Thanks for leaving me the note," she said to Josh. He was bent over a picnic table.

"Didn't want you to freak if you didn't see me. Head on or off?"

"Whatever you think. Wait, are you talking about those fish?"

"Aren't they pretty? We hit a good spot out there."

Meg searched for a neutral response before she spoke. "Prepare them the way you think best. I trust your judgement."

"Ranger Rick came by and dumped water on my cooking fire. Forest fire threat too high. How was I supposed to know? Anyway, the fish won't be as tasty on propane," Josh said.

He slid the fish onto a plate and squeezed a lemon over it.

"Impressive, hon. Where did you learn that method?"

"Dad taught me a few different versions. I watched a video online for this method."

Meg sucked the last of the fish off the bones and licked her fingers. They wrapped up the garbage and stuck it in a metal can, making sure to clamp the lid.

"Did you always want to be a housewife?" Josh asked while they cleaned up the dishes.

"I hate that term. Even more so after Candy's article."

"Well, did you know what you wanted to be when you grew up?"

"Actually, I considered going to law school and becoming an attorney, like my dad."

"Seriously? Guess that didn't work out."

"Your father was eager to get married right after college. He didn't think we needed the financial stress of more education for me.

"So he started selling houses?"

"He earned his real estate license and we moved to Lake Devine. Time for bed. It's getting cold out."

In the morning, Meg stretched and wiggled her toes, thankful for the fleece hat and socks she stuck on before falling asleep. She unzipped the tent, careful not to make any noise. Josh slept with his sleeping bag pulled up to his forehead, sheltering his ears from the threat of frost.

The sun was just beginning to tint the water, with splotches like rainbow trout, as it rose behind the jagged mountains. Crisp air tingled her nose. She pulled her sweatshirt closer to her body, stretched toward the morning sky, and headed to the outhouse. When Meg returned to their campsite, she lit their propane stove to heat water for coffee and oatmeal.

She sat on a stump and waited. A blue jay hopped around in the boughs of a pine tree. A chipmunk scurried over to her foot and paused. Meg reached in her sweatshirt for a cracker and rewarded the chipmunk. Other than the water bubbles bursting and rattling the pot, the stillness of the area continued to amaze Meg. Being alone in the world was so different from being alone at home. There, waves of loneliness often threatened her daily routine. Sometimes it was better to hide in bed all day. But this loneliness carried a sense of peace. Meg dipped her mug in the pot and added instant coffee and a packet of vanilla creamer. The tent quivered and Josh popped his head out through the door.

"Hey," he said.

"Hey yourself, sleepy head. Water's ready when you are." Meg smiled and lifted up her mug as proof.

"Cool. Give me a sec to throw on more clothes." He retreated to the tent and she heard more rustling. He soon emerged wearing a down vest over a T-shirt, flannel boxers and socks.

"That's not much more. You're going to freeze your hiney, honey," she said. "It feels colder today. I knew when we hit higher elevations it would get cold, but we haven't really climbed yet, have we?"

Josh snorted. "You just wait. I looked over the map last night after you fell asleep. We'll hit the summit today. Be ready to use your gears. Remember what I taught you? Shift down before you start the climb. Stay focused on one spot. Keep relaxed, stop if you have to."

"I know, I know. Let me just enjoy the morning as it is right now. Right now in this slice of time. Now, how about breakfast? Oatmeal? I picked up some raisins yesterday in that little town."

He nodded on his way to the bathroom. "Maybe we could leave in about forty minutes."

Meg pulled on the black leg warmers and arm warmers Duda gave her, and silently thanked him for his insight and generosity. A long-sleeved shirt covered her riding jersey. For the final layer, she threw on a windproof jacket Naomi sent her, bright fluorescent green, like those worn by highway construction workers.

They broke camp in silence and Josh checked his watch. "Perfect, forty minutes, just like I said. Let's hit the road."

Sixty-Two

Meg rode the switchbacks over the pass alone. Mindful of Josh's advice, she shifted to her lowest gear as she approached. She and Josh had started just as the sun was rising, but the boy was already out of sight. So far the climb didn't seem terribly difficult, although Meg's legs started shaking with fatigue from all the extra pedaling in her lowest gear. Like a hamster running on its little treadmill in the cage. All those revolutions and nowhere to go.

One by one, wide campers trailing boats wended down the pass on the two-lane road. Big mirrors jutting out from the drivers' side forced passing cars to swing wide. When they met Meg slowly climbing toward them, their faces distorted in surprise. She lowered her head and concentrated on the thin white line that separated her from the highway, tense to remain on the narrow shoulder. Certain death waited on either side of the line.

Meg finally found an area to withdraw from the traffic and dismounted. She retrieved a granola bar from her pack and washed it down with water from her first bottle.

The road looked clear for a few miles, so Meg pulled back on. She'd been on her bike for an hour, and every now and then tiny stars floated across her eyes. Each time the stars appeared Meg pulled over to catch her breath. The image of a medieval torture chamber, deep in the bowels of a forlorn castle soon replaced the visual of the hamster.

The bumpy surface of the road's shoulder compounded the tingling in Meg's hands. She tried to shake each hand back into a wakeful state. Two hours had elapsed since the bottom of the mountain. Two hours since she was once comfortable. Two hours since she could really breathe.

Her cadence lacked a rhythm and her wheels moved like wooden blocks through mud. As she pedaled, she reached down for a water bottle. Her numb fingers lost their grip and the bottle bounced on the pavement. It tumbled along until a gust of wind picked it up and tossed it over the edge of the mountain. Now she was forced to ration the water left in her reserve bottle. The sun refused to relinquish its hold. Meg could feel her neck begin to expand with blisters.

Three miles later, Meg was forced to stop. Her saliva could no longer compete with the grit of the road and her throat was raw. She pulled the polished pebble out of the back pocket of her jersey. She'd been carrying it since the B&B. A tale of desert survival came to mind and she dribbled what spit was left onto the pebble before she popped it into her mouth.

Each revolution brought her closer to the summit, but she feared the sun had already damaged her brain receptors. For some reason, the smells of winter holidays in her grandmother's house came spinning in her head. When little stars burst in front of her eyes, she realized it was time to get off the bike. As she walked her bike a few paces, the smell returned. She bent over a shrub near the road and inhaled. Sage, just like in her grandmother's turkey stuffing. She walked along the sagebrush, and memories of the long table crowded with relatives and friends and lots of food came to her. Once the stars faded, she pulled on the leg of her shorts, and got her leg back over the bar to straddle her bike. Even if it killed her, she was making it to the top.

With each tedious pedal, she tried to focus again. Her labored pace gave her the ability to observe the narrow ditch between the road and the mountain on her right. Carcasses—*or was that carcasi?*—in varying degrees of decomposition, assorted shoes and boots, and a faded bouquet of artificial flowers. Did a young bride change her mind after the wedding? Or did the wrong person catch them at the wedding? She passed a plastic storage bin dumped to the side, assorted shirts and pants strewn onto the rocks and grass.

This must be how it was with the settlers. They traveled this same route, carrying too many of their belongings. And then, piece-by-piece they tossed out family relics, music boxes, and possessions that brought pleasure and joy. How depressing it must've been to leave their wealth out east and come to this. Meg compared her fate to early settler sisters. At least she knew a shower and a comfortable bed awaited her that night. Meg wiped sweat off her forehead and rolled her arm warmers down to her wrists. Her pace slowed enough that a fly hitchhiked on her forearm as she chugged up the mountain.

A roadside sign announced the summit just ahead. Meg struggled the last several miles until finally reaching the top. When she safely pulled over to the scenic outlook, she glanced at her watch: *Three hours to climb this intolerable mountain*. But she made it. And the vista was spectacular. She could see for miles and viewed the switchbacks as other cars traveled up. She dismounted and slurped a long drink of water, letting it splash her cheeks and down her neck, no longer worried about running out of the precious liquid.

Three cyclists gathered by the sign at the summit, laughing and taking turns snapping photos.

"Hey, great climb, wasn't it?" one said to Meg.

She wheeled her bike over to them. "Boy, I don't know if I would classify it as great. It's great it's behind me."

"Don't worry. You'll love the descent. It's worth the hard work," he said.

Meg motioned to the backpacks they all wore. "Don't those get awfully hot?"

"You need to get one of these. They're hydration packs. We carry water this way." He grabbed the tube hanging over his shoulder and sucked on it. "You'll find them in the shop at the bottom."

Before they left, Meg handed one her camera and asked him to photograph her by the sign as proof she made it. Meg munched another granola bar before returning to her bike. Before the descent, she checked her watch. Her body shivered as she raced downhill, the air whisking away her perspiration. It was all she could do to hang on and enjoy the ride. She thrilled to the exhilarating sensation of flying and losing control while trying to maintain a steady hand on the brake. At the bottom she admired the time: *fifty-five minutes to descend.* She looked around for someone to share her victory. But she was all alone.

"Fifty-five minutes," Meg said to the shopkeeper.

"Fifty-five what?" He knelt by a box on the floor and glanced up at Meg.

"That's how long it took to descend."

"That's too bad." He stood up. "Maybe I can help you find something to increase your speed."

"I did come in for a hydration pack," she said. "But I want to explore the rest of your store first." She rummaged through the box he had just left. Like a kid plucking the winning rubber duck at the county fair, Meg grabbed a pair of red biking shorts. She chuckled at the price, almost 80 percent off. When she tried them on, it was the first time she had seen herself in a full-length mirror in weeks.

"Not bad, not bad at all," she said looking at the muscle definition in her legs and arms. Perhaps her bulges had all smoothed out.

"So, passing through the area?" The clerk eyed her.

"You bet," Meg said. "I'm from Minnesota. Heading to Missouri."

"Tell you what. I'll give you an extra discount. Five bucks and they're yours."

Sixty-Three

From the corner of her eye Meg watched the man at the bar, glued to the 24-hour sports channel. In between mouthfuls of salted peanuts, he sipped on a longneck bottle of beer. Long silver hair curled over the neck of his denim shirt. An air of self-assuredness, like a politician or a celebrity, coiled around him. Clanging of metal pans from the kitchen crew cleaning up after the noon rush broke into the low murmur from the TV.

Meg leaned back in her booth to let the sun beat through the window and warm her. The effort climbing the summit had soaked her T-shirt, making her sorry she didn't put on a jersey instead. If she didn't warm up soon, she'd have to change clothes. A fly, stuck in limbo between the panes of glass, distracted her. What kind of life span did it have and what choices were left? She wanted to liberate it, but she couldn't see its point of entry.

She dipped the edge of her grilled cheese sandwich into a dollop of catsup on the plastic plate. A lone pickle spear sat on the plate, atop a wilted leaf of lettuce. *Presentation, presentation, no matter where you go.*

A commotion at the front door stopped all thoughts and a man stumbled in. "Who's No. 1?" he asked. He looked at Meg. "Who's No. 1?" Meg looked around blankly. He stared at her and repeated, "I'm asking you, honey, who's No. 1?"

"Louie, Louie" started to play on the kitchen's radio, and the cook's singing threw off the newcomer.

"I am." He hopped up on a barstool, but a slight miscalculation caused him to land on the floor. The man roared with laughter. "Pretty good trick, man," he said as Mister Silverhair helped him to his feet. "Bartender, come here and give me and my friend a beer."

A young woman came out of the kitchen. She wiped her hands on a towel tucked in her low-cut jeans. "Have you had too much to drink already?" she asked.

The newcomer waved away the idea. "Nah, I'm just a happy guy." The bartender filled two glasses and set them on the bar.

Meg concentrated on her sandwich and contemplated fly limbo. The two men cheered at the latest scores on the TV. When someone on the small screen started extolling the latest drug for impotence, the men looked over at Meg and whispered. Meg caught them staring at her chest and she glanced down. Two wet circles emphasized the not-meant-to-be emphasized parts under her soggy T-shirt. She shifted her arms to conceal her breasts. By now, the men had swiveled on their barstools to face Meg. She stared back at them, and they returned to their beers.

She pulled a small notebook from her fanny pack and scribbled down the cost for lunch. So far her cheapest day's total was $2.35. Her new habit was to stop at a grocery store and pick up a fresh banana and a granola bar for breakfast. Her only other expenditures that day were for postcards and the hydration pack.

Another man joined the group at the bar. Their loud laughs broke their whispered conversation to the bartender. To avoid the continued glances, Meg shifted her position and hunched in her shoulders to deflate her chest. Finally, the newcomer walked over to Meg.

"We got this deal going. Me and him say you're with the circus that's come to town. Peggy the bartender says it ain't so. She says you come here on bicycle. Traveling on a bike? Sounds like a circus to me. Do you juggle bowling balls and swords while you ride?"

He looked back at his buddies and laughed. "Curly, see the bald guy—hey, Curly, wave to the lady—thinks he seen your act before. Said you were something special. We got some money riding on this thing, so what'll it be?"

"I'm sorry to disappoint you gentlemen, but I'm not in a circus," Meg said.

"C'mon, honey, I bet you can do a lot of tricks." He leered. His buddies now crowded around her booth. Meg jerked away when Curly rested his hand on her shoulder.

"What are you doing way out here by yourself anyway?" Curly winked at Mister Silverhair. "Ya know, she dresses like a guy and she's traveling all alone. And I seen her eyeballing Peggy the bartenderess. I bet she's one of them lesbos." He reached for her shoulder again. "I could help you change that, honey."

The phone in the kitchen rang shrilly. The bartender came through the swinging door and motioned to Meg. "Ma'am, I think this is for you. It sounds like the sheriff. You can take it in here."

Meg instantly thought of Josh and her heart fell. She grabbed her gear and dashed into the kitchen. When she picked up the phone, she heard nothing.

"I thought you said the sheriff was on the phone for me," Meg said. Peggy put a finger to her lips and pointed to a switch under the counter and whispered. "That activates the ringer. I found it works almost as well as a bouncer. I tell drunken guys their wives just called to order them home." She tossed a shirt to Meg. "Now put this on, get your bike and go before those guys realize you're not coming back. That handsome one, he's real trouble and he sweet-talks his victims into not pressing charges. Everyone around here knows about it though."

"Thanks for saving me. They were making me nervous. I don't know what would've happened next. Probably nothing, but just the same..." Meg drifted off. "Anyway, this dry shirt is great. What do I owe for it and the lunch?" Meg reached into her bike bag.

"Nothing. It's on the house, now go." Peggy pushed Meg toward the door. Meg pulled the dry shirt on over the wet one, and then took off the wet shirt and threaded it out through the armhole. She waved thanks and slipped out the backdoor. She strapped the soggy T-shirt on the side pack on her bike.

Once outside she looked down to fully admire the green shirt advertising Bryan and Peggy's place: *I don't have a drinking problem, I drink, I fall down, no problem.*

Sixty-Four

Meg adjusted the sound level on her headphones to allow the music to envelop her. She coasted and drank in the air, soaking up the fragrance of the rich soil along the empty county road.

She looked forward to the days when Josh would actually ride with her for more than a few miles. This putative mother-son adventure evidently existed only with Robert. Maybe this week she'd be fast enough. Raucous honking interrupted her musings. She jumped and glanced over her left shoulder. A long red car with pointy tail fins and lots of chrome roared up alongside. Mister Silverhair at the wheel blasted the horn again.

"Wait, wait, you forgot something at Bryan and Peggy's place. Pull over up ahead. I'll give it to you." Mister Silverhair smirked at her. The other passengers grinned.

"Yeah right." Meg continued pedaling. The men took turns yelling at Meg to stop. When she finally looked over again a pair of skinny bare buttocks hung out the side window. She could see the other men rocking in mirth. Meg pushed hard on the pedals and pumped until she thought her feet would burn up, leaving only bone.

The car was even with her when she glanced again at the road. A semi-truck barreled toward them. The squeal of a jake brake burst the air. Meg pulled the handlebars to the right and the bike bounced down into the ditch and Meg flew off the loaded bike. Above her on the asphalt, the two vehicles screeched and skidded. Apparently too intoxicated to avoid the collision, Mister Silverhair plowed toward the truck. The truck swerved and jackknifed, upsetting its load. Meg hunkered in the ditch, dazed at the unfolding horror.

Crates jammed with poultry catapulted from the truck. Feathers and squawking filled the air along with diesel fumes and chicken excrement. Fowl fluttered and limped through the clouds of dust on the road. Sirens soon added to the din. A sheriff's car flew toward them, followed closely by an ambulance.

A crate landed in the ditch by Meg and she was eye-to-eye with a load of stunned chickens. Paramedics tended to the human passengers, all still moving as far as Meg could tell. Mister Silverhair's hair was turning decidedly bloody red. The door to the truck groaned as the driver wrenched it open. He stumbled as he stepped out. When he stood up, he started yelling at Mister Silverhair. Emergency vehicles continued to roar to the scene. An EMT rushed over to Meg and threw a blanket over her trembling shoulders.

"What happened? Is everyone alive?" She tried to stand but the paramedic gently pushed her back down.

"Just stay still," he said.

"I'm fine, just banged up."

The sheriff's deputy came over to Meg with his notebook. "Peggy sent for us as soon as those goons left her place. She was right, they were headed for trouble."

The deputy took notes from Meg. "I want you to get checked out. You took quite a tumble. Where are you headed for tonight?"

"The next town, I think. Bayside Motel. My son should be there."

The sheriff nodded in recognition of the motel. "You'll certainly have a lot to tell him. Maybe your son can fix your bike for you too." He wheeled her bike over to her. The frame appeared intact, but both tires were flat. He stuck the bike into the patrol car's trunk.

"I can give you a lift. If we have more questions, I'll call you tonight at the motel."

Sixty-Five

Before Josh left for more pain relievers at the grocery store next door to the Bayside Inn & Supper Club, he handed Meg a plastic card from Duda. His private number was on one side and the other side said Hebrews 12:1: "Let us run with patience the race that is set before us."

Meg twirled the card in her fingers for a few minutes. That sounded like Duda, always talking about the race. She dialed Christy's number, but there was no answer. Maybe at least Malachi or Rachel would pick up. Maybe Duda was available. Her body twinged with every move and her baffled mind was about to rupture. This nightmare needed to end. No way could she go another day or another mile.

She dialed. The phone rang five times. Duda answered just as she was about to hang up. "I apologize for calling, but you said to call anytime. It's Meg. I can't do this." She tried to explain the accident and the bar scene preceding it, but frustration turned her words to mush.

"Miss Meg, take deep breaths. Are you sitting down?"

"Uh huh." She tried to slow her breathing and stop the hiccoughs.

"Are you okay? Any injuries?"

"Nothing bad." She wiped her nose. "Nothing is broken, but I think I aged three decades in one day. I'm sore all over. Josh borrowed a heating pad from the front desk for my back. And I look like a little kid with skinned up knees.

I should've listened to everybody. This is crazy. I'm not up for this. I seem to find trouble everywhere." Her breathing leveled out, and with a straw, she sipped some water.

Duda grunted.

"Duda, what are you doing?"

"Sorry, unpacking new bike frames. Don't worry. I'm listening. I'm wearing a headset with my cell phone. Now why did you think you're not up for this?"

"Honestly. Have you ever heard of such a thing to begin with?"

"Stop right there. What happened to the lady who worked hard to make it this far? The woman who spent hours at the gym and on the bike trail? Even through rain and sleet? The woman who didn't care what others said?"

Meg watched the blood seep through the gauze on her left knee. She plucked fresh cotton from the box next to the phone and gently pried off the old pad, applied ointment, and firmly placed the new one over it.

She could tell by his breathing that Duda had returned to his unpacking. After a few seconds, he said, "Meg, what do you think?"

"Maybe deep down I agree with you. But this is so difficult. I didn't realize how tough this was going to be."

"Of course it's tough. Finishing the race isn't easy, but you're on the course God set out for you. God's hand is on you, keeping you safe. If you think about it, the accident could've been fatal."

"Gee thanks."

"Go for it, Miss Meg. Don't let those wackos or the accident get in the way of your goal. With Christ behind you, you can succeed."

"Thanks coach. I feel like the quarterback, ready to run out on the field and win the big game."

She hung up with Duda and tried one more time for Malachi. She was calmer and her words came out stronger.

"Malachi, what about God's will? Is this part of His will, that I should have an accident?"

"No, I don't think we can say an accident is God's will."

"But if God's not in control, who is?" Meg balanced Duda's card in her hand. Malachi's words seemed to conflict with Duda's. Maybe she had a minor concussion and her brain was scrambled.

"Anyway, Malachi, thanks for the support. Tell Rachel hello."

"Just know we believe in you and we're praying for you. I've got the whole church covering you in prayer. By the way, send more postcards. The people love them. I've been posting them on the bulletin board."

"So now you're convinced I'm continuing?"

"Yeah," Malachi said. "Aren't you? And when you get back, Rachel and I hope to have more discussions about faith. You're cultivating your God-confidence now. We can help you grow that. So anyway, call tomorrow. Bye and God bless."

She set down the receiver and someone knocked on the hotel door. Meg hobbled over. A young man bustled in and set a tray on the low dresser by the TV. He lifted the dome to show off a steaming bowl of chicken soup, a heaping mound of creamy macaroni and cheese, and a hot fudge sundae in a tall parfait glass.

"What's all this? I just asked for a cup of soup."

He grinned. "Well ma'am, everyone heard about you and what happened back there on the road. You're practically a celebrity. Anyway, the chef thought you needed a dose of comfort. We all suggested stuff that makes us feel good and hope it works for you. Enjoy."

He turned around before he left. "And ma'am, don't worry about the charge. The manager said it's on the house. He said he wants you back on the road, having fun, riding strong."

"Mom, wake up." Josh's voice reached deep into her nightmare tangled with twisted metal and the stench of chicken waste. She felt a stiff pat on her shoulder.

"Wake up, you're moaning out loud. I mean really loud."

Meg surveyed the room, trying to get her bearings. A light from the bathroom reassured her she was no longer on the road. The nightmare crept away and she recognized the motel room they checked into after the accident.

Josh sat in a chair by Meg's bed, his headphones dangling from his neck. A yawn slipped through his lips.

"Did you know you can smell in dreams?" Meg said. "All of a sudden the chickens, the drunks, the—it was so real."

Josh picked Meg's covers up from the floor, and put them back on her bed, smoothing them around her shoulders. "Do you need a drink of water, or something? More meds?"

"I'm good," Meg said.

"Try to catch some sleep. We'll check your frame in town tomorrow."

She winced as she rolled over and slipped her hand under her pillow, hoping to latch on to Robert's old shirt. Her hand came up empty, but having Josh nearby filled her heart with comfort.

Sixty-Six

Meg's bike gripped the shoulder's edge, an inch from the ditch. She flinched with the sound of every approaching vehicle. The sun broiled their backs as they headed east again. Dust rolled off the fields and encrusted their bodies. Meg smacked her lips to get rid of the gravely coating and clamped down on the mouthpiece hanging by her shoulder. Dribbles of water mingled with air sputtered up the tube from the hydration pack on her back.

"Josh, Josh." Her voice came out cracked like the dirt alongside the road.

Josh stopped on a bridge and waited. Meg pulled next to him and leaned over the railing. She cleared her throat to spit into the creek bed, no longer home to any aquatic activity.

"See that. Nothing. No saliva," Meg said.

Josh launched a gob of spit and they watched it dampen the soil below.

"At least you still have water in your system. Let's call it a day. Perhaps we can find a nice place to camp, and buy some water. I need water. My insides are as dry as my outsides."

"Mom, you know we have to keep moving. We'll never make it to St. Louis at this rate."

"What if we hit the road super early tomorrow, to make up? That should help."

"I doubt it, at the speed you've been going."

"Humor me, Josh. I'm tired of these trucks rumbling by. Plus this sore bod needs to stop. I need to get away from this bike. My legs feel like mush in this heat. My rear is aching again..."

Josh held up his hand. "Stop. Too much information." He checked the map and after a few minutes, pointed.

"This could work up here. I think we're coming up to a little lake. Maybe a recreation area or something."

Meg peered at the map. "How far?"

"Not bad. We should hit it in an hour. If you don't stop anymore." He tossed her an extra water bottle. "Keep drinking."

"Keep drinking?" Meg grunted. "I think that's what Mister Silverhair's friends must have said right before the accident."

"What an idiot," Josh said. "You were lucky. I'm proud of how you snapped back after a few days."

Meg had to admit to herself that she was also. The old Meg would have jumped on a plane and whimpered all the way home.

"Will you be okay if I bike ahead to make sure I can find that rec area?"

"Be my guest," Meg said and opened her hand toward the road. After plodding for miles, she finally noticed movement ahead from Josh. He waved his left arm straight up and then out, pointing to some trees. Meg sped up and soon spotted a sign announcing Piney Lake campground. Close on Josh's back wheel, she bounced along the trail as he negotiated rocks the size of basketballs embedded on the gravel path. Closer to the main gate Meg inhaled deeply, eager to exchange the dusty air for something fresh. Tall pines surrounded a small lake dappled with the late-afternoon sun.

"Oh baby, we are stopping!" Meg declared. Picnic tables, fire rings and barbecue grills marked campsites along the shore.

Meg stretched out her arms. "Feel that? There's even a breeze here." Thoughts of Lake Devine and the deck returned to her homesick mind. Near the shore, Meg found a level spot under several trees. "Josh, this is it. Heaven."

They unpacked the tent and unrolled the drop cloth. Meg crawled around to check for any rocks and pinecones hidden under the cloth. Within minutes the tent was erect, its front door facing the lake. While the mattresses inflated, they shook out their sleeping bags and Josh plunked down on his.

"Feels good to stop, doesn't it?" Meg said. Josh groaned his affirmation and rolled over.

Meg grabbed a towel and walked over to a strip of sand. She pulled off her riding shoes and socks and waded into the lake. The cold water snatched away her breath and she stood for a minute until it returned. Minnows darted around her ankles in the clear water.

She waded in a few more steps and rinsed the grime from her browned arms, down to her white hands and then to her brown fingers. With one deep breath, Meg dropped her knees to the sandy bottom. The brisk water closed in around her shoulders. She gasped at the change in temperature and feared a heart attack. Numbness set in and she felt as comfortable as she guessed a polar bear must.

When she walked out of the lake, her crisp skin felt stretched over her bones. After she pulled on dry clothes, she was elated to see that Josh had already started boiling water. With her teeth, she zipped off the top of the pouch for dinner, instant lasagna. And for dessert, raspberry crumble in a pouch.

"This astronaut food isn't too bad, Mom. Maybe you can buy a bunch of packets when I move out. Don't want you to starve or anything." Josh leaned over and lightly punched Meg on the arm.

"I wonder if Dad ever tried this stuff when he biked. I wish he would've invited me. All we ever did was play ball together."

Someone nearby was grilling steak for dinner and children giggled, playing tag in the setting sun. A security light flickered to life near the outhouse and Meg could see lanterns marking nearby campsites.

"It's true your father wasn't around much when you were little. He was on the road four days out of seven. But when he was home, he was the good parent, always involved with you."

Most of the time Meg had felt like an outsider. When Robert was alive, the house was more alive. Their waterski boat seemed to operate 24/7, until its season came to a close and the snowmobile took over. Every winter they spent long weekends skiing at resorts throughout Minnesota and Wisconsin, even Colorado. Robert and Josh took to the black diamonds while she stayed on the safe green slopes. Robert coached little league baseball; Meg made the team treats.

In the middle of the night, Meg fought the urge to go to the bathroom. The more she tried to withstand it, the more intense it became. She grabbed her flashlight and left the tent and her sleeping son. The moon shimmered off the lake in bright sheets so she shut off her flashlight until she reached the outhouse. On the return trip, her flashlight illuminated an official sign. A bear was pictured in the center, with the word caution across it. As she bent over to read the fine print, something rustled in the bushes across the road. She snapped off the flashlight and stood still. Even her breathing felt too loud. The rustling stopped.

"Hey bear, hey bear," she said in a sing-song voice. Someone once advised her to let her presence be known. Better than surprising a bear.

Behind her a branch cracked. She *yelped* and whirled around and flicked the light back on. Red eyeshine from an animal glinted in the light's beam before the raccoon bounded away.

She sidestepped the rest of the way back to the tent and continued her bear song until she was zipped inside the tent, nestled next to Josh. Finally satisfied no bears were sniffing around, she relaxed her shoulders and waited for sleep.

Sixty-Seven

Orange and yellow speckled the pink morning sky above the evergreens across the lake. Josh dashed back onto shore and shook his head like a golden retriever.

"Man, that's cold water." He quickly wrapped a towel around his boxers.

Meg held up a steaming mug. "Have some coffee. It's mocha java today." Her concession to roughing it included flavored coffee packets.

He cupped both hands around the mug and inhaled. A smile crossed his face before he took a sip.

"Thanks. You know what I realized last night? I sat by the fire after you fell asleep. Anyway, we both know, I'm the stronger biker."

His muscle-bound frame looked like a younger version of Robert. Where had her baby gone? Just yesterday they were teaching Josh to ride his two-wheeler.

He tightened the towel and sat down on a nearby stump. He vigorously rubbed his long curly hair, launching droplets of water. "I think I need to see Mr. Downs for a cut. I can't believe how this feels. But I am proud of this." He stroked his furry chin.

Meg's hand shot to her eyebrows. *Oh goodness, are they as bushy as his face?* For weeks she had been avoiding a close look in a mirror.

She wondered how many girls asked to run their fingers through Josh's ringlets. That curly softness drew her to Robert so many memories ago. They had met in a coffeehouse near campus, listening to a folksinger. Corkscrews of hair ringed Robert's head. When the musician took five, Meg spoke first. "It's not fair you know. You don't have to do a thing and you get that hair."

Robert had smiled at her, the same smile her son now owned right down to the dimple in the right cheek. On their second date, she let her fingers get lost in Robert's soft hair.

Josh continued. "And I feel stronger every day out here. It's like training, only more intense. Last night, I realized your body was probably getting stronger. But your riding isn't. Today, you are going to have a bicycle lesson," he announced. "I rechecked the map. We're traveling pretty slow, so I'm going to show you some stuff I picked up from the bike club."

Meg sat in amazement. After all this time he still thought she needed a bike lesson? And the boy is just suggesting it now?

"Let's break camp, and hit the road. Soon you'll be burning rubber."

He rinsed off the skillet and poured water on the campfire. The coals sizzled and spurted. She rolled up her sleeping bag and stuffed it into a compression sack. With the side of her hand, Meg swept pine needles off the tent. In minutes, the tent was down and packed.

With Piney Lake in her rearview mirror, Meg waited for her lesson.

"Show me your cycling technique. Ride to that utility pole."

Meg jammed down on her pedals and raced to the pole. The bike buckled under its load of camping gear.

"What's up with the wobbling? You're swaying back and forth. Have you been doing this the whole time?" Josh shook his head in disbelief. "Man, no wonder you're so slow."

"Slow? Even that time?" It was her top speed. Meg stopped the bike. "Maybe if I didn't have all this gear."

"No, you're balanced. It's not the gear. It's you. Your whole upper body is too tense. Relax your arms, your shoulders."

Meg remembered the last time she felt relaxed, months ago at the beach with Aunt Naomi. She did her best imitation of a jellyfish and flopped across her handlebars.

"Now try to follow the white stripe on the side."

Meg tried it again, only this time inhaling and expelling long Lamaze breaths, *heeee-hooo, heeeee-hooo*. At least this was easier than childbirth.

"Feel yourself relax," Josh encouraged.

Her body started to travel in a straight line.

"Next, we work on the pedaling."

That was news. Hadn't she already mastered the pedaling and the toe clips? The idea of being trapped on a bike frightened her, so she never graduated to the fancy shoes that locked right on the pedals.

"Shift to a smaller gear," he commanded.

"Is that shift up or down?"

"C'mon, you're teasing. You know that by now."

Meg fumbled around with the gearshift. Under pressure she forgot what once was second nature.

"Now, picture a circle. You want a smooth continual pedaling movement. Be aware of those leg muscles pulling and pushing you all the way around the circle."

The image stuck in her mind and she focused on her legs, while trying to maintain some degree of relaxation in the upper body.

"Circle, circle, circle." She pumped her legs.

"That's it. Much better." Josh caught up to her. "Your bike isn't rocking anymore."

Josh inserted the headphones into his ears and reached to adjust the volume. "Now, try to keep up with me."

His muscled legs pumped in a circle and his speed increased. Soon he was out of reach, and once again, Meg was on her own.

Sixty-Eight

Their route cut diagonally across Wyoming and Meg thrilled at seeing the Tetons once more. On more than one occasion she was tempted to hitch a ride from one of the RVs in the park, except she knew Josh would accuse her of cheating.

Tumbleweeds skipped across the road and Meg turned her head to avoid the sudden swirl of gritty wind. The idea of prevailing westerly winds must be a myth. It seemed to be more of a crosswind.

Meg wasn't sure if it was the lesson from Josh or just time in the saddle, but she was finally thinking she could make it all the way to St. Louis.

Each day melted into the next, and Meg often got confused what day of the week it was. Except for this morning. Today was definitely a Sunday with the steady flow of pickups and cars heading to a white-steepled church perched around the bend.

Josh, a few yards in front of Meg, signaled his turn.

"Are you crazy?" Meg said when she reached him at the edge of the gravel lot.

"Duda said worshipping with others is important," Josh said.

"But here? What if they pass snakes or something?" Meg shuddered, having seen enough snakes on the road to last a lifetime. "Why now?"

"Just take a little step of faith, Mom." Josh leaned his bicycle on the side of the church. "You coming?"

Meg looked down at her biking clothes and back up at her son. "Like this?"

"Fine. Suit yourself. I'm going to get me some religion," Josh said.

Meg watched Josh walk up the steps. Immediately, other church-goers welcomed him, all eager to shake his hand. A familiar hymn on the organ drifted out through the open doors. Josh stood and looked back at Meg. She held up an index finger, "wait." Then she turned to her panniers for a cleaner overshirt before she fluffed up her hair and pulled the edge of her shorts lower.

Once inside, they slid in a wooden pew toward the back, at the invitation of a grizzled man.

As Meg listened to the voices around her lifted in praise, she began to realize the people weren't that different. After the service, she brushed off several invitations for noon dinner. Meg was savvy enough to know that a nap would be the only thing she'd want after a huge lunch. Not the way to make it to St. Louis in time.

Back on the road after church, Meg tried to remember the key points from the sermon. She was about to ask Josh for his opinion when he sped up, without a word.

Apparently worshipping with others was important. But not cycling with others. Maybe another accident would help.

She clamped down on the tube from her hydration backpack and sucked in a cool stream of water. Before church, she had stopped at a convenience store and dropped ice cubes in the pack's bladder.

Clanging from the blades of a windmill, rusted into obsolescence, rang across the field. Green vines circled the remains of the abandoned farm, left to rot like a carcass.

The sensation of rotting spread to her shorts. She twisted in her saddle and tried to relieve the weight off her rear. The bargain shorts lost their appeal the second time she wore them. The gel pad shifted with every stroke of the pedal. Now it had worked its way loose and the sensation was of mashed potatoes with nowhere to go. She pulled over and tried to rearrange her shorts by yanking on the legs. By watching the mile markers she could calculate when she'd have to pull over to readjust the shorts.

"That's it. That is absolutely it," Meg yelled. The gel bunched in a knot, now solidified right between her rear and the bike saddle. Unable to stand it any longer, Meg pedaled toward a small grove of trees. Furtively swiveling her head to watch the road, she whipped off the red shorts with relief and tossed them aside. Then she added a layer of ointment to her chafed skin and grabbed the black pair of shorts drying atop her panniers.

She was impressed by her own boldness and wanted to call Christy. The woman wouldn't have believed Meg had just stripped down to her birthday suit next to the road. Sometimes those northern inhibitions are hard to shake.

The soothing rhythm of the road and the routine was an odd comfort now. The great gaps of time gave her nothing to do but think. She still hadn't found harmony with Josh. Some days he seemed to barely tolerate her, other days he acted downright friendly.

"Robert, I need your help here." Meg pulled out the plastic bag from her handlebar pack. She talked to Robert's ashes as she rode. "You know Josh and I ride at different speeds, although he tried to help me speed up. Wasn't your point to make us travel together and bond?" She coasted a little bit, hoping for a sign from Robert. *Maybe I need to talk directly to God?*

When she eased her way into town, she passed a church that resembled the one from that morning. The sermon's topic was displayed on the marquee out front. "You can't take it with you, so why have it all now? Lighten the load before you knock on the pearly gates. Preacher Jack 10 a.m. Sunday."

Meg looked down at Robert's cremains and said, "Gee thanks, Robert. Try not to be so obvious next time."

The box outside the church was labeled GOODS FOR THE NEEDY. She stopped and rummaged through her panniers. From the bottom, she pulled out a curling iron, a full bottle of hair spray, an electric hairdryer with its cord tangled around a flannel nightgown she never wore, a hardbound book she hadn't even opened, blue jeans, hiking boots, the battery-operated coffee grinder Aunt Naomi sent. One by one she ceremoniously placed items in the drop box. Her sweat pants and tennis shoes would be fine off the bike and she didn't need to bother with her hair anymore. A bike helmet canceled any effort anyway. She withdrew her cosmetic bag from her pack on her handlebar bag and tossed it into the charity box. Lip gloss was good enough.

"God bless you, Ma'am." A small man with a plastic bottle in his hand appeared behind her. "I've been watching you through my office window. You certainly lightened your load. That sounds like the sermon I preached today. Would you like some cold water?" He handed the bottle to her.

"What about the rest of your baggage? Are you ready to meet your Maker?"

"Sure," Meg said. "My slate's clean. Listen, thank you so much for the water but I have to run." She jumped on her bike, several pounds lighter, and flew like she had wings.

Sixty-Nine

Wind gently blew on Meg's back as she pedaled along. "Now this, I could get used to," she told Josh. Josh, several lengths ahead, turned his head.

"What? You're used to the riding?" He slowed his tempo.

"No, no. I mean this tailwind. It's beautiful. I can tell this is going to be a gorgeous day." She sat up straight in the saddle, and poked her right arm up, catching the slight breeze. Seconds later, she burst out singing "Summertime, and the living's easy."

"Obviously, you didn't major in music," Josh said. "What did you study?"

"It should have been business. Then I could have taken over your dad's office."

Robert's storefront office in town had lured passersby with color photographs of lakefront property plastered in the front window. Robert had the knack to put his clients at ease, and his business profited. When the blood markers of his cancer activity offered little hope of survival, Robert made arrangements to sell his business to a colleague.

"You know, I think I'm actually relieved *not* to be responsible for the business."

"That sounds kinda strange. First you do and then you don't," Josh said.

"Maybe you're too young to understand. I get sad when I hear the stories about more and more mom-and-pop resorts disappearing in the name of progress. All that beautiful lake property getting gobbled up, and your dad carried the serving platter."

"It doesn't take a genius to figure that out," Josh said and started to pull ahead.

"Hey wait, before you get too far up there, when do you want to stop for a real breakfast?" Meg's stomach had been grumbling for the last five miles.

"I told you we should've done that before we broke camp."

Meg tried to smile patiently. "Well, we didn't. And remember Duda's words, 'You can't run a car on empty.' "

"I know. I know. Anything he says you believe." Josh glanced down at the map slipped inside a plastic covering on his handlebar bag.

"There's a little town ahead. Not too far. We can probably get 'fuel' there. See ya."

His form grew smaller and smaller. *What did I say this time?* It was another Gershwin day. Definitely.

Reaching back, Meg adjusted the volume. As "Rhapsody in Blue" intensified, so did the sky. Clouds swirled in the darkening sky. Rain hit the distant fields. Loud music pulsed through her ears, sending its message to her legs. *Pump, pump, pump.*

With the back of her glove, Meg caught a blob of sweat cascading down her forehead. A green sign alerted her to an approaching town, and its grain elevator was visible miles away.

No need to get wet. Surely Josh is going to take cover too. Meg knew she could time this just right. Find a nice cozy café to duck into and maybe get a slice of pie. Some real coffee too. She marveled at the glorious feeling of riding and eating. The freedom of not having to count calories. *What a marvelous concept! I should've discovered this years ago.*

Her bicycle bounced on a rumble strip, and she swerved to avoid the second and third ones imbedded in the pavement before the stop sign. A large American flag flapped wildly from its post on a large two-story brick farmhouse. Meg's pace quickened beneath the churning, brewing sky.

A Methodist church, with a tall steeple, marked the start of the town, followed by a gas and convenience store, and a self-serve laundry. Houses with freshly mown grass dotted the tree-lined street. Meg waved to a little boy helping his mother pull wash off the clothesline. Nearby, two teens struggled with the top of an old convertible parked in a gravel driveway.

Meg coasted along Main Street, past the post office and library, until she spotted Mr. Ted's Café. It was tucked between an abandoned fire station and Mr. Tom's Tavern. She dismounted and left her bike against the old brick building.

"Hello? Hello?" Her voice bounced off the walls.

"Back here," replied a voice from the kitchen. "I'm just getting these ready for the dinner crowd. I like to shut down midafternoon. Give myself a break, collect my thoughts, try some new recipes." A man, too tall for the doorframe, ducked his head. Atop each paw-like hand sat a pie.

"Oh, sorry. I didn't realize you were closed." Meg wistfully turned away, the aroma from the freshly baked pies spun her stomach's rumbling into overdrive.

"Don't worry about it." He set the pies down on a wooden counter and gestured with an oven-mittened hand. "Come, sit down. You're obviously not from around here." He looked her over. "These women generally don't wear spandex. You look like something off the outdoor channel on cable TV."

Meg pointed outside. "Is it okay if I bring my bike in? I think the sky is about to break wide open."

The man nodded. "Just put it right there, by the jukebox."

He held the door open while she wheeled in her bike.

"Wow, you're really loaded down. Two packs on a bike. Where's you headed?"

He grabbed the checkered dishtowel tucked in his waistband and wiped off a table for her.

"Here, sit. I'll bring you a slice of the world's best pie. In exchange, you fill me in on the details. Coffee?" he asked over his shoulder as he lumbered back to the kitchen.

"Love some." Meg glanced around the café. A huge moose head hung over a table and glass cases displayed other stuffed wildlife in various poses. TV flickered in one corner.

"This is some place you have," she said.

He set a thick slab of lemon meringue pie in front of her. "Hope you like lemon. Yep, there's a story behind this place. In a nutshell, my brother and I ran a tavern. He still does." He jerked his thumb right.

"Right next door?"

"He's Mr. Tom. We're twins, but we look nothing alike. He got Mom's side and I got Dad's. I made a pretty good bouncer, good for tossing out the rowdies.

"Anyway, I caught religion, Tom didn't. I can't stand alcohol. Didn't want to enable people, as the TV shrinks say, so we split. This was an old restaurant. Steady stream of owners. I figured I could do better so I bought it when the last guy died. I took some stuff from the bar. We had tons collected over the years and I decorated this place myself."

He glanced up at the TV. "Oh look, there's that cute gal on Channel 5. I can't believe the way she gets people to talk on her show. Why, just the other day she had an old geezer who'd been living in the mountains. A regular hermit. How she ever got him on camera I'll never know."

He jumped up and pulled a pot of coffee off the warmer. He refilled her cup. "Now your turn. What's up with the bike?"

An extra-large bite of pie filled Meg's mouth. She waved her hand and muttered.

"Take your time. Glad to see you're enjoying my pie. That's the famous Ann Landers recipe. Never fails. I've tried others, but everyone seems to like that one the best. Clipped it out her column years and years ago."

Meg grabbed a paper napkin out of the metal dispenser on the table. She wiped off her mouth and sipped her coffee.

"It's a strange story, in a way," she started. "I guess strange because of our mission."

"Who is the 'our'?"

"My son, Josh." Meg looked out the window at the water cascading over the gutter. "I sure hope he stopped somewhere. This storm looks pretty bad."

"Yup, no one would be fool enough to cycle in this mess."

Josh watched the green mile markers go by. Just when he thought Mom recognized him as an adult, she'd say something stupid and they'd be back to zero. Doesn't she realize everything he sacrificed to do this trip with her? Like Candy, the hot reporter. They went out a few times, but now she probably met someone new.

Florida was going to be incredible. He was going to be on his own, finally. He couldn't believe it. No more nagging, no more dumb questions. He'd be far away from the idiots at school. Just a waste of time anyway. Thanks to honor classes, he didn't have to worry about finals. This last semester was a joke. High school was a joke. Science was good though. Marine biology was going to be incredible. Pretty smart to pick a Florida school. Warm sunshine all the time. Girls on the beach. Tiny bikinis.

Sweet Candy. Wonder what she's doing right now? He pulled out his cell phone, but discovered he couldn't get a good signal. Maybe later.

The empty road stretched before him. Wind blowing through the overhead wires made a strange eerie sound, like something out of a horror flick.

Seventy

When the rain cleared, Meg hopped back on her bike. She passed a silo and a post office and found Josh's bike leaned against the Bluebird Cafe. The café's sign reminded her of the decision to become more appreciative since she was communing with nature all summer. Her field guide to birds helped, although her life list in the back only had three checkmarks.

A haze of old grease and cigarette smoke hung in the cramped diner. Several pairs of eyes shifted toward Meg. She quickly scanned the cafe and spotted Josh huddled in a booth.

"Well, where have you been?"

She quietly slipped into the booth, pushing aside his plate with congealed egg, toast crusts, and syrup.

"Breakfast? This late?" she said. "I guess any fuel is good fuel for the road, right?"

"Like I said. Where have you been?"

"I sat out the storm. Didn't you?"

Josh reached for his coffee cup. "Give me that coffee pot. I need a refill."

Meg jumped up and grabbed a coffeepot from a nearby table, recently vacated. A waitress appeared, pad in hand. Her eyes appeared to be lined in black crayon and her waist was no bigger than Meg's thigh. *Must be an eating disorder.* Letters spelling out "Steve" were tattooed in pen on her knuckles. Perhaps Steve was no longer in the picture, the way she was eyeballing Josh.

"Whacha want?"

Meg eyed the laminated menu. "Well, I already had dessert. Would you recommend the pancakes?"

"Yeah, sure," the girl said.

The waitress left with Meg's order of a short stack, OJ, coffee, and water. Josh tossed some dollars on the table.

"Look," he said. "I need to check on something in town. Maybe a granola bar for the road. The next town is only fifteen miles away. I'll wait for you. Just look for my bike. Try to speed up this time."

Meg finished her breakfast and scanned the headlines of the weekly newspaper on the table. The city council met to discuss loitering teens, someone lost a prized heifer, police declare foul play, gas prices stable. Satisfied the world was still in order, at least in this corner, Meg paid for breakfast. The waitress pointed out the bathroom through the kitchen, directly across from the grill.

When Meg got outside, she plunked on her helmet and turned to grab her gloves off the handlebars, their usual resting spot. She searched around her bicycle and panniers, and finally returned inside to ask the waitress.

The word "miss" had barely slipped out of Meg's lips when the girl snapped. She slammed a tray of dishes down so hard they clattered against the metal tray.

"What, are you blind? Can't you see I have to do it all today? The bus boy didn't show up so I have to clean up the mess everyone makes. I'll be with you in a minute."

Meg waited next to the counter. After delivering a tray of orders to three tables, the girl returned. She had one word for Meg, "what," except she uttered it in three syllables.

"I lost a pair of gloves."

The girl reached under the counter. She surfaced with a cardboard box and pawed through a hodge-podge of caps, scarves and sunglasses.

"Is this it?" She held up a brown work glove.
"Not exactly." Meg said.
"That's all we got."

Meg pushed open the door in time to glimpse a dog trotting around a corner, gloves dangling from its mouth.

Seventy-One

Outside the self-serve laundry, a steady rain fell. Armed with a stack of postcards, Meg dragged a plastic chair over to the washing machine. Mesmerized, she watched the clothes tumble in sudsy water. Layover days offered a chance to get off bikes and behave like normal people. Josh wanted to check the local bike shop and pick up a few extra parts, as well as new gloves for Meg. She happily sent him on his way and opted for the warm self-service laundry, with the comfortable repetitive motion of the machines and the reassuring scent of fabric softener. She was almost giddy at the anticipation of sleeping in a fresh T-shirt that night.

In addition to catching up with the laundry, Meg considered it necessary to work on her correspondence. Christy, Duda, Malachi, and Aunt Naomi insisted she mail cards at every opportunity. Naomi had even sent a stack of prestamped, preaddressed ones. Josh kept in touch electronically whenever he could.

The door opened to let a stream of crisp air in to mix with the humid layer. A man and a preschool boy ducked in from the rain. The boy carried a leash attached to a small brown-and-white dog.

"Thomas O'Brien. If I told you once, I've told you a million times. That fleabag of a dog is not allowed in here."

A woman scurried over from where she'd been emptying the change machine.

"Ah, Mrs. Martin, a delight to see you again. I must say you are looking spectacular today. And if you'll observe, Toby is behaving quite nicely. See, he's already settled down on that rug." The man pointed to the dog on the floor.

"If you'll allow us to continue, my son and I have laundry to accomplish."

"Very well. Be off with you. You know you always manage to charm me anyway," Mrs. Martin said.

The man emptied a laundry bag into one of the metal carts and wheeled it to the washing machines. After he dumped in the detergent, he lifted his son to help deposit quarters into the machine.

Meg wrote postcards until the washer's buzzer interrupted her musing. After she put everything into a dryer, she stood by a waist-high table and jotted a few more stories from the road. Shortly she felt a tug on her jacket.

The little boy had moved over and stared at her.

"Hi," Meg crouched to eye level. "What's your name?"

"Stuart." He peered up at her and waited. "Aren't you going to ask me how old I am? Everyone does."

"Sure Stuart. How old are you?"

"I'm six."

"Oh," Meg said. She looked again at the small boy.

"Dad says someday my body will catch up with my mind. Hey, do you want to play a game?"

"Sure, what do you have in mind?" Meg's brain raced to recall children's games.

"I spy. I'll go first. I spy with my little eye something red," Stuart said. "Now you have to guess what."

Meg scanned the room. "Is it on that box of detergent?"

Stuart shook his head, "Nope."

"How about that red shirt going around in the washing machine?"

"Too obvious." Stuart cackled.

Meg pivoted and pointed to the bulletin board plastered with notices.

"Aha, there it is. That red thumb tack, that has to be it." Meg said.

"Nope. Wrong again. Give up?"

"Okay kid, you've got me. What do you spy with your little eye that's red?" Meg asked.

Stuart pointed at Meg with delight. "It's your eye silly. It has little lines filled with lots of blood."

Seventy-Two

The rain had eased up by the time Josh wheeled into the entrance to a shopping plaza. He swerved to avoid a pothole. Several girls flagged him to their carwash area. He stopped in front of the girls. His mom had turned off earlier when they rode past a self-serve laundry.

"What's up, ladies?" Josh flashed the smile that made him famous at school when his braces finally came off. It never failed.

"Cash for cheerleading camp. But you can get a discount," A blonde, armed with a garden hose, playfully sprayed water near his feet. The T-shirt over her swimming suit was already soaked and Josh admired every curvy inch of her body. "We'll even let you sit down while we work." She pointed to a nearby lawn chair.

Josh grinned at her and lifted up his shirt to wipe sweat from his face. "The bike could use a little cleaning. Me too. The ride here was pretty hot and dusty." He undid his biking shoes, pulled off his socks then beckoned to the girl with the hose.

"Hit me," Josh said and stepped away from his bicycle. A spray of water cascaded over his body and he shivered at the contrast in temperature. The girls giggled even more and launched a full water fight.

"Girls, let's stick to business. You're scaring away customers." The coach returned, carrying a stack of towels. She tossed one to Josh.

After he dried off, Josh turned to concentrate on cleaning his bike. "I don't want the packs to get soaked," Josh said. "Maybe just a little soapy water, no hose."

A cheerleader brought over a bucket of water and another girl handed him a brush. While Josh scrubbed off a layer of grime, they bombarded him with questions about his trip. Finally satisfied with the bike's condition, Josh pointed to the faded beach towel the adviser had tossed him. Two girls dove to retrieve it for him.

"Thanks, I can take it from here." With his left hand, he steadied the bike and wiped off the frame.

"Oh man," he groaned. His index finger traced a hairline crack in the head tube of the bike. "Is there a bike shop in town? I forgot I need some gear too."

"There's Dellert's Hardware. He carries bikes," one girl said.

"Hardware? I doubt he can help. This doesn't look too good."

"Can we help?" The girls crowded around the bike.

"Nah, thanks. I need to make a phone call." He fished out his cell phone and set his bike next to the fence before sinking into the lawn chair. The girls resumed their attempts to flag passing traffic.

Duda answered on the second ring.

"Duda, I'm in trouble," Josh said.

"What? What happened?"

"It's the bike man. The frame is cracked. What do I do now?"

"No problem. How bad is it? The manufacturer guarantees it. I can send it in."

"I just noticed it. A sliver, about five inches long."

"Ooh," Duda said. "It could stay that way for a while, or it could go fast. You still have about a month to go, true?"

"Yup. This is bad. I can't quit now." Josh stood up and started to pace.

"Tell me the name of the town you expect to hit in two days. I'll ship one out to you. Do you think you can keep riding that one?"

"Yeah, maybe. I guess so." He named the town.

"Hang on," Duda said. "Let me look that up on-line. Hmm, computer is slow today. Wait, here it is. Not much there. Bank? Motel? The Sleepy Inn?"

"Motel. We'll need one by then."

"Beautiful. Now do not worry. I will put together a bike for you and ship it out yet this afternoon. You'll see," Duda said. "Now what about your mama? How is she doing?"

"Oh you know, hanging in there," Josh said.

"That's all man? Just hanging in there?"

"Well, I admit she's doing better each day. She's not as grumpy and she's getting better on the bike. Still slow, but not bad for an old lady."

"Old, you wait brudda." Duda laughed. "Put her on the phone."

"She's checking out the town, maybe doing laundry. I offered to..."

Duda cut him off. "Sure you did."

Josh protested. "No, for real. But she wanted to do it by herself."

Before Duda hung up, he tossed one more tidbit to Josh, "Just remember man, play nice."

Seventy-Three

Meg circled downtown until she found the old library, right where the kids running a lemonade stand said it would be. Marigolds bobbed in the breeze in front of the two-story building. An older woman clipped wayward strands of grass next to the building. Meg pulled up to a bike rack and parked her bicycle near an assortment of kids' bikes.

Inside, a group of children circled a teen-aged girl. She held up a large picture book. The kids sat cross-legged on a round braided rug on the polished wooden floor.

Meg stood and listened, charmed by their rapt expressions and excitement. Then she looked around for the reference desk and waited for the librarian to acknowledge her. Finally Meg coughed politely and spoke.

"Do you have Internet access here?"

The woman nodded and stood. "We do." She waved toward to a row of six computers, three back-to-back. Meg was relieved to see an open one.

"I don't believe I know you. Have you a card?"

Meg shook her head. "No, I'm on the road and I need to send a lengthy email."

"In that case, I can give you a guest card for today."

After Meg filled out the requisite forms, the librarian handed her a slip of paper with a password and directed her to the computers.

Meg typed in the code and promptly was in. She scanned the score of mail that had accumulated since she last checked and quickly deleted requests for prescriptions and investment opportunities. She scrolled through and smiled at one from Christy.

"Hey girl, if you're reading this, you must still be alive! Give me a call sometime. Call me collect if you want. I'm dying to know how life on the road is."

The email she expected was there. Actually there were several from Candy Cane at the newspaper. The subject lines were first marked "pls read" and then "impt" and then from the previous week, "URGENT." Meg opened the most recent one first.

"Oops," Meg said. "I guess I should've checked in with her."

Candy's terse message said, "Pls respond ASAP. Editor ready to kill me. U let me down. (Candy had inserted a little frowny face.) BUT we cn still do this. Remember BIG story at end. Pls pls rite."

Meg stared at the ceiling, and pondered where to start. She drummed her fingernails on the table.

"Ah hem." Someone cleared a throat. "Ma'am. Do you mind? I'm trying to concentrate here."

Meg stared at the person to her left. The woman twisted her lips and glared at Meg.

"Ma'am. Please, your fingers. They're loud. They're bothering me. And you're talking out loud. I have work to do."

Meg quickly tucked her hand under her thigh. "Sorry." The woman turned back to her monitor with a loud *humph*. In the reflection of her own computer, Meg mimicked the woman. Someone snickered and Meg glanced up to see a man smiling over his monitor across from her.

"Don't worry," he whispered and returned to his computer.

She started typing her response to Candy.
Hi Candy:

> *Believe or not, we're still on the road. So far we've logged more than 1,000 miles. Just ask my body how many that is. We've had a few mishaps along the way, but I guess that's to be expected. I have been impressed by how nice everyone is, for the most part.*

Meg stopped and looked again to her left. She continued pecking away:

> *The scenery has been fantastic. There's a lot of rugged beauty out here. I don't know what more I can say. What exactly did you want from me? I thought you just wanted a before and after story, not a during story. When we return, you may interview Josh. I'm sure he'd love to talk with you. Well, that's it for now.*

Meg logged off and drifted back to story time. She drew closer to the children, all leaned forward, glued to the book. She slipped into an empty chair next to the circle and listened. Soon, she reached out and absently patted a little boy's head.

His head swirled around and he jumped at Meg's touch.

"You're not my mother," he called out. "And you smell!"

Meg yanked her hand back. "I'm so sorry," she stammered. The kids scampered to get away.

"Ma'am." The librarian flew to her side. "I have to ask you to leave. We maintain a safe environment for these children. If you're looking for a shelter, I recommend the church down the street. They also have a food pantry if you need something to eat."

Meg looked down at herself. Sure she was a little gritty and grimy, but homeless? Embarrassed, she collected her bags and slunk out.

Seventy-Four

While she was on the bike, Meg decided to do her stretches. She had found a list in Duda's shop and memorized the routine. First up, neck and shoulders. Move your shoulders up to the ears and hold. Meg realized she held her breath for the five counts. She expelled the air when she released her shoulders. Look left, look right. She let her head swivel and heard cracking up her neck.

She had just started the exercises to relieve tension in her facial muscles when Josh coasted next to her.

"What in the world?"

Meg still had her mouth open wide. She snapped it shut. "Face exercises."

"You look funny."

"I have a full routine, if you don't mind," Meg said. "From my head to my toes."

"Don't let me stop you." Josh stood up on his pedals and wiggled his body. "All better. That's what we call stretching."

"Wise guy." Meg resolved to resume the routine later. Later when there'd be plenty of time and plenty of miles to go. She inhaled deeply and counted to five. It was time for something else, time for a new approach.

"So, I bet you're excited for college," she said.

Josh glanced over at her, and matched her pace.

"Yeah?" His answer was slow, loaded with questions of its own. "If there's a lecture behind this, save it."

"Doggone it, Josh." Meg dashed her hand against the handlebar. "I'm just asking a simple question."

"It sounded like more."

They pedaled in silence, neck and neck. A station wagon with Kentucky plates passed them. The kids inside waved. Meg tried again.

"It will be a nice to leave Minnesota. You were smart to pick a school in Florida."

"Dad helped me narrow the choices."

"Just remember the choices you make in college can affect you your whole life."

"Mom. Stop. Remember that one time you forced me to go to youth group at that church? You and Stephanie's mom?"

It was right around the time of Robert's death. She remembered Stephanie's mother had walked over with a plate of cookies and suggested the meeting for Josh.

"There I was in a room with kids who called themselves Christians. And you know what? Half those kids were at the kegger that weekend."

"Kegger?"

"They hide behind their masks at group. Saying one thing, doing another. The topic that night was choices. What a bunch of fakes. They said they made the choice not to sin. They wanted me to come clean too." Josh pointed to a green sign. "Only nine miles to the town. Let's stop for something cold to drink." Josh pedaled ahead.

A kegger? Something cold to drink? Surely he didn't mean alcohol. Meg tried to deal with her son's latest announcement. How much of his life had been lived in secret?

Josh's bike was easy to find, propped up next to the sign for the gas station. Its red packs stood out against the gravel parking lot. Meg leaned hers against the building.

"Good day for traveling, huh?" The clerk behind the counter nodded to the loaded bicycles.

"Some people might think so," Meg said. She aimed for the refrigerated cases in the back and selected a bottle of cranberry juice. She counted out the change and spotted Josh standing near the food counter. He looked up when she approached.

"Wonder how old those hot dogs are?" he said.

Meg watched frankfurters rotate on the rack inside the glass. Grease glistened along the length of each.

"You really don't want one of those in your belly. Not now." Meg moved past Josh and slid into one of three booths. With a grubby hand, she twisted off the lid. Cool, tart liquid replaced the dryness in her throat. A small, satisfied moan, almost a hum, came out of her mouth. Then she let her shoulders drop and rolled her head around. From the small speaker on their booth, a guy crooned about the gal he lost to the rodeo champ.

Josh slipped into the seat across from her. He had a paper tray of nachos and cheese and a cola from the fountain. Bubbles danced around the ice cubes. He tossed a packet of salted nuts on the table.

"Here, go crazy." He ripped open the plastic and turned the package toward Meg.

Meg popped a peanut in her mouth and let her tongue absorb the salt. Nothing had ever tasted so wonderful in her entire life.

"Josh, about what you were saying. About those other kids at church." Meg played with the package of nuts to avoid looking at her son. With an index finger, she spun the package first at one end and then at the other. Her next move was a little too vigorous, and peanuts spilled out.

"Whoops." Meg kept her head lowered, afraid for her son's reaction. Everything she did seemed to be stupid. By the time she looked up, he was gone. A blob of artificial yellow cheese congealed on the table next to the empty tray.

Meg corralled the nuts back into their package and swallowed the last of her juice. With a napkin, she wiped away Josh's mess.

"Five more minutes," Josh called out from the front. He walked outside and Meg headed toward the bathroom.

Five more minutes of air conditioning. Five more minutes of not being the mom.

Seventy-Five

The chirping cell phone threatened to drive Meg crazy. Why did Aunt Naomi insist on a daily inquisition? Meg grabbed the phone to check the caller ID. Relieved to see Christy's name, she flipped it open.

"Hi hon, didn't want to bug you while you're on your big adventure, but I've been following your itinerary. Are you near Pueblo?"

"Let me see." Meg peeked out the tent at Josh perched near the campfire, stirring a pot.

"Josh, when will we hit Pueblo?

Josh glanced up. "Tomorrow. We'll spend the night there. At Breezy Point Motor Lodge and Supper Club."

Meg passed the information on to Christy. "Why?"

"Oh, just curious. I once dated a guy from that area and when I noticed it on your itinerary I just started reminiscing. It was an old summer camp romance. So, tell me, how's it going?"

After Meg filled her in on the latest, she hung up and joined Josh by the fire.

"Well, that was certainly odd," Meg said.

Josh looked around. "What?"

"Christy called out of the blue, just to see if we were near a town she once heard of."

"Mom, I hate to tell you, but she's a little on the strange side herself. Maybe she's just sitting around getting bored. Here, have some dinner." Josh passed the pot of noodles to Meg.

Today's mileage had ripped away at Meg's body. Her fingers were so numb she doubted she could raise a fork to her mouth. Her shoulders stung from hours of fighting a headwind. Josh waved her off of cleanup duty, and Meg stretched out in the tent, no longer able to battle the overwhelming sense of fatigue.

In the morning, she slipped out of the tent to the shower house. Refreshed, she returned to camp and started pulling towels and clothes off the rope strung between the trees. By the time the sun's rays reached them, Meg and Josh were packed and ready to roll. It was the perfect time of the day. A robin's egg sky, dotted with wispy strands of white, and air so fresh Meg hung open her mouth to welcome it. For that one moment, the world stood at peace. *And, miracle of all miracles, wonder of all wonders, fewer miles today. Thank you, Father, for the joy today!*

Meg and her son kept an even pace. For her, it was miles and miles of uneventfulness made palatable by the magic of Gershwin. Something about that music lifted her heart and soul, and helped the miles vanish. She hoped Josh had a similar companion in his headphones.

Lunch was a five-minute stop to peel a banana and slather peanut butter on crackers. Meg untwisted the waxed pouch of crackers and passed it to Josh.

"Today, we're flying economy. Tonight, though, honey, we'll be in first class."

Dinner at Breezy Point promised to be top of the line, at least for that part of the country. The lure of a giant sirloin, baked potatoes smothered with real butter, sour cream and bacon bits, a smattering of fresh green beans, lots of homemade rolls, and fresh apple pie, topped with vanilla ice cream motivated Meg.

Soon, billboards for Breezy Point sprouted along the road and visions of real food encouraged Meg and Josh to increase their speed. They found the motel just off the county highway, right on the edge of town. Only a couple cars sat in the dusty lot. Meg and Josh rode over to the office and left their bikes near the screen door.

Josh dinged the bell on the wooden counter, scratched from years of use. The manager hobbled to the desk from his adjacent residence. His body, crippled at a permanent 90-degree angle, forced him to turn his head sideways to greet the newcomers. "Just working on my supper. What may I do for you?"

"Albertsons, I called you yesterday about a reservation?"

The manager opened the ledger and followed each line with a gnarled index finger. He stopped at an entry highlighted in yellow marker. A smile crossed his weathered face. He looked up intently at Meg and Josh.

"Oh, so that's who you are. I have your rooms ready."

Meg cleared her throat. "Excuse me, but one is sufficient. I'm his mother."

The man shook his head. "No problem, no problem. We don't have many guests with us today. Plus I have a big package for one Josh Albertson." He handed them fist-sized plastic holders with metal keys to 201 and 203. "They're adjoining. You can open the doors between if you want. Ma'am, I put you in 201. Need any help getting settled? I've got a handyman around here somewhere. He could deliver your belongings."

Meg assured him they'd be fine on their own. She unhooked her handlebar bag and followed Josh up the stairs. "We'll be back down for the bikes in a minute."

"Take your time, take your time." The manager shuffled off to his apartment, but left the door open. Meg's stomach grumbled at the aroma of fried chicken that teased them all the way to their rooms.

"I think I'm about to pass out. Maybe we could find somewhere to eat right away," she said.

"Yeah, real soon. But I got to unpack the new frame. I can't believe it's here." Josh inserted the key in his door.

Meg walked in 201, flipped on the light switch and shrieked.

"What in the world?" The stranger in Meg's room was no stranger. Christy sat on one of the beds, wearing a big grin. Meg sank down onto the bed across from her. "Are you really here?"

"You bet." Christy stood up when Josh raced in the room. "Hey Josh, I feel like I already know you. You've got one incredible mom. I can't believe she's doing this."

Josh thrust out his hand. "You have to be Christy. I've heard a lot of things about you too."

Meg sputtered, unable to form intelligible words. How could those two carry on as though they were meeting at the bagel shop back home? A gleam of understanding flashed across her brain. She wagged her finger at Christy. "I get it. You're the reason the clerk said we have two rooms."

Christy stuck out her chest and nodded. "I thought you two might need a little break from each other, at least for a night. This is my treat, well, actually one from my ex. Now, Josh, you go off and enjoy yourself. The supper club next door is supposed to serve some pretty fine chicken."

"I get it, you're trying to get rid of me." Josh grinned. "I can take a hint." He waved an arm and backed out of the room.

"Meg, such a handsome boy. That little dimple? And he seems rather pleasant too. I thought you said he was a bit prickly. But you, you look wonderful, even plain like that with your funky hair and no makeup."

"I'm afraid I look a little worn from the road. But I'm hanging in there."

Christy stood up and hugged Meg. "You really are doing it. I'm so proud of you! You've come a long way since that Pilates class at the Y."

Meg straightened her arms so Christy stood an arm's length away. "But I still don't understand what you're doing here. What was that story about a summer camp romance?"

"I made that up so I could surprise you. Ready?"

"Ready for what?" Just then a loud rap sounded on the motel room's door.

Christy sprung up. "I'll get it."

A man gripping a folding table stood in the doorway. Christy jumped up to embrace him. "Stephen, it's so good to see you! How long has it been? Since Aunt Esther's funeral?"

She pulled Stephen into the room. "Meg, meet my cousin, Stephen. Can you believe he lives in this town? When I recognized the town on your itinerary, the light bulbs went off in my head."

Meg pointed to the object he was carrying. "What in the world is that for?"

He unfolded the legs and set up a table. Christy clapped her hands. "It's a massage table. My cousin is the best massage therapist around."

Meg felt her face flush. Thank goodness the tan would cover it. "A massage? Oh, Christy, that's awfully nice of you, but I've never..."

Christy held up her palm. "Don't say no before you try it."

Meg pulled Christy aside. "But I can't get naked and hop on that table," she whispered. "I'd sooner die than do something like that."

Stephen busied himself with the table and pulled an assortment of towels out of a duffel bag.

Christy said, "Don't be silly. You can wear a swimsuit. Now go take a shower and wash away the sweat. No offense, but you sort of smell, too. We'll be out here waiting. I might even let him get warmed up on my shoulders."

An embarrassed Meg dashed downstairs to her bike and rummaged through a pack for her swimsuit. *Maybe Josh and I have just grown accustomed to the smell.*

She counted the flowers on the hall carpet all the way back to her room. No one had really touched her since Robert. Well, except Duda and his magical touch on her hands. But her whole body? *Maybe I shouldn't do this. Could this be considered a sin?*

She shivered in her damp clothes and pushed open the door. Christy sat in a chair, while her cousin kneaded her shoulders.

"Mmm, Meg, you are in for such a treat," Christy groaned and rolled her head.

Meg cleared her throat. "Well, you go ahead. I don't think I really need this. But I do need a shower."

Christy opened her eyes. "Meg Albertson, forget your conservative roots. For once, I'm not pushing sex. This is therapy, pure and simple. Stephen, tell her."

Stephen stepped toward Meg. "It's true. Massage is documented to have great therapeutic benefits. Plus, I'm a licensed professional, I'm happily married to the woman of my dreams, and you are simply a client, nothing more. Any questions?"

Meg meekly retreated. After she showered, she pulled on her suit, wrapped a towel around her waist, and walked out.

"So you don't get chilled, I'm going to drape you with a sheet while I work on your muscles. I'll only expose the area I'm concentrating on. Let me know if anything hurts. I imagine your legs, back, and shoulders all need attention? Let's get started, roll to your stomach please." Stephen's quiet tones matched the soothing notes of Pachelbel's Canon from the CD player.

"Meg," Christy whispered, "I'll be back in a little bit. Relax and enjoy Stephen's wonderful touch. You'll feel so much better, I promise."

Meg inhaled deeply and allowed herself to succumb to the massage and the peace that permeated the motel room.

Gentle shaking at her elbow roused Meg from a restful nap.

"Oh my goodness, Christy, how long have I been out? And what happened to your cousin?" Meg found herself on top of the massage table. She wrapped the sheet around herself and sat up.

"I told you he was good." Christy smiled and set down two large brown paper bags. "He'll be back later for the table. He did say your muscles were pretty well knotted. Could feel the stress in your neck."

"It was heavenly," Meg said. "Thank you. That was an amazing gift. How'd you know that's what I needed?"

"Call me psychic. Now, are you ready for the next treat?"

Grease started to seep through the bags. Christy reached in and pulled out a small container and stuffed it into the room refrigerator's freezer. Out of a small suitcase, she pulled out a purple sweatshirt and pants. "Put on these fresh clothes and let's eat."

Meg brought the stack of clothes to her face and inhaled. "It's been weeks since I smelled fabric softener. You really are psychic," Meg said. She eagerly pulled the sweats on over her swimsuit and sighed in pleasure at the soft, clean fabric.

Christy pulled out container after container, placed them on the table and flipped open the lids. "We have fried chicken, mashed potatoes and gravy, lasagna, a little salad. I didn't know what you'd be in the mood for, so I just picked up a bunch of stuff. Dig in."

After dinner, they both rolled back on their beds and groaned. Christy patted her belly, "You know, I probably shouldn't have inhaled my dinner. I haven't been riding a bike for weeks like you."

"Oh, you always look good. That was fabulous."

Christy sat up. "What if I give you a ride to St. Louis? You've done great getting this far, but do you need to finish on the bike? You could still fulfill your husband's silly request about the ashes."

"That wouldn't be right. Besides, I doubt Josh would go for it. He's pretty into this whole thing after all."

"You two look as though you're getting along. Good thing you have him around. You do ride with him all the time, right? What about drunk drivers? Isn't it dangerous being out on the road?"

Meg dismissed her friend's concern with a wave. "I can handle myself. In fact, some guys probably ended up in jail after they tried to tangle with me."

The tale of Mister Silverhair and the clucking chickens strewn across the highway entertained Christy. She started to laugh and tried to choke out an apology. "I'm sorry, I can't help it, but that cracks me up."

Her mirth was contagious and Meg joined in with big belly laughs. Tears streamed from Meg's eyes and she began to snort. Christy doubled over, convulsed with laughter. "Oh-oh, I gotta go." Christy jumped out of her bed and dashed for the bathroom.

When she returned, she said, "I just hate getting old. Maybe I need to do those exercises, what are they, Kegels?" Christy tossed a spoon to Meg and opened the refrigerator.

"Nutty chocolate or strawberry banana?" She held up two pints of ice cream.

"Christy, you are just the best friend ever." Meg dug into her pint and devoured it in five spoonfuls.

"Wow, impressive. I never knew you were such a hog," Christy said. Meg wadded up a napkin and threw it at Christy.

Christy's spoon rattled in her container of ice cream. "All done," she said. Meg switched off the bedside lamp, the room black except for a soft light slipping in under the door. Tucked in, she stretched out to all four corners of the mattress, absorbing as much softness as possible. Most motel beds felt lumpy, like a stuffed animal that's seen a little too much loving. This one was fresh off the toy store shelf.

"Meg, Meg, you asleep?"

"Nope."

"Other than your muscles, how's your body holding up? It sounds so uncomfortable. I can't even imagine the abuse you're heaping on your body. What about blisters, and eeooh, what about chafing? Do you even have a butt anymore?"

"Two words," Meg said. "Diaper ointment."

"Seriously? That's too much." Christy giggled. "What about the other stuff? Do you ever get scared at night, camping out all alone? Don't you get bored?"

"I listen to music, I talk to the cows. I even talk to God."

Christy launched herself out of bed and landed with a *thump*. "Did you see that creepy swimming pool downstairs? I think they filmed the Midnight Monster Horror series down there. The place is so dark and secluded. Hey, let's sneak in and go skinny dipping."

"Now? You're crazy."

Christy countered. "C'mon, I dare you."

Honestly, that woman transported Meg straight back to junior high slumber parties and painful Truth-and-Dare games.

Christy lobbed the final volley, "Or are you still a prude?"

"That's not it. If you were closer you'd want to check my breathing to make sure I'm still alive. I'm glued to this bed. Like fresh roadkill, I can't move. A possum, with my legs splayed."

"You really have been on the road too long, girl. You sound a little batty. Let's go jump in. Are you sure this has nothing to do with religion? After all, you came into this world naked, and that's how you'll depart. How could God frown on that?"

"Christy, I really am exhausted. The idea of dragging myself out of this bed, the best bed I've been in since June, possibly since forever, doesn't excite me."

"Meg, don't change on me."

"The only change I can feel is that I'm getting stronger. Duda or Malachi once talked about developing God-confidence, not self-confidence. Well, I think that's what is going on. I don't have to go along with anyone else. I let Robert control me, Josh too. I don't think I'm going to let you either."

"Well, I'm just trying to have some fun. Good night. Don't get all witchy."

Seventy-Six

In the morning, Josh saw his mom slip a note under the door to Christy before they loaded up. The sun was just beginning to show, and the TV in the lobby talked about another record high.

The sun held its intensity all day long, and Josh obliged his mom with all the rest breaks she requested. When they hit town, she begged for a lukewarm shower and a cool bed in a quiet motel. At the Hideaway Inn, the desk clerk told them about the carnival and the big Fourth of July celebration.

"Not for me, thanks," Mom raised up her palm. "Just tell me where the room is."

Dank musty air slammed into them when they opened the door. Josh flipped the air conditioner to blast and the thin curtains fluttered overhead. He flopped on a bed, grabbed the TV's remote, and discovered a lack of channels. Disgusted, he stood up.

"Let me take the first shower and then I'm outta here. I know you're not leaving this place," Josh said.

When Josh pedaled up to the park, people started to gather around him and his loaded bicycle. It was kind of cool how he almost felt famous. Word quickly spread that he was cycling coast-to-coast. Coast to Midwest didn't sound that awesome. He also left out the part about his mother. No one needed to know he traveled with the extra weight.

He soaked up the attention until two girls began to giggle. "Do you always talk like that?" one girl asked. "You have a funny accent."

"Well maybe you sound funny too," Josh said.

The girls giggled again and flashed big smiles. Then one girl signaled, "Follow me. I'm Mandie and that's Tricia. You can win us a prize at the carnival."

Before the sun disappeared, he had finally toppled enough bottles with baseballs to win two stuffed bears. The girls hugged their prizes and led Josh to the ball field. The smell of fried elephant ears drifted over the blanket where he sat next to Tricia and Mandie. He leaned back on his elbows.

The crowd *oohed* and *aahed* at the cascading bursts of scarlet and gold overhead. Clouds of smoke floated across the field and the ground rumbled with the percussive blasts.

"Mandie and her boyfriend up in a tree." A chant rose from behind the trees.

"Shut up, twerp, or I'll tell Mom."

A volley of pinecones landed on the blanket. "It's just my stupid little brother and his stupid little friends," Mandie said.

Josh touched her on the shoulder. "Maybe there's somewhere else we can go, like down there?" He pointed away from the celebration.

The girls looked at each other and twittered at his accent again.

"You goof," Mandie said. "We can't leave now. The show just started. As soon as I get the call I need to head to the stage because my choral group is singing the "Star Spangled Banner" for the grand finale. Then I get to present a flag to the widow of a war hero."

Tricia was on her back, her stomach exposed between her short top and low-slung shorts. A silver ring in her navel winked in the light from the staccato bursts. She twirled her long hair and gazed up at Josh.

"Ya know, it's almost like you're from another country. The way you talk, and the way you act. You're not like the guys from around here. And you're so mature." She sat up and moved a little closer to Josh. "I'm planning on getting my tongue pierced."

She wiggled her tongue at him. "I think that's so sexy. I've been saving up my babysitting money."

"I'm going to do it too," Mandie added. Her phone beeped and she jumped up. "Well, I have to head. Will you be here when I finish?" she asked Josh.

"Probably," Josh said.

Mandie dashed off to the stage. Tricia put her head on Josh's shoulder.

"Do you have a girlfriend?" she asked.

For a reply, Josh leaned over and kissed Tricia. She opened her lips and returned the kiss with sloppy enthusiasm, throwing her arms around his neck.

The bright beam of a flashlight momentarily blinded Josh.

"Mandie's gone, you little freaks. Quit bugging us," Tricia said. She covered her eyes from the light.

Holding the flashlight was a lanky man dressed in a police uniform.

"Tricia," the man bellowed. "You get your rump on home. And you there, boy. Did she tell you she's only 13? If I see you sniffing around here again, you're all mine."

Seventy-Seven

Crisp white sheets enveloped Meg's body. The air conditioner rattled in the window and citrus air freshener filled the tiny room. Because they had logged hundreds of hot miles the last several days, it was high time to reward themselves with a stop at a little roadside motel. It even had an old concrete swimming pool, kept immaculately clean.

Meg slipped out of her narrow bed, careful not to wake Josh, sound asleep in the bed next to her. She pulled on her swimsuit and headed toward the pool.

Someone else beat her for an early-morning dip. The swimmer pulled steady strokes, breathing rhythmically. Meg pulled a plastic chair over and dropped her towel and room key on a little metal table. The sun was already warming the air, a little steam was coming off the pool. Clear sky, no clouds in sight.

"Hey, little missy. The water's wonderful. C'mon in." The swimmer motioned with a dripping arm.

She walked over to the edge and stuck in her toe. Satisfied, she slipped into the water. "Oh, this is nice. Much warmer than I thought it'd be." She sighed and sank up to her neck.

"I crank up the heat over night so it's perfect for my morning swim," the swimmer said. He pulled his goggles up to his forehead. "Name's Sam. Berniece and I have owned this motel for ages. Ever since the interstate came through, not much traffic comes down this road anymore, but I didn't want to give up my pool. I figured if I let the town use it for swimming lessons, that will pay for the heating bill. Course, the minute I finish my laps, I turn the heat way down. Sometimes off."

His tanned upper body rippled with muscle and his long white hair was slicked back. "I swam on the Olympic team, back in the 1950s. You probably weren't even born then. Missed the bronze by a tenth of a second. Boy, did I want to stand on that platform. I'll still never forget that crazy race. I was doing freestyle, and this guy from France did a false start. We were all a bit jumpy. So I didn't dive off the stand when I should've. I still swim whenever I can. Figure I need something to stay in shape."

Meg paddled around in the clear water.

"My parents ran the motel for years. They had second jobs too, while I was training. Here, I'll let you enjoy your peace. You looked pretty ragged when you and the boy pulled in last night. Did you catch any of the fireworks?"

"No, I missed them. But my son was down there. I'm sure they were glorious." Meg waved her thanks and arched to float on her back. Under the water, the vibrations from the pump echoed. She slowly moved her arms and legs up, sort of a modified backstroke and glided through the smooth water. A jet trail snaked across the sky. Meg watched the jagged lines crisscross above her. *All those people on board, so many life stories waiting to be shared, if only the passenger in the next seat would listen.*

An inflatable raft floated under the diving board and Meg swam over and jumped on. Once on her back, she closed her eyes and hung a foot over to latch onto the pool's edge. Birds darted about the flowering bushes that surrounded the pool enclosure, calling out to each other.

"Sam said I'd find you here. I just brewed you a nice pot of coffee." A gnome-like woman moved Meg's towel to a chair and placed a tray on the metal table. "It will keep warm for hours in this thermal pot. So go ahead, honey, enjoy your swim."

The woman disappeared before Meg could offer any gratitude. Meg swam a few more lengths of the pool before she got out. Under the lid next to the coffeepot, a cinnamon roll the size of the plate oozed with creamy white frosting. Meg wrapped the towel around her and sat down. She poured herself a steaming mug of coffee and prepared to sink her teeth into the pastry.

"Hey Mom, get off your rear. Let's move. Daylight's burning." Josh wheeled up, helmet on and bike packed.

Seventy-Eight

The morning air was calm and every few seconds Meg routinely checked the rearview mirror attached to the handlebars. A shiny blue oversized pickup followed in the distance.

"Truck back," Meg yelled ahead to Josh. He signaled with a wave and kept to the shoulder of the blacktop. His bike slowed until he was right in front of Meg.

Meg kept watching the truck in her mirror. He was like the tourists that puttered behind the bikers and never passed. The road was clear.

"I don't know what this guy's up to," she cautioned Josh.

"Probably just out checking the crops."

"I guess you're right, hon."

The truck inched its way up until it was side-by-side with Meg. She looked over. The passenger had hiked his body out his window. His hand missed her, but he managed to punch Josh's arm before the driver stepped on the gas and flew down the road.

Josh tried to regain control, but it was too late. The bike teetered and he skidded on his shoulder. His body and bike stopped on a rough patch of grass, littered with gravel and broken glass. Meg jumped off her bike faster than a mother bear with cub.

"Josh, honey. Are you all right? Can you move? I can't believe they did that. What an idiotic stunt." Meg's emotions whirled. The maternal side was concerned; the cyclist side was outraged.

Josh had skidded several yards on his left side and lay on the ground for a few minutes, trying to figure out what just happened. His favorite Italian jersey was torn and his new bike was scratched. His mom screamed at the driver, but the nimrod never stopped. She never yelled like that before.

Another pickup truck pulled over on the shoulder. The driver jumped out and ran toward Josh.

"Hey, you all right? Hang on, I'll come help." The guy trotted over. Josh's mom pulled out a towel and dabbed at the blood dripping from his arm. Josh was more worried about his shoulder. It was killing him.

The guy stood next to Josh's mom. "Ma'am, don't ya think this boy needs to get to a hospital? His shoulder looks pretty bad. We can throw your bikes in the back of my truck. There's plenty of room for both of you to ride. The bad thing is nothing's real close."

"Oh, thanks, but I'm sure he'll be fine. I can clean him up. See, I think the bleeding stopped already." Josh's mom lifted the towel, but quickly clamped it back on his arm. "We don't want to impose. I'm sure you have things to do."

Josh couldn't believe her. What if his shoulder was really broken? He opened his mouth to protest.

The driver beat him to it. "No, I insist. I'd feel like a real heel if I left you two out here alone. Call me Big John. Let me take you into town." The driver slipped off his baseball cap and swiped his brow with his forearm.

"Besides, the truck is air conditioned."

Josh let the guy help him to his feet. His mom wheeled his bike to the truck. With his good arm, Josh spun the front tire. "Can you believe that? It still rolls."

Big John lifted the bikes into the truck and closed the gate. Josh's shoulder felt every bump in the road on the way to town. Maybe Big John really was aiming for potholes during the hour-long ride to the hospital.

Josh's mom locked the bikes near the entrance before they signed in. After a nurse entered his medical history, Josh took a seat. They paged through dog-eared copies of *Field and Stream* and *Cat Fancy* while they waited in the empty emergency room. Finally, a door opened and a nurse called Josh's name.

Josh and his mom followed her to the bay and she pulled a curtain, rattling on its track overhead. She patted the examining table and Josh gingerly stepped up and sat down. When the attending physician walked in the exam room, a puzzled expression crossed her face.

"Admitting said it was a bike accident. Usually that means a drunken guy on a motorcycle. From the looks of you two, it must've been a bicycle accident. I'm sorry. We should've called you in sooner. We let the drunken guys chill for a while. Let's take a look."

"Is this your mom?" The doctor gestured. "Let's take off his shirt, or what's left of it." The doctor's sparkling dark eyes mesmerized Josh. She didn't seem too old either. Josh held his breath while she pulled the shirt over his shoulder and head. At least he didn't need to suck in his gut. She probably noticed.

"There, that wasn't too bad, was it?" She placed a hand gently on the opposite shoulder. "Your shoulder is rather raw, but probably not broken. We can take an X-ray after I clean this up. I'm going to put some topical numbing gel on it. That should deaden the pain a little while I work on your shoulder. Mom, you can sit right there, if you want."

Josh's mom briefly stroked his knee before she sat down in the corner.

"Now, if I didn't remove these cinders and rock chips, your arm would heal and look like tattoos." The doctor held a metal pan under Josh. With a scalpel she scraped his shoulder. "Feel that?"

Josh shook his head. His arm was rubber.

Ping, ping, ping, the pieces from the road plunked into the metal pan. The doctor continued to grate his skin. "This is certainly embedded, isn't it?"

Josh caught his mom's eye. He was surprised she hadn't passed out yet. He knew she hated blood and gore. She once told him she had enough blood and mucus from the hockey games. Her smile came out more like a grimace. Kind of like the gargoyles on the edge of the courthouse.

"It's fine Mom. I can't feel a thing. Maybe you better just read a magazine or something." *Maybe you could just go to the waiting room while I talk to this sweet-looking doc.*

"That's it. We're finished here." The doctor placed a light dressing on his arm and shoulder. "Now that you're not dripping all over the place, we'll get some X-rays."

The X-ray showed no break. The physician sent Josh and his mom on their way, much too soon, if he had any say. Before they left, the admitting clerk called a nearby motel and booked a room for them. The motel was only a few blocks away, so they wheeled their bikes over. Josh noticed a spaghetti shop on the way.

"Pasta tonight?"

"Sure, honey," Mom said. "We'll order after we get settled. I'll run over and pick it up while you rest. And then we'll figure out how to fly home and end this cockamamie thing before one of us gets killed."

Seventy-Nine

Meg came out of the bathroom, toweling her wet head. Josh flicked the remote past a constant stream of infomercials. An array of white containers covered his motel bed. Spaghetti and meatballs, Caesar salad, and thick slices of garlic bread. The enormous meal reminded her of the one she had shared with Christy.

Christy. Sometimes it's better to just stick to your zone, complete your goal. Meeting the real world while dealing in a solitary, simplified existence threw Meg off, and she was in no hurry to mix it up again with people they knew.

"Mom?"

"What's up, hon?" Meg moved over to the mirror and picked up a comb from the low dresser. "Need more food? Something to drink?"

"Nah. Thanks. We need to talk."

Meg scooted a chair over to his bed. "Mute the TV please."

"I heard you on the phone with Aunt Naomi. You told her we weren't going to finish the trip."

"Well, I told her we were discussing it."

"That's not what I heard. Want some of this?" He handed her a container of pasta.

"Oh, Josh. I don't know about continuing. First me, now you. Thank goodness you weren't seriously hurt. But I don't think we should press our luck anymore. I doubt Dad would want us to."

Josh stared at her for a few minutes. "You're calling it quits? Now?"

"We've ridden far," Meg said, "And we can be proud we covered as many miles as we did."

"C'mon, Mom. Look at it this way, we're getting closer. My shoulder's fine, I've seen guys ride in major races with broken bones. This is nothing." He worked his arm in windmills to prove its stability.

"Maybe we should discuss this in the morning, when we're refreshed," Meg said.

"No. We need to decide now. And the decision is to continue."

Meg abruptly stood. She picked up the damp towel and twisted it with each step around the small room.

"Anyway, what'd the guy from that funny little church, what was it, the Four Ls, say to you after your accident?" Josh stretched out on his bed.

Meg smiled at the recollection of Malachi's encouragement and weighed his words. "Well, perhaps we can continue. I guess we have a lot of people counting on us. Are you sure you're up to it though?"

"I'm fine, just fine," Josh said.

"Just the same, I'm going to call Malachi and ask for some new recruits to pray for us. You should think about sending a few prayers of your own."

"Did you forget I was the one who made us stop at that little church the other week? What about you? You sure were quiet about God when Dad was sick. Now look at you, you're almost as bad as Duda. That guy always wants to talk about God."

"I thought you only went to his shop a couple times," Meg said.

Josh laughed. "It was a few more. I didn't want you to know I was taking the trip seriously. How do you think I got to be so fast changing tires? I often helped out in his shop after school. There was another kid there, a Buddhist, I guess. We talked about reincarnation and how maybe Dad is in another form. Kinda weird stuff. Duda always smiled and explained the differences between Buddhism and Christianity. Duda did say that if God could make Adam out of ashes, he could give Dad a new body. I guess I overreacted about the cremation thing."

Meg stood over Josh and patted his head. "I think your dad is hanging out in heaven, smiling down at the two of us right this minute."

Meg noticed Josh grimace when he lifted the bag with the tent and poles, and his pace was slower. She debated her approach to the boy. *Talk or no talk.* She tried to erase the thought that her baby could be in pain, but oh, how she longed to comfort him. It was too early in the day for a confrontation. She didn't want to be left alone on the road and watch his rear disappear over the horizon. With self-loathing, she realized she should've picked up a book at Ned's about teen psychology. Those mood swings seemed worse than a premenstrual woman.

Eighty

Josh had slammed both hands flat on the director's desk and stood up. "You are not going to burn my father!"

The funeral director had *hemmed* and *hawed*, while Josh explained that the ambulance attendant who took his dad away told him not to worry, his father would receive a new body in heaven. Josh glared at Meg and the director through the swollen slits of his eyes.

Meg's heart lurched now at the memory of her son's agony. It had taken an hour to finally convince Josh that his father's soul had long departed. Besides, Robert stipulated cremation. And he always got his way.

At the funeral, the searing pain erupted again when Meg overheard countless well-wishers try to console a stone-faced Josh. A flock of the old guard ladies, resplendent in proper funeral hats and somber dresses, reminded Josh that his father was free from pain, he'd be made new in heaven. How, Josh had argued, could you make something new out of something that was destroyed, burnt to a crisp?

Right now, watching the campfire, Meg willed her sick mind to veer away from thoughts of cremation.

With a long stick, Josh poked the glowing embers. Meg, fatigued after another long day on the road, spread out on her sleeping bag next to the fire and watched her son and the night sky.

Lying on her back, Meg pointed up to the blackness. "Look, see that? There's a falling star."

Josh glanced up. "Maybe a satellite. But over there is the archer, you know, Sagittarius. It's kinda hard to see the exact figure. You have to use your imagination."

"I didn't realize you took astronomy in school. When did you pick up all this information?"

"When I was a little kid, Grandpa would take me outside at night. By the lake. He showed me all that stuff."

Meg remembered the times her father tried to share that same passion. But as a young teenager, she was too busy with friends and boys to bother learning constellations.

"Hey, Mom, you know what I just realized? You've really lost a lot of people. I'm about all you have left. Except for crazy Aunt Naomi."

Meg sat up. "Honey," she patted the sleeping bag. "Come sit by me. How's the shoulder now?"

"It didn't feel too bad today." He tossed the stick into the fire and plunked down next to her.

"Sitting here by the fire reminds me of all the times we camped out in the backyard. Your dad would sneak out of the tent and run around it, grunting, scaring you half to death. Then he'd get the fire going again and we'd toast marshmallows."

"Yeah. Remember the time I got Dad back?"

"What were you, twelve or thirteen then?"

"I was going into seventh grade. That was the summer the skunk kept coming around. Dad fell asleep early, but I was wide-awake. I decided to scare him. So I crawled around outside, scratching the tent, making little animal noises. Boy did Dad bolt!"

They laughed at the memory of Robert with his wild eyes and frizzy hair when he stormed out of the tent.

Meg touched Josh's arm. "This feels good to talk about your dad. Sometimes I get depressed thinking about everyone who has died. And I wonder why I'm still here. There has to be a reason, right?"

Eighty-One

The towering thunderhead in the distant sky signaled the end to the streak of clear weather. Meg and Josh pulled on rain gear and cycled while fat drops of rain splattered on the pavement. When the driving rain finally obscured their vision, they sought refuge huddled under a tarp in a drainage ditch next to the desolate road. Marbles of ice bounced off the ground around them. Bursts of lightning crackled from gray and black layers in the sky.

"This is awful," Meg yelled over the wind. "I didn't think the storm was going to be this severe. And what's with this hail? We're getting pelted to death."

Meg grabbed her son by the shoulders. "Why isn't anyone else on the road? Do you think they have tornadoes out here? What if one touched down and everyone is hunkered in their basements?"

He shook off her death hold. "Mom, listen to me. If there is a tornado, we're fine here. The funnel would probably go right across us. We're lucky there was a ditch here. It could've been flat instead." Josh struggled to keep his grip on the billowing tarp. The weight of the bicycles secured the opposite edge.

Meg tried to squelch her whining, but another one slipped from her lips. "What about the lightning?"

"What about it?" Josh raised his voice, matching the tenor of the storm.

"We could be struck dead, right here. Right now."

"This is about Grandpa, isn't it?" The boy rearranged his grip on the tarp overhead to avoid the water cascading down the edge.

Meg stammered her denial. But Josh pursued his theory.

"Just because lightning killed him doesn't mean it will us," he said. "Ever consider therapy for that phobia?"

"Therapy! Phobia!" Meg stood up to her full height. "This is silly. Here we are, about to die in a storm and you're talking nonsense." She grabbed the edge of the tarp from Josh. "Take a break, kid."

Meg's bravado lasted until the next clap of thunder and she dropped her hands and released the tarp as if it were in flames. The wind sucked it aloft and Josh leapt to grab hold.

"Think sometimes," he yelled at her, his face splashed with rain.

Surprised by his furor, Meg inhaled another whine. Just for a minute. Finally, she couldn't hold it in.

"Don't you think this storm has to stop soon? It's been pouring for ages."

Her son clenched his eyes close. His lips moved, but no sound emanated from them. When he spoke, it was in measured tones.

"Remember that storm last spring when I had to come get you at Malachi's church? You were holding that figure from the nativity scene?"

"Malachi gave me the baby Jesus."

"Right, so look at your situation now. Jesus is holding you and not going to let you down."

His burst of profound spirituality caught Meg off guard and rendered her speechless. She looked at Josh again, just in time to see him bite back a satisfied grin.

They crouched and dripped in silence, except for the storm raging above their tarp. Up until today, they had made good time across Kansas.

"Josh, look down!" Meg jumped up and pointed to the water spreading toward them. "I thought you said this was a good idea. The ditch is filling. Now what?"

"It won't get high, it has to drain sometime." Josh popped his head out to scan the area. Soaked, he ducked back under the tarp.

"I think the clouds are breaking up," he said.

Meg danced around the puddles growing around her feet. "Maybe we should take off our biking shoes, before they get ruined." She peeled off her shoes and socks and connected them to her bike. Muddy water covered her feet. Rumbling drilled through the cacophony of the storm.

"Josh, did you hear that? Is it a tornado?" Meg whimpered and grabbed her son, trying to pull him down to the ground with her.

"Mom, get a grip." A series of honks pierced their tarp and they peeked out to see a delivery truck pulling to a stop.

"Hey," the driver yelled out the window. "Get in." He jumped out of the truck and ran to the back and pulled down the gate. "Throw your bikes back here and get in front with me."

Josh hustled to get the bikes quickly loaded. Meg teetered trying to put her shoes back on so she'd have less to carry. She ran to the truck and Josh pushed her into the front seat and flung himself after her.

"Whew," Meg said. "I can't believe this storm. Thank you so much for saving us."

"You bet. I drove by here, saw bikes sticking out under that tarp. The more I drove on, the more I thought that was kind of strange. Why would there be bikes out here? I turned around when I realized there had to be people under there too. This storm sure doesn't want to let up. What in the world are you doing out in it?"

"It caught us off guard, completely. I guess we should've checked the forecast before we took off," Meg said.

"Tell you what. I'm heading to the next town. I'll drop you off at a fast food place there." He turned around and reached behind the seat. "Here, use these." Meg took a handful of paper towels from a roll and pressed them against her face and head.

The truck's wipers beat to the rhythm of the country tune on the radio. The driver reached over and flipped on the heater. Warm air blew on Meg's legs and she pulled on her soggy socks and adjusted her shoes. Soon she could see the town and the golden arches.

The driving rain switched to a gentle soaking by the time they turned into the restaurant's parking lot. Meg tried to press a ten-dollar bill into the trucker's hand, but he refused. Josh retrieved their bicycles and gear. He balanced the bikes against the building, spread the tarp over them and headed inside.

Meg's feet squished with each step. One mushy sock slipped below the heel of her shoe. She waved to Josh in line and disappeared into the restroom. Relieved to find it empty, she took off her shoes and socks. She wrung her socks out over the sink and used the electric hand dryer mounted on the wall. Her long rain pants hid her bare feet. She padded out to Josh and two large cups of steaming coffee.

"I never thought we'd leave that ditch this afternoon." She plunked down into the booth. "It's going to take forever for our gear to dry out. Maybe the motel will have a hairdryer we can use."

A latex-gloved employee walked by. He held a soggy sock at arm's length and pointed to a trail of damp footprints that led to Meg. "Are these yours, ma'am? We have a no shirt, no shoes, no service rule. Could you at least slip your shoes back on?"

Eighty-Two

"Hey, you okay if I take off for a while? I have a need for speed this morning." Josh grinned and rocked his bike frame underneath him.

"Go," Meg said. "Not too many places to get lost around here."

Midday, Meg glanced over her shoulder at a commotion behind. Some sort of motorcycle advanced toward her. One of those enormous motorcycles. And there, plopped in the sidecar was Aunt Naomi, wearing a flowing scarf, old-fashioned aviator goggles, and a helmet. "Yoo-hoo," she called out to Meg.

The swirl of dust settled and Harry tapped on the horn. A rendition of "Let Me Call You Sweetheart" closed the gap between the motorcycle and the bicyclist.

Harry pulled in front of Meg. "I can't believe we finally found you. Naomi got this hare-brained idea to surprise you. We've been looking for miles," he said.

Meg stopped her bike and walked it over to the giggling couple. "What in the world are you two doing here? I haven't seen anyone for hours. And now I turn around, and there you are."

"Meg, Meg, honey! Can you believe it?" Naomi popped out of the sidecar onto the road and enveloped Meg in a bear hug. Her eyes, magnified under goggles, bulged like frog eyes.

"Look, prescription goggles. Isn't that grand?" She pulled off her helmet and slipped off the goggles. With a finely lacquered nail, she chipped at the dirt lodged around a lens.

Harry parked and walked over to hug Meg, lifting her off the ground while she tried to balance her bicycle. "Where's the boy?" he asked.

Meg gestured down the road.

"He left you here by yourself?"

"I'm fine. Really. All I have to do is get on my bike and ride. It's a piece of cake."

"Cake," Naomi's eyes lit up. "Oh honey, wait till you see what I brought. I think I outdid myself." Naomi rubbed her hands with glee.

"Outdid yourself with what?" Meg asked. "So really, what in the world are you two doing here?"

"It's a surprise. We wanted to come and cheer you on the road. You know, like you see on TV." Naomi couldn't contain herself any longer and began to bounce from foot to foot.

"So when do you get a rest stop?" Harry asked.

"Anytime I want. But our next official one is up there." Again, Meg pointed down the road. "There's a town where we were going to meet. Josh said there's a roadside park at the edge."

Naomi eyed her. "Think you can go a few more miles on your own? I don't think we could stuff you in the sidecar. Maybe we could carry some of your parcels."

"No, no, I'm fine. But a stop would be good. I'm dying to hear about you, about life." Most of Meg's news now came while she scanned headlines in checkout lines at the grocery stores. "What's going on in the world? What's the president up to these days?"

"Oh honey, you wouldn't believe it." Naomi rolled her eyes. "More scandals on the Hill." Naomi was a political gossip sponge. "Don't get me started out here in the middle of nowhere. That reminds me, how is your hair?

You don't look like an old woman, even with that helmet on. I knew my Jack could help you. Guess you found someone local to help."

Harry pulled a plastic bottle of water out of the cooler and tossed it to Meg.

"Here, this will help make those miles fly. Naomi, let's load 'em up. We'll signal the boy and wait at the park for Meg."

Naomi snapped her goggles back on and stuck the helmet over her curly head. Once settled into the sidecar, she said, "Are you sure you'll make it?"

Meg took a slug of cool water and wiped her mouth. "I'll be fine," she reassured her aunt. "See you in a little bit."

Meg set her bike against an oak tree. Its massive branches shaded a wide area.

"Meg, Meg, over here." Naomi flagged her with gusto. "And look, here's Josh."

Naomi commandeered a wooden picnic table so no other picnickers could steal it, although the park was deserted. A plastic red-and-white tablecloth covered a decade's worth of bird droppings, if the benches gave any clue. Josh circled the table once, and then grinned at Meg.

"Come sit. You won't believe what I have." Naomi pointed to the bench. "First, here's a newspaper." Meg grabbed it and spread it out along the bench.

Naomi grunted. "Hmm, I meant for you to read it. And I brought you your own scarf, the one with a map of France, you know, like the Tour de France?"

Harry mopped his brow with one of the cloth napkins. "Whew. Has it been this hot the whole time?"

"You betcha," Meg said, "and then some."

Naomi scurried around the table, lifting lids off various plastic tubs. The enormous spread included plump strawberries, white and red grapes, bagels, cream cheese, crackers, seafood spread, pita bread, cherry tomatoes, fried chicken, coleslaw, and peanut butter cookies. "Eat, eat, we don't want to carry any food back." Naomi said.

Meg dove into the fresh fruit. Josh kept nodding his head, his mouth too full to converse. He sampled everything Naomi pulled out. Halfway through a bucket of fried chicken, Josh groaned and raised his grease-smeared face.

"Honey, maybe you better slow down," Meg said.

"Nah, this is incredible." He gnawed on a drumstick.

Naomi cleared her throat. "And now," she said, "the *pièce de résistance*." With a flourish she lifted the cover off a three-layer cake adorned with miniature bicycles. She sliced a thick piece, ladled fudge sauce on top, and slid it to Josh. He dipped a finger in the frosting and smiled. Then he picked up the whole piece and crammed it into his mouth.

"Mmm, that was something. But I can't figure out the flavor." Josh looked at his great-aunt.

"One of my favorites," Naomi beamed. "It's prune cake!"

"You're looking a little green, boy," Harry said. "What's wrong?"

They all glanced up in time to see Josh bolt for a group of bushes.

Eighty-Three

The route was not exactly as everyone predicted. Whoever said Kansas was completely flat was wrong. Dead wrong. Plus it was hot. They awoke early to mount their bikes just before the sun rose, before the humid air smothered the state. The heat obliterated any desire for conversation. Many miles went by before any words were exchanged. By mid-day they would search for a shady spot to rest.

At a small booth by the café's window, Meg sipped coffee and watched pickup trucks roll by. Every now and then a motorcycle roared by. But she hadn't seen one with a sidecar since Naomi and Harry left after their feast and a long nap in the shade. It took a day for Josh's stomach to fully recover from the overload of rich and greasy food. Now he was back up to full speed and Meg was left on her own.

A lone slice of blueberry pie rotated lazily in the glass container on the counter. The waitress appeared with a coffeepot.

"Refill?" She nodded to Meg's cup.

"Sure, and is that pie homemade?"

"Made fresh this morning. Want that last slice honey?"

"That'd be wonderful," Meg said.

"Are you with that bike group? I made a boatload of extra pies because we heard a group is coming through town. I've got more in the back."

"Cyclists? Or motorbikes?"

"Well, they didn't really say. Probably cyclists. I know there's a big bicycle ride across the state every year, so I just guessed that was it."

Meg finished her pie and coffee. Her theory of ingesting something warm to counteract the heat seemed worthless. Right now she'd love to stick her feet in a bag of ice.

Sated with blueberry pie and a dab of vanilla ice cream, she got back on the road and fiddled with the menu on her mp3 player before she found some music to inspire her. More Gershwin. She was at a loss to explain the Gershwin kick. Gradually warming up to the song and the liberating feeling along the empty country highway, Meg serenaded the undulating wheat fields with a little bit of "Ain't Misbehavin'." The empty two-lane road snaked through shimmering pools of water on the pavement, just out of Meg's reach. A brief gust of wind kicked up a dust devil and spun it across to a field of sunflowers.

The squawk of a dime store bike horn interrupted her singing. The rider's legs stretched out in front of him on the long bike frame low to the ground.

"Hi," the rider said. "Where you from?"

"Minnesota," Meg said.

"Boy, you came far to do this ride. I'm from Wichita. That last lunch stop at the school was something. Homemade kolaches and everything. They sure have been feeding us right this week."

"Oh, I'm not with a group. I'm traveling on my own, with my son."

"Well, you can certainly ride with me for a while. There are hundreds ahead of us, they left when it was still dark this morning. I didn't feel like pushing it that much. It's a pretty low mileage day anyway, so what's a few hours in the heat?"

A fleet of bicycles flew past and people called out "hellos."

"What's that microphone for?" Meg pointed to the set under his helmet.

"My wife is behind me. She's on the tandem with our 9-year-old son. I prefer riding this."

"And just what exactly is that?"

"Ah, it's a recumbent. Best way to ride. You should try one. It takes a lot of the pressure off your body. Don't your hands tingle sometimes? And doesn't your rear get sore?"

They pedaled and chatted while he shared the merits of his bike. Soon Meg had absorbed enough material to produce a TV infomercial on the device. The man's jarring voice pierced the shroud of silence Meg had come to enjoy. Weeks ago she had made peace with her solitude, and now, surrounded by a group of chattering bikers, she felt disoriented. Unable to alter her pace, Meg was stuck until their paths diverged.

The man radioed his wife to stop at the next town. "Just wait," he said to Meg. "You're in for a treat."

Meg's mouth watered at the thought of homemade ice cream with chocolate syrup, ice-cold lemonade with chocolate chip cookies, maybe fresh, ice-cold watermelon.

At the edge of town, signs proclaimed the world's largest ball of twine. The time/temperature sign over the brick bank building blinked 94 degrees. Across the street, a handful of bikers gathered at the display.

"This is it? The surprise?" Meg stared at the immense ball of twine.

"I can't believe I did this to myself." Josh massaged his calf.

"Did what honey?" Meg stirred the noodles in the boiling water. The coals under the metal grate shifted and sparks drifted up through the grate.

"Nothing."

"I bet I could help." Meg dumped the pasta into a strainer and let the water trickle away from their campsite. They had stopped at a public site. A sign on the gate announced the presence of bears. She was relieved other campers would be around to hear her screams.

Josh limped over to the picnic table. He sat down and swung both legs up on the bench, stretched out. He bent over to touch his toes. "Yikes."

Meg opened a bag of pasta sauce and poured it over the noodles before she returned it to the pot. With a stick, she lifted the pot to the side of the grate.

"Come on, let the pro in." She motioned to the top of the table. "Hop up. Let me take care of those legs. Wait though." Meg grabbed a beach towel off the line strung between two trees and tossed it on the picnic table.

"Okay, up you go." She patted the table.

Josh struggled to stand up and then stretched across the table, his nose in the towel.

"Ick, the towel is wet. Mildew even." He sat up.

"Fine." Meg tried to yank the towel from under him. "You want a rub or not?"

"Yeah, yeah, I need it. I raced with the big dogs today. A little variety."

Meg looked over to a nearby campsite where a group of college-age men sprawled in camp chairs. They'd been traveling the same route and ran into each other periodically.

"Again Josh? Why?"

"I dunno. It's fast. Not boring."

Meg began to knead his calf and could feel the knots in there. Her fingers worked on his muscles and she remembered what it felt like to knead bread. Robert was not a big fan of her sourdough bread, so she had quit making it.

"Yow. Not so hard." Josh's yelp brought her out of the kitchen in her head.

She applied a more gentle touch, pushing and pulling the muscles in a rhythmic pattern.

That night, Josh hobbled over to join the college group. Meg listened to them laugh and share turns picking out tunes on a guitar and a banjo long into the night.

Eighty-Four

A water tower and then a grain elevator popped up in the distance and Josh signaled Meg.

"Mom, I'm going ahead to find us some shade. I promise to be right back for you unless I find something right away. You should not be out here any more under this sun." Josh waved a gloved hand and was gone.

Meg clamped the nozzle in her mouth and forced herself to keep drinking and moving. *Pedal*, she told herself. *Persevere*. The heat and the endless road lulled her into a zombie state. A shrill whistle snapped her out of it. She swiveled to look for the source. Behind her, a figure jumped up and down.

"Mom, Mom. Back here." Josh flagged his arms. He had discovered a little roadside park.

Meg stopped her bike and tried to focus. Then she turned around and slowly pedaled back to her son.

"Let's stop and rest." He pointed to his sleeping bag unrolled under a scrawny tree. "You can stretch out over there."

With great effort, Meg clambered off her bike and handed it to Josh. She stumbled over to the sleeping bag.

"You don't look too great. Have you eaten anything today?"

Meg shook her head. "I don't think so. The eggs looked too slimy this morning at that cafe. I couldn't stomach them. Toast wasn't even calling me."

"Well, you need to have something." Josh rummaged around in one of his packs. "How about a granola bar? Or this?"

She winced at the mottled brown banana in his hand. "No, let me just curl up here..." She groaned and clutched her stomach. "Help me over to those bushes. I'm going to be sick. There's only water sloshing around in my stomach."

Josh stroked her back when she finished retching. "I remember you used to do this for me when I was sick when I was a kid."

Meg nodded and pointed to the sleeping bag. "Just let me lie down for a while. I'll be fine."

She sat cross-legged on the ground near their tent and rested her head in her hands. Her head felt hollow, reminding her of the feeling before her ears popped on the flight to Oregon. Even her voice sounded muddy to her own ears. With the tip of her tongue she probed her cracked lips. Josh kneeled by her and offered a bowl.

"Eat this," he said.

Meg leaned over to glance at the contents and recoiled. "No way. It looks like paste from elementary school."

Runny oatmeal dripped off the spoon Josh dangled in front of her. "It's about all that's left. Want me to make you?" He smiled as he spoke and teased her with the spoon.

Meg blocked his efforts with her hand. "Water. I need water. And then we can take the tent down."

Back on her bike, Meg forced herself to nibble on a granola bar she had stashed in her handlebar bag. By noon she was ready for more food and they stopped at a grocery store for a fresh banana. Josh pressed a cold bottle of apple juice in her hand and watched her drink every drop. He smiled as she slurped the last sip.

"So, what do you think, Mom?"

"I think you'd make a great doctor. I'm back to normal."

"That depends on what you're calling normal." Josh swatted her with his cycling gloves.

Their route through Missouri took them on the smaller, lettered roads, instead of the main country roads. The two cyclists played on the undulating ribbons of road, pedaling up and then coasting down the hills, trying to crest the next hill.

"Times like this make me understand your father a lot better," Meg said. "I might consider joining one of those rides across a state next summer. You could join me."

"Seriously?"

"Very."

With a burst of energy, Meg powered up the next hill. Josh passed her at the top and then tucked in his body to race to the bottom.

He coasted and waited for Meg to join him. "Mom, how long was Dad sick before you told me?" His brows peeked out under his helmet, but sunglasses hid his eyes. His elbows rested on the handlebars, and his palm held his chin. Meg recognized his contemplative posture, developed after miles on the road.

"Not that long," she said. "We discussed withholding the news. But I told your father you should be in on it."

"Why?"

"When my daddy died, we had no warning. I caught a flight home for the funeral." Meg studied her pedals for a while and straddled the white stripe on the road's shoulder.

"There were a lot of things left unsaid. I wanted to apologize for the years of grief I put him through. I never did get to tell him I was sorry, that I loved him. And I never did receive his forgiveness or love out loud."

Josh pedaled for a few yards and took a slug of water. "I bet he forgave you in his heart," he said.

Meg smiled at his consolatory attempt.

"So what about my dad? What happened with him?"

"What do you mean?" Meg was about to continue when the stench of manure and urine from a nearby hog confinement building jarred her. "Wow, we are in the country, that's for sure."

Josh shook his head as if to dispel the smell. He continued his questioning: "I mean, he was sick and dying. Obviously the treatments weren't working. Why did you give up on him?"

"Me, give up on him? Where'd you get that idea?"

"He could've tried those experiments in Mexico. There was something on TV one night when I flipped around channels. Right after you told me he had cancer. This show came on and the guy was in total remission. You should've let Dad try it."

"I was all for it. He was the reticent one."

"No way," said Josh. "I don't believe it. You were always the conservative one."

"Not really. I suggested he stay at a clinic in Tijuana—"

"Sprint." Josh hollered and stomped on his pedals. A barking dog raced from a farmyard and sped across the road.

"Sprint?" Meg's ability to sprint had disappeared miles ago. She grabbed a water bottle and aimed a spray at the dog's face. The mongrel snapped at her right ankle until she kicked it free. The dog whimpered and scampered to a nearby culvert.

Josh stood on the side of the road just past the barn waiting for Meg.

"I figured you could handle that little guy," he said.

"Sometimes it's the little guys that are the worst." Meg looked at her foot, happy to have escaped a severe bite.

"You were on to something back there," Josh said. "What was that about Dad in Mexico?"

"I was the one who wanted him to go, to try the alternative therapy. What did he have to lose? His cancer had metastasized. It kept popping up. But he said his body had taken enough. It was time to go home to God. I conducted the research for him. I found a wealth of information online. He still wasn't interested. He said they were quacks."

Meg's pace evened with Josh and she reached over to touch his arm. "So now you know."

Josh shook his head. "And when he quit eating, toward the end? I blamed you for not fixing what he wanted. I guess he was just too sick anyway. He probably was ready to die."

Meg nodded. "He was in a lot of pain then. I think he was ready to let his earthly body go." Robert's last days were spent at home and Meg was grateful for Joyce, the hospice worker. "I regret we didn't have you talk to Joyce while she was helping. You would've gotten a better perspective."

"Nah, I doubt it," Josh said. "Back then, I was too mad."

Eighty-Five

Raindrops splatted alongside Meg's tires as she skimmed along the county road. Lightning snaked across the darkening Missouri sky. Caught by the storm, Meg crouched and continued to pedal, too late to put on the raingear. She regretted sending Josh on ahead, but she convinced him she really needed quiet time for contemplation. A spine-jarring crack overhead made her jump, causing the bike to wobble. The bike's front tire struck loose gravel and sent the bike sliding.

Words she had never used before exploded from her mouth. Wincing, she untangled herself and glanced down at the blood and rain trickling down her knee. Her right elbow was a pulpy mess of flesh and gravel, but the churning clouds made shelter her first concern.

As the rain bit into her, Meg clenched her teeth and carried her bike through thigh-high grass to the faded barn she had spotted minutes earlier. A pungent smell met her at the door. While rain streamed through the roof's rotted timbers, Meg ducked into a dry corner stall. Feeling through her pack, she unearthed her first-aid kit. A peculiar rustling nearby made her stop. Meg shuddered, hoping to avoid a rodent.

She remembered the palm-sized canister clipped to her handlebars. If pepper spray stops mangy curs on the road, it should easily drop a rat, she reasoned.

The rustling got louder. Meg grabbed her ammunition.

"Dickens of a storm, ain't it, ma'am."

Eighty-Six

Meg screamed. A faded felt hat covered the top half of the man's grizzled face. He flipped open a heavy silver lighter to light the cigarette dangling from his lips.

"Did you want a smoke?" he asked.

"No, I don't smoke. Not that I'm against it, go ahead. I'm sorry I had no idea someone was in this old barn. I'll be off soon. I just need to straighten the handlebars and I'll hit the road."

"Lady, there's no need to rush. You're safe from the storm here. There's plenty of room for the three of us."

Meg's eyes darted around the dark barn. He flicked on his lighter and held it up toward a stable.

"Hey, Major," he called out.

A low whinny responded.

"That's my traveling buddy. We've been traipsing across the old US of A for many years. He pulls the cart. Man, I hate it though when we have to go through a town. Those idiot drivers get too close, trying to have a lookie-see at us. Major hates them too. He gets spooked. The cart got dumped yesterday. I stopped here to try to strengthen the axle."

Meg assessed the situation and willed her breathing to deepen.

"Major and me won't bother you none." He turned back to the axle. The rhythmic clanging of his hammer filled the barn. Heavy fatigue, coupled with shakiness from the accident, forced Meg to sit. She pulled out her sleeping bag and shook it before she wrapped it around her body. Through narrow slits, she eyed the man and tried to relax and wait out the storm. Malachi's song played in her head and she longed for the comfort it offered. She tried to recite Bible verses to herself, but her memory stumbled.

After many silent hours, she lost the battle to exhaustion and drifted off. She dreamed she and Robert were lying on their dock back in Lake Devine. Robert was stroking her hair and she smiled at the warm sun.

"You sure are purty when you smile like that."

She bolted upright and clutched her sleeping bag around her chest.

"Now, little lady, just lie back down. I think we could be real good friends." He crouched next to her bag. Then he clamped his hand on her shoulder. As his hand moved up to her face, the smell of his unwashed body mixed with that of his horse and moldy straw. His fingers moved up her face, almost touching her eyelids. Meg swallowed the sudden rush of bile.

"I've been watching you for a long time. I figure you being on the road by yourself, with that nice fancy bike of yours, that you're looking for some fun." He winked and grinned at her, displaying a row of stubby dirty teeth.

The storm had passed through during the night and the early sun darted in through the missing timbers in the walls. Now she could really see the stranger.

"I let you sleep last night..." he continued.

"You know," she said, "We have all day to get to know each other. You're right. I'm just traveling around by myself, like you. Why don't you let me make you some coffee or tea? I think I have that with me." She almost let it slip that it could be packed in Josh's gear.

He looked at her. "Coffee'd be mighty fine. I ran out last week. Some guy in Marysville gave me a coupla pounds. Didn't last too long." He went to work building a small fire.

Meg tried not to tremble while she searched her packs for the little coffee pot. When she discovered her Swiss Army knife, she angled her back away and stuck the knife in her waistband. While the coffee brewed, Meg collected her gear and rolled up the sleeping bag and squished it into the compression bag.

"Mmm, smell that, wouldja?" The man bent over the little pot and inhaled. Meg darted in, grabbed the pot and swung it toward his head.

Hot coffee scalded his face. He toppled over on the glowing logs before he caught himself on his hands.

"You whore, what have you done?" he screamed at her. "My face, my hands."

Meg scrambled to her feet, hoisted her bike and dashed out of the barn. Wheezing, she collapsed in the ditch among knee-high prairie grass. A red farm truck lumbered by, stopped and backed up.

"Hey, you okay?" the driver yelled and lifted the brim of her dusty seed cap to get a better look at Meg. "I can see you there. You in trouble?"

Meg stared at the woman. An exposed strip of white skin contrasted with the dark tan of the bottom half of the driver's face.

"I said, 'you in trouble?'"

Meg's body began to shake uncontrollably. She saw the driver push against the door of the old truck and jump out across the road.

"Look, I can take you into town. It's just seven miles down the road. Someone can help you there."

Meg tried to relax a little at the woman's insistence, but she kept checking over her shoulder. The woman reached out a hand to Meg.

"It's fine, I don't see anything or anyone behind you now," the woman said. "Just grab my hand and you will be fine."

Meg searched the woman's eyes, but found only reassurance radiating from them. She took the outreached hand

and allowed herself to be pulled to a stand. Together they lifted her bike and bags into the bed of the truck and Meg limped in the front.

The driver got in and locked the doors. Meg jumped when she heard the click. "I hope I can find my son in town."

Meg gulped a little more air and willed her body to stop shaking. "There was the strangest guy back there in the barn. I spent the night out of the rain there. Then he tried coming on to me this morning. Real creepy guy. I whacked him with my coffee pot. But now I don't have one. I'm Meg. I'm biking cross-country with my son, only we split up for just a little bit yesterday. We should've stayed together. This would never have happened."

"Carol," her driver said, and reached across to shake hands. "Now relax, slow down, take a deep breath and you can fill me in on the details."

Meg obliged and inhaled deeply before she began. Carol nodded at suitable intervals, and waved to each truck they passed. Straight rows of corn and soybeans marched across the landscape. Beyond the next hill, a peeling water tower displayed faded remnants of the artistic talents from the Class of '74.

"The fields are too wet for me to do much today, so I was heading into town for coffee," Carol said. "You want to join me? I sit with a bunch of old guys. I graduated to their table after my dad died. He was a regular. Now Mom and I are running the farm, thanks to hired help. Are you sure you're all right? That leg of yours doesn't look too good."

Meg glanced down at her knee, caked in dried blood and rimmed with purple bruises. At this rate, she'd never heal. "I just need to find a restroom to clean up."

The truck pulled into the diner's lot, next to a rack of pickups and farm trucks.

"Looks like Dusty is busy today," Carol said.

The smell of fried food, hot coffee and warm bodies greeted them at the entrance. A little bell jingled when

Carol pushed the door open. A hearty group of "hellos" met them, and Carol directed Meg to the table. The men stared at Meg in her jersey and black shorts.

"Hey, are you that biker lady that's missing? That kid over there said he lost his mom."

Meg followed the direction of his gaze. Josh hunkered over a cup of steaming coffee, a faded cap pulled over his eyes.

"Mom!" Josh jumped off his chair. "How'd you make it here? I thought you got lost in the storm. The cell phone didn't have any service. I didn't know how to reach you. I didn't know what to do. I hitched a ride here and was getting ready to call the authorities, or someone." In his exuberance, he reached out and hugged her.

Eighty-Seven

Click. Clickety click. Click. The calypso beat of Meg's chain punctuated the silence between the mile markers.

"You should probably fix that, you know." Josh looked down at Meg's chain as they pedaled side-by-side.

"It won't be long now anyway. Maybe I can just nurse it along," Meg said. She fiddled with the shifter and watched below as the chain jumped along the cogs. She cocked her head to the side for a moment.

"Better?" She looked up at Josh.

"Yeah. Maybe you didn't really hurt your bike. How's the knee?"

Meg reached down to tap the ragged bandage over her scrapped knee. Its dirty edges pulled away from the stiff wound. Keeping the bandage clean and white was near to impossible on the dusty roads.

Cows grazed near the road. Meg guessed them to be Holsteins. Or maybe Jerseys. She berated her ignorance. You'd think after all this time on the road she would know by now.

Josh broke the silence. "When I emailed Candy Cane the other night, it sounded like she plans to show up in St. Louis. She asked a bunch of questions about your night with the freaky guy. She thought that could be a front-page report. Did you take a picture of him?"

"A picture? Are you insane?" Meg shook her head.

"I didn't think you did, but Candy wondered. She wanted some art other than photos of our bikes and us."

"Get me lined up with a police sketch artist and I could figure something out. The turnoff is probably near if that hotel clerk was right," Meg said.

Meg and Josh turned off the road on to a trailhead for a route on abandoned railroad tracks.

"This is kind of fitting we finish on a trail, considering that's how I started," Meg said.

Josh's front tire bounced a little on the crushed limestone. "I know I'm happy to get away from cars and dogs. And crazy drivers."

"You know, as strange as this sounds, I'm sad this trip is almost over," Meg said. "This is all I've focused on for so long. And soon, nothing. At least you have college and Florida ahead of you."

"I can't wait. It's going to be awesome."

"Awesome, I'm sure, but I feel as though I need to impart some final nuggets of wisdom before you go. I'm not finished parenting you yet."

"You mean you actually have some advice left? You've given me plenty over the years. Especially since we left Minnesota in June." Josh grinned.

"There's always more, hon. Remember who you are, work hard for your dream and give back to God and the world. Do something for someone else. And I don't just mean the cute college girls. Maybe you could volunteer somewhere?"

They approached a pair of bikers heading the opposite way. Meg pegged them for newcomers, since their packs still had the pristine store exterior. She nodded as they crossed.

"What about you Mom? What's going to happen once we get back and I take off?"

"Maybe I'll redecorate your room. Make it an exercise room." Meg laughed.

"No, seriously Mom."

"I've been thinking about that lately. I became too dependent on your dad and in the process I disappeared. I wasn't always like that you know. Maybe if I would've had a career. Once you were born, you became my career. Someone had to be the room mother, party planner, den parent."

Josh looked over at her. "Maybe it's time you found a real career. Maybe you could try for law school. Don't get me wrong." He hesitated. "Dad was a good guy, but he was a big control freak. I don't think it was your entire fault. You just let yourself get swept up in his flow."

"That noticeable, huh?" Meg said. "When he started getting sick, I started losing it too. I'm surprised I made it out of that spiral before I crashed. It must have been lousy for you."

"Yeah, you could say that. Does that mean you're going to start cooking again? I got tired of cereal."

"I could show you how to cook, at least survive on your own. Meatloaf would be easy," Meg said. "Speaking of food, we have one night left on the road. Let's look for a good restaurant and somewhere comfy to sleep."

Saddened by the realization that the ability to consume food with no weight gain was coming to an end, Meg dug into the steak sizzling on a platter. With her eyes closed, she savored the meat tender enough to yield to her fork. She peeled back the aluminum foil on her baked potato, added a dollop of sour cream and two pads of real butter. Then she sprinkled chives over the fluffy pulp. A server in gingham and blue jeans maneuvered around tables passing out softball-sized rolls. Meg grabbed two and slathered on honey butter. Unable to decide which dessert to order, they had the server bring the top four favorites. Meg raked her fork through the meringue and puckered at the tart snap of the lemon pie. It was a close second to Mr. Ted's back in Kansas.

Josh tipped back in his chair and patted his belly. "I am going to miss these meals," he said. Then he sat back up and speared a chunk from his apple crisp.

Meg tugged at the waistband of her sweatpants, relieved that she jettisoned her jeans weeks ago at the little church. She and Josh ambled back to their cabin. Josh showered first. When it was Meg's turn, she stood and let the hot water cascade over her body as steam filled the shower stall. She soaped her shoulders and arms, marveling at the definition and strength she felt, no longer the overweight, sedentary housewife. Water swirled about her white feet, a sharp contrast to her suntanned legs.

As the water cleansed her body, she realized this was the end. The end to a journey she never thought she would take. The end to her mother-son adventure. The end to her chapter as a mother. Soon, she really would be all alone. Before she knew what was happening, tears mingled with the rushing water. Emotions flowed out of her system until she was empty. She yanked off the bandage and turned off the shower. Exhausted, she pulled on the last clean T-shirt she'd been saving and a pair of baggy cotton shorts.

No TV cluttered their small cabin. Just the sound of crickets drifted through the walls. Josh was already in his bed, so Meg flicked off the light switch by the door and jumped between the cool clean sheets on her bed.

"Hey, you know this trip wasn't as rotten as I thought it'd be," Josh said. "You're not a bad biker for an old lady."

"Old lady?" Meg sat up.

"Okay, okay, you did learn how to work those hills." Josh kept silent for a while. "But Mom, back to this fall. What are you going to do?"

"It's hard to believe it'll be a year in September since your father died. I followed his advice and didn't make any major decisions for a year. Especially about the house. It's a little too big just for me. But I sure love it out on the lake."

"Maybe you could run a B&B, like the one we stayed in at the beginning of the trip."

"By myself Josh? That'd be rather difficult. Law school might be worth a shot, after all these years."

"Get a friend to help you out with the B&B. What about Christy? Think she'd do it?"

"I suppose I could hire someone to help out too." Meg warmed to the idea. The kitchen was spacious enough, and it'd be easy to whip up wild rice pancakes and deer sausage in the morning. She could convert the upper floor to several cute bedrooms. Haul Josh's stuff to the basement. Turn the den into her room on the main floor. A true northern retreat, with more loons and pine furniture, she thought as she drifted off to sleep. Maybe nature photographs framed in birch bark.

In the morning after they packed up their gear, Josh stopped to grab Meg's wrist.

"You know Mom, how Christmas morning is always so exciting? And Christmas day is sort of anti-climatic. That's what today is like," he said.

Meg turned her hand over to grasp Josh's hand. "It's like you don't know if we should speed up or slow down."

"Exactly."

"Let's just ride and enjoy the day," Meg said.

For the next five miles, they rode in silence until Meg blurted, "Canoe paddles."

"I thought you'd be thinking of breakfast." Josh looked at her.

"Breakfast, definitely. My stomach is rumbling," Meg said.

"What about canoe paddles?"

"Are they still in the boathouse?"

"Yeah. I guess." Josh pedaled alongside Meg.

"You got me thinking about that B&B idea. Maybe a pair of canoe paddles over the doorway might look quaint, touristy."

"Over the boathouse? That'd work. There are some old duck decoys in the basement."

"What's going to happen once we hit St. Louis?" Meg realized they were getting closer. Her stomach released its desire for breakfast.

"I emailed a bike club there," Josh said. "Someone will meet us at the trailhead about 20 miles west of St. Louis. They'll give us a lift to Forest Park, on the edge of the city. From there, we'll head for Busch Stadium."

"On bikes?"

"The streets are supposed to be wide. We'll be fine. And then I guess we're finished," Josh said.

"Just like that," Meg said.

She kept her cadence steady next to Josh until she blurted out, "We need to stop."

"Right this minute? Or turn off the trail to a town?"

"Right now. I have something to confess."

Eighty-Eight

Meg's head swirled to match her stomach. Maybe Josh didn't need to know. *God,* she cried out in her heart, *send me words. Now!*

Josh wheeled his bike over to Meg. "So spill it. What's so important we had to stop now?"

She leaned her bike against a tree and waited for Josh to do the same. She reached in her handlebar pack for a bag of peanuts. With her teeth, she tore off the top strip of plastic and passed the peanuts to Josh. He tossed a few into his mouth.

"Last night, I couldn't find your father," she said. "The bag is gone, the ashes are gone."

Peanuts flew out of Josh's mouth. He wiped his mouth with the back of his hand and turned away. After a few paces he whirled back to face Meg and slammed his hand against a tree trunk.

"That's the whole point of this trip," Josh said.

"I know, but—"

"I can't believe it. You lost Dad? Seriously? We might as well quit now."

"Josh, listen to me."

"No. You listen to me. Dad asked me to do something. Both of us. And we failed him."

Meg tugged on his sleeve. "Remember Duda talking about the race and how we finish it? He was talking about life as a Christian. The end is important to God. We're going to finish the race in eternity. The ashes were just a pretense to get us together."

"We had a mission. It's dead. Like Dad." Josh turned to his bike. "It's over."

"Over?"

"Why finish now?"

Meg reached for his face, but Josh jerked away from her touch. "We have to finish," she said.

"Just do whatever you want." Josh slumped down next to a tree and stared down the trail. "Where did you lose him?"

"First of all, I didn't really lose him. His spirit lives on. Especially in you. The ashes were just the earthly wrapping."

"Tell me Mom. For real."

"Probably when I unloaded a lot of extra weight, ages ago, at a funny little church. That's the last time I remember talking to them, the ashes."

"So what do we do now? Everyone is expecting this grand ceremony."

"Did you ever look closely at the cremains?"

"No," Josh said.

"Then no one else will know either. Let's scoop some dirt, grind it up a little, and put it in a bag."

"That's disgusting. You do it. I'm finished."

Meg watched him mount his bike, his helmet swinging from its strap on the handlebars.

"You're going to leave me here? Alone? What am I supposed to do Josh?"

Josh's cell phone chirped. He let it go to voicemail before he fished it out of his back jersey pocket. An image of a smiling Duda flashed on his screen. Josh scanned the trail ahead and then pushed the button to listen to his message.

"Hey, you must be close now. Can you believe you and your momma did this? Your dad would be so proud.

Not many guys would accept such a challenge. When you first came in the bike shop, I was not too sure. But the more we chatted, the more I knew you were a good boy. See you in St. Louis."

Josh stared at the phone before he returned it to his pocket. With a heavy sigh, he turned his bike around and pedaled back to his mom. She stood by her loaded bike on the side of the trail.

"Mom?"

She looked up as he approached. Her tan and dusty face was veined with tears. He yanked a bandana out of his pocket and handed it to her.

"Guess I better do something about that short fuse of mine." Josh reached over and gave her a hug.

Several quiet miles later, they left the trail and pulled into an adjacent parking lot. Meg scanned the area until she spotted a van with a small flatbed trailer. A person next to the van signaled them with both arms.

"Josh, you were right."

"See Mom, just like I told you. There's our way into the city." Josh pedaled over to the waiting vehicle. After a brief round of introductions, they loaded the dusty bikes onto the trailer and hopped into the van.

"I wonder if anyone is going to be there?" Josh turned around from the passenger seat to face Meg in the back.

"You can bet we'll see Aunt Naomi and Harry. She probably set up camp waiting for us."

Josh laughed. "She better have tons of food again."

They unloaded at Forest Park, snapped on their helmets and straddled their bikes for the last time. Their host rode his bike with them, eager to share the area's history.

"Over there is where the World's Fair was in 1904."

Too excited to listen to his long descriptions, Meg just nodded at appropriate intervals.

"Up here, we're going to turn right, out of the park. Just stick with me," the guide said.

They pedaled past multi-storied brick homes, with tall white columns and well-kept lawns. Despite a *Share the Road* sign, Meg tensed as traffic increased. She kept her eyes trained to the parked cars to her right, in case any driver attempted to open a car door. The air was peppered with car horns and sirens from a fire truck racing through the intersection.

She breathed easier when they biked past a section with diagonal parking, even if the cars parked backwards, unlike in Lake Devine. Meg marveled at the complex old churches with turrets and spires, unlike the simple churches that dotted the back roads of the Midwest.

The guide pointed ahead. "There's the Gateway Arch behind those structures. You'll want to take a tram ride up there sometime."

Meg's bike wobbled when she craned her head to look at the top of the buildings lining the block. After months of open roads, she felt suffocated and suddenly small.

Soon the guide signaled to the right and they turned onto a one-way street.

"Mom, there it is. There's the stadium on the left," Josh said.

Meg looked up and saw *Busch Stadium* in large letters on the top. At the corner was a cluster of statues of baseball players in various poses.

When the traffic light turned green, the trio continued toward the stadium.

"Which one is Stan Musial?" Meg asked Josh. "That's where Naomi said she'd be. Oh my goodness, listen to that!"

With each turn of their pedals, the cheering became louder. Josh turned around and grinned at her.

"Is this great or what?" he said. He pumped his fist in the air.

"This is for us? Maybe there is a game going on," Meg said.

"Check it out, Mom." He pointed to a group of women holding cardboard signs: *Minnesota Moms for Meg*.

Several people ran forward and helped Meg and Josh with their bicycles. The pair walked toward the largest statute near the third base entrance to the stadium. Naomi nearly toppled from the weight of the huge American flag she was waving. Her husband, Harry, balanced a portable stereo on his shoulders and the theme from "Chariots of Fire" blared out of the compact speakers. Christy jumped up and down and raced to hug Meg.

"Look at you girl! You did it," she yelled. She wrapped a feathered pink boa around Meg's neck. "You're a regular biking diva now."

"Where did all these people come from?"

"That young pastor drove his bus here. They made him park over there," Christy said. Meg looked to where she pointed and gasped at the yellow banners rippling from Malachi's white school bus.

Duda broke from the crowd. He grabbed Meg and twirled her in the air. "Miss Meg, you are one tough biking machine."

The little newspaper reporter, Candy Cane, hustled over and stuck her recorder in Josh's face. "I want to know everything. I told my editor I had an exclusive. This story is going to make me famous. Maybe the New York Times will publish it in their magazine."

"Harry, hurry and uncork the champagne," Naomi said. She quickly rolled up the flag and passed it along in the crowd. From a cardboard box she produced a tray of plastic cups. Harry poured and she wove through the crowd distributing the cups.

Duda raised his cup. "A toast to the Albertsons. To Meg and Josh for their incredible adventure."

"Hear, hear," responded the group.

Naomi lifted hers. "And a toast to Robert for the inspiration behind the journey. A fitting tribute to the man we all loved."

"Mom?" Josh put his hand on Meg's shoulder. "Do you think it's time? Time to finally tell Dad goodbye?"

"Uh-huh. Good bye and thanks." Meg bit her lower lip so hard she could taste blood. She grabbed the plastic bag from her handlebar pack and linked elbows with Josh. Arm in arm, they marched to the stadium gate.

The End

About the Author

As a journalist, **Sarah (Bunce) Kohnle** covered stories across the Midwest. Her roots were planted in North Dakota and she and her husband currently reside in Missouri.

CPSIA information can be obtained
at www.ICGtesting.com
Printed in the USA
FSOW01n0447191017
39898FS